Jerry Bauer

---

*About the Author*

---

MARIAN KEYES is Irish, but lived in London
for ten years before returning to Dublin. After
receiving a law degree and studying accounting,
she began writing short stories in 1993. She is
the author of six novels—*Watermelon, Lucy
Sullivan Is Getting Married, Rachel's Holiday,
Sushi for Beginners, Last Chance Saloon*, and
*Angels*—all major bestsellers in the United
Kingdom and elsewhere.

# MARIAN KEYES

# Lucy Sullivan is Getting Married

Perennial

*An Imprint of HarperCollinsPublishers*

A hardcover edition of this book was published in 1999 by William Morrow and Company.

HarperCollins books may be purchased for educational, business, or sales promotional use. For information please write: Special Markets Department, HarperCollins Publishers Inc., 10 East 53rd Street, New York, NY 10022.

First Perennial edition published 2002.

Library of Congress Cataloging-in-Publication Data

Keyes, Marian.
    Lucy Sullivan is getting married / Marian Keyes.—1st Perennial ed.
        p.   cm.
    ISBN 0-06-009037-5
    1. Female friendship—Fiction. 2. Roommates—Fiction. 3. Psychics—Fiction. I. Title

PR6061.E88 L83 2001
823'.914—dc21                                                    2001059143

02  03  04  05  06  RRD  10  9  8  7  6  5  4  3

For Liam

## acknowledgments

thank you to everyone who has worked on this book. Thanks to my agent, Russ Galen; thanks to all at Avon Books; and special thanks to my editor, Jennifer Hershey, for her enthusiastic support and careful, sensitive editing.

# Lucy Sullivan is Getting Married

*1*

When Meredia reminded me that the four of us from the office were due to visit a fortune-teller the following Monday, my stomach lurched.

"You've forgotten," accused Meredia, her chubby face aquiver.

I had.

She slapped her hand down on her desk and warned, "Don't even *think* of trying to tell me that you're not coming."

"Damn," I whispered, because that was just what I had been about to do. Not because I had any objections to having my fortune told. On the contrary—it was usually good for a laugh. Especially when they got to the part where they told me that the man of my dreams was just around the next corner. That part was always *hilarious*.

Even *I* laughed.

But I was poor. Although I had just been paid, my bank account was a post-holocaust, corpse-strewn wasteland because the day I'd been paid, I'd spent a fortune on aromatherapy oils that had promised to rejuvenate and energize and uplift me.

And bankrupt me, except it didn't say that on the packaging. But I think the idea was that I'd be so rejuvenated and energized and uplifted that I wouldn't care.

So when Meredia reminded me that I'd committed myself to paying some woman thirty pounds so that she could tell me that I would travel over water and that I was quite psychic myself, I realized that I'd be going without lunch for two weeks.

"I'm not sure that I can afford it," I said nervously.

"You can't back out now!" thundered Meredia. "Mrs. Nolan is giving us a discount. The rest of us will have to pay more if you don't come."

"Who's this Mrs. Nolan?" Megan asked suspiciously, looking up from her computer where she had been playing Solitaire. She was supposed to be running a check on debtors overdue a month.

"The tarot reader," said Meredia.

"What kind of name is Mrs. Nolan?" demanded Megan.

"She's Irish," protested Meredia.

"No!" Megan tossed her shiny, blond hair in annoyance. "I mean, what kind of name is 'Mrs. Nolan' for a *psychic?* She should be called Madam Zora or something like that. She can't be called 'Mrs. Nolan.' How can we believe a word that she says?"

"Well, that's her name." Meredia sounded hurt.

"And why didn't she change it?" said Megan. "There's nothing to it, so I'm told. Isn't that right, so-called Meredia?"

A pregnant pause.

"Or should I say 'Cathy'?" Megan continued with triumph.

"No, you shouldn't," said Meredia. "My name is Meredia."

"Sure," said Megan, with great sarcasm.

"It is!" said Meredia hotly.

"So let's see your birth certificate," challenged Megan.

Megan and Meredia didn't see eye to eye on most things

and especially not on Meredia's name. Megan was a no-nonsense Australian with a low bullshit threshold. Since she had arrived three months ago as a temp, she had insisted that Meredia wasn't Meredia's real name. She was probably right. Although I was very fond of Meredia, I had to agree that her name had a certain makeshift, ramshackle, cobbled-together-out-of-old-egg-cartons feel to it.

But unlike Megan I couldn't really see a problem with that.

"So it's definitely not 'Cathy'?" Megan took a little notebook out of her purse and drew a line through something.

"No," said Meredia stiffly.

"Right," said Megan. "That's all the *C*s done. Time for the *D*s. Daphne? Deirdre? Dolores? Denise? Diana? Dinah?"

"Shut up!" said Meredia, clearly on the verge of tears.

"Stop it." Hetty put a gentle hand on Megan's arm, because that's the kind of thing that Hetty did. Although Hetty was rich, she was also a good, kind person, who poured oil on troubled waters. Which meant, of course, that she wasn't much fun, but no one was perfect.

Immediately upon meeting Hetty, you could tell that Hetty came from old money—mostly because she had horrible clothes. Even though she was only about thirty-five she wore awful tweed skirts and flowery dresses that looked like family heirlooms. She *never* bought new clothes, which was a shame because one of the chief ways that office workers bonded was by displaying the spoils of the post-payday shopping run.

"I wish that Aussie bitch would leave," Meredia muttered to Hetty.

"It probably won't be long now," Hetty said soothingly.

"When are you going to leave?" Meredia demanded of Megan.

"As soon as I've got the cash," Megan replied.

Megan was doing her grand tour of Europe and had temporarily run out of money. But as soon as she had enough money to go, she was going—she constantly reminded us—to Scandinavia or Greece or the Pyrenees or the west of Ireland.

Until then Hetty and I would have to break up the vicious fights that broke out regularly. Megan was tall and tanned and gorgeous; Meredia was short and fat and not gorgeous. Meredia was jealous of Megan's beauty, while Megan despised Meredia's excess weight. When Meredia couldn't buy clothes to fit her, instead of making sympathetic noises like the rest of us did, Megan barked, "Stop whining and go on a bloody diet!"

But Meredia never did. And in the meantime she was condemned to cause cars to swerve whenever she walked down the road. Because instead of trying to disguise her size with vertical stripes and dark colors, she seemed to dress to enhance it. She went for the layered look, layers and layers and layers of fabric. Really, *lots*. Acres of fabric, yards and yards of velvet, draped and pinned and knotted and tied, anchored with broaches, attached with scarves, pinned and arranged along her sizeable girth.

And the more colors the better. Crimson and vermilion and sunburst orange and flame red and magenta.

And that was just her hair.

"One of us has got to go. It's either me or her," muttered Meredia, as she glared balefully at Megan.

But it was just bravado. Meredia had worked in our office for a very long time—to hear her tell it, since the dawn of time; in reality, about eight years—and she had never managed to secure another job. Nor had she been promoted.

This she bitterly blamed on a sizeist management. (Although there seemed to be no bar to any number of tubby men on the fast track to success, reaching all kinds of exalted positions within the ranks of the company.)

Anyway, wimp that I was, I gave in to Meredia about the visit to the fortune-teller. I even managed to persuade myself that having no money would be a good thing—being forced to go without lunch for two weeks would be good for my diet.

And Meredia reminded me of something I'd overlooked.

"You've just split up with Steven," she said. "You were due a visit to a fortune-teller *anyway*."

Although I didn't like to admit it, she was probably right. Now that I had discovered that Steven wasn't the man of my dreams, it was only a matter of time before I made some sort of psychic inquiries to find out exactly *who* was. That was the kind of thing that my friends and I did, even though no one *believed* the fortune-tellers. At least none of us would *admit* to believing them.

Poor Steven. What a disappointment he'd turned out to be.

Especially as it had started with such promise. I had thought he was gorgeous—his only average good looks were upgraded, in my eyes, to Adonis class, by blond curly hair, black leather pants and a motorcycle. He seemed wild and dangerous and carefree—well, he would, wouldn't he? What were motorcycles and black leather pants if not the uniform of a wild, dangerous and carefree man?

Of course, I thought I hadn't a hope with him, that someone as beautiful as him would have his pick of the girls and that he certainly wouldn't have any interest in someone as ordinary as me.

Because I really *was* ordinary. I certainly looked ordinary. I had ordinary brown curly hair, and I spent so much money on antifrizz hair products that it would probably have been more efficient if I'd had my salary paid directly to the drugstore near work. I had ordinary brown eyes and, as a punishment for having Irish parents, I had about eight million ordinary freckles—one for every single Irish person who died in the potato famine, as my father used to say when he was a bit drunk and maudlin.

But despite all my ordinariness, Steven had asked me out and acted as if he liked me.

At first I could barely understand why such a sexy man like Steven wanted to be with me.

And, naturally, I didn't believe a word that came out of his mouth. When he said that I was the only girl in his life, I assumed that he was lying, when he told me I was lovely, I looked for the angle on it, walked all around it, inspecting it, to see what he wanted from me.

I didn't even really mind not taking his compliments at face value; I just assumed that those were the kind of terms on which you went out with a man like Steven.

It took a while for me to realize that he was sincere and that he *wasn't* saying it to all the girls.

At this point, I tentatively decided that I was delighted, but what I really was was confused. I had been so sure that he had a whole secret other life, one that I was supposed to know nothing about—middle-of-the-night dashes on the Harley to have sex on the beach with unknown women and that sort of thing—he looked that type.

I had expected a short-lived, passionate, roller-coaster of an affair, where my nerves would be stretched to the snapping point waiting for his call; my whole body flooded with ecstasy when he *did* call.

Unfortunately, he always called when he said he would.

And he always said that I looked gorgeous, no matter what I wore. But instead of being happy, I felt uncomfortable.

What I saw was what I got, and I began to feel strangely short-changed by life.

He had started liking me too much.

One morning I woke up and he was propped on his elbow, staring down at me. "You're beautiful," he murmured, and it felt so *wrong*.

When we had sex he said, "Lucy, Lucy, oh God, Lucy," millions of times, all feverishly and passionately and I tried to join in and be all feverish and passionate also, but I just felt silly.

And the more he seemed to like me, the less I liked him until in the end I could barely breathe around him.

I was suffocating from his adulation, smothering in his admiration. I wasn't *that* attractive, I couldn't help thinking, and if he thought that I was, it meant there was something wrong with him.

"Why do you like me?" I asked him, over and over.

"Because you're beautiful," or "Because you're sexy," or "Because you're all woman," were the nauseating replies that he gave me.

"No, I'm not," I would reply desperately. "How can you say that I am?"

"Anyone would think you were trying to convince me not to like you." He smiled tenderly.

The tenderness was probably what drove me over the edge. His tender smiles, his tender gazes, his tender kisses, his tender caresses, so much *tenderness*, it was a nightmare.

And he was so touchy-feely! Mr. Tactile—I couldn't bear it.

Everywhere we went he held my hand. When we were driving he planted his hand on my thigh, when we were watching television he almost lay on top of me. He was always stroking my arm or rubbing my hair or caressing my back, until I could bear it no more and had to push him away.

Velcro man, that's what I called him in the end.

And eventually to his face.

As time went on, I wanted to tear my skin off every time he touched me, and the thought of having sex with him made me feel sick. One day he said he'd love a huge backyard and a houseful of kids and that was it!

I broke up with him immediately.

And I couldn't understand how I had once found him so attractive, because by then I couldn't think of a more repulsive man on the face of the earth. He still had the blond hair and the leather pants and the motorcycle, but I was no longer fooled by them.

I despised him for liking me so much. I wondered how he could settle for so little.

None of my friends could understand why I had broken up with him. "But he was great" was their cry. "But he was so good to you" was another one. "But he was such a catch," they protested. To which I replied, "No, he wasn't. A catch isn't supposed to be that easy."

He had disappointed me.

I had expected disrespect and instead got devotion, I had expected infidelity and instead got commitment, I had expected upheaval and instead got predictability and (most disappointing of all) I had expected a wolf and had gotten a sheep.

It's upsetting when the nice guy you really like turns out to be a complete, lying, two-timing bastard. But it's nearly as bad when the guy that you thought was an unreliable heartbreaker turns out to be uncomplicated and nice.

I spent a couple of days wondering why I liked the

guys who weren't nice to me? Why couldn't I like the ones who were?

Would I despise every man who ever treated me well? Was I fated only to want men that didn't want me?

I woke up in the middle of the night wondering about my sense of self-worth—why was I comfortable only when I was being ill-treated?

Then I realized that the saying "Treat 'em mean, keep 'em keen" had been around for hundreds of years. And I relaxed—after all, I didn't make the rules.

So what if my ideal man was a selfish, dependable, unfaithful, loyal, treacherous, loving flirt who thought the world of me, never called when he said he would, made me feel like the most special woman in the universe and flirted with all my friends? Was it my fault that I wanted a Schrödinger's cat of a boyfriend, a man who was several directly conflicting things simultaneously?

 2

There seemed to be a direct link between how difficult it was to get to a fortune-teller's house and how good their reputation was. The more inaccessible and off-putting the venue, the higher the quality of the predictions, was the widely held view.

Which meant that Mrs. Nolan must have been brilliant because she lived in some awful, faraway suburb on the outskirts of London.

On Monday, at five on the dot, Megan, Hetty, Meredia

and I assembled on the front steps of our place of work. Hetty went and got her car from where it was parked, several miles away—because that was parking in central London for you—and in we got.

The journey was a nightmare. We spent hours either stuck in traffic or traveling through anonymous suburbs, then we went onto a highway. After driving for ages more, we turned off an exit and finally turned into a housing project.

And what a neighborhood! It was downright apocalyptic. The neighborhood I'd grown up in was pretty poor, but not this bad!

Two huge gray blocks loomed like watchtowers over what seemed like hundreds of miserable little gray box houses. A couple of stray dogs roamed aimlessly, half-heartedly looking for someone to bite.

There were no plants, no trees, no grass.

In the distance there was a small concrete row of shops. It was nearly all boarded up except for a sandwich shop and a bookies' office and a liquor store. It was probably just my overactive imagination but through the evening gloom I could have *sworn* I saw four horsemen loitering outside the sandwich shop. So far, so good—Mrs. Nolan was obviously better than I had already realized.

"My God," said Megan her face twisted in disgust. "What a dump!"

"Yes, isn't it?" Meredia smiled with pride.

In the middle of all the grayness was a small patch of ground that some urban planner had obviously anticipated would be a little oasis of abundant greenness where laughing families would play in the sunshine. But it looked like it had been a long time since grass had grown there. Through the twilight gloom we could see a group of about fifteen children gathered. They were clustered around something that looked suspiciously like a burned-out car.

Even though it was a bitterly cold March evening, none of them was wearing coats and, as soon as they saw us, they paused from whatever criminal activity they were up to and ran toward us, whooping loudly.

"Good God!" cried Hetty. "Lock your doors!" All four locks snapped shut as the children swarmed around the car, staring at us with their old and knowing eyes.

What made them look even more scary was that they were smeared with black stuff, which was probably only oil or charred metal from the burned car, but it looked like war paint.

They were mouthing something at us.

"What are they saying?" asked Hetty in terror.

"I think they're asking us if we've come to see Mrs. Nolan," I said doubtfully.

I opened the window a fraction of an inch and through the babel of childish voices established that that was indeed what they were asking us.

"Phew! The natives are friendly," smiled Hetty, making a great show of wiping the sweat from her forehead and breathing deeply with relief.

"Talk to them, Lucy."

Nervously, I opened the window a bit more.

"Er . . . we've come to see Mrs. Nolan," I said.

A cacophony of shrill voices answered us.

"That's her house."

"She lives over there."

"That's the one."

"You can leave your car here."

"That's her house."

"Over there."

"I'll show you."

"No, I'll show you."

"No, *I'm* showing them."

"No, *I'm* showing them."

"But I saw them first."

"But you got the last lot."

"Fuck you, Cherise Tiller."

"No, fuck *you,* Claudine Hall."

A vicious fight broke out between four or five of the little girls while we sat in the car and waited for them to stop.

"Let's get out." Megan sounded a bit bored. It took more than a crowd of semisavage children to frighten her. She opened the door and stepped over a couple of children wrestling on the pavement.

Then Hetty and I got out.

As soon as Hetty put foot outside the car a wiry, skinny little girl with the face of a thirty-five-year-old cardsharp began tugging at her coat. "Hey, me and my friend'll guard your car," she promised.

Her friend, who was even more skinny, nodded silently.

"Thank you," said Hetty, her face a picture of horror, trying to shake the little girl off.

"We'll make sure that nothing happens to it," said the wizened little girl, a bit more threateningly, still holding on to Hetty's coat tightly.

"Give them some money," suggested Megan in exasperation. "That's what she's really saying."

"Excuse *me!*" said Hetty, outraged. "I will not. That's blackmail."

"Do you want the wheels to be on your car when you get back or don't you?" Megan demanded.

The little girl and her friend patiently watched the exchange with folded arms. Now that a sensible streetwise woman like Megan was on the case, they knew that the outcome would be to their liking.

"Here," I said, giving the thirty-five-year-old little girl a pound.

She accepted it with a grim nod.

"*Now* can we please go and have our fortunes told?" asked Megan impatiently.

Meredia, the big wimp, had cowered in the car during the entire exchange with the Children from Hell. She waited for them to drift away before levering herself out.

But the minute they saw her emerging from the car they returned at high speed. It wasn't often that they got a two-hundred-pound woman dressed head to toe in crimson crushed velvet, with matching hair, in their neighborhood. But when they did, they knew how to make the most of it. The screeches of laughter that emerged from the children were blood curdling.

Poor Meredia, her face as crimson as the rest of her, lumbered the short distance to Mrs. Nolan's front door like the Pied Piper, with swarms of horrible brats running and dancing after her, laughing and shouting insults. A carnival atmosphere prevailed, as though the circus had come to town, while Hetty, Megan and I jostled protectively around Meredia, making half-hearted attempts to shoo the children away.

Then we saw Mrs. Nolan's house. You couldn't miss it.

It had double-glazed windows and a little glass porch stuck onto its front. All its windows had scalloped, lacy net curtains and elaborately looped Austrian blinds. The windowsills were crammed to capacity with ornaments, china horses and glass dogs and brass jugs and little furry things on little wooden rocking chairs. Evident signs of prosperity that set it apart from all the other houses around it. Mrs. Nolan was obviously a bit of a superstar among tarot readers.

"Ring the bell," Hetty told Meredia.

"No, you do it," said Meredia.

"But you've been here before," said Hetty.

"*I'll* do it," I sighed, reached over and pressed the button.

When the first couple of verses of "Greensleeves" began chiming in the hall, Megan and I both started to snigger.

Meredia turned and glared.

"Shut up," she hissed. "Have some respect. This woman is the best. She's the master."

"She's coming. Oh my God. She's coming," whispered Hetty in hoarse excitement as a shadowy shape moved behind the frosted glass of the porch.

The door opened and instead of an exotic, dusky, psychic-looking woman, an unfriendly-looking young man stood there. A small child with a dirty face peeped out from between his legs.

"Yes?" he said, looking us over. His eyes widened with mild shock as he registered Meredia in all her crimsonness.

None of us spoke. Hetty gently nudged Meredia and Meredia elbowed Megan and Megan elbowed me.

"Say something," hissed Hetty.

"No, you," muttered Meredia.

"Well?" inquired the creepy looking man again, none too civilly.

"Is Mrs. Nolan here?" I asked.

He eyed me suspiciously, then apparently decided that I could be trusted.

"She's busy," he muttered.

"Doing what?" demanded Megan impatiently.

"She's having her tea," he said.

"Well, can we come in and wait?" I asked.

"She's expecting us," volunteered Meredia.

"We've come a long way," explained Hetty.

"We were led by a star from the East," sniggered Megan from the back.

All three of us turned and frowned at her.

"Sorry," she muttered.

The young man looked mortally offended at the disrespect shown to his mother or granny—or whatever Mrs. Nolan was to him—and began to close the door.

"No, please don't," pleaded Hetty. "She's sorry."

"I am," called Megan cheerfully, not sounding a bit of it.

"All right then," he said grudgingly and let us into a tiny hall.

There was barely space for the four of us.

"Wait here," he ordered and went into another room. It must have been the kitchen, judging by the smoke and the clinking of teacups and the smell of fried eggs that emerged when he opened the door and disappeared when he shut it again.

There was hardly an inch of wall space in the hall that wasn't covered with pictures or barometers or tapestries or horseshoes. Meredia moved slightly and knocked a photograph of a very large family off the wall. She bent down to pick it up and brushed against ten other pictures that went tumbling to the floor.

We loitered in the hall, totally ignored, while sounds of talk and laughter came from behind the closed door. The minutes ticked by.

"I'm *starving*," said Megan.

"Me too," I agreed. "I wonder what they're having for tea."

"This is stupid," said Megan. "Let's go."

"Please wait," said Meredia. "She's wonderful. She really is."

Eventually Mrs. Nolan finished her tea. I couldn't help feeling disappointed when I saw her—she looked so ordinary. There wasn't a red head scarf or a gold hoop earring in sight.

She had glasses and a short perm and was wearing a beige sweater and sweat pants and, worst of all, *slippers.* And she was *minute!* I wasn't very tall myself but she barely came up to my waist.

"Right girls," she said, brisk and businesslike, in a Dublin accent. "Who's first?"

Meredia went first. Then Hetty. Then me. Megan wanted to wait until last to see if the rest of us thought it was worth the money.

 3

When it was my turn I went into what was obviously the family "good room." I barely got past the door because the room was so crammed with furniture and stuff. An embroidered fireguard stood next to a huge mahogany sideboard, which groaned under the weight of yet more ornaments. There were footstools and nests of tables everywhere you looked and a sofa and chairs in brown velvet. They still had their plastic covers.

Mrs. Nolan was sitting on one of the plastic-covered chairs and she gestured to me to sit on the other.

As I fought through the furniture to get to the seat, I

began to feel nervous and excited. Although Mrs. Nolan looked like she would be more at home on her knees scrubbing Hetty's kitchen floor, she had obviously earned her wonderful reputation as a fortune-teller, *somehow.* What would she tell me? I wondered. What was in store for me? "Sit down, me dear," she said.

I sat, balanced on the edge of the plastic-covered chair. She looked at me. Shrewdly? Wisely?

She spoke. Prophetically? Portentously?

"You have come a long way, me dear," she said.

I gave a little jump. So accurate! Yes, indeed I *had* come a long way from my working class childhood. "Yes," I agreed tentatively, quite shaken by her perception.

"Was the traffic bad, me dear?"

*"What?* The *what?* Er . . . oh . . . the traffic? No, not really," I managed to reply.

Oh I see. She had only been making conversation. The reading hadn't started yet. How disappointing. Well, never mind. "Yes, me dear," she sighed. "If they ever finish that bloody bypass it'll be a miracle."

"Er, yes." I nodded.

But then it was straight down to business. "Ball or cards?" she shot at me.

"S . . . sorry?" I asked politely.

"Ball or cards? Crystal ball or tarot cards?"

"Oh! Well, let's see. What's the difference?"

"Five pounds."

"No, I meant . . . never mind. The tarot cards please."

"Right," said Mrs. Nolan and with that she started shuffling the deck with the finesse of a riverboat poker player.

"Shuffle them, me dear," she said, handing me the

cards. "And whatever you do, don't drop them on the floor."

It must be bad luck to drop them on the floor. I nodded knowingly.

"I have a bad back," she explained. "The doctor said no bending."

"Now, ask yourself a question, me dear," she advised. "A question that the cards will answer for you, me dear. Don't tell it to me, me dear. I don't need to know it"— a little pause, meaningful eye contact—"me dear."

I could have chosen one of several questions. Like, would there be an end to world hunger? Would they find a cure for AIDS? Would there be peace on earth? Will they manage to fix the hole in the ozone layer? But interestingly enough, the question that I wanted to ask was the "Will I ever meet a nice man?" one. Funny.

"Have you decided on the question, me dear?" she asked, taking the deck back from me.

I nodded. She started flinging cards on the table at high speed. I didn't know what any of the pictures meant, but I thought that they didn't look very promising. There seemed to be a lot of them with swords, and surely that couldn't be good? "Your question concerns a man, me dear?" she said.

Even *I* wasn't impressed with that.

I mean, I was a young woman. I had few concerns in my life. Well, actually, I had plenty. But the *average* young woman would only seek guidance from a fortune-teller for two reasons—her career and her love life. And if she was having problems with her career, she would probably do something constructive about it herself.

Like sleep with her boss.

So that just left the love life option. "Yes," I answered wearily. "It concerns a man."

"You have been unlucky in love, me dear," she said sympathetically.

Once again, I refused to be impressed.

Yes, I had been unlucky in love. But show me a woman who hasn't.

"There is a fair-haired man in your past, me dear," she said.

I suppose she meant Steven. But I mean, who *hadn't* got a fair-haired man in their past? "He was not the one for you, me dear," she continued.

"Thanks," I said, a bit annoyed, because I'd already figured that out myself.

"But waste no tears on him, me dear," she advised.

"Don't worry."

"For there is another man, me dear," she said, giving me a big smile.

"Really?" I asked, delighted, leaning closer to her, the plastic covers squeaking against my thighs. "Now you're talking."

"Yes," she said, studying the cards. "I see a marriage."

"Do you really?" I demanded. "Whose? Mine?"

"Yes, me dear," she said. "Yours."

"Really?" I said. "When?"

"Before the leaves have fallen on the ground for the second time, me dear."

"Sorry?"

"Before the four seasons have rolled by a time and half a time again," she said.

"Sorry, I'm still not sure what you mean," I apologized.

"In about a year," she snapped, sounding a bit annoyed.

I was slightly disappointed. In about a year, it would still be winter, and I'd always seen myself getting married in the spring. On the rare occasions that I could see myself getting married at all, that is. "You couldn't make it a bit longer than a year, could you?" I asked.

"Me dear," she said sharply. "I do not ordain these things. I am simply the messenger."

"Sorry," I muttered.

"Well," she said, in a nicer tone, "let's say up to eighteen months just to be on the safe side."

"Thanks," I said, thinking that was very decent of her. So I was getting married, I thought. Momentous stuff. I would just have settled for a boyfriend.

"I wonder who he is?"

"You must be careful, me dear," she warned me. "At first you may not recognize him for who he truly is."

"You mean I'll meet him at a costume party?"

"No," she said ominously. "At first he may not be who he appears to be."

"Oh, you mean he's going to lie to me," I said, understanding. "Well, fair enough then. Why should this one be any different?"

I laughed.

Mrs. Nolan looked annoyed.

"No, me dear," she said irritably. "I mean that you must take care not to wear cupid's blinkers. You may have to seek this man out and look at him with clear and fearless eyes. He may not have money, but you must not humble him. He may not have looks, but you must not humble him."

Oh great, I thought. I might have known! A deformed pauper.

"I see," I said. "So he's going to be poor and ugly."

"*No*, me dear," said Mrs. Nolan, in exasperation and dropping her mystical language. "I just mean that he mightn't be your usual type."

"I *see!*" I said.

If only she'd said that to begin with. Clear and fearless eyes, indeed! "So," I continued, "when Jason, the seventeen-year-old with all the pimples and those awful baggy clothes, meets me at the photocopier and asks me out, I shouldn't laugh in his face and tell him that I'll see him ice-skating in hell?"

"That's the idea, me dear," said Mrs. Nolan, sounding pleased. "For the flower of love may flourish in the most unexpected of places, and you must be ready to pluck it."

"I understand," I nodded.

All the same, I'd want to be pretty desperate before Jason would have any kind of chance. But there was no need to tell Mrs. Nolan that.

Anyway, if she was worth her salt, she already knew. She started pointing briskly at cards and barking out staccato sentences, thus indicating that the audience was nearing its end. "You will have three children, two girls and a boy, me dear," and "You will never have money, but you will have happiness, me dear," and "You have an enemy at work, me dear. She is jealous of your success." I had to laugh—slightly bitterly—at that one. She would have laughed too if she knew how menial and awful my job was.

Then she paused.

She looked at the cards, then she looked at me. Something like concern was on her face.

"There has been a cloud over you, me dear," she said slowly. "A darkness, a sadness."

Suddenly, to my horror, I had a lump in my throat. A dark cloud was exactly how I described the bouts of depression that I sometimes got. Not the usual "I wish I owned that suede skirt" type of depression—although I suffered from *that* kind of depression too. But since I had been seventeen, I had had bouts of actual clinical depression.

I nodded, almost unable to speak.

"Yes," I whispered.

"For many years you have carried this," she said quietly, looking at me with great sympathy and understanding.

"Yes," I whispered again, feeling my eyes fill with tears.

"You have carried it almost entirely alone," she said gently.

"Yes," I nodded, feeling a tear make its way slowly down my cheek. Oh my God! It was awful! I thought that we had come for a laugh. But instead this woman, who was almost a complete stranger, had seen through to the essence of me, had touched me in a place where few human beings had ever been.

"Sorry," I sniffed, wiping my face with my hand.

"Don't worry, me dear," she said, handing me a tissue from a box that was obviously there for this very reason. "This happens a lot."

She waited for a few moments while I recovered my composure and then she began to speak again.

"Okay, me dear?"

"Yes." Sniff. "Thanks."

"This can get better, me dear. But you must not hide from people who wish to help you. How can they help you if you won't let them?"

"I don't really know what you mean," I mumbled.

"Maybe you don't, me dear," she agreed kindly. "But I hope that you will learn."

"Thanks," I sniffed. "You've been very nice. And thanks, you know, for the guy and me getting married and all that. It was nice to hear."

"Not at all, me dear," she said pleasantly. "Now that'll be thirty pounds, please."

I paid her and launched myself out of the crackling plastic.

"Good luck, me dear," she said. "And will you send the next young lady in?"

"Who's next?" I wondered. "Oh it's Megan, isn't it?"

"Megan!" exclaimed Mrs. Nolan. "Isn't that a lovely name? She must be Welsh."

"Australian, actually," I smiled. "Thanks again. Bye now."

"Bye, me dear," she nodded, smiling. I went back out into the tiny hall, where the other three fell on me with urgent questions. "Well?" and "What did she say?" Megan asked, "Was it worth the money?"

"Yes," I told her. "You should go."

"I'll only go if you all promise not to tell anything until I'm back out and we're all together," said Megan sulkily. "I don't want to miss anything."

 4

When Megan emerged smiling about twenty minutes later, it was time to go back out into the cold night to see what Satan's children had done to the car.

"The car will be all right, won't it?" asked poor Hetty anxiously, as she broke into a run.

"I sincerely hope so," I answered, walking briskly after

her. I really *did* sincerely hope so. The chances of getting home any other way were apparently very slim indeed.

"We should never have come," she said miserably.

"Yes, we should have," said Megan gregariously. "I've had a great time."

"So've I," came Meredia's voice, as she lumbered along about fifty yards behind the rest of us.

Unbelievably, the car was fine.

As soon as we rounded the corner, the little girl who was supposed to be guarding the car appeared as if from nowhere. I don't know what kind of threatening look she gave Hetty, but it was enough to make her immediately grope around in her purse for another couple of pounds to give to the girl.

We couldn't see any of the other children, but we could hear whooping noises and shrieks and the sound of smashing glass coming from somewhere nearby.

As we drove out of the project we passed a crowd of them. They were doing something to a camper van. Completely destroying it, I think.

"Don't they have to be in bed at any time?" asked Hetty anxiously, appalled by her first brush with a ghetto. "I mean, where are their parents? What are they doing? Surely *something* can be done?"

The children were delighted to see us. As our car approached them, they began laughing and shouting and pointing and cackling. Obviously they were still greatly interested in Meredia. Three or four of the boys gave chase to us and managed to run alongside us, laughing and making revolting faces at us, for quite a distance before we managed to shake them.

As soon as it became obvious that we had made good our escape from the little brats, we relaxed. It was time for the postmortem on what Mrs. Nolan had said and the four of us were a bit excitable. The noise in the car was deafening, with Meredia and Megan competing to tell their stories.

"She knew that I was Australian," burst in Megan excitedly. "And she says that I'm going to have some sort of split in my life, but that good will come of it and I'll cope with it marvelously, the way I do with everything." She said the last piece a bit smugly.

"So maybe it's time to go traveling again," she continued. "Either way it looks as if I won't have to be looking at your ugly mugs for much longer."

"She said I'd come into money," said Meredia happily.

"Good," said Hetty, sounding oddly bitter. "Then you can give me back that twenty-pound note you owe me."

I noticed that Hetty was quieter than usual. She wasn't joining in with the general hilarity and excitement but was just driving the car and staring straight ahead.

Was her upper-crust conservative body still in shock from such close contact with working-class children? Or was it something else?

"What did she say to you, Hetty?" I asked, a bit concerned. "Did she tell you something bad was going to happen?"

"Yes," said Hetty, in a little voice. She even sounded a small bit tearful!

"What was it? What did she say?" we all blurted out at once, drawing our faces nearer to hers, eager to hear predictions of terrible things—accidents, illness, death, bankruptcy, mortgage companies foreclosing, boilers bursting—whatever.

"She said that very soon I'm going to meet the love of my life," said Hetty tearfully.

A silence fell in the car. Oh dear! That was bad. Very bad.

Very bad indeed.

Poor Hetty!

It's unsettling to be told you're going to meet the love of your life when you're already married with two children.

"She says I'm going to be completely smitten with him," sniffed Hetty. "It's going to be awful. There's never been a divorce in our family. And what about Marcus and Montague?" (Or it might have been "Troilus and Tristan" or "Cecil and Sebastian.") "They're finding boarding school difficult enough without the embarrassment of their mother having a love affair and leaving home."

"Oh dear," I said sympathetically. "But it's only a fortune-teller's prediction. It probably won't happen."

But that just made her tears flow faster. "But *why* shouldn't I meet the love of my life? I *want* to meet him."

Megan, Meredia and I exchanged shocked looks. Good lord! It was most irregular. Was the normally sane and calm—I'd even go so far as to say boring—Hetty having some kind of nervous fit?

"Why can't *I* have some fun? Why do *I* have to be stuck with boring old Dick?" she demanded.

She thumped the steering wheel every time she said "I" and the car lurched alarmingly into the other lane. All around us cars were beeping their horns, but Hetty didn't seem to notice.

I was amazed. I had worked with Hetty for two years and, while we were never soul mates, I thought I knew her quite well.

There was a nonplussed silence in the car while Meredia, Megan and I swallowed and tried and failed to think of comforting things to say.

It was Hetty who rescued the situation. She didn't have

a fourteenth cousin, three times removed, as a lady-in-waiting to the Queen for nothing. She hadn't gone to a hugely expensive finishing school without learning to smooth over awkward social situations. "Sorry," she said, suddenly seeming to become Hetty again, the veneer of polite calm and reserve firmly clipped back in place. "Sorry, girls," she said again. "You must forgive me."

She cleared her throat and squared her shoulders, indicating that there was nothing further to say on the subject. Dick and his boringness were not to be topics for discussion.

Such a pity. I had always wanted to know. Because to be honest, Dick did seem *extremely* boring. But, then again—and I mean this in the nicest possible way—so did Hetty.

"So then, Lucy," she said crisply, deflecting the last few remaining crumbs of interest away from her. "What did Mrs. Nolan predict for you?"

"Me?" I said. "Oh yes. She says I'm getting married."

Another silence fell in the car.

Another stunned one.

The disbelief of Megan, Meredia and Hetty was so tangible it was like a fifth person in the car. If it wasn't careful it would end up having to contribute to the cost of the gas for the trip.

"Really?" asked Hetty, somehow managing to get sixteen syllables from the one word.

"You!" shouted Megan. "She said that *you* are getting married."

"Yes," I said defensively. "What's so wrong with that?"

"Nothing really," said Meredia kindly. "It's just that, you know, you haven't been exactly lucky with men."

"Not through any fault of your own," said Hetty hurriedly, tactfully.

Hetty was good on tact.

"Well, that's what she said," I said sulkily.

They didn't really know what to say and conversation remained subdued until eventually we reached civilization again. I was the first to be dropped off because I lived in Ladbroke Grove. The last thing I heard as I got out of the car was Meredia telling anyone who cared to listen that Mrs. Nolan had said that she would travel over water and that she was very psychic herself.

 5

I shared an apartment with two other girls, Karen and Charlotte. Karen was twenty-eight, I was twenty-six and Charlotte was twenty-three. We were a bad example to each other and spent a lot of time drinking bottles of wine and not very much cleaning the bathroom.

When I let myself in, Karen and Charlotte were asleep. We usually went to bed early on a Monday night to recover from the excesses of the preceding weekend.

There was a note on the kitchen table from Karen saying that Daniel had phoned me.

Daniel was my friend and, while he was the closest thing that I had to a steady man in my life, I wouldn't have become romantically involved with him if the future of the human race depended on it. So that will give some idea of just how male-free my life was.

My life was the Reduced-Male variety, the Male Lite life.

Daniel was wonderful, really. Boyfriends came and boy-friends went (and believe me, they went), but I could al-ways rely on Daniel to be the boyfriend figure in my life, to annoy me with sexist comments and say that he pre-ferred the shorter, tighter skirt.

And he wasn't unattractive, or so I was told. All my friends thought he was adorable. Even Dennis, my gay friend, said that he wouldn't kick Daniel out of the bed for eating potato chips. And whenever Karen answered the phone to him she made faces like she was having an or-gasm. Sometimes Daniel came to our apartment and, after he'd gone, Karen and Charlotte would lie on the bit of the couch where he'd been sitting and roll around and make noises like they were in ecstasy.

I couldn't see what all the fuss was about. Because Daniel was a friend of my brother Chris, I'd known him for years and years and years. I just knew him too well to have a crush on him. Or for him to have a crush on me, for that matter.

There might have been a time, once, several thousand light-years in the past, when Daniel and I smiled shyly across a Duran Duran record and contemplated kissing each other. But then again, there might not have been, I couldn't actually *remember* ever feeling like that about him, I just assumed that I had because, in the free-for-all of emotions that was my adolescence, I had a crush on just about everyone.

It was really for the best that Daniel and I didn't like each other that way because, if we *did*, Chris would have to go to all the bother of beating Daniel up for violating his sister's honor and I didn't want to cause anyone trouble.

Karen and Charlotte—quite mistakenly—envied my relationship with Daniel.

They would shake their heads in wonder and say, "You lucky bitch, how can you be so relaxed around him? How are you able to be funny and make him laugh? I can never think of a thing to say."

But it was easy because I didn't have a crush him. When I *did* like someone I panicked and knocked things over and opened conversations by saying things like, "Do you ever wonder what it's like to be a radiator?"

I looked at the note that Karen had left for me—there was even a little stain on it that she had labeled "dribble"—and wondered if I should ring Daniel. I decided not to, he might be in bed.

Accompanied, if you follow me.

Damn Daniel and his active sex life. I wanted to talk to him.

What Mrs. Nolan had said had given me food for thought. *Not* what she had said about me getting married—there was no way that I was fool enough to actually take that seriously. But what she had said about me being under a dark cloud had reminded me of my bouts of Depression and how awful they'd been. I *could* have woken Karen and Charlotte, but I decided against it. Apart from the fact that they could turn nasty if roused from their slumber for any reason other than an impromptu party, they didn't know about my Depression.

Of course, they knew that sometimes I said I was depressed, and then they said, "But why?" and I would tell them about an unfaithful boyfriend or a bad day at work or not fitting into last summer's skirt, and they would be more than sympathetic.

But they didn't know that I sometimes got depressed

with a capital *D*. Daniel was one of the few people outside my family who actually knew.

That's because I felt ashamed of it. People either thought that depression was a mental illness and that consequently I was completely nuts or, more often they thought that there was no such thing as depression, other than a vague, neurotic concept. That I was merely indulging myself, wallowing in teenage angst that was way past its use-by date. And that all I had to do was to "pull myself together" and "snap out of it" and "take up sport."

I could understand that attitude, because *everyone* got depressed sometimes. It was part of being alive, part of the deal, sunny days and earaches.

People got depressed about money (about not having enough of it, I mean). Unpleasant things happened to people—relationships fell apart, jobs were lost, televisions broke down two days after the guarantee ran out and so on and so on—and people felt miserable about them.

I *knew* all that, but the depression that I suffered from wasn't just an occasional bout of the blues or a dose of Holly Golightly's mean reds—although I got them also, and fairly regularly at that. So did a lot of people, especially if they had just had a week of heavy drinking and very little sleep, but the blues and the mean reds were mere child's play compared to the savage black killer demons that descended on me from time to time to play crucifixion with my head.

Mine was no ordinary depression, oh *no,* mine was the super, deluxe, top-of-the-range, no-expense-spared version.

Not that any of it was immediately obvious on first meeting me. I wasn't miserable *all* of the time, in fact a lot of the time I was bright and personable and entertaining. And even when I felt dreadful I tried very hard to act as though I didn't. It was only when things got so desperate that I couldn't conceal it any longer that I took to my bed and waited for it to pass. Which it invariably did, sooner or later.

The worst bout of depression that I ever had was actually my first one.

I was seventeen and it was the summer that I had left school, and for no reason—apart from all the obvious ones—I got the idea into my head that the world was a very sad, lonely, unfair, cruel, heart-breaking kind of a place.

I got depressed about things that were happening to people in far-flung corners of the world, people that I didn't even know and wasn't ever likely to know, especially considering that the main reason that I felt depressed about them was that they were dying of hunger or of a plague or from their house falling in on top of them during an earthquake.

I cried at every piece of news that I heard or saw—car crashes, famines, wars, programs about AIDS victims, stories of mothers dying and leaving young children, reports on battered wives, interviews with men who had been laid off in their thousands from coalmines and knew that even though they were only forty they would never work again, newspaper articles about families of six who had to feed themselves on fifty pounds a week, pictures of neglected donkeys.

I found a child's blue-and-white mitten on the pavement near my house one day and the grief that it triggered was almost unbearable. The thought of a tiny chilled hand, or of the other mitten, all alone without its mate was so poignant that I cried wet, hot, choking tears every time I saw it.

After a while I wouldn't leave the house. And shortly after that I wouldn't get out of bed.

It was horrendous. I felt as though I was personally in touch with every ounce of grief in the world, that I had an Internet of sorrow in my head, that every atom of sadness that had ever existed was being channeled through me, before being packaged up and transported to outlying areas, like I was a kind of centralized misery depot.

My mother took charge. With the efficiency of a despot being threatened with a coup d'état, she imposed a total news blackout. I was banned from watching television.

And every evening when my brothers came home, my mother frisked them at the front door to relieve them of any copies of newspapers that they may have had secreted about their persons, before they could gain admittance to the house.

Not that her media clampdown made any difference. I had the admirable skill of being able to locate a tragedy—however small—in absolutely anything. I managed to cry at the description of little bulbs dying in a February frost in the gardening magazine that was my only permitted reading material.

Eventually Dr. Thornton was sent for, but not before a day or so was spent tidying and cleaning frantically in honor of his arrival. And he diagnosed depression and—surprise, surprise—prescribed antidepressants for me, which I didn't want to take.

"What good will they do?" I sobbed at him. "Will the antidepressants give those men in Yorkshire back their jobs? Will the antidepressants find the pair to this . . . to this . . ." (by now I was gasping and incoherent with crying) ". . . to this MITTEN!?" I wailed.

"Oh, would you ever shut up about that bloody mitten," tisked my mother briskly. "Yes, doctor, she'd be delighted to start on the pills."

My mother was like a lot of people who hadn't been allowed to finish their schooling in that she believed that anyone who had been to a university, especially doctors, were almost Popelike in their infallibility, and that taking prescribed narcotics was a mystic and sacred kind of a thing.

("I am not worthy to receive them but only say the word and I shall be healed.")

Also she was Irish and had a huge inferiority complex and thought that everything English people suggested had to be right. (Dr. Thornton was English.)

"Leave it to me," my mother grimly assured Dr. Thornton. "I'll see that she takes them."

And she did.

And after a while I felt better. Not happy or anything like that. I still felt that we were all doomed and that the future was a vast wasteland of bleak grayness, but that it mightn't hurt if I got up for half an hour to watch some TV.

After four months, Dr. Thornton said it was time for me to stop taking the antidepressants and we all held our breath, waiting to see if I could fly on my own or if I would dive-bomb back to that salty, single-mittened hell.

But by then I had started at secretarial college and I had faith, however fragile, in the future.

My world opened up at college, I learned many strange and wondrous things—I was amazed to hear that the quick brown fox jumps over the lazy dog, that *i* comes before *e,* except and *only* except after *c,* that if I began a letter with "Dear Sir" and ended it with "Yours sincerely" that the world would come crashing to an immediate end.

I mastered the demanding art of sitting with a wirebound notebook on my lap and covering the page with squiggles and dots, I strove hard to be the perfect secretary, quickly working up to four Bacardis and diet Cokes on a night out with the girls, and my knowledge of the stock of the local department store was, at all times, encyclopedic.

It never occurred to me that perhaps I could have done something else with my life—for a long time I thought it was such an honor to get the chance to train as a secretary that I didn't realize how much it bored me. And even if I *had* realized how much it bored me, I wouldn't have been able to wriggle out of it because my mother—a very determined woman—was adamant that it was what I would do. She actually cried with joy the day I got my certificate to say that I could move my fingers quickly enough to type forty-seven words a minute.

In a fairer world, *she* would have been the one to enroll in the typing and shorthand course and not me, but that's not the way it happened.

I was the only girl from my class at school who went to secretarial college. Apart from Gita Pradesh, who went to Physical Education college, everyone else either got pregnant, got married, got a job stacking shelves in Safeway, or a combination of the three.

I was quite good at school, or at least I was too afraid of the nuns and my mother to be a complete failure.

But I was too afraid of some of the other girls in my class to be a complete success either—there was a gang of "cool" girls, who smoked and wore eyeliner and had very developed chests for their age and were rumored to have sex with their boyfriends. I badly wanted to be one of them but I hadn't a hope because I sometimes passed my exams.

Once, I got sixty-three percent in a biology exam and

I was lucky to escape with my life, which wasn't really fair because the exam was on the reproductive system, and they probably knew a lot more about it than I did, and would have all got high marks if they had only turned up.

But every time there was an exam they brought faked sick notes from their mothers.

Their mothers were even more scary than they were and if the nuns cast doubts on the authenticity of the sick notes and administered punishment accordingly, the mothers— and sometimes even the dads—came to the school and caused an uproar, accusing the nuns of calling their daughters liars, and shouting wildly of "reporting" them.

Once, when Maureen Quirke brought three sick notes in one month, each of them asking for her to be excused because she had her period, Sister Fidelma slapped her and said, "Do you take me for a fool, girl?," and within hours Mrs. Quirke arrived at the school like an avenging angel. (As Maureen said later, the funniest part of all was that she was actually pregnant at the time, although she didn't know it when she wrote the notes.) Mrs. Quirke shouted at Sister Fidelma, "No one lays a finger on any of my children. No one! Except me and Mr. Quirke! Now get yourself a man, you dried-out old mickey-dodger, and leave my Maureen alone."

Then she marched imperiously out the gate, dragging Maureen with her, and slapped Maureen all of the way home. I knew that for a fact because when I got home from school at lunchtime my father fell on me eagerly and said, "I saw that Quirke child passing up the road earlier with her mother, and the mother slapping forty shades of shite out of her. Tell us, what happened?"

So when I stopped taking antidepressants and went to secretarial college, my depression didn't return in all its savagery, but it hadn't entirely gone away either. And because I was terrified of being depressed again and didn't want to take pills, I dedicated my life to finding out the best ways of keeping it at bay, *au naturel.*

I wanted to banish depression entirely from my life, but had to be content with just stemming it by constantly reinforcing my emotional sandbags.

So along with swimming and reading, fighting depression became a hobby. In fact, strictly speaking, swimming wasn't really a hobby in its own right, it was more accurate to say that it came under the heading of Fighting Depression, subheading Exercise, category Gentle.

I read everything on the subject of depression that I could lay my hands on, and nothing raised my spirits like a good, juicy story of a famous person who suffered agonies from it.

Accounts of people who spent months on end in bed, not eating, not speaking, just staring at the ceiling, tears trickling down the sides of their faces, wishing they had the energy to kill themselves, thrilled me.

I was in very exalted company.

Churchill called his depression his "black dog," but, at eighteen, that confused me because I loved dogs. However, that was before the media had invented pit bull terriers. Once that happened, I understood exactly what Winston had been getting at.

And everytime I went to a bookstore, I pretended that I was just aimlessly browsing but, before I knew it, I had bypassed the new releases, the fiction, crime, science fiction, cookbooks, home decoration and horror sections, kept going through the biography section (pausing only briefly to see if any depressed person had recently published their life story) and somehow, as if by magic, always ended up at the self-help section, where I would spend hours reading through books that I hoped might fix me, that might have the magic solution, that would take away, or even just ease, the corrosive gnawing that was nearly always with me.

Of course a lot of self-help books were so full of garbage that they could reduce the most happy, well-balanced person to despair. Nevertheless, I usually parted with money for a little volume that encouraged me to perhaps "feel the fear and walk through it" or maybe to "heal my life" or it mightn't be a bad idea to "rediscover" my "child within" or asked me to consider "why I need you to love me before I can like myself."

What I really needed was a self-help book to help me stop buying self-help books, because they didn't help. They just made me feel guilty. It wasn't enough just to read the books. For them to work, I had to *do things*— like stand in front of a mirror and tell myself a hundred times a day that I was beautiful, which was called affirmation. Or spend half an hour every morning imagining myself being showered in love and affection, which was called visualization. Or writing lists of all the good things in my life, which was called writing lists of all the good things in my life.

I usually read the book and did what it suggested for about two days and then got tired, or bored, or caught by my brothers as I spoke seductively to my reflection in the mirror. (I never forgot The Great Scorning that followed *that.*)

And then I would feel depressed *and* guilty. So I would say that the hypothesis of the book must be fundamentally faulty because it hadn't made me feel any better and then I could abandon the whole project with a clear conscience.

I tried lots of other things also—evening primrose oil, vitamin $B_6$, excessive exercise, subliminal self-help tapes that you play when you're asleep, yoga, pilates, a flotation tank, aromatherapy massage, shiatsu, reflexology, a yeast-free diet, a gluten-free diet, a sugar-free diet, a food-free diet, vegetarianism, a "lots of meat" diet (I don't know if there's a name for it), an ionizer, an assertiveness course, a positive-thinking course, dream therapy, past-life regression, praying, meditating and sunlight therapy (a holiday in Crete, to be precise). For a while I ate nothing but dairy products, then for a while I gave up dairy products completely (I'd misread the article the first time), then I felt that if I had to go another day without a bar of chocolate, I would be killing myself anyway.

And while none of my measures turned out to be the Final Solution, at least they all worked for a while and I never again got as depressed as I had the first time. But Mrs. Nolan had said something about help being available if I only asked for it. I wished now I'd brought a tape recorder into the room with me because I couldn't remember exactly what she'd said. What did she mean?

The only thing I could think of was that maybe she meant that I should go for professional help, and see some kind of therapist or counselor or psychologist something or other. The problem was that about a year ago I *had* seen a therapist, about eight weeks or so, and that had been a complete waste of time.

 6

Her name was Alison and I used to go to see her once a week where we sat in a bare, tranquil little room and tried to figure out what was wrong with me.

Although we had discovered all kinds of interesting things—like the fact that I still held a grudge against Adrienne Cawley for giving me a game that the box said was "suitable for two-to-five-year-olds" at my sixth birthday party—I didn't seem to have learned anything more than what I had already managed to figure out for myself on many a sleepless night.

Naturally, the first thing that Alison and I did was the psychotherapy witch hunt called "Cherchez La Famille," where we tried to hold my family responsible for everything that was wrong with my damaged psyche.

But there was nothing funny about my family, unless normal was funny.

I had a perfectly normal relationship with my two brothers Chris and Peter—that is, I spent my childhood hating their guts and they reciprocated in traditional fraternal fashion by making my life a misery. They made me go to the store for them when I didn't want to, they hogged the TV set, broke my toys, scribbled on my homework, told me that I was adopted and that my real parents were in prison for robbing a bank. Then they told me they were joking about that and that my real mother was actually a witch. And when Mum and Dad went out to the pub they told me that they had really run away and were never coming back and that I'd be sent to an orphanage. The usual sibling playfulness.

I told all of this to Alison and when I got to the bit about Mum and Dad going to the pub she seized on it joyfully.

"Tell me about your parents' drinking," she said, settling back in her chair, making herself comfortable for the great pouring forth of revelations that she expected to follow.

"I can't really tell you anything," I said. "My mother doesn't drink."

Alison looked disappointed.

"And your father?" she asked, hopefully, realizing that all was not lost.

"Well, *he* drinks," I said.

She was delighted!

"Yes?" she said, in her extragentle voice. "Do you want to talk about it?"

"Well, yes," I said, confused. "Except there's nothing really to talk about. When I say he drinks, I don't mean that he has a problem."

"Mmmmmm," she nodded gently, knowingly. "And what do you mean by 'having a problem'?"

"I don't know," I said. "I suppose I mean being an alcoholic. And he isn't."

She said nothing.

"He's not," I laughed. "Sorry, Alison, I'd love to be able to tell you that my father was drunk throughout my childhood and we never had any money and that he hit us and shouted at us and tried to have sex with me and told my mum that he wished he'd never married her."

Alison didn't join in with my laughter and I felt slightly silly.

"*Did* your father tell your mother that he wished he'd never married her?" she asked quietly and with dignity.

"No!" I said, embarrassed.

"No?" asked Alison.

"Well, hardly ever," I admitted. "And it was only when he was drunk. And that was hardly ever either."

"And *did* you feel that your family never had enough money?" she asked.

"We were never short of money," I said stiffly.

"Good," said Alison.

"Well, that's not really true," I felt forced to admit. "We were always short of money, but it wasn't because of Dad's drinking, it was just because we . . . didn't have much money."

"Why didn't you have much money?" asked Alison.

"Because my dad couldn't get a job," I explained eagerly. "You see, he didn't have any qualifications because he had to leave school when he was fourteen because his father died and he had to look after his mother."

"I see," she said.

In fact, Dad used to say an awful lot more on the subject of his unemployment but I felt strangely reluctant to tell Alison.

One of the clearest memories of my childhood was Dad sitting at our kitchen table, passionately explaining the faults in the system. He used to tell me that in the English workplace the Irishman will always get "the shitty end of the stick" and that Seamus O'Hanlaoin and Michael O'Herlihy and all the rest of them were nothing but a crowd of crawlers and "arse-lickers" because they sucked up to their English bosses, but that you should hear what they said behind their backs. And that although Seamus O'Hanlaoin and Michael O'Herlihy and all the rest of them might have jobs, at least he, Jamsie Sullivan, had integrity.

That must have been very important to him, because he said it a lot.

He said it an awful lot the time that Saidbh O'Herlihy and Siobhán O'Hanlaoin were going with the school to Scotland and I wasn't.

I didn't want to tell Alison because I was afraid that I might offend her, in case she took my father's condemnation of his English would-be bosses personally.

I started to tell Alison about all the jobs my father went for and didn't get, when she cut into my memories.

"We're going to have to leave it there for this week." She stood up.

"Oh, is the hour up already?" I asked, shaken by how abruptly the session had ended.

"Yes," said Alison.

A wave of guilty fear overwhelmed me. I hoped that I hadn't sounded disloyal about Dad.

"Look, I don't want you to think that my dad wasn't a nice man or anything," I said desperately. "He's lovely and I really love him."

Alison gave me her Mona Lisa smile, giving nothing away and said, "See you next week, Lucy."

"Honestly, he's great," I insisted.

"Yes, Lucy," she smiled, not showing her teeth. "See you next week."

And the next week was worse. Somehow Alison got it out of me about not going on the school trip to Scotland.

"Didn't you mind?" she asked.

"No," I said again.

"But why not?" She had sounded quite despairing at that point—the first time I'd ever seen her show any emotion.

"Because I just didn't," I said simply.

"How did your father react when it became clear that you couldn't go?" she asked. "Can you remember?"

"Of course I can remember," I said in surprise. "He told me that his conscience was clear."

In fact, "My conscience is clear" was something Dad often said. And, "I can sleep easy in my bed at night" was another. And he was right. Very often he would sleep easy even before he got to his bed. That usually happened on the nights when he had a few drinks.

Somehow I ended up telling all of this to Alison also.

"Tell me about the nights when he . . . er . . . had a few drinks," she gently demanded.

"Oh, you make it sound so bad," I complained. "It wasn't bad at all, it was nice. He just kind of sang and cried a bit."

Alison looked at me without saying anything and to fill the silence I blurted out, "But it wasn't sad when he cried because I knew that in a funny way he was glad to be sad, if you know what I mean?"

Alison obviously didn't.

"We'll talk about it next week," she said. "Our hour is up."

But we didn't talk about it next week because I never went back to Alison.

I had felt manipulated by her into being mean about Dad and the guilt was awful. Besides, I was the one who was depressed so I couldn't understand why two whole sessions had been devoted to my father and how much he did or didn't drink.

In the same way that dieting makes you fat, I felt that analysis gives you problems. So I sincerely hoped that Mrs. Nolan hadn't been suggesting that I go and see another Alison because I really didn't want to.

7

We would have all forgotten about Mrs. Nolan—the whole experience would have been consigned to some dark and dusty room somewhere in the attic of our memories—if a couple of things hadn't occurred.

The first thing that happened was that Meredia's prediction came true. Well, sort of . . .

The day after we had had our fortunes told, Meredia arrived into work waving something above her tie-dyed head in a triumphant fashion.

"Look," she commanded. "Look, look, look."

Hetty, Megan and I hopped up from our desks and went over to Meredia's to have a look. The thing that she had been waving above her head was a check.

"She said I'd come into money and I *have*," shouted Meredia excitedly as she attempted to do an ill-advised little dance, knocking nine or ten files off her desk and sending shudders throughout the entire building.

"Show me, show me," I begged, trying to grab it from her. But, for such a large woman, she was surprisingly deft.

"Do you know how long I've waited for this money?" she demanded, looking from one of us to the other. "Have you *any* idea how long?"

Mutely, the three of us shook our heads. Meredia certainly knew how to create a captive audience.

"Well, I've waited *months!*" she bellowed, throwing her head back. "Literally *months!*"

"Wonderful," I said. "Isn't that amazing?"

"Who's it from?" asked Hetty.

"How much is it for?" asked Megan, asking the only truly important question.

"It's a refund from my book club," sang Meredia joyfully. "And you simply cannot *imagine* the number of letters I've had to write to get it. I was on the verge of going to Swindon in person to complain."

Megan, Hetty and I exchanged puzzled looks.

"Your . . . *book* club?" I asked slowly. "A refund from your book club?"

"Yes," said Meredia, sighing dramatically. "It's been awful. I said I didn't want the book of the month and they sent it anyway and—"

"So how much did you get?" interrupted Megan abruptly.

"Seven fifty," said Meredia.

"Is that seven hundred and fifty or seven pounds fifty?" I asked, fearing the worst.

"Seven *pounds* fifty," said Meredia, sounding annoyed. "What do you mean, seven hundred and fifty? The book of the month would need to be made of solid gold for me to spend that much on it. Honestly, Lucy, sometimes I wonder about you!"

"I see," said Megan, very matter-of-factly. "You got a check for seven pounds fifty—a *quarter* of the cost of the reading from Mrs. Nolan—and you're saying that her prediction that you would come into money has come true? Have I got that right?"

"Yes," said Meredia, all indignant. "She didn't say how *much* money I'd come into. She just said that I would. . . . And I did," she added defensively. "What's wrong?" she shouted, as we all drifted back to our desks, disappointment on our faces. "Your expectations are too high. That's your trouble."

"For a moment there I thought the predictions were going to come true. But it doesn't look like I'll be meeting the love of my life," said Hetty sadly.

"And I won't be having my big split," said Megan. "Unless it's a banana split."

"And I won't be getting married," I said.

"Not a hope," agreed Megan.

"None," said Hetty, sighing heavily.

Our conversation was cut short by the arrival of our boss, Ivor Simmonds. Or "Poison Ivor" as we sometimes called him. Or "that mean bastard" as we called him at other times.

"Ladies," he nodded at us, the expression on his face indicating that he thought we were anything but.

"Good morning, Mr. Simmonds," said Hetty with a polite smile.

"Mumble, mumble," said the rest of us.

That's because we hated him.

For no particular reason. Not for his complete absence of a sense of humor—as Megan said, he must have had all charisma surgically removed at birth—or his shortness, or his receding wispy red hair, or his hideous red beard, or his salesman's tinted spectacles, or his plump red lips that always seemed to be wet, or, worst of all, for his round, low-slung, womanly bottom, or for his nasty, cheap, shiny suit that covered—just about—the aforementioned bottom, or the visible panty line you could see through the shiny seat of the suit.

Of course all these factors *helped*. But mostly we just hated him because he was our boss. Because it was the *rule*.

His disgustingness did come in handy on several occasions. Once, when Megan was feeling really nauseous after a night on the Fosters and peach schnapps, it was a great help.

"If only I could puke," she complained. "Then I'd be fine."

"Imagine having sex with Ivor," I suggested, anxious to help.

"Yes," said Meredia gleefully. "Imagine having to kiss him, that mouth, that beard, Ugh!"

"Christ," muttered Megan, heaving slightly. "I think it's working."

"And I bet he's a real slurper," said Meredia, her face twisting in delighted horror.

"And think about what he'd look like just in his underpants," I suggested. "Think hard. I bet he doesn't wear normal ones. No nice boxers or anything."

"No, he doesn't," said Hetty, who didn't usually join in. We all swiveled around.

"How do *you* know?" we asked in unison.

"Because . . . er . . . you can see . . . you know . . . the line." Hetty blushed delicately.

"Fair enough," we conceded.

"I bet he wears knickers," I said gleefully. "Women's knickers. Big, pink, interlock ones that come up to his armpits, that his wife has to buy for him in an old ladies' shop because he can't get any normal ones to fit him."

"And imagine what his willy looks like," suggested Meredia.

"Yes," I said, feeling my stomach begin to turn. "I bet it's tiny and skinny and that he has red pubic hair and . . ."

"That was enough to do it. Megan bolted from the office and returned, beaming, about two minutes later.

"Wow," she grinned. "Projectile! Anyone got any toothpaste?"

"Honestly, Megan," said Hetty coldly. "You're just too much sometimes."

Megan, Meredia and I exchanged raised eyebrow looks,

wondering what had annoyed the normally pleasant and polite Hetty.

By a happy coincidence Mr. Simmonds seemed to hate us as much as we hated him.

He glared at us, went into his office and slammed the door.

Meredia, Megan and I made desultory attempts to switch on our computers. Hetty didn't, because hers was already on.

Hetty did most of the work in the office.

There was a very scary period when Megan first arrived and she had worked really, really hard. Not only did she start work on time, but she actually *started work if she came in early*. She didn't unfold a newspaper and look at her watch and say, "Three more minutes. Those bastards aren't getting a second more out of me than they're owed," like the rest of us did.

Meredia and I took her aside and explained that not only was she putting our jobs in jeopardy, but that she could even end up working herself out of a job. ("And *then* how would you get to Greece?") So she slowed down, even managed to make a few mistakes. We all got along a lot better after that.

"Get Hetty to do it," was the office motto. Only Hetty didn't know about it.

I couldn't ever really figure out why Hetty had a job. She certainly didn't need the money. But Meredia and I decided that the boards of all the charities in London must have been oversubscribed when Hetty decided that she was bored and needed amusing, so she lowered her sights and came to work for us instead.

Which wasn't *unlike* working for a charity.

Indeed, Meredia and I often joked that working for Wholesale Metals and Plastics was exactly the *same* as working for a charity, so pitifully small were our stipends.

\*     \*     \*

The day progressed. We went about our work. Sort of. No further mention was made of Mrs. Nolan, loves of lives, big splits, coming into money or of me getting married.

Later that day my mother called and I braced myself for news of a disaster, because she never called me just for a chat, to shoot the breeze, to aimlessly while away a few minutes of my employer's time. She only rang to breathlessly report catastrophes—deaths were her favorite, but most things would do. A chance of layoffs at my brothers' place of work, a lump on my uncle's thyroid, a fire in a barn in Monaghan or an unmarried cousin falling pregnant (a particular favorite, up there with deaths in the works of a combine harvester).

"D'you know Maisie Patterson?" she demanded excitedly.

"Yes," I said, thinking "Maisie *who?*" but knowing better than to say so because we could have been there all day while I got the Maisie Patterson family tree. ("She was one of the Finertans before she married . . . but, of *course* you know the Finertans, don't you remember when you were small I took you over to their house, a fine big house with a green gate, just behind the Nealons, but you *know* the Nealons, don't you remember Bridie Nealon, the day she gave you two Marietta biscuits, sure you know what a Marietta biscuit is, don't you remember squeezing the butter out through the holes . . .")

"Well . . ." said my mother, building up some suspense. Maisie Patterson had obviously gone to meet her maker, but it wasn't enough just to say it like that.

"Yes," I said patiently.

"They buried her yesterday!" she finally exclaimed.

"Why did they do that?" I asked mildly. "Had she annoyed them? When are they letting her out?"

"Oh, you're very smart," my mother said bitterly, annoyed that her news hadn't sent me gasping and reeling. "You're to send them a Mass card."

"How did it happen?" I asked, hoping to cheer her up. "Did she catch her head in the combine harvester? Drown in the grain silo? Or was she savaged by a hen?"

"Not at all," she said, annoyed. "Don't be ridiculous, sure, hasn't she been living in Chicago this long time?"

"Oh, er . . . yes."

"No, t'was terribly sad," she said, dropping her voice a couple of decibels as a mark of respect and for the next fifteen minutes she gave me Maisie Patterson's medical history. The mysterious headaches that she got, the glasses she was prescribed to correct the headaches, the CAT scan she was given when the glasses didn't work, the X-rays, the medication, the spells in the hospital being prodded and poked by bewildered specialists, the eventual all-clear and, finally, the red Toyota that knocked her down, ran her over, ruptured her spleen and sent her somersaulting into the next world.

 8

On Thursday morning the day started badly and got worse.

When I woke up feeling totally miserable, I wasn't to know that Megan's "prediction" was due to come "true" that day.

If I *had* known I might have found it easier to get up.

As it was, it was touch and go whether I'd manage to break free from my bed's loving, warm embrace.

I always found it hard to get up in the mornings—one of the legacies of my teenage bout of depression, at least that's what I liked to say. It was probably just laziness, but calling it depression made me feel a lot less guilty. I could barely drag myself into the bathroom and once I was there I had my work cut out to force myself to have a shower.

My bedroom was freezing and I couldn't find clean underpants and I hadn't ironed anything so I had to wear the same clothes that I had worn to work the day before and that I'd just thrown on the floor the previous night and I couldn't find any clean underpants in Karen's or Charlotte's rooms either so I had to go to work wearing my bikini bottoms from my swimsuit.

And when I got to the tube station all the newspapers were sold out and I'd just missed a train. And while I was waiting I thought I'd try and buy a chocolate bar from the machine on the platform and for once the bloody thing worked and then I ate the candy bar in two seconds and immediately felt really guilty and then I started to worry that maybe I had an eating disorder if I was internalizing chocolate first thing in the morning.

I was miserable.

It was cold and wet and there seemed so little to look forward to and I wanted to be at home in my warm bed, eating potato chips, weighty piles of glossy magazines beside me.

Megan looked up from her newspaper when I dragged myself in, twenty minutes late.

"Didn't you get undressed last night?" she asked cheerfully.

"What do you mean?" I asked wearily.

"I mean did you sleep in your clothes?" she said.

"Oh shut up," I said. On days like that one, Megan's Australian plain speaking was just too much for me.

"And anyway," I said, "if you think I look bad on the outside, you'd want to see what I've got on as underpants."

Even if Megan had only had five minutes sleep, she still got up in time to iron her clothes. And if she didn't have any clean panties, she gave herself enough time to stop somewhere on the way to work and buy a pair. Not that Megan ever didn't have clean panties because she always did her washing long before her underwear drawer was empty. But that was Australians for you. Organized. Hardworking. Capable.

The day proceeded along normal lines. Every now and then I would fantasize about a Lockerbie-style disaster where a plane would fall from the sky and land on my office. Preferably on my desk, just to be on the safe side. Then I wouldn't have to come to work for ages. I might be dead, of course, but so what? I still wouldn't have to come to work.

The door to Mr. Simmonds's office would open regularly and he'd stomp out, bottom wobbling, and throw something on my desk or Meredia's desk or Megan's desk and shout, "There's forty-eight mistakes in that. You're getting better," or "Which one of you has bought shares in Liquid Paper" or something equally unkind.

He was never mean to Hetty, because he was afraid of her. Her poshness reminded him that he was a middle-class boy made average and that he wore suits of man-made fibers.

It was about ten to two, when I was slumped over my desk reading some article about how coffee is actually good for you again, and Meredia was snoring gently at her desk, a large bar of chocolate by her hand, that a small drama burst into the office, and lo and behold Megan's prediction proceeded to come true.

Kind of . . .

Megan lurched in, her face as white as a ghost, blood pouring from her mouth.

"Megan!" I shouted in alarm, jumping up from my desk. "What *happened* to you?"

"Eh? What?" said Meredia, jerking awake, all confused, the merest hint of a dribble exiting her mouth by the left side.

"It's nothing," said Megan, but she looked a bit wobbly and sat on my desk. Blood was pouring down her chin and onto her shirt.

"I've got to ring an ambulance," said Megan.

"Jesus, no you don't," I said panicking, giving her a handful of tissues, which were soaked red in an instant. "I'll do it. You'd better lie down. Meredia, get up off your fat ass and help her to lie down!"

"No, it's not for me, you fool," said Megan irritably, shaking Meredia off her. "It's for the bloke who fell off his bike and landed on me."

"Oh my God!" I exclaimed. "Is he badly hurt?"

"No," said Megan shortly, "But he bloody well will be by the time I've finished with him. He'll need a body bag, not an ambulance."

Before I could do it, she had picked up the phone and, through a mouthful of blood, called the emergency services and asked for an ambulance.

"Where is he?" asked Meredia.

"Out front, lying on the road, holding up the traffic," said Megan.

She was in a *very* bad mood.

"Is someone looking after him?" asked Meredia, an acquisitive gleam appearing in her eyes.

"Loads of people," barked Megan. "You Brits love a good accident, don't you?"

"Well, I'd better check on him anyway," said Meredia, lumbering toward the door. "He may be in shock so I'll cover him with my shawl."

"No need," complained Megan, blood bubbling as she spoke. "Someone's already put a coat over him."

But Meredia was gone. She had heard opportunity knocking. Although she had a pretty (if extremely fat) face, she had little success with men. The only men who actively pursued her were the odd ones who had a definite "thing" for obese women. And as Meredia said, with dignity, "Who wants a man who just wants you for your body?"

But the alternative was nearly as bad, I thought. She liked meeting men when they were vulnerable, either emotionally or physically, taking care of them, making herself indispensable, giving them all the support a weak person might need.

The only fly in the ointment was that the moment they were well enough to move, that's exactly what they did. Headed for the hills and away from Meredia's loving embrace as fast as their recently healed legs could carry them.

"Well, I'd better clean up this mess," said Megan, wiping her mouth on her sleeve.

"Don't be ridiculous," I said. "You're going to need stitches."

"No, I'm not," said Megan scornfully. "This is nothing. Have you ever seen what a combine harvester can do to a man's arm . . . ?"

"Oh stop being so . . . so . . . *Australian!*" I exclaimed.

"You need stitches. You need to go to the hospital. I'll come with you."

If she thought I was going to miss the chance to have an afternoon off work, then she had another think coming.

"No, you bloody well won't come with me," she said tartly. "What do you think I am? Some kind of kid?"

Just then the office door opened and in came Hetty back from lunch. She looked suitably appalled at the showing of *Apocalypse Now* that was taking place on Megan's face.

Two seconds later, Mr. Simmonds arrived, also back from lunch. A separate lunch from Hetty's lunch, he seemed peculiarly keen to emphasize. Apparently they had just bumped into each other at the front door—not that anyone cared.

He too looked appalled. He was obviously upset about Megan's blood being spilled, but I think he was more upset about *where* Megan's blood was being spilled. On the desks and files and phones and letters and documents of his precious little empire.

He said that of course Megan must go to the hospital, and that of course I must go with her and when Meredia returned to say that the ambulance had arrived he said that she could go too. He said that Hetty had better stay behind because he wanted someone to hold the fort.

As I joyfully turned off my computer and got my coat, it suddenly struck me that whatever it was Mr. Simmonds wanted Hetty to hold, it certainly wasn't his fort.

*9*

When we got to the ambulance, there was no room for Meredia. Undeterred, she said she'd get a taxi and see us there. As we drove away from the curb, I felt a bit like a pop star—it must have been the tinted windows and the small crowd of onlookers staring after us.

They were reluctant to leave, wringing the last few drops of excitement from the accident before they started to drift back to their lives, disappointed that the drama was over, and even more disappointed that someone hadn't died.

"He looked okay, didn't he?" said one bystander to another.

"Yes," came the bitter reply.

We spent four hours sitting on hard chairs in a crowded, manic, overworked emergency room. People with injuries far worse than Megan's or Shane's (the cyclist—by now we were all fairly intimate) sat waiting also, stoically holding in their laps whatever limbs they had severed and managed to retrieve. Trolleys with dying people on them were rushed past us regularly. No one seemed able to tell us what was happening or when Megan or Shane would be seen. The coffee machine wasn't working. The place was freezing.

"Just think." I closed my eyes in bliss. "We could be at work now."

"Yes," sighed Megan, bits of dried blood flaking away from her face as she spoke. "What a stroke of luck, eh?"

"God." I smiled. "I was so *miserable* earlier. I wish I'd known what a treat I had in store for me."

"I hope I'll be seen soon," said Shane, looking anxious and confused. "Because they're waiting for those documents in WC1. They said they were urgent. Has anyone seen my radio?"

Shane was a bike messenger and had been en route to a delivery when he veered off his path and landed on Megan.

He kept kind of dozing off to sleep and then jerking awake and going on about his delivery in WC1. Megan and I exchanged long-suffering looks when he launched into it for about the tenth time, while Meredia smiled at him like he was a sweet little child and it gradually dawned on us that maybe he wasn't a moron and that perhaps he was concussed.

Apart from these regular bursts from Shane, conversation was desultory.

"Well, look on the bright side." I smiled at Megan, referring to her mutilated mouth. "You got the big split that you were promised by the fortune-teller. But I bet you weren't expecting it to be a split lip."

At that, Meredia jerked up straight like she'd been shot in the back and grabbed my wrist, digging her nails into me.

"My God," she hissed, staring straight ahead, a peculiar light in her eyes. Mad, actually, that was the word I needed. A *mad* light in her eyes. "She's right!" she said, still talking in the hissy voice, still staring into the middle distance. "My God, she's right!"

"I've got a name," I said, annoyed at her histrionics. And my wrist hurt.

"Hey, you're right," said Megan, starting to laugh.

"Ouch!" she complained, as her laughter started her face bleeding again. "What a blast," she went on, laughing in earnest, blood pouring in Niagraesque fashion down the side of her face. "Yeah, I got my big split, all right. Just like she said. I can't see what good has come out of it, though."

"Maybe all will become clear with time," said Meredia, in a mysterious voice and giving Shane pseudo-covert looks and winking meaningfully at Megan and then jerking her head in Shane's direction again.

"If you know what I mean . . ." continued Meredia, with heavy emphasis.

"Yeah, maybe," laughed Megan lightheartedly.

I wasn't sure if Meredia had Shane in mind for herself or Megan, but past experience told me that Meredia wanted him for her own. That situation had her hallmark stamped all over it.

Although, by rights, he really should have been Megan's. Didn't she break his fall? And she handled the whole trauma so bravely that she deserved a treat.

"So now it's just you and Hetty, Lucy," said Megan. "Soon it'll be your turn for your fortune to come true."

"Do the words 'cold day' and 'in hell' mean anything to you?" I asked, laughing.

"Oooh, you doubting Thomas," admonished Meredia. "But you have to admit that it *is* peculiar."

"No, I don't," I said. "Don't be so silly! You can adjust any facts to fit into any predictions if you try hard enough."

"Such cynicism in one so young," said Meredia, shaking her head sadly.

"Has anyone seen my radio?" croaked Shane, coming to again. "I've got to talk to my controller."

"Shush, lovie, it's fine," said Meredia comfortingly, as she forced his head down onto her shoulder.

He mumbled some kind of protest, but it didn't do him any good.

"Just you wait," Meredia said threateningly to me, talking over Shane's confused head. "You'll see. It'll all come true. And then you'll be sorry."

I smiled longsufferingly at Megan, expecting her to smile longsufferingly back but to my great alarm, she didn't. She was too busy nodding agreement with Meredia.

Golly, I thought, my stomach tightening with shock, could her brain have been affected by the accident? I mean, Megan was possibly the most cynical person that I'd ever met, including myself—and I prided myself on having the highest standards of cynicism. I had my days when I was sure I could out-cynic some of the best cynics currently operating on the circuit.

Megan, like me, was so cynical that she didn't even like Daniel. "He doesn't fool me with his nice manners and his good looks," she had said after she first met him.

So what had happened to her?

*Surely* she didn't think that the predictions for herself and Meredia had come true? And worse again, surely she didn't think that because of that, that the predictions for Hetty and me would come true?

Eventually, when the nurses had run out of heart-attack victims and other nearly dead people to deal with, they stitched up Megan's face and said that Shane wasn't concussed, that he was just diligent.

We were all finally allowed to leave.

"Where do you live?" Meredia asked Shane, as we stood in the hospital carpark.

"Greenwich," he said warily.

That was in south London. *Very* south London.

"What a stroke of luck," said Meredia quickly. "We can get a taxi home together."

"But . . ." I started to protest, about to remind Meredia that she lived in Stoke Newington—which was northeast London—nowhere *near* Greenwich.

But Meredia fixed me with a murderous glare and my protests died away.

"But I've got to get my bike," said Shane backing away in fear. "And I really have to deliver these documents."

"Don't be so silly," said Meredia, all faux-cheerful. "You can do that tomorrow. Come on now. Night, girls, see you both at work in the morning.

"If I'm able to walk," she muttered in an aside—one that was loud enough for Shane to hear and flinch at.

"Know what I mean, eh?" she leered, gesturing in the direction of her crotch. And with a final meaningful wink off she went, dragging the terrified Shane along by the arm.

He looked back pleadingly at Megan and me, his face one big cry for help, but there was nothing we could do for him.

An innocent lamb to the slaughter.

 10

The following day all hell broke loose, when Megan and Meredia notified everyone in the whole world that I was getting married. They didn't actually tell everyone in the whole world, they just told Caroline, the receptionist at work. But that was as good as—better probably than, actually—telling everyone in the whole world.

Meredia and Megan had decided, notwithstanding my lack of boyfriend, that Mrs. Nolan's predictions for me would come true, just as her predictions for them had.

Of course they apologized later and said they hadn't meant to do any harm and that they had really only been joking, etc., etc., but by then the damage was done and the idea had been planted in my mind and I had got to thinking that maybe a boyfriend would be a nice thing, a soul mate, someone to feel safe with, someone to be intimate with.

It opened up old longings. I began to *want* something from my life, which was always a mistake.

But all that was still ahead of me when my alarm went off, and I thought I felt miserable *then*. The only good thing was that it was Friday.

When I woke up I was as badly organized as I had been the previous day. I still hadn't washed my clothes, so I still hadn't any clean underwear, so I had to wear Steven's boxers that he had left behind when I forced him to leave my apartment rather suddenly about three weeks before. I had washed them, with the vague intention of returning them to him, so at least they were clean.

At the station, the candy machine was a bastard, it worked for me—again! Machinery hated me. It gave me a bar of chocolate and I didn't have the willpower not to eat it. I was becoming more and more convinced that I had an eating disorder.

I finally got to work and I was very, very late indeed, even by my standards.

As I rushed past reception I was almost knocked to the ground by Mr. Simmonds going at high speed in the direction of the Gents, his butt scurrying along about three yards behind the rest of him, trying hard to keep up. He looked flustered and agitated and he was a small bit red about the eyes. In fact, if I had thought the man was capable of human emotion, I would have sworn that he was crying. Something had obviously upset him.

My spirits rose.

I smiled brightly at Caroline, the receptionist, because it was more than my life was worth not to. She took offense easily and withheld my personal calls if she felt that I had slighted her. She smiled brightly back. As I raced past I thought I heard her call something after me—in fact it sounded oddly like "Congratulations"—but I was too eager to find out what disaster had befallen Mr. Simmonds to stop.

I breezed into the office, no longer so worried about being late. Mr. Simmonds obviously had bigger fish to fry.

Megan's bruises had come up beautifully and a white bandage covered the lower right-hand corner of her face.

I stopped in my tracks when I noticed that Megan and Meredia weren't fighting. Indeed, they compounded my confusion by talking civilly to each other.

How peculiar, I thought! Some kind of cease-fire must be in process. The pair of them were huddled around the cookies—always a great bonding area, the office cookies—and were whispering furtively.

It was unlikely that they were discussing Megan's injuries or Meredia's sex life. It would take a bigger event than either of those to bring Megan and Meredia together.

This had to mean that something was definitely up.

Great! My spirits rose even further. I loved a bit of excitement. Maybe Mr. Simmonds had been fired. Or his wife had left him. Something good like that, I hoped.

I gave a quick glance around the office. Where was the diligent Hetty?

"Lucy!" declared Meredia dramatically. The way she

often did. "Thank God you're here. There's something you *have* to know."

"What?" I demanded, a thrill of anticipation running through me.

"Is it you? Did you get lucky with Shane?"

A brief shadow passed over Meredia's face. "We'll talk about that later," she said. "No, it's something to do with here."

"*Really?*" I gasped in excitement. "I thought something must be up. I just passed Poison Ivor in the hall and he was . . ."

"Lucy, I think you'd better sit down," Megan interrupted.

"What is it?" I demanded, absolutely *dying* to know.

"Something has happened," said Meredia, in a dramatic whisper, keen to create an atmosphere. "Something that you should know."

"Well, if I should know it, why won't you bloody well tell me?" I demanded.

"It's Hetty," said Megan solemnly, talking out of the uninjured side of her mouth.

"*Hetty?*" I hooted incredulously. "But what's Hetty got to do with Poison Ivor? Or me? Oh God—she's not having an affair with him, is she?"

"No, no, no," said Meredia, shuddering. "No, it's a *good* thing. But she won't be in for a couple of days because something has happened to her."

"Well, would you mind telling me just what that something is," I said querulously. "Or do I have to sit here all day while you draw this out?"

"Hetty has met the love of her life," Meredia finally intoned.

A silence followed. You could've heard a tab of acid drop. "Really?" I managed to ask, my voice hoarse.

"You heard me," said Meredia with a smug smile. I looked at Megan. Hoping for a bit of sanity and normality. But she just nodded at me and she had the same smug smile.

"She's met the love of her life and she's left Dick and she's moving in with Roger immediately.

"And Poison Ivor's heart is broken," guffawed Megan, slapping her slim, golden thigh.

"Don't be ridiculous," I said absently. "He hasn't got a heart."

More chortling from Megan and Meredia but I couldn't bring myself to join in.

"He must have the hots for Hetty big-time," said Megan. "Yuk, poor Hetty, how awful. Imagine! He must have been going around with a constant hard-on."

"Shut up, Megan!" I begged. "Or I'll throw up."

"Me too," said Meredia.

"So, have I got this right?" I asked weakly. "Roger is the other guy?"

"Yes," smiled Megan.

"But Hetty doesn't do this sort of thing," I said.

I was upset and confused. I mean, Hetty really *didn't* do that sort of thing. Well, at least, she certainly didn't used to. It felt all wrong. Hetty was steady and steadfast and stable and stalwart and all those other words beginning with *st*. She just didn't go around meeting the love of her life and leaving her husband and that kind of thing. She just *didn't*.

I would have felt as upset and disoriented if the earth changed direction and the sun rose in the west instead of the east. Or if I dropped a slice of toast on the floor and it landed with the buttered side facing up. Hetty's leaving Dick contradicted everything that I believed to be true, the very foundations of my universe were shaken.

"Aren't you happy for her?" asked Meredia.

"Who is he?" I blurted out. "Who's this love of her life?"

"Wait till you hear," said Meredia with relish.

"Yes, get this," interrupted Megan, also with relish.

"The love of her life is none other than Dick's brother," said Meredia with a flourish.

"Dick's brother?" I whispered. Things were getting more bizarre by the second. "So what happened? She's known the guy for all these years and she suddenly decides that she loves him?"

"No, no, no," said Meredia, smiling at me as though I was a naughty child. "It's so romantic. She'd never met him until three days ago and they just clapped eyes on each other and *'voilà!' a coup de foudre, l'amour, je t'adore,* er . . . um . . . *la plume de ma tante . . .*" she trailed off, having run out of French phrases to describe Hetty falling in love.

"How come she'd never met him before?" I asked. "She's been married for years." A thought struck me. "Oh no," I said in alarm. "Oh no. Don't let it be so."

"What?" gasped Megan and Meredia in unison.

"Please don't tell me that this is Dick's younger brother and he's been out in foreign parts—maybe Kenya or Burma or somewhere—for the past twenty years or so, like something out of *Last Days of the Raj* and that he's come back and he's all tanned and has blond floppy hair and he's lounging around in a white linen suit, and sitting in a rattan chair and drinking gin and looking at Hetty with lazy, come-to-bed eyes. I mean, I just couldn't *bear* it! It would be too much of a cliché."

"Honestly, Lucy," scolded Meredia, "you have such an overactive imagination. No, it's nothing like that."

"He hasn't given her an ivory bracelet?" I asked.

"Well, if he did she didn't mention it," said Meredia doubtfully.

"Phew." I breathed a sigh of relief. "Good."

"It's Dick's *older* brother," said Megan.

"Good," I said again. "Already this is going against the stereotype."

"And she had never met him before because there had been some kind of family fight," continued Meredia. "Dick and Roger hadn't spoken for years. But they're the best of friends now. . . . Although maybe not, now that Hetty has . . ."

I stared at the pair of them, at their happy, excited faces.

"What's wrong with you, you miserable cow?" demanded Megan.

"I don't know," I said. "It doesn't feel right."

"Yes it does," sang Meredia. "The fortune-teller told her that she'd meet the love of her life. And now she has!"

"But it's all wrong," I said desperately. "There's something wrong with Hetty and Dick. I mean, that was obvious when she got upset on the drive home from Mrs. Nolan's."

Meredia and Megan sat silently and sullenly.

"But instead of doing something about it, she believes some cock-a-mamie story from a charlatan of a fortune-teller . . ."

"She *wasn't* a charlatan," interrupted Meredia angrily. "I didn't see her changing color."

"That's a chameleon, not a charlatan," I said in exasperation. "Anyway, she's told that she'll meet the love of her life, so she latches on to the first man she meets, one who hasn't even got the decency to have a linen suit or a rattan chair, and without giving any thought to the consequences, she ups and runs off with him!

"In fact," I added, "I think she was having some kind

of flirtation or something going with Poison Ivor—that's how miserable she was.''

I paused in case either of them needed to vomit. They both looked pale and sweaty, so I waited a short while before I continued.

''We weren't wrong to get our tarot cards read, but we weren't supposed to take it seriously. It was only a bit of fun. Not some kind of solution to real problems.''

They were both silent.

''Can't you see?'' I begged them, but they avoided my eyes and looked at their shoes. ''This isn't the right thing for Hetty.''

''But how do you know?'' demanded Meredia. ''Why don't you have any faith? Why don't you believe Mrs. Nolan?''

''Because Hetty has real problems with her marriage,'' I said. ''And they're not going to be fixed because she wants to believe she's met the love of her life. That's just escapism.''

''You're just scared,'' Megan suddenly blurted out, lop-sided but passionate. She sounded angry and her face was flushed and emotional.

''Of what?'' I asked in surprise.

''You're just afraid to admit that the predictions have come true for me and Meredia and Hetty, because you'll have to admit that your prediction will come true also.''

''Megan,'' I said in desperation. ''What's wrong? I rely on you to be the sane one around here. The voice of reason.''

Meredia bristled angrily and visibly expanded, which was quite something, as I had thought she was already at bursting point.

''Look, Megan,'' I continued. ''You don't really believe all this nonsense about predictions. Tell me you don't.''

''The facts speak for themselves,'' she said haughtily.

"Yeah," sneered Meredia, much braver once she knew she had Megan on her side. She even tried to curl her lip. "Yeah. The facts do speak for themselves. So you'd better face it! You're getting married!"

"I can't listen to any more of this," I said calmly. "I don't want to have a falling out with either of you about this, but as far as I'm concerned the subject is closed."

The pair of them exchanged a look, a funny one—worried? Guilty maybe?—which I chose to ignore.

I sat down at my desk, switched on my computer, fought back the urge to hang myself—which passed fleetingly, but intensely, through me—and started my day.

After a little while I noticed that the two of them still weren't doing any work—not that there was anything unusual about it, especially considering that Mr. Simmonds hadn't yet returned—but instead of making personal calls to Australia or flicking through *Marie Claire* or eating their lunch (which Meredia did most days around ten-thirty) they just sat and looked at me in an odd way.

I stopped typing and looked up.

"What's wrong?" I asked in exasperation. "Why are you both being so weird?"

"Tell her," muttered Meredia to Megan.

"Oh no," said Megan with a grim little laugh. "Oh no, not me. It was your idea so you get to tell her."

"You bitch!" exclaimed Meredia. "It was not my idea. It was *our* idea."

"Fuck you!" cried Megan. "You're the one who started all . . ."

My phone rang, interrupting the exchange. I managed to answer it without taking my eyes off the pair of them. I hated to miss a good fight, and you could depend on Meredia and Megan to have some humdingers. It was amusing to see how short-lived their detente had been.

"Hello," I said.

"Lucy!" said a voice.

Oh dear. It was my roommate Karen. She sounded angry. I must have forgotten to leave a check for the gas or the phone or something.

"Karen, hi!" I said quickly, trying to cover my nervousness. "Look, I'm sorry I forgot to leave the check for the phone. Or is it the gas? I got home late last night and . . ."

"Lucy, is it true?" she interrupted.

"Of course it's true," I said indignantly. "It was well after midnight when I got in and . . ."

"No, no, no," she said impatiently. "I mean about you getting married?"

The room tilted slightly.

"Excuse me?" I said faintly. ".Who on earth told you that?"

"The receptionist who answers the phone at your office," said Karen. "And I must say that it's a bit much having to find out from her. When were you going to tell Charlotte and me? I thought we were your best friends. And now we'll have to put an ad in for a new roommate and we all get along so well and what if we get someone horrible who doesn't drink and who doesn't know any good-looking men and it won't be the same without you and . . ."

Her voice continued plaintively.

Megan and Meredia had gone suspiciously quiet. They were both sitting very, very still, guilt and fear written on their fool faces.

The guilt on their faces? Karen talking about me getting married? Megan and Meredia's insistence that Hetty's prediction had come "true"? Mrs. Nolan foretelling that I would be getting married.

*The guilt on their faces.*

 *11*

The penny finally dropped. It was so outrageous I could hardly believe it.

Was it really possible that, because they thought that Mrs. Nolan's predictions for Meredia, Megan and Hetty had come true, her predictions for me were also bound to come true? Could it really be that this pair of idiots had gone around telling people that I was getting married, as if it was a *fact* and not the prediction of a tarot reader?

Rage surged through me. And bewilderment. How could they be so stupid?

I realized that I was not one to talk. My life had been a series of one stupid thing after another, interspersed with some really ridiculous things and one or two downright insane things. But I was pretty sure that I'd never have done anything as crazy as that!

I narrowed my eyes at them. Meredia shrunk back in her chair, the very picture of craven fear. Megan set her mouth—well one side of it anyway—in a stubborn and brazen fashion. She wasn't so easy to scare.

Karen continued to talk at high speed.

". . . I suppose we could get a guy for a roommate but what if he got a crush on one of us and . . ."

"Karen," I said, trying to get a word in edgewise.

". . . and he'd pee all over the bathroom, you know what men are like . . ."

"Karen," I said again, a bit louder.

". . . of course *he* might have good-looking friends, in fact he might even be good-looking himself, but we wouldn't be able to walk around with no clothes on although if he was good-looking maybe we'd want to and . . ."

"Karen!" I shouted.

She shut up.

"Karen," I said with relief, glad to have arrested the unstoppable train of her stream of consciousness. "I can't really talk right now, but I'll call you back as soon as I can."

"It's Steven, I suppose," she interrupted. "I'm glad, he's great. I don't know why you had to go and dump him, unless you *wanted* him to ask you to marry him, all along. Smart move, Lucy, I wouldn't have expected that from you . . ."

I hung up. I had to. I didn't know what else to do. I stared hard at Meredia and then at Megan and then back to Meredia. And then quickly flicked another glare at Megan just to let her know that I was still on her case.

After a few seconds I spoke. "That was Karen," I said, in a daze. "And she seems to be under the impression that I'm getting married."

"Sorry," muttered Meredia.

"Yeah, sorry," muttered Megan.

"Sorry for what?" I said unkindly. "Perhaps you'd care to tell me just what exactly is going on?"

I mean, I had a fairly good idea of what was going on. But I wanted to know the full facts and I also wanted to put the pair of them through the very awkward experience of having to explain. To have to say, out loud, in words, in front of people, the exact nature of their stupidity. The door opened and Catherine from the director's office breezed in and flung something in the in-tray. "Lucy," she called. "Congratulations! I'll be down later to hear all the details."

And breezed out again.

"What the fu . . ." I began.

The phone rang.

It was my other roommate Charlotte.

"Lucy," she said breathlessly. "Karen's just told me! And I want to tell you that I'm really happy for you. I know Karen says that you're a stupid bitch for not telling us, but I'm sure you had your reasons."

"Charl—" I tried to say. But, as with Karen, there was no getting a word in edgewise with her.

"And, Lucy, I'm so glad things have finally worked out for you," she chattered on. "To be quite honest, I never thought that they would. I know I always disagreed with you when you went on about how you were going to end up as an old maid with forty cats, but I was beginning to be afraid that that really was what was going to happen. . . ."

"Charlotte," I interrupted her angrily, "I've got to go."

And I slammed down the phone.

Which rang again immediately.

This time it was Daniel.

"Lucy," he croaked, "tell me it's not true. Don't marry him! No one could love you as much as I do."

I waited grimly for him to shut up.

"Lucy," he said after a while. "Are you there?"

"Yes," I said shortly. "Who told you?"

"Chris," he said, sounding surprised.

"*Chris?*" I yelled. "Chris, my brother?!!"

"Er, yes," said poor Daniel. "Is this supposed to be a secret or something?"

"Daniel," I tried to explain. "Look, I can't go into this, right now. But I'll call you as soon as I can, okay?"

"Okay," he agreed. "And I was only joking earlier. I really am very hap . . ."

I hung up.

The phone rang again.

And I let it ring.

"One of you two better answer it," I said grimly.

Meredia picked up the phone.

"Hello," she said nervously.

"No," she said, looking fearfully at me. "She can't come to the phone right now."

A pause.

"Yes, I'll tell her," she said, and hung up.

"Who was it?" I asked, feeling like I was dreaming.

"Er, the boys in the mailroom. They want to take you out for a drink to celebrate."

"Just how bad is this?" I asked, my head spinning in horror. "Have you e-mailed everyone in the entire organization? Or just several hundred of my closest friends? I mean, how does my *brother* know?"

"Your brother?" asked Megan, alarm flitting across her face.

Meredia swallowed. "Lucy," she said nervously. "We haven't e-mailed anyone. Honestly."

"No," chimed in Megan, laughing slightly in what I can only hope for her sake was relief. "We've told hardly anyone. Just Caroline. And Blandina and . . ."

"Blandina!" I interjected sharply. "You've told *Blandina.* If you've told Blandina, we don't need bloody e-mail. The whole world must already know. They probably know on Mars. In fact I bet my mother knows."

Blandina was the PR person at our company, and gossip was her currency, the air that she breathed.

My phone rang again.

"One of you better answer that," I said threateningly.

"If it's anyone else calling to congratulate me on my impending nuptials I may not be responsible for my actions."

Megan picked up the phone.

"Hello," she said, a nervous quaver in her voice.

"It's for you," she said, handing the phone over to me as if it were red-hot.

"Megan," I hissed, gesturing to her to cover the mouthpiece. "I don't want to talk to anyone. I'm not taking this call."

"I think you'd better," she said miserably. "It's your mother."

 12

I stared pleadingly at Megan, then at the phone, then at Megan again.

This did not bode well. Surely it was too soon for someone else to have died? And she definitely wasn't just calling for a chat—my mother and I had never had the, "Oh go on, buy it, I won't tell Daddy, no one would believe you've got a grown-up daughter, it looks better on you than it does on me, can I have a squirt of your perfume, you've a better figure now than the day you got married, now let's go for several gin and tonics because you're my best friend," type of relationship. So it meant that my mother must somehow have gotten wind of the whole me-getting-married fiasco and I was very reluctant to talk to her.

To be honest, I was quite afraid of her.

"Tell her I'm not here," I hissed desperately at Megan. Immediately there was an eruption from the receiver, which sounded like two parrots fighting, but which was actually my mother yelling that she had heard that. I took the phone.

"Who's dead?" I said, playing for time.

"You are," she roared, with an uncharacteristic flash of wit.

"Ha, ha," I said nervously.

"Lucy Carmel Sullivan," she sounded furious. "Christopher Patrick just telephoned me and he tells me that you're getting married. Married!"

"Mum . . ."

"What a lovely state of affairs that your own mother has to find out such a thing through the grapevine!"

"Mum . . ."

"Of course I had to act as if I knew all about it. But I knew this day would come, Lucy. I always knew it. Since you were a child you've been flighty and feckless. We couldn't depend on you to do anything—except to get it wrong. There's only one reason that a young woman gets married in such a hurry and that's if she's stupid enough to get herself into trouble. Although you're bloody lucky that you've got the guy to say he'll stand by you, although what kind of a useless idiot he is, God only knows . . ."

I didn't know what to say, because it was kind of funny—there was a long-standing joke in my family that whatever I ever did, my mother found fault with it. I had so much experience of her disapproval and disappointment that it no longer really bothered me.

And years ago, I'd given up hoping that she'd approve of my boyfriends, that she'd admire my apartment, that she'd be in awe of my job and that she'd like my friends.

"You're just like your father," she said bitterly.

Poor Mum—nothing I ever did was good enough for her. When I finished secretarial college, I got a job with the London office of a multinational company. On my first day my mother rang me, not to congratulate me and wish me well, but to tell me that the company's shares had dropped ten points on the FTSE index.

"Mum, listen to me, you fool," I interrupted loudly. "I'm not getting married."

"I see. So you're going to shame me by presenting me with an illegitimate grandchild," she exclaimed, still sounding furious. "And where do you get off calling me names . . ."

"Mum, I'm not pregnant and I'm not getting married," I said briskly.

There was a confused pause.

"It's a joke." I tried to sound a bit friendlier.

"Oh, it's a joke, that's right," she snorted, back in her stride. "The day you come home to me and tell me that you've got some decent man to marry you, that'll be a great joke. Oh, I'll laugh that day. I'll laugh till I cry that day."

To my surprise, I suddenly felt very angry. Out of the blue I wanted to shout at her that I wouldn't ever come home and tell *her* that I was getting married, that I wouldn't even invite her to the wedding.

Of course, the funniest thing of all was that, in the unlikely event of me ever winding up with a respectable man, one who had a job and a stable home and no ex-wives or criminal records, I wouldn't be able to stop myself from parading him in front of my mother and smugly inviting her to try and find some fault with him.

Because even though I often felt as if I hated her, there

was still a part of me that wanted her to pat me on the head and say, "Good girl, Lucy."

"Is Dad there?" I asked her.

"Of course your beloved father is here," she said bitterly. "Where else would he be? Out at work?"

"Can I talk to him, please?"

If I could talk to Dad for a few moments, I would feel a bit better. At least I could console myself that I wasn't a complete failure, that one of my parents loved me. Dad was always good at cheering me up and making fun of Mum.

"I doubt it," she said harshly.

"Why?"

"Think about it, Lucy," she said wearily. "He got his unemployment check yesterday so what kind of condition do you expect him to be in?"

"I see," I said. "He's asleep."

"Asleep!" she barked mirthlessly. "The man is *comatose*. And has been, off and on, for twenty-four hours. The kitchen looks like a bottle recycling center!"

I said nothing. My teetotaling mother thought that anyone who had an occasional drink was automatically an alcoholic.

"So you're not getting married?" she said.

"No."

"So you've created all this fuss for nothing."

"But . . ."

"Well, I'm going now," she said before I was able to think of something scathing to say. "I can't stand around here all day chatting."

Fury surged through me. *She* had called *me*, after all, but before I could shout at her she was off again.

"Did I tell you that I'm working at the dry cleaners

now?'' she said, changing, without warning, to a much more conciliatory tone. "Three afternoons a week."

"Oh."

"As well as doing the laundry service washes on Sunday and Wednesday."

"Oh."

"They closed down the minimart, you see," she went on.

"Oh."

I was too annoyed to bother talking to her.

"So I was delighted to get the few hours at the dry cleaners," she went on. "The extra money comes in handy."

"Oh."

"So between doing the cleaning at the hospital and the flowers for Saint Dominic's and organizing a retreat with Father Colm, I've been keeping busy."

I *hated* when she did this. This was almost worse than when she was being bitter and horrible. How was I supposed to suddenly switch into a civilized conversation with her after the things she had just said to me?

"And are you all right yourself?" she asked awkwardly.

All the better for not seeing you, I felt like saying, but managed not to. "Fine," I said vaguely.

"We haven't seen you in so long," she said in a tone that was meant to be cheerful and slightly teasing.

"I suppose."

"Why don't you come over some night next week?"

"I'll see," I said, starting to feel panicky. I couldn't think of anything more awful than spending an evening in my mother's company.

"Thursday," she said firmly. "Your dad will have run out of money by then so there's a good chance he'll be sober."

"Maybe."

"Thursday," she said, with finality. "And now I'd better go."

She was trying to sound good-humored and friendly, but her inexperience showed. "All those . . . *yuppies* or whatever it is they're called, from the new townhouses, will be lining up for their lovely Armada suits and their expensive silk shirts and whathaveyou. Do you know some of them even get their ties dry-cleaned? I ask you! Their *ties*. What next!"

"Well, you'd better go then," I said, with a sick heart.

"God bless. See you on Thu . . ."

I slammed down the phone.

"And it's *Armani!*" I shouted at it.

I stared tearfully at Megan and Meredia who had been sitting silent and shamefaced throughout the lengthy conversation.

"Now look at what you've done!" I said, surprised by the hot, angry tears that were spilling down my face.

"Sorry," whispered Meredia.

"Yeah, Lucy, sorry," muttered Megan. "It was Elaine's idea."

"Shut up," hissed Meredia. "My name is Meredia and it was your idea."

I ignored them both.

They tiptoed around, shocked and frightened at how angry I was. I very rarely got angry; at least that was what they thought. In fact, I often got angry, I just very rarely showed it. I was much too afraid of people not liking me to court confrontation, and that had both pluses and minuses. The minus being that I would probably have burned a hole all the way through my stomach lining by the time I was thirty, but the plus being that on the rare occasions when I did give vent to my anger, it commanded some respect.

I wanted to put my head down on my desk and sleep. But instead I got a twenty-pound note out of my purse and put it in an envelope and addressed it to my father. If Mum was no longer working in the minimart, money must be even tighter than usual.

The news that I wasn't getting married spread through the company at least as fast as the original news that I *was*. There was a constant flow of people visiting my office on the most unlikely of pretexts. It was a nightmare. Groups of people fell silent, then sniggered, as I walked past them in the corridors. Apparently someone in Personnel had started a collection for an engagement present and a nasty scuffle had broken out when attempts were made to return the donations because the sums being reclaimed were a lot more than the sums that were originally contributed and although it wasn't my fault I still felt, somehow, that it was.

The awful day seemed to last forever but it finally came to an end.

It was Friday evening and on a Friday evening it was traditional for me to go for ''just one or two drinks'' with the people from work.

But not that Friday.

I was going straight home.

I didn't want to be with anyone.

I was taking my embarrassment and my humiliation and other people's pity at my single status home. I'd had enough of being a laughingstock for one day.

Luckily, on a Friday evening Karen and Charlotte also traditionally went for ''just one or two drinks'' with their respective workmates.

As ''just one or two drinks'' usually entailed a good

seven hours of solid drinking, ending up in the early hours of Saturday morning in an anonymous, tourist-trap night-club in a basement somewhere near Oxford Circus, dancing with young men in cheap suits wearing their ties knotted around their heads, there was a good chance that I would have the apartment to myself.

I was glad about that. Whenever I had a tussle with life and came out the loser—and I usually did come out the loser—I would hibernate. I hid myself away from people. I didn't want to talk to anyone. I tried to limit human contact to ordering in a pizza and paying the delivery man. And I preferred it if the delivery man kept his bicycle helmet on because it cut down on eye contact. The feeling always passed after a while.

After a couple of days I'd have regained the energy I needed to go out into the world and deal with other human beings. I'd have managed to reassemble my protective armor so that I wasn't a whining, miserable pain in the neck. So that I was able to laugh at my misfortunes and actively encourage others to do so also, just to show what a good sport I was.

 13

By the time I got off the bus, it had started raining and was bitterly cold. Although I was mute with misery and desperate for the shelter of home, I stopped at the row of shops beside the bus stop to buy supplies for my couple of days of isolation.

First I visited the newsstand and bought four chocolate bars and a magazine, which I managed to procure without one word being exchanged between me and the shopkeeper. (That was one of the many benefits of living in central London.)

Then I went next door to the liquor store and guiltily bought a bottle of white wine, uncomfortably sure that the man knew I intended to drink the entire bottle on my own. I don't know why I was so worried because he probably wouldn't have raised an eyebrow even if I was knifed in the line, just so long as he got paid. But it was hard to shake my inherited small-town mentality.

Next I stopped at the fish and chips shop and, apart from a rudimentary discussion involving salt and vinegar, I was able to avoid any real human contact *and* buy a bag of chips.

Then I went into the video shop, hoping that I could very quickly pick up something light and diverting, with the minimum of conversation.

But it was not to be.

"Lucy!" called Adrian, the video shop man, sounding all excited and delighted to see me.

I could have kicked myself for coming in! I had forgotten that Adrian would want to talk to me, that his customers were his social life.

"Hi, Adrian." I smiled demurely, hoping to calm him down.

"Great to see you," he shouted.

I wished he hadn't. I was sure that the other people were looking at me. I tried to make myself smaller inside my inconspicuous brown coat. I quickly—a lot more quickly than I had originally intended—found what I wanted and took it to the desk.

Adrian smiled broadly.

If I wasn't so curmudgeonly I would have had to admit that he really was sweet. Just a bit too enthusiastic.

"So where've you been?" he asked loudly. "I haven't seen you for, oh . . . *days!*"

The other customers paused from perusing the racks and looked at me, waiting for my answer. Well at least that was how it felt to me, but I *was* self-conscious to the point of paranoia.

My face burned with embarrassment.

"So you went and got yourself a life?" asked Adrian.

"I did," I murmured. (Shut up Adrian, *please.*)

"And what happened?" he asked.

"It fell through," I smiled wistfully.

He guffawed. "You're a laugh, do you know that?"

I gave a tight smile. I was sure that I could feel all the other customers craning their necks, looking at me and thinking "Her?—*that* insignificant little thing. Are you sure? She doesn't *look* like a laugh."

"Well, it's good to see you again," announced Adrian. "And what are you going to watch this evening?" He looked down at the box in my hands.

"Oh no!" he said. His broad smile vanished in disgust and he almost threw my choice of video back at me. "Not *Four Weddings and a Funeral.*"

"Yes, *Four Weddings and a Funeral,*" I insisted, sliding it back across the counter at him.

"But, Lucy," he pleaded, sliding it firmly back to me, "it's sentimental crap. I know, I know! What about *Cinema Paradiso?*"

"I've seen it," I told him. "And on your recommendation. That was the night you wouldn't let me take out *Sleepless in Seattle.*"

"Aha!" he said triumphantly. "But what about *Cinema Paradiso, The Director's Cut?*"

"Seen it."

*"Jean de Florette?"* he asked hopefully.

"Seen it," I said.

*"Babette's Feast?"*

"Seen it."

*"Cyrano de Bergerac?"*

"Which version?"

"Any of them."

"Seen them all."

*"La Dolce Vita?"*

"Seen it."

"Something by Fassbinder?"

"No, Adrian," I said, fighting back despair, but trying to sound firm. "You never let me take out anything I want. I've seen every cult and foreign film that you stock in here. Please, *please,* just this once, let me watch something lighthearted. . . . That's in English," I added hastily, before he attempted to find me something lighthearted in Swedish.

He sighed.

"Well, okay," he said sadly. *"Four Weddings and a Funeral* it is. What have you got for your dinner?"

"Oh," I said, thrown slightly by the abrupt change in subject.

"Give up your bag," he said.

I reluctantly put my bags up on the counter.

This was a ritual that Adrian and I usually went through. A long time ago he had confessed to me that his job made him feel very isolated. That he never had his meals at the same time as anyone else. And that it made him feel as though he still belonged to the real world if he kept in contact with the nine-to-fivers and what they did with their evenings and, more specifically, what they ate.

Normally I had a lot of sympathy for him, but that

evening I wanted to get out of the outside world and be alone with my chocolate and my wine so that I could revel in the complete absence of any other human beings.

Also I was ashamed of the high-sugar, high-saturated-fat, low-protein, low-fiber purchases.

"I see," he said, poking through my carrier bags. "Chocolate, chips, wine—the chocolate will melt if you leave it next to the chips, you know—are you feeling a bit depressed?"

"I suppose," I said, trying to smile, trying to be polite. While every atom in me ached to be at home, with the door locked behind me.

"Poor you," he said kindly.

Again I tried to smile, but I wasn't able. For a moment I thought I might tell him about the whole me-getting-married fiasco, but I couldn't find the energy.

Adrian was sweet. Really sweet. And cute, I realized vaguely. And I kind of thought that he had a crush on me. Maybe I should consider him, I thought halfheartedly. Maybe that's what Mrs. Nolan meant when she told me that at first I may not recognize my future husband.

Then, with a little burst of irritation, I realized that even *I* had started to believe Mrs. Nolan, that I was just as bad as Megan and Meredia. Angrily, I told myself to get a grip, that I wasn't marrying anyone and *certainly* not Adrian. It would never work.

To begin with, there were financial considerations. I wasn't sure what kind of money Adrian was earning, but it couldn't have been much—it certainly couldn't have been much more than the pittance I earned. I certainly wasn't mercenary, but face it, I thought—how could we possibly keep a family on our combined incomes? And what about our children? Adrian seemed to work twenty hours a day, seven days a week, so they'd never even get to see their dad.

In fact, I'd probably never get to see him long enough for him to actually impregnate me. Oh well.

Adrian had keyed in my account number, which he knew by heart and was telling me that I owed a late charge for something that had been taken out ten days previously and hadn't yet been returned.

"Really?" I asked, turning pale at the thought of the amount I owed and the fear that I might never actually get out of that shop.

"Yes," he said, looking concerned. "That's not like you, Lucy."

He was right. I never did anything risky. I was far too afraid of annoying someone or of being told off.

"Oh God," I said in alarm. "I don't even *remember* taking out something in the last fortnight. What is it?"

*"The Sound of Music."*

"Oh," I said, worried. "That wasn't me. That must have been Charlotte using my card."

My heart sank. That meant that I was going to have to tell Charlotte off for impersonating me. And I'd have to get money from her for the late charge. Extracting teeth would be easier.

"But why *The Sound of Music?*" asked Adrian.

"It's her favorite film."

"Really? Is there something wrong with her?"

"No," I said defensively. "She's very sweet."

"Ah, come on," scoffed Adrian. "She must not be too bright."

"She's not dumb," I insisted. "She's just young."

"If she's over the age of eight, she's out of the 'just young' category," he snorted. "How old is she?"

"Twenty-three," I muttered.

"Old enough to know better," he said.

"I bet she has a pink duvet cover," he added, his lip curled in disgust. "And she loves children and animals and gets up early on Sunday mornings to watch *Little House on the Prairie.*"

If he only knew how close he was.

"You can tell an awful lot about a person by the video they choose," he explained. "Anyway, why is it charged to *your* card?"

"Because you closed her account. Remember?"

"She's not the blond who took *Planes, Trains and Automobiles* to Spain?" said Adrian, his voice rising in alarm. He looked appalled at the realization that he'd lent out one of his precious videos to the awful girl who had taken one of his babies across Europe and then refused to pay the late charge on her return. That somehow the trade sanctions that he'd imposed against Charlotte had been breached.

"Yes."

"I can't think how I didn't recognize her," he said, looking upset.

"Don't worry, don't worry," I said soothingly, willing him to clam down and let me go home. "I'll get it back. And I'll pay the fine."

I would have agreed to pay *anything* so that I could leave.

"No," he said. "Just get it back." The way tearful mothers of missing children do on television appeals.

"Just get it back," he repeated. "That's all I ask."

I left. I was exhausted. So much for not wanting to talk to anyone. But I wouldn't speak to anyone else that evening, I decided. I *couldn't* speak to anyone else that evening. I was taking a vow of silence. Although it felt more like a vow of silence was taking me.

 14

The apartment was in a terrible mess. The kitchen was in a shambles, with dirty dishes and pans piled higgledy-piggledy in the sink. The trash needed to be taken out, the radiators were covered with drying clothes, two pizza boxes were flung on the living-room floor, perfuming the air with onion and pepperoni, and there was a funny smell coming from the fridge when I opened it to put in my bottle of wine.

Although the state of the place made me more depressed than I already was, I couldn't summon the strength to do anything more than put the pizza boxes in a trash bag.

But at least I was home.

As I foraged gingerly around in the kitchen for a cleanish plate to put my chips on, the phone rang. And before I had realized what I was doing I had answered it.

"Lucy?" said a man's voice.

At least, for a moment, I *thought* it was a man. But then I realized that it was just Daniel.

"Hello," I said, trying to sound polite but cursing myself for answering the phone. He was obviously calling to gloat over the fortune-teller marriage nonsense.

"Hello, Lucy," he said in a friendly, concerned tone. "How are you?"

I had been right. He was *definitely* calling to gloat.

"What do you want?" I said coldly.

"I called to see how you are," he said, doing a passable imitation of a surprised voice. "And thank you for the warm welcome."

"You're calling to laugh at me," I said huffily.

"I'm *not,*" he said. "Honestly!"

"Daniel," I sighed. "Of course you are. Whenever something bad happens to me you call to rub it in. The same way as whenever something bad happens to you, I laugh myself hoarse. It's the *rule.*"

"It's *not* actually," he said mildly. "I can't deny that you seem to get great enjoyment whenever I have bad luck, but it's not true to say that I laugh at any of your misfortunes."

A pause.

"Let's face it," he said kindly. "I'd spend my entire life laughing if that was the case."

"Goodbye, Daniel," I said coldly, pulling the phone toward me.

"Wait, Lucy!" he shouted. "It was a *joke.* Good lord," he muttered. "You're so much nicer when you have your sense of humor plugged in."

I said nothing, because I wasn't sure whether or not to believe that he had been joking. I was very sensitive about the seemingly disproportionate amount of disasters that befell me. I was terrified of being ridiculed and, even more so, of being pitied.

The silence continued.

What a waste of a phone bill, I thought sadly. Then I tried to pull myself together. Life was bad enough, I thought. There was no need whatsoever for me to go into a total slump about the tragedy of unspoken words on a telephone call. To pass the time I flicked through my magazine. I found an article on colonic irrigation. Ugh, I thought, that looks disgusting. It must be good.

Then I ate two Rolos. One on its own wasn't enough.

"I hear you're not getting married," Daniel finally said, after the silence had stretched taut.

"No, Daniel, I'm not getting married," I agreed. "I hope I've made your weekend. Now I want to go. Goodbye."

"Lucy, *please*," he begged.

"Daniel," I interrupted wearily, "I'm really not in the mood for this."

I didn't even want to talk to someone, let alone bicker with him.

"I'm sorry," he said apologetically.

"Are you?" I asked suspiciously.

"I am," he said. "Really."

"Fine," I said. "But I really want to go now."

"You're still pissed off with me," he said. "I can tell."

"No, Daniel, I'm not," I said wearily. "But I just want to be left alone."

"Oh no," he said. "Does this mean that you're going to disappear until next weekend with a box of cookies?"

"Maybe." I laughed slightly. "See you in a week."

"I'll stop by every so often to turn you," he said. "I don't want you getting bedsores again."

"Thanks."

"No, look, Lucy," he said. "Why don't you come out with me tomorrow night?"

"Tomorrow night?" I asked. "*Saturday* night. That's the night for going to parties and trying to meet men, not for going out with old friends. That's what God invented Monday nights for."

An alarming thought suddenly struck me.

"Where are you?" I demanded suspiciously.

"Er, at home," he said, sounding shamefaced.

"On a Friday night?" I asked in astonishment. "And

you want to go out with me on a Saturday night?
What's wrong?''

Then I knew. And my spirits lifted perceptibly.

''She's dumped you, hasn't she?'' I said, coaxingly.
''That woman Ruth has come to her senses. Although I
have to admit that up until now I didn't actually think she
*had* any senses to come to.''

I always made unkind remarks about Daniel's girlfriends. I thought that any woman stupid enough to become involved with someone so obviously flirtatious and
commitment-shy as Daniel deserved to have disparaging
things said about her.

''Now aren't you glad that I called?'' he said nicely.
''Aren't you glad that you didn't just pawn me off on the
answering machine?''

''Thanks, Daniel,'' I said, feeling slightly better.
''You're very thoughtful. A trouble shared is a trouble
doubled. So what happened?''

''Oh,'' he said vaguely. ''Just one of those things. I'll
tell you all about it when I see you tomorrow night.''

''Daniel,'' I said gently, ''you're not seeing me tomorrow night.''

''But Lucy,'' he said reasonably. ''I've made a reservation for dinner.''

''But Daniel,'' I said, equally reasonably, ''you shouldn't
have done that without consulting me. You know how
unpredictable my moods are. And at the moment I'm no
fun at all.''

''Well, you see,'' he explained, ''I had the reservation
weeks ago and I was supposed to go with Ruth, but with
me and her no longer being an item . . .''

''Oh, I see,'' I said understanding. ''You don't specifically want *me* to go with you. You just need *someone*.
Well, that should be no trouble at all to organize consider-

ing how women love you. Although, quite frankly, it's beyond me why . . .''

"No, Lucy," he interrupted. "I do specifically want you to come with me."

"Sorry, Daniel," I said sadly. "But I'm just too depressed."

"Hasn't the news that my girlfriend has left me cheered you up?" he asked.

"Yes, of course," I said, starting to feel guilty. "But I just couldn't face going out."

Then he played his trump card.

"It's my birthday," he said hollowly.

"Not until Tuesday," I said quickly.

I had forgotten that it was his birthday, but, quick as a flash, I had my excuse in place. I'd had a lot of practice in getting out of things I didn't want to do, and it showed.

"But I really want to go to this particular restaurant," he said wheedlingly. "And it's so hard to get a table."

"Oh, Daniel," I said, starting to feel despairing, "why are you doing this to me?"

"You're not the only one who feels miserable, you know," he said quietly. "You haven't got a monopoly on it."

"Oh, I'm sorry, Daniel." I felt both guilty and resentful. "Are you heartbroken?"

"Well, you know how it is," he said, still sounding all quiet and defeated.

"And have I ever abandoned you when you've been upset?" he asked, sealing my fate.

"That's blackmail," I said heavily. "But I'll come with you."

"Good," he said gleefully.

"Are you very miserable?" I asked. I was always interested in other people's despair. I would compare and contrast it with my own just to make me feel like I wasn't such an oddity.

"Yes," he said sorrowfully. "Wouldn't you be? Not knowing when you'll next get laid?"

"Daniel!" I said outraged. "You bastard! I might have known that you were only pretending to be upset. You haven't got a sincere emotional bone in your body!"

"A joke, Lucy, a joke," he said mildly. "That's just *my* particular way of dealing with unpleasant things."

"I never know when you're joking and when you're being serious," I sighed.

"Neither do I," he agreed. "Now let me tell you about this wonderful restaurant that I'm taking you to."

"You're not *taking* me to it." I felt uncomfortable. "When you say it like that it sounds like we're going on a date—which we're not. You mean this restaurant that you've forced me into going to."

"Sorry," he said. "This restaurant that I've forced you into going to."

"Good," I said. "That's better."

"It's called The Kremlin," he said.

"The *Kremlin?*" I said, sounding alarmed. "Does that mean that it's Russian?"

"Well, obviously," he said, anxiety in his voice. "Is that a problem?"

"Yes!" I said. "Won't it mean that we'll have to wait in line for hours and hours and hours for our food? In subzero temperatures? And that although there'll be delicious food on the menu, the only thing that they'll actually be serving is raw turnip?"

"No, no, honestly," he protested. "It won't be anything like that. It's *pre*-Bolshevik and it's supposed to be wonderful. Caviar and flavored vodka and very plush. You'll love it."

"I'd better," I said grimly. "And I still don't understand why you're insisting that I come. What about Karen or Charlotte? They both like you. You'd have much more fun with either of them. Or *both* of them, now that I think of it. Wouldn't you like a little flirtation with your borscht? A threesome with your blinis?"

"No thanks," he said firmly. "I'm a bit battle-scarred. I'm off women for a while."

"You?" I hooted. "I don't believe it! Womanizing comes as naturally to you as breathing."

"You have such a low opinion of me," he said, sounding amused. "But, honestly, I'd much rather be with someone who didn't have a crush on me."

"Well, I mightn't be much good for most things, but at least I can oblige you in that respect," I said, in an almost cheerful tone.

I seemed to have perked up a little.

"Great!" he said.

There was a small pause. Then he spoke.

"Lucy," he said awkwardly, "can I ask you something?"

"Of course."

"Well, it's not really important, or anything," he said. "I'm just slightly curious, but, er, *why* don't you have a crush on me?"

"Daniel!" I said in disgust. "You're pathetic."

"I just want to know what I'm doing wrong . . ." he protested.

I hung up.

I had just managed to get my lukewarm chips onto a plate when the phone rang again, but this time I was smarter. This time I switched on the answering machine.

I didn't care who it was, I wasn't speaking to them.

"Er, ah, hello. This is Mrs. Connie Sullivan ringing for her daughter Lucy Sullivan."

It was my mother.

How many Lucys did she think lived in my flat, I thought in irritation. But at the same time joy at my narrow escape ran through me! I was so relieved that I hadn't picked up the phone. So what did the old bag want?

Whatever it was, she wasn't too comfortable sharing it with the answering machine.

"Lucy, love, er, um, eh, it's, um, Mammy."

She sounded a bit humble. Whenever she called herself Mammy it was a sign that she was trying to be friendly. She was probably calling to grudgingly apologize for being so nasty to me earlier that day. That was her usual pattern.

"Lucy, love, I, er, think I might have been a bit hard on you on the phone today. If I was it's only because I want the best for you."

I listened with curled lip and disdainful expression.

"But I had to call you. It was on my conscience," she went on. "I got a bit of a shock, you see, when I thought you might be . . . *in trouble* . . ." She whispered "in trouble," doubtless as a precaution against anyone else inadvertently listening to her message and hearing such a filthy notion being uttered.

"But, I'll see you on Thursday and don't forget that Wednesday is a Holy Day of Obligation and the start of Lent . . ."

I threw my eyes heavenward, even though there was no one there to see me do it, and walked back to the kitchen to get some more salt. It would have killed me to admit it, but, you know, I felt a bit better now that my mother had rung, now that she had kind of apologized. . . .

\* \* \*

I ate my chips, I ate my chocolate, I watched my video and I went to bed early. I didn't drink the bottle of wine, but maybe I should have, because I slept badly.

All night there seemed to be people coming in and out of the apartment. The doorbell being rung, doors opening and closing, the smell of toast being made, "How Do You Solve a Problem Like Maria" coming from the front room, stifled giggles coming from the kitchen, bangs and thumps of falling furniture from someone's bedroom, more giggles, not so stifled this time, rattling in the silverware drawer while someone was probably searching for a corkscrew, male voices laughing.

That was one of the downsides of having an early night on a Friday in an apartment where the two other occupants went out and got drunk. Very often I would be one of the ones giggling and banging and thumping so I wouldn't mind anyone else doing so either.

But it was a lot harder to put up with when I was sober and miserable and wanted oblivion. I *could* have gotten out of bed and marched down the hall in my pajamas, my hair all messy, my face bare of makeup and begged Karen and Charlotte and whatever guests they had to keep the noise down, but it wouldn't have done me any good. Either they would have drunkenly ridiculed me and my pajamas and my hair, or else I would have been forced to drink half a bottle of vodka in a "If you can't beat them, join them" exercise.

Sometimes I wished I lived by myself. I had been thinking that a lot lately.

I eventually got to sleep and then, what seemed like a little while later, I woke up again. I didn't know what time it was but it was still pitch dark. The house was quiet and my room was cold—the heat must not have come on yet. Outside I could hear that it was raining and the wind rattled my bedroom's shaky Victorian windows. The curtains moved slightly from a stray draft. A car passed, its wheels hissing on the wet road.

A pang of something unpleasant shot through me—emptiness? loneliness? abandonment?—if it wasn't one of those emotions, it was at least a member of their extended family.

"I'm never going out again," I thought. "Not while the world is the way it is. Bad weather and people laughing at me. I want none of it."

After a while I couldn't help noticing that, even though it was five-thirty on a Saturday morning, I was awake. That was always happening to me—from Monday morning to Friday morning I couldn't open my eyes, even with the help of the alarm clock and the threat of losing my job if I was late one more morning. Getting out of bed was almost impossible, as though the sheets were made of Velcro.

But come Saturday morning, when I didn't have to get up, I woke of my own accord and couldn't persuade myself, under any circumstances, to turn over and shut my eyes and snuggle under the covers and go back to sleep.

The only exception to this pattern occurred on the occasional Saturdays when I had to go to work. Then I found it as hard to wake up as I had done on the previous five mornings.

If my mother knew, she would probably have held it up as evidence of my—at least according to her—contrariness.

"I know," I thought, "I'll eat something."

I got out of bed—the room was freezing—and ran down the hall to the kitchen. To my dismay, someone was already there.

"I don't care who it is," I thought belligerently. "I'm not talking to them."

It was a young man whom I had never seen before. He was dressed only in red boxer shorts and he was energetically gulping tap water from a mug.

That was not the first Saturday morning I had bumped into a strange man in our kitchen. The only difference on this particular Saturday morning was that I hadn't brought him home myself.

Something about him—it might have been the way he was drinking the water like he was dying of thirst—made me feel like being nice to him.

"There's Coke in the fridge," I told him, hospitably.

He jumped and turned around.

"Oh, er, hello," he said, his hands going automatically to his groin in protective fashion. "Sorry," he stuttered. "I hope I didn't frighten you. I came home with . . . er . . . your roommate last night."

"Oh," I said. "Which one?"

Who had had the attentions of this person forced upon them the previous evening? Karen or Charlotte?

"Er, this is rather embarrassing," he said sheepishly. "But I can't actually remember her name. I had quite a bit to drink."

"Well, describe her," I said nicely.

"Blond hair."

"That's no use," I told him. "They both have blond hair."

"Er, big, um," he said, sketching something expansive with his hands.

"Oh, you mean big tits." I suddenly understood. "Well, once again, it could be either of them."

"I think she had a funny accent," he said.

"Scottish?"

"No."

"Yorkshire?"

"Yes!"

"That's Charlotte."

I got my bag of cookies and went back to bed.

A few minutes later the boy walked into my room.

"Oh," he said, looking confused and flustered, his hand going to his crotch again. "But where's . . . ? I thought . . ."

"Next door," I said sleepily.

 15

When I awoke again, it was almost midday. Someone was in the bathroom and steam was billowing out from under the door so that I could hardly see down the hall. I found Karen lying under her duvet on the couch in the front room. She was coughing and smoking, there was an overflowing ashtray on the floor beside her and she looked like a panda because she hadn't taken off her previous night's makeup.

"Morning." She smiled, looking a bit pale and wan. "What were you up to last night?"

"Nothing," I said absently. "Why is the apartment like a sauna? Who's in the bathroom? Why are they taking so long?"

"It's Charlotte. She's purging herself with the scalding water and the Brillo pads, scrubbing herself till she bleeds, atoning for her sin."

I felt a powerful rush of sympathy.

"Oh no, poor Charlotte. So she slept with that guy?"

"When did you see him?" asked Karen, attempting to sit up in her excitement and then thinking better of it.

"I bumped into him in the kitchen about five-thirty this morning."

"Awful, wasn't he? But Charlotte was wearing her beer goggles, well, her tequila goggles, actually, so she thought he was gorgeous."

"Judgment impaired?"

"Very much so."

"Was she being all raunchy and dancing seductively around the place?"

"Yes."

"On no."

Charlotte was a lively but well-brought up, respectable girl from a small town outside Bradford. She had only been living in London for about a year and was still going through the painful process of trying to find out who she really was. Was she still the sprightly, cheeky, but very decent, apple-cheeked girl from Yorkshire? Or was she the blond, busty temptress that she turned into when she drank too much? It's an odd thing, but when she was behaving like a temptress her hair really did seem to turn a couple of shades lighter and her bust really did seem to increase at least one cup size.

She found it very, very hard to marry these two different aspects of herself. When she acted like the blond, busty temptress she spent the following days bitterly berating herself. Guilt, self-loathing, self-hatred, fear of retribution, disgust with herself and her behavior were her constant companions.

She took far too many very hot baths during those times. It was unfortunate that Charlotte was blond and busty

because she was also a bit slow, and it confirmed too
many stereotypes. People like Charlotte gave blondes a
bad name. But I was very fond of her and she was a
lovely person and an amiable roommate.

"But never mind her. Tell me about *you*," said Karen
gleefully. "Tell me the whole story of you and the getting
married thing and all."

"No."

"Why not?"

"I don't want to talk about it."

"You always say that, Lucy."

"Sorry."

"Please."

"No."

*"Please!"*

"Well, all right, but you can't laugh at me and you
can't feel sorry for me."

Then I told Karen everything about going to see Mrs.
Nolan and her predictions and about Meredia coming into
money and Megan getting a split lip and Hetty running
off with Dick's brother and Meredia and Megan telling
everyone that I was getting married.

Karen listened awestruck.

"My god," she breathed. "How awful. And how
embarrassing."

"Indeed."

"Are you upset?"

"A bit," I admitted reluctantly.

"You should kill Meredia. You shouldn't let her get
away with this. And I can't believe that Megan got involved. She always seemed so *normal*."

"I know."

"It must have been some kind of mass hysteria," suggested Karen.

Charlotte shuffled into the room, wearing a heavy, shapeless polo-necked purple knitted dress that came almost to her ankles. It was her version of a hairshirt.

"Oh, Lucy," she wailed, bursting into tears and rushing toward me.

I wrapped my arms around her as best I could, bearing in mind that she was eight inches taller than me.

"I'm so ashamed," she sobbed. "I hate myself. I wish I were dead."

"Shush, shush," I said with the ease of practice. "You'll feel better soon. Don't forget that you were drinking a lot last night and that alcohol is a depressant. You're bound to feel depressed today."

"Really," she said, looking at me hopefully.

"Honest."

"Oh, Lucy, you're so good. You always know the right things to say when I'm miserable."

And of course I did. I'd had so much first-hand practice myself that it would have been churlish not to share what I had learned the hard way.

"I'm never going to drink again," she promised.

I said nothing.

"Ever!"

I inspected my nails.

"At least I'm never going to drink tequila again," she said vehemently.

I gazed out of the window.

"I'm going to stick to wine."

I stared at the television (though it wasn't on).

"And every second drink will be a mineral water."

I straightened a cushion.

"And I'm not going to have more than four glasses of wine in an evening."

I looked at my nails again.

"Well, six, maybe."

Another gaze out of the window.

"Depending on the size of the glass."

The television again.

"And I won't have more than fourteen glasses a week."

And on and on she went until she had finally persuaded herself that a bottle of tequila a night was fine. I'd heard it many times before.

"Lucy, I was terrible," she confided. "I took off my blouse and I danced around in my bra."

"Just your bra?" I asked solemnly.

"Yes."

"No panties?"

"Of *course* I had my panties on. And my skirt."

"Well, that wasn't so bad then, was it?"

"No, I suppose not. Oh, Lucy, cheer me up. Tell me a story. Tell me . . . let me see, tell me . . . *tell me* about the time that your boyfriend dumped you because he'd fallen for another guy."

My heart sank.

But I could only blame myself. I had carefully cultivated a reputation for myself as a bit of a comic raconteur—at least among my close friends—with my own life tragedies in the starring roles. A long time ago it had dawned on me that one way I could avoid being a tragic and pitiful figure was to be a witty and amusing figure instead. Especially if I was being witty and amusing about my tragic and pitiful aspects.

That way no one could laugh at me, because I'd already beaten them to it. But right then I just couldn't manage it.

"Oh no, Charlotte, I can't . . ."

"Oh go on!"

"No."

"Please! Just tell me about when he made you cut your hair short and he *still* dumped you."

"Oh . . . oh . . . damn you! All right then."

Who knows, I thought, it might cheer me up.

So, as amusingly as I could, I regaled Charlotte with the story of one of my many humiliating losses in love. Just to make her feel that no matter how much of a disaster her life was, it could never be as bad as mine.

"There's a party tonight," said Karen. "Are you coming?"

"I can't."

"Can't or won't?" asked Karen shrewdly. As she was Scottish, she was good at asking things shrewdly.

"Can't."

"Why not?"

"I got strong-armed into saying that I'd go out for dinner with Daniel."

"Dinner with Daniel. Lucky *you*," breathed Charlotte, her face aglow.

"But why did he ask *you?*" shrieked Karen in disgust.

"Karen!" said Charlotte.

"Oh, you know what I mean, Lucy," said Karen impatiently.

"I do."

Karen didn't mince words but, in fairness, she was absolutely right—I couldn't understand either why Daniel had wanted to take me.

"He's split up with whatshername," I said, and immediately there was uproar. Karen sat bolt upright on the couch, like a corpse risen from the dead.

"Are you serious?" she asked, an odd, manic look on her face.

"Absolutely."

"Wow," breathed Charlotte, with a beatific smile. "Isn't this wonderful?"

"So he's a free man?" asked Karen.

"He is indeed," I said solemnly. "Repaid his debt to society and all that."

"Not for long, if I've anything to do with it," said Karen, her voice full of steely determination, her head full of images of herself and Daniel walking hand-in-hand into posh restaurants, herself and Daniel smiling at each other radiantly on their wedding day, herself and Daniel tenderly tickling their first-born child.

"Where's he taking you?" asked Karen, when she had returned to the present and the general fuss had died down a bit.

"Some Russian place."

"Not The Kremlin?" asked Karen, sounding shocked.

"Yes."

"You lucky, lucky, lucky, lucky, *lucky* girl."

The pair of them stared at me, naked jealousy on their faces.

"Don't look at me like that," I said fearfully. "I don't even want to go."

"How can you say that?" asked Charlotte. "A good-looking . . ."

"Rich," interjected Karen.

"A good-looking, rich man like Daniel wants to take you to some posh restaurant and you don't even want to go?"

"But he's not good-looking and rich . . ." I protested lamely.

"He is!" they chorused.

"Well, maybe he is. But, but . . . but it's no good to me," I said weakly. "*I* don't think he's good-looking. He's just a friend. And I think it's a total waste to have to go out with a friend on a Saturday night. Especially when I'd rather not go out at all.''

"You're weird," muttered Karen.

I didn't deny it. She was preaching to the converted.

"What are you going to wear?" asked Charlotte.

"Don't know."

"But you've *got* to know! You're not just going to the pub for a pint.''

Daniel arrived at about eight and I wasn't ready. But I would still have been in my pajamas if Charlotte and Karen hadn't bullied and cajoled me into having a bath and putting on my glamorous gold dress.

Not that I thanked them for it. I just accused them of dressing up and going out with Daniel vicariously.

They gave me lots of advice on what to wear and what way to do my makeup and my hair, and they started every sentence with, "Now, if *I* was going out with Daniel . . ." and, "If Daniel had asked *me* . . ."

"Wear these, wear these," said Charlotte in excitement, pulling some silky, lacy stockings out of my underwear drawer.

*"No,"* I said, taking them from her and putting them back.

"But they're beautiful."

"I know."

"So why don't you wear them?"

"What for? It's only Daniel."

"You're so ungrateful."

"I'm *not*. What's the point in wearing them? It's a waste—who's going to see them?"

"Jesus," said Karen, pulling out a bra, "I didn't know they made bras this small."

"Show me," demanded Charlotte, pulling it from her

and then dissolving into convulsions. "My God! It's like a doll's bra! My nipple would just about fit into it."

"You must have tiny nipples," laughed Karen, elbowing Charlotte. "I didn't know they made triple A cups."

I stomped around the bedroom, my face red with shame, waiting for them to finish making fun of me.

Just as the doorbell rang, Karen raced into my room and sprayed me energetically with her perfume.

"Thanks," I said, my eyes watering, waiting for the clouds to disperse.

"No, silly," she said. "It's so that you'll smell like me. You're paving the way for me with Daniel."

"Oh."

Charlotte and Karen fought over who was going to answer the door to him and Karen won because she had lived in the flat longer.

"Come in," she said brightly and exuberantly, flinging wide the door for him. Karen was always bright and exuberant when Daniel was around and the door was probably not the only thing she would have liked to be flinging wide for him.

Daniel looked just like Daniel, but no doubt at some later date, I'd have to listen to Karen and Charlotte blab on and on about how beautiful he was.

It was funny that women liked him so much because there was nothing really remarkable about him.

It wasn't as if he had piercing blue eyes and blue-black hair and a sexy, sulky mouth and a jawbone the size of a handbag. Nothing of the sort.

He had gray eyes, which weren't a bit piercing—gray eyes were boring, I thought.

And his hair was that noncolor—brown. As indeed was mine, except that he had been touched by the Good-Hair

Fairy so his hair was straight and shiny. While mine was springy and curly and after I'd been caught in the rain, I looked like I'd had a home perm.

He smiled at Karen. He smiled a lot. And everyone that ever found Daniel attractive kept going on about what a nice smile he had and I couldn't see why. It was only a row of little lumps of enamel.

Okay, so he seemed to have a full set and they looked like they were real. And none were missing, or black, or at right angles to his face, but so what?''

The secret of his success, I reckoned, was that he looked like the boy next door, like a decent, friendly man, one with old-fashioned values, who'd treat you like a lady.

Which was so far from the truth that it was funny. But by the time his women found that out, it was far, far too late.

"Hello, Karen," said Daniel, doing the smile thing again. "How are you?"

"Wonderful!" she declared. "Just great!"

And immediately she launched straight into unashamed flirting. She gave him lots of level looks and knowing smiles. And with supreme self-confidence she possessively brushed imaginary fluff from his dark winter coat.

"Hello, Daniel." Charlotte sidled slowly out of her bedroom. She also flirted unashamedly with him, but she played the sweet shy smiles and fleeting eye contact card. All rosy cheeks and delicate blushes and clear-eyed, clearskinned, milk-drinking wholesomeness.

Daniel stood in our little hall, and smiled and looked very tall.

He resisted Karen's attempts to steer him into the living room. "Thanks, but no," he said. "I've got a taxi waiting outside."

He looked at me rather meaningfully as he said that, and then he looked at his watch.

"You're early," I accused. I rushed up and down the hall trying to find my high heels.

"Actually, I'm exactly on time," he said mildly.

"Well, you should have known better," I called from the bathroom.

"You look nice," he said, grabbing me as I hurried past again and attempting to kiss me. Charlotte looked woebegone.

"Ugh," I said, wiping my face. "Stop it, you'll ruin my makeup."

I found my high heels in the kitchen, in the gap between the fridge and the washing machine. I put them on and stood beside Daniel. He was still far too tall.

"You look beautiful, Lucy," said Charlotte wistfully. "I love that golden dress on you. You look like a princess."

"Yes," agreed Karen, smiling straight into Daniel's eyes and holding his gaze for far longer than was necessary—not that he seemed to mind, the womanizer.

"Don't they make a lovely pair?" asked Charlotte, smiling from me to Daniel and back again.

"No, we don't," I grumbled, shifting from high heel to high heel in embarrassment. "We're ridiculous. He's far too tall and I'm far too short. People are going to think the circus is in town."

Charlotte made shocked and effusive denial of this, but Karen didn't contradict me.

Karen was very competitive. She couldn't help it. She was one of those people who never put herself down, was never self-deprecating, never made rueful little jokes at her own expense. Whereas I, on the other hand, rarely did anything else. I really think she actually *couldn't*.

She was perfectly nice most of the time but if things went wrong, you crossed her at your peril—especially when she was drunk, when she could be quite terrifying. She had a big thing about respect. In fact, she was nearly obsessed about it if you asked me.

About two months previously her boyfriend Mark had timidly suggested that they might be getting a bit too serious, and she barely let him finish the sentence before she ordered him to get out of the apartment and never to come back. She hardly even gave the poor guy time to dress himself. (In fact, she still had his underpants which she waved in triumph out the window after him as he slunk off home.) Then she bought three bottles of wine and insisted that I stay in with her while she drank her way through it.

It was a terrible night—she sat there, looking like thunder, saying nothing, just occasionally muttering "bastard" while I nervously sipped wine by her side, murmuring what I hoped were comforting platitudes. Then out of the blue, she turned nasty.

She turned to me and grabbed the front of my dress and slurred, "Eff ah doan' respec' mahsell, then who's goan to?"

"Eh?" she asked me again, her Scottish accent pronounced, her eyes half-closed and her face too close to mine. "Ansairr me!"

"Indeed," I agreed nervously. "Who's, er, goan to?"

But she apologized the following day and hadn't behaved the same way since. Apart from being competitive, she was a great roommate. She was good fun, had great clothes that she would loan without too much begging, she could be extremely vulgar and she always paid her rent on time. Of course, I was aware that if our interests ever clashed I should be prepared to either back out gracefully or start enjoying hospital food. But our interests hadn't ever clashed yet—and they were hardly likely to start clashing over Daniel.

She was making the most of her close proximity to him.

"There's a party tonight," she told him, addressing him and him alone. "Perhaps you'd like to come along afterward."

"That sounds good," he agreed, smiling at her. "I'd better write down the address."

"It's all right," I said, quite touched by the air of romance in the hall. "I have it."

"You're sure?" Karen asked anxiously.

"I'm sure. Now let's go. Let's get this over and done with."

"Please come to the party," called Karen. "Even if Lucy doesn't want to."

*Especially* if Lucy doesn't want to was what she really meant, I thought with a laugh.

We left, Daniel bestowing his game-show-host smile on Karen and Charlotte, me bestowing an amused look on Daniel.

"What?!" he demanded as we went down the stairs. "What've I done?"

"You're outrageous!" I laughed. "Have you ever met a woman that you *didn't* flirt with?"

"But I wasn't flirting," he protested. "I was just being normal. I was only being polite."

I gave him a "You don't fool me" look.

"You look beautiful, Lucy," he said.

"You're such a bullshit artist," I replied. "In fact, you should be forced to wear a warning. To protect women from you."

"I don't know what I've done wrong," he complained.

"Do you know what your sign should say?" I ignored him.

"What should it say, Lucy?"

"Beware of the bull."

He opened the front door for me and the cold air, the outside world, hit me like a slap. "Oh God," I thought bleakly. "How am I ever going to get through tonight?"

 16

We arrived at the restaurant and the saddest-looking man I have ever seen confirmed our reservation.

"Dmitri will take your cloaks," he said heavily, in a thick Russian accent.

He paused, as if he could barely summon the energy to continue speaking. "And then," he sighed, "Dmitri will see you to your table."

He halfheartedly clicked his fingers and about ten minutes later Dmitri arrived, a short, lumpy man in a badly fitting dinner suit. He looked on the verge of tears.

"The Vatson party?" he murmured, like a mourner at a funeral.

"Er, sorry?" said Daniel.

I nudged him. "He means us. *You're* Mr. Vatson."

"Am I? Oh right, yes."

"This vay please," Dmitri whispered hoarsely.

First he led us to a little counter where we gave our coats to a very beautiful but very bored-looking young woman. She was all angular bone structure and porcelain skin and raven hair and long-suffering ennui. Even Daniel's hundred-watt grin didn't get a flicker of response from her.

"Dyke," he muttered.

Then we followed Dmitri through the restaurant, in what he obviously thought was stately fashion, but which was in fact just very, very slowly. I kept bumping into him. Then I stepped on the back of his shoe and he stopped and turned around and gave me a look that was more in sorrow than in anger.

Even though I had made much of not wanting to be there, I had to admit that the place was beautiful. There were glittering chandeliers and lots of red velvet and huge gilt-framed mirrors and big palm plants. The place hummed and clinked and tinkled with the sound of young, good-looking people laughing and drinking flavored vodka and spilling caviar down their fronts and onto their laps. I was very, very grateful that I'd let myself be bullied into wearing the gold dress, I may not have felt like I belonged, but at least I looked like I did.

Daniel put his arm lightly around my waist.

"Stop it," I muttered, squirming away from him. "What do you think you're doing? Stop treating me like I'm one of your women."

"Sorry, sorry," he said earnestly. "Second nature. For a moment I forgot it was you and went straight into restaurant mode."

I gave a little laugh and immediately Dmitri's head whipped around to glare at me.

"Er, sorry . . ." I muttered, feeling somehow ashamed, as if I had been disrespectful or blasphemed or something.

"Your table," said Dmitri, with a feeble flourish, indicating acres of snow-white, starched linen and hundreds of glinting, winking crystal glasses and several miles of dazzling silverware. We might only be getting raw turnip to eat, but The Kremlin provided **very nice** surroundings to eat said raw turnip in.

"This is very nice." I smiled at Daniel.

Then Dmitri and I did a little dance where we both tried to pull my chair out and then we both pulled away from it and then we both lunged for it again.

"Er, can we order a drink please?" asked Daniel, when we were both finally installed on opposite sides of the vast round table.

Dmitri sighed, his sigh indicating that he had known that a request such as this was probably going to be made, that the request was entirely unreasonable, but that he was a good, hardworking man and he would do his best to oblige.

"I'll fetch Gregor, your vine vaiter," he said and plodded away.

"But . . ." said Daniel to his retreating back.

"Oh god," he said, "I only want to order us some vodka."

Gregor arrived promptly and, smiling sadly, produced a very long list of drinks, which included every flavor of vodka under the sun.

I liked the look of it very much indeed. I nearly felt glad that I had come.

"Mmmm," I said, getting excited, "what about strawberry flavor? Or mango? Or, no, no, wait . . . what about blackcurrant?"

"Whatever you want," called Daniel from the far side of the table. "You choose for me."

"Well, in that case," I said, "why don't we try the lemon flavor to start with and then maybe try a different one in a while?"

When I had been younger, I had been dazzled by cocktail lists, wanting to try everything, wanting to work my way through the menu in alphabetical order, never having the same thing twice, but I had been far too frightened of getting drunk to actually do it. And I suppose what I was suggesting with the flavored vodkas was just the grown-up version of that. I was still frightened of getting drunk, but that evening, somehow I felt I could live with it.

"Lemon it is," said Daniel.

As soon as Gregor had left, Daniel hissed across at me, "Come over here. You're too far away."

"No," I said nervously. "Dmitri told me to sit here."

"So what? You're not in school."

"But I don't want to annoy him . . ."

"Lucy! Don't be such a wimp. Come over here."

"No!"

"Okay, I'll come over to you then."

He stood up and moved his chair several feet around the table, and sat down almost on my lap.

The two glamorous young-professional couples at the next table looked appalled and I threw them a kind of rueful, poor-me, look-at-this-maniac-I'm-with, I'm-very-refined-and-I'd-never-do-that-kind-of-thing-myself     look, but Daniel just looked delighted.

"There!" he smiled. "That's much better. Now I can see you." Then he started moving his knives and forks and glasses and napkin over to near mine.

"Daniel, please," I said desperately, "people are looking."

"Where?" he asked, looking around. "Oh yes, I see."

"Now will you behave?" I thundered with righteous indignation. But I had lost him because he'd made eye contact with the better looking of the two women at the next table and was up to his usual tricks. He looked at the woman and she blushed and looked away. Then he looked away and she looked discreetly at him again. Then he looked at her and caught her looking at him and gave her a smile. Then she smiled back at him and I have him a thump on his arm.

"Look, you stupid bastard, I didn't even want to come out with you tonight!"

"Sorry, Lucy, sorry, sorry, sorry."

"Just cut it out, okay? I'm not going to spend my evening with you talking over my shoulder to the woman at the next table."

"Fair enough, sorry."

"You were the one who wanted me to come here with you, so you'd better have the bloody manners to talk to me. If you wanted to flirt with someone then why did you invite me?"

"Sorry, Lucy; you're right, Lucy; forgive me, Lucy."

He *sounded* humble but he certainly didn't look it.

"And you can knock off that naughty little boy smile," I continued.

"Sorry."

Gregor arrived with two hefty glasses filled with a bright yellow liquid. It looked as if it had come straight from Chernobyl, but I thought it might seem ungracious to say so.

"Christ," said Daniel doubtfully, holding his glass up to the light. "It's rather radioactive looking."

"Shut up," I said. "Happy birthday."

We clinked glasses and threw the vodka back.

I immediately felt a tingling, warm kind of glow start to radiate out from my stomach.

"Oh God." I giggled.

"What?"

"It's *definitely* radioactive."

"Nice, though."

"Oh very."

"More?"

"Oh, yes, I think so."

"Where's Gregor?"

"Here he is."

Gregor was making his way toward us and Daniel flagged him down.

"We'll have two more of those Gregor, thanks," said Daniel.

Gregor looked pleased. If it was possible for someone to look totally heartbroken and pleased simultaneously.

"Pink ones please," I called.

"Strawberry?" said Gregor.

"Is it pink?"

"Yes."

"Strawberry then."

"And I suppose we'd better think about having something to eat."

"Fine," I said, picking up my menu. The strawberry ones came and they were so good that we decided to have two more.

As I said, "They're only small. There can't be much harm in them."

The two new drinks came—blackcurrant this time—and we drank them.

"They don't last long, do they?"

"More?" inquired Daniel.

"More."

"Food?"

"I suppose we'd better. Ah, here's Dmitri now. Anytime you like with the raw turnip, Dmitri," I said jovially. With a shock I realized that I was enjoying myself.

"I've something to tell you, Lucy," said Daniel, suddenly getting all serious on me.

"Well, go on then," I said. "For a moment there I

thought I was cheering up but I think it's best if we put a stop to that."

"Sorry, I shouldn't have said anything. Forget it."

"I can't forget it, you idiot. You'll *have* to tell me now."

"Oh all right, but you're not going to like it."

"Tell me."

"It's about Ruth."

"*Tell* me."

"I broke up with her. Not her with me."

Was that it? I thought, slightly dazed. And then I remembered about my mission to keep Daniel in his place.

"You bastard! How could you?"

"But I was *bored,* Lucy. I was so bloody bored. It was a nightmare."

"But she had big tits."

"So what?"

"You're very callous."

"Oh, Lucy, I'm not. I tried to be nice to her."

"Did you make her cry?"

"No."

"You're still a bastard."

Daniel looked slightly upset, a bit tearful. The vodka was making us both a bit emotional.

"I'm sorry I told you now," he said, sulkily. "I knew you wouldn't like it."

"Maybe not, but I'll have to put up with it."

I gave him a little smile. Suddenly I didn't seem to care that much about Ruth. None of it seemed to really matter somehow.

"That's very philosophical of you, Lucy."

"I know, I feel very philosophical."

"That's funny, so do I."

"What do you think it is? Maybe it's the vodka?"

"It's got to be."

"I feel kind of funny, Daniel, sort of sad like I always do, but happy too. Happy in a sad way."

"I know," he said eagerly. "That's exactly how I feel. Except I think I feel happy like I always do but sad in a happy way."

"This must be how Russians feel all the time." I giggled. I felt very light-headed and knew that I was being silly, but it didn't matter. It didn't sound silly, it seemed very important and true. "Do you think Russians drink so much vodka because they're philosophical and miserable, or are they philosophical and miserable because they drink so much vodka?"

"That's a tough one, Lucy."

"Why don't I ever meet the right woman, Lucy?" asked Daniel, seriously.

"I don't know, Daniel. Why don't I ever meet the right man?"

"I don't know, Lucy. Will I always be lonely?"

"Yes, Daniel. Will I always be lonely?"

"Yes, Lucy."

There was a little pause while we both smiled sadly at each other, united in our bittersweet melancholy. Thoroughly enjoying it, actually. At some stage food arrived. It might have been then.

"But, Dan, you see, it doesn't matter, because at least we're being *essentially* human. We're in touch with the pain of being alive. Will we get another drink?"

"What color?"

"Blue."

Daniel leaned back in his chair, trying to grab a waiter. "The lady wants two more of these," he called, waggling a glass around. "Well, she doesn't want two for herself . . . or maybe she does, actually. Do you, Lucy?"

"The same again, sir?" asked Gregor. At least I think it was Gregor. I gave him a melancholy smile and he gave me an identical one back.

"The exact same as this," said Daniel. "Except two of them. No, make it four. And . . . oh yes," he called after him, "they have to be blue."

"Now, where were we?" said Daniel, smiling sweetly.

I was so glad I had come; I felt so *fond* of him.

"We were talking about existential pain, weren't we?" said Daniel.

"Yes," I said. "Indeed we were. Would I look good with my hair the way that girl has hers?"

"Where?" he asked, turning around. "Oh yes, you'd look even better than her."

"Good." I giggled.

"What's it all about, Lucy?"

"What's what all about?"

"All of it, you know, any of it? Life, things, death, hair?"

"How do I know, Dan? Why do you think I'm so depressed all the time?"

"It's good, though, isn't it?"

"What is?"

"Being miserable."

"Yes." I giggled. Again. I couldn't stop. He was right. We were both miserable, but we were soaring, almost ecstatic, in our misery.

"Tell me about you getting married."

"No."

"Please."

"No."

"Don't you want to talk about it?"

"No."

"That's what you always say about everything."

"What?"

"That you don't want to talk about it."

"Well, I *don't* want to talk about it."

"Did Connie go berserk?"

"Totally. She accused me of being pregnant."

"Poor Connie."

"Poor Connie, my eye!"

"You're very hard on her."

"No, I'm not."

"She's a good woman, you know, who only wants the best for you."

"Ha! That's easy for you to say because she's always nice to you."

"I'm very fond of her."

"I'm not."

"That's a terrible thing to say about your mother."

"I don't care."

"You can be very stubborn, Lucy."

"Oh, Daniel." I laughed. "Stop it, for god's sake. Has my mother paid you to tell me nice things about her?"

"No, I genuinely like her."

"Well, seeing as you like her that much, you can come with me on Thursday to see her."

"Fine."

"What do you mean, 'fine'?"

"I mean, 'fine.' "

"Don't you mind?"

"No, of course I don't mind."

"Oh. I mind."

A little pause.

"Can we stop talking about her now, please?" I asked. "It's making me feel depressed."

"But we were miserable anyway."

"I know, but it was a different kind of miserable. A nice miserable. I liked it."

"Okay. Will we talk about the fact that we're all going to die anyway and that none of this matters?"

"Oh yes, please. Thanks, Dan, you're an angel."

"But first," declared Daniel, "more drinks. What color haven't we tried?"

"Green?"

"Kiwi fruit?"

"Perfect."

More drinks came and I know we both ate a lot, but afterward I was at a complete loss to actually say what I'd had. I believe I liked it though. Daniel said that I kept saying that it was delicious. And we had a wonderful conversation. I can't really remember much of it now, but I know that it had something to do with everything being pointless and meaningless and that we were all doomed and at the time it made perfect sense to me. I was completely at peace with myself and the universe and with Daniel. I can vaguely remember Daniel thumping the table and saying fervently, "I couldn't agree more" and stopping one of the waiters (Gregor? Dmitri?) and shouting, "Listen to this woman, she speaks the truth."

It was a wonderful evening and I probably would still be there shouting "Purple! Have you any purple ones?" if Daniel and I hadn't noticed at some stage that we were the only customers left and that a row of short, bulky, dinner-jacketed waiters were lined up behind the bar staring at us.

"Lucy," he hissed, "I think it's time we left."

"No! I like it here."

"Really, Lucy, Gregor and the rest of them have to get home."

I felt very guilty then.

"Of course they do. Of course they do. And it'll take them *hours* to get back to Moscow on the night bus, the poor things."

Daniel shouted for the bill—the reverential behavior we had assumed on our arrival had long disappeared—and the bill came, very promptly. Daniel looked at it.

"That national debt of Bolivia?" I inquired.

"More like Brazil," he said. "But what does it matter?"

"Exactly," I agreed. "Anyway, you're loaded."

"Actually, I'm not. It's all relative. Just because you get paid a pittance, you think anyone who earns above a pittance is loaded."

"Oh."

"All it means is the more you earn the more you can owe."

"Dan, that's wonderful! That's such a profound economic truth—in the midst of life we are in debt. No wonder you have such a good job."

"No, Lucy," said Daniel sounding hoarse with excitement. "*That's* wonderful, what you just said, it's so true—in the midst of life we are *indeed* in debt. You must write that down. In fact we should write down everything we've talked about tonight."

My head was spinning slightly with how wise both Daniel and I were. I told him how wise and wonderful I thought he was.

"Thanks, Daniel," I said. "This has been fabulous."

"I'm glad you enjoyed it."

"It's been great. So much makes sense now."

"Like what?"

"Well it's no wonder I never felt like I belonged anywhere, because I'm obviously Russian."

"How do you figure that?"

"Because I'm miserable but I'm happy. And I feel like I belong here."

"You might just be drunk."

"Don't be silly. I've been drunk before and I've never felt like this. Do you think I could get a job in Russia?"

"Probably, but I don't want you to go."

"You can come and visit me. You'll probably have to anyway, when you run out of girls to go out with here."

"Smart thinking, Lucy. Should we go to this party Karen told us about?"

"Yes! I'd forgotten about that."

 17

"Did you give them a big tip?" I hissed at Daniel as we finally left The Kremlin, waved off by the assembled staff.

"Yes."

"Good. They were nice."

I laughed all the way up the stairs out of The Kremlin and I laughed even more when we got out into the cold night air.

"What a laugh. That was great fun," I said, leaning against Daniel.

"Good," he said. "Now behave, or we'll never get a taxi."

"Sorry, Dan, I think I'm a bit drunk, but I feel so *happy*."

"Good, but please shut up for a minute."

A taxi stopped. It had an angry-looking man driving it.

"Smile," I sniggered. Luckily he didn't hear me.

In I clambered, Daniel pulling the door behind us.

"Where to?" asked the man.

"Anywhere you like," I said dreamily.

"Eh?"

"Wherever you want," I said. "What does it matter? Because in a hundred years' time you won't be here, I won't be here and your cab *certainly* won't be here!"

"Stop it, Lucy." Daniel elbowed me, trying not to laugh. "Leave the poor man alone. Wimbledon, please."

"We'd better stop at a liquor store and get some booze for the party," I said.

"What'll we get?"

"Vodka? It's my new favorite drink now."

"Fine."

"No, I've changed my mind."

"Why?"

"Because I'm drunk enough."

"So what? Aren't you enjoying yourself?"

"Yes, but I think I'd better stop."

"Don't."

"No, I must. We'll get something else, something not so strong."

"Beer?"

"I don't mind."

"Or will I get a bottle of wine?"

"Whatever you like."

"How about Guinness?"

"It's up to you."

"Lucy, for God's sake. Stop being so meek and tell me what you want! Why are you always so self-effacing and . . ."

"I'm not being meek and self-effacing," I laughed. "I really don't mind. You know I'm not much of a drinker."

The taxi driver gave an outraged snort. I don't think he believed me.

We could hear the music as soon as the taxi turned into the street.

"Sounds like a good party," said Daniel.

"Yes," I agreed. "I wonder if the police will come—the true mark of a great party!"

"Oh no. The neighbors are bound to call the local cop shop, so we'd better get in there and start enjoying ourselves fast before the whole thing is closed down."

"Don't worry," I said soothingly. "Many cop shops are called but few parties are closen."

Daniel laughed.

A bit too much, I thought.

The vodka was obviously still doing its job.

Then there was a little scuffle while both Daniel and I tried to pay the taxi driver.

"I'll get it."

"No, *I'll* get it."

"But you paid for dinner."

"But you didn't want to come."

"All the same, fair's fair."

"Why can't you ever relax and let someone be nice to you? You're so . . ."

"I don't have all night!" said the driver, who was quick to interrupt Daniel's thumbnail psychoanalysis of me before it got into full flight.

"Pay him," I muttered. "Quick."

Daniel paid the man who grumpily accepted Daniel's no doubt lavish tip.

"You take too much lip from that lady," was his parting comment. "I hate a lippy woman." And the taxi roared away.

I stood shivering, staring balefully at the back of the disappearing taxi.

"The audacity of him! I'm *not* lippy."

"Lucy, relax."

"Oh, all right."

"Actually though, he had a point. You *are* quite lippy sometimes."

"Oh shut up."

I tried to be annoyed with Daniel, but I couldn't help laughing.

That was unusual behavior for me, but, all in all, it had been an unusual night.

We rang the doorbell of the house where the party was, but no one came.

"Maybe they can't hear the bell," I said, as we stood shivering in the misty night air, our cans of Guinness under our arms, listening to the sounds of music and laughter behind the heavy wooden door. "Maybe the music is too loud."

And still nothing happened and we remained where we were, shivering and expectant.

"At least let me give you half of it," I said.

Daniel looked at me like I'd gone crazy.

"*What* are you talking about?"

"The taxi. At least let me pay for half."

"Lucy! Sometimes I could happily sock you! You drive me . . ."

"Shush! Someone's coming."

The door opened and a young man in a yellow shirt stared at us.

"Can I help you?" he asked politely.

It was then that it dawned on me that I had no idea of who was having the party.

"Er," said Daniel.

"Um, John invited us," I muttered.

"Oh right!" said yellow shirt, grinning, suddenly a lot friendlier. "So you're John's friends. Crazy bastard, isn't he?"

"Er, yes," I agreed brightly, throwing my eyes to heaven. "Crazy!"

That was obviously the correct thing to say, because the door swung wide and we were admitted to partake of the festivities and merriment within. I noticed, with a sinking heart, that there were an awful lot of girls there. About a thousand to every man, which seemed to be par for the course for London parties. They were all eyeing Daniel with interest.

"Who's this John?" hissed Daniel as we pushed into the estrogen-sodden hall.

"Didn't you hear? He's a crazy bastard."

"Yes, but who *is* he?"

"No idea," I whispered furtively, making sure we were out of yellow shirt's earshot, "but I thought there was a good chance that someone called John either lived here or was a friend of the people who live here. Law of averages and all that."

"You're amazing," said Daniel admiringly.

"No, I'm not," I said. "You've just gone out with too many stupid women."

"You're right, you know," he said thoughtfully. "Why do I always pick dumb ones?"

"Because they're the only ones who'll have anything to do with you," I said kindly.

He threw me a bitter look. "You're very mean to me."

"No, I'm not," I said reasonably, "It's for your own good. It hurts me more than it hurts you."

"Really?!"

"No."

"Oh."

"Now, no sulking. It'll ruin your manly jawline and you'll scare the girls away."

Our fledgling fight was interrupted by a bright, vivacious, Scottish voice shouting, "Great, you're here!

Karen made her way toward us, through the crowds of people standing around in the hall with cans of beer in their hands. She must have been watching the front door all evening, I thought uncharitably, and then immediately felt guilty. It wasn't a criminal offense to find Daniel attractive, it was just a terribly unfortunate lapse of taste and judgment. Karen looked lovely—very much Daniel's type—all blond and vivacious and glamorous. If she played her cards right and toned down her sharp intelligence I was sure she was in with a very good chance of being Daniel's next girlfriend. She, very gaily, told us how delighted she was to see us and threw questions at us with the speed of raindrops hitting the ground in a thunderstorm. How was the restaurant? Was the food lovely? Were there any famous people there?

For a few moments I was foolish enough to think that it was a real conversation and that I was part of it. Until I noticed that Karen received my would-be hilarious stories of Gregor and Dmitri with stony silence and that every time Daniel opened his mouth she collapsed with squeals of laughter. And whenever I caught her eye she gave me very energetic, meaningful frowns—her eyebrows ricocheted from her hairline to her cheekbones and back again—and then I noticed that she was mouthing something at me. I squinted, following the shape of her mouth, trying to make out what it was. She did it again. What was it? . . . What could it be? . . . First letter? Sounds like? Two syllables?

"Fuck *off!*"

She leaned over and hissed it into my ear while Daniel was momentarily distracted taking off his coat. "For God's sake, fuck off!"

"Oh, er, righto."

My conversational seed was falling on barren ground and I was definitely excess baggage. It was time for me to go. As it was, I knew that I was probably in for it the following day. Karen would read me the riot act.

I knew when I wasn't wanted. In fact, I was usually exceptionally good at it, very often knowing it even before the other person did. I had been uncharacteristically thick-skinned that evening.

My face reddened with embarrassment—I hated feeling like I'd done something wrong—and murmuring "I'll, er, be over here," discreetly shifted away from the pair of them and stood by myself in the hall.

Neither of them objected. I felt the faintest flicker of disappointment that Daniel hadn't tried to stop me, or at least asked me what I was doing but I knew that if the situations were reversed, I wouldn't appreciate him being around.

But then I felt a bit mortified—I was alone and I couldn't see anyone that I knew and I was still wearing my coat and I was sure that everyone was looking at me and thinking that I had no friends. The earlier euphoria had worn off and my usual acute self-consciousness had returned. Suddenly I felt very, very sober.

I had spent most of my life feeling that life was a party to which I hadn't been invited. Now I really was at a party to which I hadn't been invited and it was almost reassuring to discover that the feelings I'd had for most of my life—isolation, awkwardness, paranoia—were indeed the correct emotions to have had.

In the confined space I managed to inch off my coat. I fixed a bright smile on my face, hoping to convey to the noisy, happy people around me that they weren't the only ones who were having a good time. That I too was happy and that I had a fulfilled life and lots of friends and that I was only alone because I had decided to be, but that I could be in the middle of a huge crowd of people any time I liked. Not that it mattered because no one paid the slightest bit of attention to me. From the way one girl bumped into me and stood on my toe while she was excitedly running to answer the door and the way another girl tipped her glass of wine on me when she tried to look at her watch, I felt as if no one could even see me.

It wasn't so much my wet dress that upset me, it was the way she tisked at me like it was all my fault, because then I felt like it really *was* all my fault, that I shouldn't have been standing there in the first place.

I seemed to spend my whole life oscillating between feeling horribly conspicuous and then feeling totally invisible.

Then, through a parting in the crowd, I spotted Charlotte and my heart lifted. I gave her a big smile and called to her that I was on my way over. But she gave me an infinitesimal, but nevertheless quite definite shake of the head. She seemed to be talking to a young man.

After what seemed like ages of grinning like the village idiot, I finally thought of something I could do—I could put the beer in the fridge! I was delighted to have a purpose. A use. A function. In my own tiny way I mattered!

Thrilled with myself and my new-found worth I fought

my way through the crowds of people in the hall and the even bigger crowds in the kitchen and put four cans of Guinness in the fridge. Then I tucked the other two under my arm and attempted to fight my way back out again, making for the big front room where all the fun seemed to be happening.

And it was then that I met him.

 *18*

In the months that followed I replayed that scene in my head so often that I remembered absolutely everything about it, down to the smallest details.

I was just on my way out of the kitchen when I heard a man's voice saying admiringly, "Behold—a vision in gold! A goddess. A veritable goddess."

Naturally I kept pushing and shoving to leave the room because, although I was wearing a gold dress, I was also wearing my well-tailored inferiority complex. So I didn't, for a second, think that I was the one being called a goddess.

"And not just any kind of goddess," the voice continued. "But my favorite kind of goddess, a Guinness goddess."

The bit about the Guinness broke through my humility barrier, so I turned around and there, wedged in beside an upright freezer, leaning against the wall, was a young man. Not that there was anything unusual about that because it was, after all, a party, and the place was full of people, even a couple of men, leaning against household appliances.

The young man—and it was hard to say just how young he was—was very cute, with longish black curly hair and bright green, slightly bloodshot eyes, and he was smiling straight at me, as though he knew me, which suited me just fine.

"Hello." He nodded in a civil and friendly fashion.

Our eyes met and I had the oddest sensation. I felt as though I knew him too. I stared at him and, although I knew I was being rude, I couldn't stop. Hot confusion swept over me and at the same time I was totally intrigued because, although I was certain that I had never met him, that I had never before in my life seen him, somehow I knew him. I don't know what it was but there was *something* about him, something very familiar.

"What's kept you?" he said cheerfully. "I've been waiting for you."

"You have?" I swallowed nervously.

My head raced. What was happening, I wondered? Who was he? What was this instant recognition that had flashed between us?

"Oh aye," he said. "I wished for a beautiful woman with a can of Guinness and here you are."

"Oh."

A pause where he lounged against the wall, the picture of relaxation, happy and good-looking, if a little bit bleary-eyed. He didn't seem to find anything unusual about the conversation.

"Have you been waiting long?" I asked. In an odd way it felt like a very normal thing to ask, as though I was making conversation with a stranger at a bus stop.

"The best part of nine hundred years." He sighed.

"Er, nine hundred years?" I asked, raising an eyebrow.

"But they hadn't invented cans of Guinness nine hundred years ago."

"Exactly!" he said. "My point exactly! God knows, but wasn't I the sorry one. I've had to wait for them to come up with the technology and it's been so boring. If I'd only wished for a jug of mead or a pitcher of ale I could have saved both of us a whole lot of trouble."

"And you've been here all this time?" I asked.

"Most of the time," he said. "Sometimes I've been over there"—he pointed to a spot on the floor about a foot away from where he was standing—"but mostly I've been here."

I smiled—I was totally captivated by him and his story-telling. He was *exactly* the kind of man I liked, not dull or staid, but imaginative and inventive and so *cute.*

"I've been waiting for you so long that it's hard to believe you're finally here. Are you real?" he asked. "Or just a figment of my Guinness-starved imagination?"

"Oh, I'm perfectly real," I assured him. Although I wasn't at all sure myself. And I wasn't sure whether *he* was real either.

"I want you to be real and you're *telling* me that you're real, but I might be imagining it all, even the bit where you're telling me that you're real. It's all very confusing—you can see my problem?"

"Indeed," I said solemnly. I was *enchanted.*

"Can I have my can of Guinness?" he asked.

"Well, I don't know," I said anxiously, forgetting for a moment that I was enchanted.

"Nine hundred years," he reminded me gently.

"Yes, I know," I said. "I see your point perfectly, but they're Daniel's. I mean, he paid for them and I was just about to give him one, but . . . oh never mind. Have one."

"Donal may have paid for them, but destiny says

they're mine,'' he told me in a confidential tone, and somehow I believed him.

"Really?'' I asked, my voice wobbling, torn between a desire to just surrender to whatever supernatural forces were operating around this man and me and the fear of being accused of giving away other people's Guinness.

"Donal would have wanted it this way,'' he went on, gently removing something from under my arm.

"Daniel,'' I said absently, casting a glance down the hall. I could see Daniel's head and Karen's head close together and I didn't think Daniel looked as if he cared about a can of Guinness, one way or the other.

"Maybe you're right,'' I agreed.

"There's only one problem,'' said the man.

"What's that?''

"Well, if you're imaginary, then, by definition, your Guinness will also be imaginary and imaginary Guinness isn't half as nice as the real stuff.''

He had such a beautiful accent, so gentle and so lyrical, it sounded familiar, yet I couldn't quite place it.

He opened the can and poured the contents down his throat. He drank the whole lot in one go as I stood looking at him. I have to say I was impressed. I'd seen very few men able to do that. In fact the only one I'd ever seen do it was my dad.

I was delighted—completely captivated by this man-child, whoever he was.

"Hmmm,'' he said thoughtfully, looking at the empty can and then looking at me. "Hard to tell. It *could* have been real and then again it might have been imaginary.''

"Here,'' I said, pushing the other can at him. "It's real, I promise.''

"Somehow I trust you.'' And he took the second can and repeated the performance.

"Do you know," he said thoughtfully, wiping his mouth on the back of his hand, "I think you might be right. And if the Guinness is real then that means that you're real too."

"I think I am," I said sorrowfully. "Even though a lot of the time, I'm not sure."

"I suppose you sometimes feel invisible?" he asked.

My heart leaped. Nobody, *nobody*, had ever asked me that before and that was *exactly* how I felt for huge chunks of my life. Had he read my mind? I was mesmerized. So much recognition! Somebody understood me. A total stranger had just looked straight into my soul and seen the essence of me. I felt light-headed with exhilaration and joy and hope.

"Yes," I said faintly. "I sometimes feel invisible."

"I know," he said.

"How?"

"Because so do I."

"Oh."

There was a pause and the two of us just stood looking at each other for a little while, smiling slightly.

"What's your name?" he asked suddenly. "Or will I just call you the Guinness Goddess? Or, if you like, I could shorten it to GG. But then I might mistake you for a horse and try to back you and let's face it, you don't look anything like a horse and although you have nice legs . . ." (At this point he paused and leaned over sideways so that his head was level with my knees.) "Yes, very nice legs," he continued, straightening up, "I'm not sure if you could run fast enough to win the Grand National. Though you might come in the first three, so I suppose I could do an each way bet on you. We'll see. We'll see. Anyway, what's your name?"

"Lucy."

"Lucy, is it?" he said thoughtfully, looking at me with his green, green, slightly bloodshot eyes. "A fine name for a fine woman."

Although I was certain that it was the case, I had to ask him anyway: "You're not . . . by any chance . . . *Irish,* are you?"

"Sure," he said, in a stage Irish accent, and did a little dance. "All the way from County Donegal."

"I'm Irish too," I said excitedly.

"You don't sound it," he said doubtfully.

"No, I am," I protested. "At least both my parents are. My surname is Sullivan."

"That's Irish all right," he admitted. "Are you of the species Paddius, variety Plasticus?"

"Sorry?"

"Are you a plastic paddy?"

"I was born here," I admitted. "But I *feel* Irish."

"Well, that's good enough for me," he said cheerfully. "And my name's Gus. But my friends call me Augustus for short."

"Oh." I was charmed. It got better and better.

"I'm very pleased to meet you, Lucy Sullivan," he said, taking my hand in his.

"And I'm very pleased to meet you, Gus."

"No, please!" he said, holding up his hand in protest, "Augustus, I insist."

"Well, if it's all the same to you, I'd rather call you Gus. Augustus is a bit of a mouthful."

"Am I?" he said, sounding surprised. "A mouthful? And you've only just met me!"

"Er, you know what I mean . . ." I said, wondering if perhaps we were slightly at cross-purposes.

"No woman has ever said that about me before," he said, looking at me thoughtfully. "You're a most unusual woman, Lucy Sullivan. A most *perceptive* woman, if I may say so. And if you will insist on formality, then Gus it is.''

"Thank you.''

"It shows that you were well brought up.''

"It does?''

"Oh yes! You've a lovely manner, very gentle and polite. I suppose you can play the piano?''

"Er, no, I can't.'' I wondered what had sparked the abrupt change of subject. I wanted to tell him that I could play the piano because I was desperate to please him, but at the same time too afraid to tell a barefaced lie, in case he suggested that we play a duet there and then.

"It'd be the fiddle then?''

"Er, no.''

"The tin whistle?''

"No.''

"In that case it must be the accordion?''

"No,'' I said, wishing he would stop. What was all this about musical instruments?

"You don't look like you've got the wrists to be a bodhrán player, but you must be one all the same.''

"No, I don't play the bodhrán.''

*What was he talking about?*

"Well, Lucy Sullivan, you have me well and truly bet. I give up. So tell me, what *is* your instrument?''

"What instrument?''

"The one that you play?''

"But I don't play an instrument!''

"What! But if you don't play, then you're surely a poet?''

"No,'' I said shortly, and started thinking about how I could escape. It was too weird, even for me, and I had a very high weirdness threshold.

But, as if he had read my mind, he put his hand on my arm and suddenly became a lot more normal.

"Sorry, Lucy Sullivan," he said, humbly. "I'm sorry. I've scared you, haven't I?"

"A bit," I admitted.

"I'm sorry," he said again.

"That's okay," I smiled, relief filling me. I had no objection to people being quirky, slightly eccentric even, but when they started to display psychotic tendencies, I knew when to throw in the towel.

"It's just that I had a great feed of class A drugs earlier this evening," he continued, "and I'm not quite myself."

"Oh," I said faintly, not sure what to think now. So he took drugs? Did I have a problem with that? Well, not really, I supposed, so long as he wasn't mainlining heroin. We were short of teaspoons in the flat as it was.

"What drugs do you take?" I asked tentatively, trying not to sound condemnatory.

"What have you got?" He laughed. Then he stopped abruptly, "I'm doing it again, aren't I? I'm scaring you?"

"Weeell, you know . . ."

"Don't worry, Lucy Sullivan. I'm partial to the odd mild hallucinogenic or mood-relaxant, nothing more. And in small quantities. And not very often. Hardly ever, really. Apart from pints. I have to admit to a fondness for a great feed of pints early and often."

"Oh that's all right," I said. I had no problem with men who drank.

But, I wondered, if he was currently under the influence of some narcotic, did that mean that normally he didn't tell stories and dream up things and was just as dull as everyone else? I desperately hoped not. It would be unbearably disappointing for this gorgeous, charming, unusual man to disappear along with the last traces of drugs from his bloodstream.

"Are you normally like this?" I asked cautiously. "You know, er, imagining things and telling stories and all that? Or is it just the drugs?"

He stared at me, his shiny curls falling into his eyes.

Why can't I get *my* hair to shine like that, I wondered absently. I wonder what conditioner he uses.

"This is an important question, isn't it, Lucy Sullivan?" he asked, still staring at me. "A lot depends on it."

"I suppose," I mumbled.

"But I've got to be honest with you, you know," he said sternly. "I can't just tell you what you want to hear, now can I?"

I wasn't at all sure whether I agreed with that. In an unpredictable and unpleasant world it was both unusual and very pleasant to hear what I wanted to hear.

"I suppose." I sighed.

"You won't like what I'm going to tell you, but I'm morally bound to tell you anyway."

"Fine," I said sadly.

"I have no choice." He touched my face gently.

"I know."

"Oh!" He shouted suddenly and theatrically threw wide his arms. He attracted worried looks from all around the kitchen—people as far away as the back door turned to look. " 'O, what a tangled web we weave, when first we practice to deceive!' Wouldn't you agree, Lucy Sullivan?"

"Yes." I laughed. I couldn't help it, he was just so crazy and funny.

"*Can* you weave, Lucy? No? Not much call for it these days. A dying art, a dying art. I'm no good at it myself—two left feet, that's me. Now, to tell you the God's honest truth, Lucy Sullivan . . ."

"I wish you would."

"Here goes! I'm even worse when I'm in a drug-free zone. There! I've said it! I suppose you'll be getting up and leaving me now?"

"Actually no."

"But don't you think I'm a lunatic and an embarrassment?"

"Yes."

"You mean to tell me that lunatics and embarrassments are your particular bag, Lucy Sullivan?"

I had never really thought of it that way before but now that he had mentioned it . . .

"Yes," I said.

 19

He took me by the hand and led me through the hall and I let myself be led. Where was he taking me, I wondered in excitement. I pushed past Daniel and he raised his eyebrows questioningly, then waggled his finger admonishingly, but I ignored him. He was a fine one to talk.

"Sit here, Lucy Sullivan." Gus pointed at the bottom stair. "We can have a nice, quiet chat."

That seemed to be very unlikely in view of the fact that there was more traffic up and down the stairs than there was up and down Oxford Street. I wasn't quite sure what was going on upstairs—the usual, I suppose, drug-taking, sex with your best friend's boyfriend on your best friend's coat and the like.

"Now, I'm sorry I scared you back there, Lucy, but I just

assumed that you had to be some kind of creative person,'' Gus said when I was installed on the foot of the stairs.

"I'm a musician myself and music is something I feel very passionately about,'' he went on. "And I sometimes forget that not everyone else feels the same way.''

"That's fine,'' I said, delighted. Not only was he not mad, but he was a musician, and my favorite men had always been musicians or writers or anything that involved the creative process and behaving like a tortured artist. I had never fallen in love with a man who had a real job and I hoped I never would. I couldn't imagine anything duller than a man with a regular income, a man who was sensible with money, a man who knew how to live within his means. I found financial insecurity a great aphrodisiac. My mother and I disagreed rather violently on that point, but the difference was that she didn't have a romantic bone in her body while I would be hard-pressed to find a portion of my skeleton that wasn't. The radius, the ulna, the patella, the femur, the pelvic girdle (especially that!), the sternum, the humerus, the scapula—both of them in fact—sundry vertebrae, a wide selection of ribs, a whole plethora of metatarsals, nearly as many again metacarpals, the couple of tiny ones in my inner ear—you name it, they were romantic.

"So you're a musician?'' I asked with interest. Maybe that was why I felt I knew him—maybe I'd seen him or heard of him or seen a picture of him somewhere.

"I am.''

"Are you a famous musician?''

"Famous?''

"Yes, are you a household name?''

"Lucy Sullivan, I'm not a household name, not even in my own household.''

"Oh.''

"I've disappointed you now, haven't I? We've only just

met and already we're at a crisis. We'll have to go for counseling, Lucy. You stay here and I'll go and find a phone book and look up the number.''

"No you won't." I laughed. "I'm not disappointed. I just felt like I knew you, but I didn't know from where, and I thought that if you were famous, that might be how.''

"You mean we don't know each other?'' he asked, sounding shocked.

"I don't think so,'' I said, amused.

"We *must*,'' he insisted. "At least in a previous existence, if not in this one.''

"That's all very well,'' I said thoughtfully. "But, even if we knew each other in a previous existence, who's to say we liked each other then? I've always had a problem with that—just because people recognize each other from another life doesn't mean they have to *like* each other, does it?''

"You're absolutely right,'' said Gus, gripping my hand tight. "I've always thought that too but you're the first person I've met who's ever agreed with me.''

"I mean, imagine if I had been your boss in another life—well you wouldn't be too pleased to meet me again, would you?''

"No! Oh Christ, wouldn't it be awful? Dying and traveling through space and time and getting born again and meeting the same terrible people that you met the last time around. Remember me from Ancient Egypt? Good, because you did a terrible job on that pyramid, so go back and do it again.''

"Exactly. Or what about, remember me? I was the lion that ate you when you were a Christian in Rome? Remember me now? Good, let's get married.''

Gus laughed delightedly. "You're wonderful. All the same, the two of us must have got along in whatever life we met in before now. I have a good feeling about you— you probably explained Pythagaros's theorem when Pythagaros had run out of patience with me—he was a very short-tempered man, that fella—or lent me money at the turn of the century or *something* nice. Now is there any more of that Guinness?''

I sent Gus to the fridge and I sat on the stairs and waited. I was thrilled, delighted, bursting with happiness. What a lovely man. I was so glad I had come to the party—my blood ran cold at the thought that I could so easily not have come and then I'd never have met him. And maybe Mrs. Nolan had been right after all. Gus could be The One, the man I'd been waiting for.

Speaking of waiting, where the hell was he?

How long did it take to go to the fridge and steal the rest of Daniel's Guinness?

Hadn't he been gone forever? While I'd been sitting on the step with a dreamy, half-wit's· grin on my face, had he started chatting to some other young woman and forgotten all about me?

I started to get nervous.

How long could I wait before I started to look for him, I wondered? What could be considered a decent interval?

And wasn't it a little *early* in the relationship—even for me—for him to start giving me the runaround?

My state of dreamy, happy introspection abruptly dispersed. I should have known that it was too good to be true. I became aware of the noise and the jostling of the other people around me—I had totally forgotten about them all while I'd been talking to Gus—and I wondered if they were all laughing at me? Had they seen Gus do this to thousands of women? Could they sense my fear?

But, no, here he was, looking a bit disheveled.

"Lucy Sullivan," he declared, sounding anxious and distracted. "I'm sorry I was gone for so long but I've been involved in a terrible fracas."

"Oh God," I laughed. "What happened?"

"When I got to the fridge, some man was trying to help himself to your friend Donal's Guinness. 'Unhand them,' I shouted. 'I won't,' says he. 'You will,' says I. 'They're mine,' says he. 'They're not,' says I. A tussle ensued, Lucy, where I sustained minor injuries, but the Guinness is safe now."

"Is it?" I said, in surprise, because Gus had a bottle of red wine in his hand and there was no sign of Guinness anywhere.

"Yes, Lucy, I made the ultimate sacrifice and it's safe now. No one else will try to steal it."

"What've you done?"

"Done? But, I drank it, of course, Lucy. What else could I do?"

"Err . . ."

I looked over my shoulder nervously and, sure enough, through the bars of the banisters I could see Daniel making his way through the hall, his face like thunder.

"Lucy," he shouted. "Some little bastard has stolen . . ."

He paused when he saw Gus.

"You!" he yelled.

Oh dear. Daniel and Gus had obviously met.

"Daniel, Gus. Gus, Daniel," I said weakly.

"That's him," said Gus, in great annoyance. "That's the light-fingered character who was stealing your friend's Guinness."

"I might have known," said Daniel, shaking his head in resignation, ignoring Gus's accusatory finger. "I just might have bloody well known. How do you pick them, Lucy? Just tell me how?"

"Oh go away, you sanctimonious pig," I said, annoyed and embarrassed.

"Do you know this person?" Gus demanded of me. "I

don't think he's the type of person you should be friends with. You should have seen the way he . . ."

"I'm going," said Daniel, "And I'm taking Karen's bottle of wine with me." And he whipped the bottle of wine out of Gus's hand and disappeared back into the throng.

"Did you see that?" shouted Gus. "He's done it again!"

I tried not to laugh, but I couldn't help myself—I obviously wasn't as sober as I had thought.

"Stop it," I said, pulling Gus by the arm. "Sit down and behave."

"Oh, sit down and behave is it?"

"Yes."

"I see!"

There was a short pause while he looked down at me, a fierce frown on his handsome little face.

"Well, if you say so, Lucy Sullivan."

"I say so."

He meekly sat down beside me on the stairs, wearing an overdocile expression. We sat in silence for a few moments.

"Ah well," he said, "it was worth a try."

 20

Suddenly I had run out of things to say. I sat squashed up against him on the step, racking my brain for something to say.

"Well!" I said, too cheerfully and trying to hide my sudden shyness. What happens now, I wondered? Should we say it had been nice meeting each other and easily slip away from each other, like ships leaving their mooring bays? I didn't want that.

I decided to ask him a question—most people seemed to like talking about themselves.

"What age are you?"

"As old as the hills and as young as the morn, Lucy Sullivan."

"Would you mind being a bit more specific?"

"Twenty-four."

"Fine."

"Well, nine hundred and twenty-four, actually."

"Are you indeed?"

"And what age are you Lucy Sullivan?"

"Twenty-six."

"Hmmm, I see. You realize that I'm old enough to be your father?"

"If you're nine hundred and twenty-four, you're old enough to be my grandfather."

"Older, I'd say."

"But you look really good for your age."

"Clean living, Lucy Sullivan, that's what I put it down to. That and the deal I did with the devil."

"What was that?" I was *loving* this, I was having such a good time.

"I didn't age for any of the nine hundred years that I was waiting for you but, if I ever put foot inside an office to do a real job, I'll age instantly and die."

"That's funny," I said, "because that's exactly what happens to me every time I go to work, but I didn't have to wait nine hundred years for it to happen."

"You don't work in an office, do you?" he asked in horror. "Oh my poor wee Lucy, this can't be right. You shouldn't have to work at all, you should spend your time lying on a silken bed in your golden dress, eating sweet-meats, surrounded by your admirers and your subjects.''

"I couldn't agree more," I said warmly, "except for the bit about the sweetmeats. Would you mind if I had chocolate instead?''

"Not at all," he said expansively. "Chocolate it is. And speaking of a silken bed, would it be terribly forward of me if I asked if I could accompany you home tonight?''

I opened my mouth, feeling light-headed with alarm.

"Forgive me, Lucy Sullivan," he said, gripping my arm, his face a picture of stricken shock. "I can't believe I said that. Please, please, banish it from your mind, try to forget that I ever said it, that such a crass suggestion ever passed from my lips. May I be struck down! A bolt of lightning is too good for me, though."

"It's okay," I said nicely, reassured by his mortification. If he was that embarrassed, then surely he didn't make a habit of inviting himself home with women he'd just met?

"No, it's not okay," he said in alarm. "How could I have said something like that to a woman like you? I'm just going to walk away from you now and I want you to forget that you ever met me, it's the least I can do. Goodbye, Lucy Sullivan."

"No, don't go," I said, seized by alarm. I wasn't sure that I wanted to sleep with him, but I certainly didn't want him to go.

"You want me to stay, Lucy Sullivan?" he asked, an anxious look on his face.

"Yes!''

"Well, if you're really sure . . . hold on here while I get my coat.''

"But . . .''

Oh God! I had wanted him to stay as in stay talking to me at the party, but he seemed to think that I had invited him to stay with me in the silken bed with the sweetmeats and I was too afraid to upset him by explaining the misunderstanding to him, so it looked as if I had an overnight guest.

He was back, a lot more promptly than the last time, trailing scarves and a coat and a sweater under his arm.

"I'm ready, Lucy Sullivan."

I bet you are, I thought, swallowing with nerves.

"There's only one thing, Lucy."

What now?

"I'm not sure I have quite enough money to pay my full share of the taxi fare. Ladbroke Grove is a long way away, isn't it?"

"Well, how much money do you have?"

He pulled a handful of change out of his pocket. "Let me see, four pounds . . . five pounds . . . no, sorry, they're pesetas. Five pesetas, a dime, a miraculous medal and seven, eight, nine, *eleven* pence!"

"Come on." I laughed. After all, what had I expected? I couldn't wish for a penniless musician and then complain when he didn't have any money.

"I'll treat you right, Lucy, just as soon as I get my big break."

 21

𝒜 long time later we arrived at Ladbroke Grove. Gus and I held hands in the taxi but we hadn't kissed yet. It was only a matter of time and I felt very nervous about it. An excited sort of nervous.

Gus insisted on chatting with the taxi driver, asking him

all kinds of annoying questions—who was the most famous person he'd ever had in his cab, who was the least
famous person he'd ever had in his cab, that kind of
thing—and only stopped when the taxi driver screeched
to a halt somewhere around Fulham and, in a volley of
short, brusque, Anglo-Saxon words, conveyed to us that if
Gus didn't shut up we could both get out and make our
own travel arrangements for the rest of the way.

The planets were not aligned in my house of taxi drivers
that evening.

"My seals are lipped," shouted Gus and we spent the
rest of the journey whispering and nudging each other and
giggling like schoolchildren, speculating on why the taxi
driver was so bad-tempered.

I paid for the taxi and Gus absolutely insisted that I
take his handful of foreign change.

"But I don't want it," I said.

"Take it, Lucy," he insisted. "I've got my pride, you
know," he added with more than a hint of irony.

"Well, okay." I smiled, happy to humor him. "But I
don't want your miraculous medal, I've got thousands of
my own, thanks all the same."

"I bet your mother gave them to you."

"But of course."

"Yes, Irish mothers are like a bottomless pit of miraculous medals. They always have one hidden *somewhere.*
And do you find that she's always forcing things on you?"

"How d'you mean?"

Gus prodded me in my side with his finger, as I tried
to open the front door, "Will you have a cup of tea? Yes,
you will. Give her a whole pot, it'll warm her up."

He thumped up the stairs calling after me, "Will you
have a slice of bread, go on, you'll have the entire loaf.
Have a ten-pound bag of potatoes, have an eight-course

banquet, go on, sure, you need fattening up. I know you've just had your dinner, but another can't hurt.''

I couldn't help laughing, even though I was worried that the other residents of the building would complain about being awakened at two in the morning by a drunken Irishman insisting that they would like a haunch of beef.

"Go ahead," he shouted. "I'll even cook it for you."

"Shush," I said, giggling.

"Sorry," he stage whispered. "But will you?" he said, pulling on my coat sleeve.

"Will I what?"

"Will you eat an entire pig?"

"No!"

"But we'll only be throwing it away if you don't eat it. And we killed it specially for you."

"Stop it."

"Well, you'll at least have a drop of holy water and a miraculous medal, won't you?"

"Okay, just to please you."

We got into the flat and I suggested tea, but Gus wasn't interested in tea.

"I'm really tired, Lucy," he said. "Will we go to bed?"

Oh God! I knew what that meant.

There was so much to worry about, not least the question of contraception and Gus didn't strike me as being in any kind of condition to care about such matters. Or even for them to occur to him. Perhaps he was a more responsible citizen when he wasn't drunk—although I wouldn't have counted on it—so it looked as though it was up to me to be the sensible, careful party. Not that I minded—I preferred men who erred on the side of wildness rather than caution.

"How about it, Lucy?" He smiled at me.

"Sure!" I said, trying to sound bright, breezy, unconcerned, like a woman in control. Then I thought that perhaps I had sounded too eager and while I didn't want him to realize that I was a bag of nerves, neither did I want him to think that I was desperate to go to bed with him.

"Er, come on," I muttered, hoping my tone was striking a neutral middle ground.

I realized that I hadn't been entirely wise. I had invited a complete stranger, a complete *male* stranger, a very strange stranger, into my empty apartment. If I ended up raped and robbed and murdered, then I would only have myself to blame. Although Gus wasn't acting like he had rape and pillage on his mind. He was too busy dancing around my bedroom opening drawers, reading my credit card bills and admiring my fixtures and fittings.

"A real fireplace!" he shouted. "Lucy Sullivan, you realize what this means?"

"What does it mean?"

"It means that we must pull up our chairs and sit in the flickering firelight and tell stories."

"Yes, but you see, we don't actually use the fireplace, because the chimney needs to be . . ."

But I'd lost him because he opened my wardrobe and was flicking through the hangers.

"Aha! A rough-hewn cloak," he said, pulling out an old coat of mine, a long velvet one with a hood. "What do you think?"

He tried it on (and, in fairness, that was all he seemed to be interested in trying on), pulled up the hood and stood in front of the mirror swishing it around.

"Beautiful," I laughed. "It's you."

He looked a bit like an elf, but quite a sexy elf.

"You're laughing at me, Lucy Sullivan."

"I'm not."

And I wasn't because I thought he was gorgeous. I was

delighted with his enthusiasm, the way he found everything interesting, his unusual way of looking at things.
There's no other word for it—I was enchanted.

I was also very relieved that he was playing dressing-
up instead of trying to get me into bed. I did find him
attractive—very attractive—but it seemed a little bit soon
to be hopping into bed with him. But I had, after all, said
that he could come home with me and I felt that in that
case etiquette dictated that I couldn't really *not* go to bed
with him.

In theory, I knew that it was my right not to go to bed
with anyone I didn't want to, and to change my mind at
any stage in the proceedings, but the reality was that I
would be far too embarrassed to say no.

I suppose I felt that after he had come all this way it
would be inhospitable to send him away empty-handed. It
went back to my childhood, where generosity to our visitors mattered above all else, where it didn't matter if we
had to do without dinner so long as the guests were fed.

I also felt that Gus and I were somehow meant to be
together and *that* was very seductive. Not only would it be
unforgivably rude to refuse to sleep with him, but it would
be actively flying in the face of fate, calling the wrath of the
gods to be delivered down on top of me. It was a great
relief to think that, actually, because it took all the "Will
I, won't I?" out of it. I had no choice. I *had* to sleep with
him. No agonizing, everything was nice and simple.

All the same, I was still nervous. I suppose the gods
can't think of everything.

I sat on my bed and fiddled with my earrings, while
Gus roamed around the room, picking things up, putting
them down, and making all kinds of comments.

"Nice books, Lucy. Apart from all this California
stuff," he muttered, reading the back of *Who Gets the Car*

*in the Dysfunctional Family of the Nineties.* I was glad to see that, while Gus was slightly eccentric, he wasn't totally neurotic.

I put my earrings back on so that I could take them off again. I had always found that wearing jewelry was a good idea in a seduction-type situation because, while it gave me the appearance of taking things off and made me seem as if I was a good sport and game for anything, in actuality the other person was down to his undergarments long before I ever was, giving me the chance to back out or change my mind without exposing, among other things, my own hand.

I learned that trick the summer I was fifteen and Ann Garrett and Fiona Hart and I used to play strip poker with some of the boys from our road. Ann and Fiona both had bosoms and in a summer that was awash with sexual undertones and overtones—none of them emanating to or from me, I have to say—they were dying to be forced into a situation where they had to display themselves. I had no bosoms, and even though I was delighted to feel that I had friends, I would rather have died than sit in the field behind the shops on a balmy summer evening in my undershirt and panties with Derek Wheatley and Gordon Wheatley and Joe Newey and Paul Stapleton.

So I solved the problem by wearing as much jewelry and accessories as I could lay my hands on. My ears weren't pierced—I didn't get that done until I was twenty-three—so I had to wear clip-on earrings, which stopped the circulation and turned my earlobes into two throbbing red balls of agony, but it was a small price to pay. (Although it was always a relief to lose the first couple of hands of poker.) And I smuggled out and wore my mother's cameo ring that she kept wrapped in tissue paper in a box in the bottom of her wardrobe and only wore herself on her wedding anniversary and her birthday. It was far too big for me and I lived in terror of losing it. And with three pink plastic bracelets and my Confirmation cross and chain, I made sure that I never had to take off more than my socks and sandals. But just to be on the safe side I wore three pairs of socks.

Curiously enough, Ann and Fiona never wore *any* jewelry.

And they seemed to be no good at the game either, throwing away aces and kings like they were going out of fashion and in what seemed like no time at all, they were down to their bras and panties, giggling and saying how embarrassed they were and sitting up straight with their stomachs in and their shoulders back and their chests thrust out. While I remained fully clothed, with just a neat little pile of pink bracelets and earrings on the grass beside me.

It was odd. I hardly ever won at anything but I somehow nearly always managed to win at strip poker. But the oddest thing of all was that none of the other players acted very impressed. It took me several years to realize that they hadn't been, as I so smugly thought, sore losers.

I was a very naïve teenager.

I went on taking my earrings on and off while Gus familiarized himself with the contents of my bedroom.

"I'll just have a little lie-down, Lucy, if that's okay."

"Fine."

"Do you mind if I take my boots off?"

"Er, no, not at all." I had been expecting him to take off a lot more than his boots. If he just took off his boots I'd be getting away lightly.

He lay down on the bed beside me.

"This is nice," he said, holding my hand.

"Mmmm," I murmured. It *was* nice.

"D'you know something, Lucy Sull . . . ?"

"What?"

He said nothing.

"What?" I said again, turning to look at him.

But he was asleep. Stretched out on my bed, still in his jeans and shirt. He looked so *sweet,* his eyelashes black and spiky, throwing shadows onto his face, faint stubble on his jaw and chin, his mouth smiling slightly.

I stared down at him.

*That's what I want,* I thought. He's the one.

 22

I tugged the duvet out from under him and covered him with it, which made me feel very caring and tender. I pushed back a lock of hair from his forehead just to enhance the feeling. Was it all right to let him sleep fully clothed, I wondered? Well, it would have to be because I wasn't going to undress him. I certainly had no intention of rummaging around in his undergarments and taking covert looks and sneak previews.

Then feeling a bit, well, *at loose ends,* I suppose, I got ready for bed. I put on my pajamas—I was pretty sure that Gus wasn't a sexy negligée type of man, which was good because I didn't have a sexy negligée. Gus was probably more likely to be frightened by a sexy negligée than turned on by it. Although, then again, you never know . . .

And I brushed my teeth. Of *course* I brushed my teeth. I brushed them so much my gums were raw. I knew that brushing my teeth was the single most important thing I had to do when sharing my bed with an unfamiliar man. Magazines and past experience could not stress just how important it was. It was a bit sad to think that a man who liked you enough to have sex with you in the night would make a break for the door if your breath was less than fragrant the following morning, but that, unfortunately, was the way things were. Being sad about it wouldn't change it.

And instead of removing my makeup, I put on lots more. I wanted to look lovely in the morning when Gus woke up and I figured that my extra makeup would compensate for his sobriety, even it out, if you like. Then I climbed into bed beside him. He looked so cute asleep.

I lay staring into the darkness, thinking about everything that had happened that evening and, call it excitement or anticipation or disappointment or even relief, but I couldn't sleep.

After a while I heard the front door and then I heard Karen and Charlotte and someone with a man's voice talking and tea being made and murmured conversation and muffled laughs. It was a lot more peaceful than the previous night—no *Sound of Music,* no falling furniture, no raucous screeches of laughter.

After what seemed like hours more of lying in the dark I decided to get up again and see what was going on out in the apartment. I was feeling a bit left out of things. But that was nothing new. I inched out of bed carefully, not wanting to disturb Gus, and tiptoed out of my room and, as I backed out into the hall, quietly closing my bedroom door, I bumped into something big and dark that wasn't usually positioned just outside my room.

I jumped a mile!

"Jesus!" I exclaimed.

"Lucy," said a man's voice. The thing put its hands on my shoulders.

"Daniel!" I sputtered, as I turned around. "What the hell are *you* doing? You scared the life out of me, you idiot!"

Instead of being apologetic, Daniel found this hilarious. He collapsed into convulsions.

"Hello, Lucy," he wheezed, barely able to speak he was laughing so much. "What a lovely welcome you always give me. I thought you'd be halfway to Moscow by now."

"What were you doing lurking in the dark outside my door?" I demanded.

Daniel leaned against the wall, still laughing. "The look on your face," he said, wiping tears from his eyes. "I wish you could have seen it."

I was shaken and annoyed and I didn't think anything was funny, so I punched Daniel in the arm.

"Ouch," he said, still laughing, holding his arm where I'd hit him, "you're dangerous."

Before I could hit him again, Karen arrived in the hall and suddenly it all became clear. She gave me a meaningful wink and said, "*I* invited Daniel back. Nothing to do with you, don't worry."

Hats off to Karen. I was impressed. Very impressed. It seemed as if she had made definite progress on her Daniel project.

"I was just about to leave, actually," said Daniel. "But seeing as you're up I think I'll stay a bit longer."

We trooped into the front room, me feeling a bit awkward about Daniel catching me in my blue pajamas, where Charlotte was stretched out on the sofa, looking blissfully happy. The room bore signs of recent tea drinking.

"Lucy," said Charlotte in delight. "Wonderful! You're

up. Come over here and sit beside me.'' She sat up and patted the place beside her on the sofa and I snuggled up next to her, modestly pulling my legs under me. I had chipped nail polish on my toes and a blister on my instep and I didn't want Daniel to see.

"Any tea left?" I asked.

"Lots," said Charlotte.

"I'll get you a cup," said Daniel, making for the kitchen. He was back in a moment and poured tea into a mug and added milk and two spoons of sugar and stirred it and handed it to me.

"Thanks. You have your uses sometimes."

He stood beside the sofa, looming over me.

"Oh, take off your coat," I said in exasperation. "You look like an undertaker."

"I *like* this coat."

"And sit down. You're blocking out the light."

"Sorry."

Daniel sat on the armchair nearest me and then Karen sat on the floor leaning her head on the arm-rest of his chair. Her eyes were shining and she looked all dreamy and romantic. I was, in all honesty, shocked.

She was behaving so out of character. Karen always played damn near impossible to get. She tied men into knots of uncertainty, turned many a well-balanced guy into Insecurity in a Suit. She was always a bit, I suppose, *hard,* and now she looked soft and pretty and sweet.

Well, well, well.

"I met a guy," Charlotte announced.

"So did I," I said gleefully.

So had Karen, but perhaps this wasn't quite the right time for her to talk about it.

"We know," said Charlotte. "Karen's been listening at your door, trying to see if you were going at it with him."

"You blabbermouthed—" said Karen in a fury.

"Oh shush," I said. "Don't fight. I want to hear all about Charlotte's guy."

"No, I want to hear all about yours," said Charlotte.

"No, you first."

"No, you."

Karen affected a bored, grown-up face, but she only did that for Daniel's benefit, to make him think that she didn't do silly, girly things like indulge in gossip. But that was all right— we had all done the same when the guy we were crazy about was present. No one was more culpable than I was. It was just a ploy and as soon as she was sure that Daniel was interested, Karen could be herself again.

"Please, Lucy, you go first," intervened Daniel.

Karen looked surprised and then she said, "Yes, come on Lucy. Stop being so coy."

"Okay," I said, delighted.

"Great." Charlotte hugged her knees in excitement.

"Where do you want me to start?" I asked, grinning from ear to ear.

"Look at her," said Karen dryly. "She's like the cat that got the cream."

"What's his name?" said Charlotte.

"Gus."

"*Gus!*" Karen was horrified. "What an awful name. Gus the Gorilla. Gussie Goose."

"And what's he like?" asked Charlotte, ignoring Karen's noises of disgust.

"He's wonderful," I began, my description gathering steam. And then I noticed that Daniel was looking at me rather oddly. He sat forward in his chair, with his hands on his knees and was staring, looking sort of puzzled, sort of sad. "What are you looking at me like that for?" I said indignantly.

"Like what?!"

But it was Karen who shouted it, not Daniel.

"Thank you, Karen," said Daniel politely to her, "but I think I can manage to cobble together a couple of words."

She shrugged and haughtily tossed her blond hair. Apart from the slight pinkness in her cheeks no one would have known that she was embarrassed. I envied her her poise and aplomb.

Daniel turned back to me. "Where were we?" he said. "Oh yes, Like what?!"

I began to laugh.

"I don't know," I giggled. "Funny. Like you knew something about me that I didn't know."

"Lucy," he said gravely. "I would never be foolish enough to presume that I knew something that you didn't. I value my life."

"Good," I smiled. "Now can I tell you about my guy?"

"Yes," hissed Charlotte. "Get on with it, would you."

"Weeell," I said, "he's twenty-four and he's Irish and he's brilliant. Really funny and a bit, you know, off the wall. He's not like anyone I've ever met before and . . ."

"Really?" said Daniel, sounding surprised. "But what about that Anthony guy that you had a thing with?"

"Gus is nothing like Anthony."

"But . . ."

"Anthony was crazy."

"But . . ."

Gus isn't," I said firmly.

"Well, what about that other drunken Irishman you went out with?" suggested Daniel.

"Who?" I said, starting to feel slightly annoyed.

"Whatshisname," said Daniel. "Matthew? Malcolm?"

"Malachy," murmured Karen helpfully. The traitor.

"That's right. Malachy."

"Gus is nothing like Malachy either," I exclaimed. "Malachy was always drunk."

Daniel said nothing. He just raised an eyebrow and gave me a meaningful look.

"Okay!" I burst out. "I'm sorry about your Guinness. But I'll replace it, don't worry. Anyway, since when did you get so mean and stingy?"

"But I'm not . . ."

"Why are you being so nasty?"

"But . . ."

"Aren't you happy for me?"

"Yes, but . . ."

"Look, if you can't say something nice, don't say anything at all!"

"Sorry."

He sounded so contrite that I felt guilty. I leaned over to him and rubbed his knee, apologetically, awkwardly. I was Irish—I wasn't equipped to deal with hot weather or spontaneous affection.

"I'm sorry too," I muttered.

"Maybe you're getting married after all," suggested Charlotte. "This Gus could be the man your fortune-teller told you about."

"Maybe," I agreed quietly. I was embarrassed to admit that that was what I had thought too.

"You know," said Charlotte, looking a bit shamefaced. "For a little while I thought that Daniel might be your mystery man, your husband-to-be."

I burst out laughing.

"Him! I wouldn't touch him with a ten-foot pole—you never know *where* he's been."

Daniel looked all offended and Karen looked absolutely

*furious.* Hastily I backtracked and winked affectionately at Daniel.

"Only joking, Daniel. You know what I mean, but if it's any consolation, my mother would be delighted. You're her ideal son-in-law."

"I know," he sighed. "But you're right, it would never work. I'm too ordinary for you, isn't that right, Lucy?"

"How d'you mean?"

"Well I have a job and I don't show up to meet you blind drunk and I pay for you when we go out and I'm not a tortured artist."

"Shut up, you bastard," I laughed. "You make all my boyfriends sound like drunken free-loaders."

"Do I indeed?"

"Yes. And you'd better watch it because they're not."

"Sorry."

"That's okay."

"All the same," he said. "I don't think Connie's going to be too thrilled when she meets Gus."

"She won't meet him," I said.

"She'll have to if you're going to marry him," he reminded me.

"Daniel, please shut up!" I begged. "This is supposed to be a happy occasion."

"Sorry, Lucy," he murmured.

I caught his eye. He didn't look very sorry. Before I could complain he said, "Come on, Charlotte, tell us about your guy."

Charlotte was only too happy to oblige. Apparently his name was Simon, tall, blond, good-looking, twenty-nine, in advertising, had a great car, at the party had been all over her like a rash and was calling her the following day to take her out for lunch. "And I just know he'll call," she said, her eyes shining. "I have such a good feeling about this."

"Great!" I said, delighted. "It seems like we all got lucky this evening."

Then I left and slipped back into bed beside Gus.

 23

Gus was still asleep and still looked gorgeous. But what Daniel had said had upset me slightly. It was true—my mother wouldn't like Gus. In fact, my mother would hate Gus. The good had gone out of the evening slightly. I marveled at my mother's unerring ability to tarnish all the happy things she touched.

She always had, as far back as I could remember.

When I was a little girl and Dad came home in a good mood because he'd just got a job, or won money at the races or whatever, she always managed to defuse any celebrations. Dad would come into the kitchen, all smiles, his coat pocket filled with candy for us and a bottle in a brown paper bag under his arm. And instead of smiling and saying, "What's happened, Jamsie? What are we celebrating?" she ruined it all by making a face and saying something awful like "Oh Jamsie, not after the last time" or, "Oh Jamsie, you promised."

And even at six or eight or whatever age I was, I felt terrible. Appalled at her ingratitude. Anxious to let him know that I thought she was behaving dreadfully, that I was on his side. And not just because candy was a rare event. I wholeheartedly agreed with Dad when he said, "Lucy, your mother is a right old misery."

Because there was no one else to do it, I felt that it was my job to provide an upbeat mood.

So when Dad sat down and poured himself a glass, I sat at the table with him, to keep him company, to show solidarity, so that he wasn't celebrating whatever he was celebrating alone.

It was nice to watch him. There was a rhythm to his drinking that I found comforting.

My mother indicated her disapproval by banging and clattering and washing and wiping. Intermittently Dad tried to get her to cheer up. "Eat the candy bar I brought you, Connie," he said.

If the phrase, "Lighten up," had been invented, he probably would have made good use of it.

And after a while he usually got out the record player and sang along to "Four Green Fields" and "I Wish I Was in Carrickfergus" and other Irish songs. He played them over and over again and occasionally between songs he said, "Eat the candy bar!"

And after a while more he usually began to cry. But he kept singing, his voice hoarse with tears. Or it might have been the brandy.

I knew that his heart was breaking because he wasn't in Carrickfergus—I often felt so sad for him that I cried also. But my mother would just say "Jesus! Sure that idiot doesn't even know where Carrickfergus is, never mind wishing he was there."

I couldn't understand why she had to be so miserable. Or so cruel.

And he'd say to her, in a kind of slurred voice, "It's a state of mind, my dear. It's a state of mind."

I wasn't really sure what he meant by that.

But when he slurred at her, "But how would you know, because you don't have a mind," I *did* know what he meant by that. I'd catch his eye and we'd both snigger conspiratorially.

Those evenings always followed the same pattern. The uneaten candy bar, the rhythmic drinking, the banging and clattering, the singing and crying. Then, when the bottle was nearly all gone my mother usually said something like, "Here goes. Get ready for the grand finale."

And Dad would get to his feet. Sometimes he wouldn't be able to walk too straight. Most times, actually.

"I'm going home to Ireland," my mother would say in a bored voice.

"I'm going home to Ireland," my dad would shout in the slurred voice.

"If I leave now I can catch the mail-train boat," my mother said, still in the bored voice, as she leaned against the sink.

"If I leave now I can catch the mail-train boat," my dad would shout.

"I was a fool ever to have left," Mum would say idly, inspecting her fingernails. I couldn't understand her complete lack of emotion.

"I was a bloody idiot ever to have left," Dad would shout.

"Oh, it's a 'bloody idiot' this time, is it?" Mum might say. "I liked 'fool' myself, but a bit of variety is nice."

Poor Dad would stand there, swaying slightly, hunched over and looking a bit like a bull, staring at Mum but not quite seeing her. Probably seeing the end of his nose, actually.

"I'm going to pack a bag," Mum would say, like a stage prompter.

"I'm going to bag a pack," Dad would say lurching toward the kitchen door.

Even though it happened lots of times and he never got further than the front door, every time I thought he was really leaving.

"Dad, please don't go," I beseeched him.

"I won't stay in a house with that woman who won't even eat the candy bar I bought her," he usually said.

"Eat the candy bar," I begged Mum, as I tried to block Dad from leaving the room.

"Don't stand in my way, Lucy, or I won't be brespon . . . I mean I won't be rospensible . . . I mean, ah fuck it!" and he'd fall out into the hall.

Then we'd hear the sound of the hall table falling over and Mum would mutter, "If that man has broken my . . ."

"Mum, stop him," I'd beg frantically.

"He won't get further than the gate," she'd say bitterly. "More's the pity."

And although I never believed her, she was right. He very rarely did.

Once he made it up the road as far as the O'Hanlaoins, clutching a plastic bag that contained four slices of bread and the rest of the bottle of brandy under his armpit. His sustenance for the journey home to Monaghan. He stood outside the O'Hanlaoins for a while and shouted things. Something about the O'Hanlaoins being dishonest and how Seamus had to leave Ireland to avoid a prison sentence. "Ye were run outta the place," my dad shouted.

Mum and Chris had to go and get him and bring him back. He came quietly. Mum led him by the hand past the censorious stares of all our neighbors who were standing, arms folded, looking over their small gates, silently watching the spectacle. When we got as far as our house

Mum turned back and shouted at them, "You can go back in now. The circus is over."

I was surprised to see that she was crying.

I thought it was with shame. Shame for the way she'd treated him, for ruining his good mood, for not eating the candy bar he'd bought for her, for urging him to try and leave. Shame that she richly deserved.

 24

I awoke to find Gus leaning over me, anxiously looking down into my face.

"Lucy Sullivan?" he asked.

"That's me," I said sleepily.

"Oh thank God for that!"

"For what?"

"I thought I might have dreamed you."

"That's so sweet."

"I'm glad you think so, Lucy," he said ruefully. "But I'm afraid it's not really. With my track record, I very often wake up and wish that I *had* dreamed the previous evening. It makes a change for me to hope that it wasn't a dream."

"Oh."

I was confused, but I *thought* it sounded like a compliment.

"Thank you for letting me avail of your lying-down facilities, Lucy," he said. "You're a wee angel."

I sat up in alarm. That sounded valedictory. Was he leaving?

But no, he didn't seem to be wearing a shirt, so he wasn't going just yet. I snuggled back into bed and he lay down beside me. Though the duvet was between us, it felt wonderful.

"My pleasure." I smiled.

"Now, Lucy, I'd better ask you how many days I've been here?"

"Less than one, actually."

"Is that all?" he said, sounding disappointed. "That was very restrained of me. I must be getting old. Although it's early days yet. Still plenty of time."

Fine with me, I thought. Stay as long as you like.

"And now can I avail myself of your bathroom facilities, Lucy?"

"Down the hall, you'll see it."

"But I'd better cover my shame, Lucy."

I eagerly hoisted myself up onto my elbow—all the better to get a good look at his shame before he covered it—and saw that at some stage during the night Gus had removed his clothing and was now only wearing his boxer shorts. And what a lovely body he had. Beautiful smooth skin and strong arms, and a tiny waist and a flat stomach. I couldn't get a good look at his legs because he was nearly lying on top of me, but if they were anything like the rest of him, they were bound to be delicious.

"Wear my robe, it's on the back of the door."

"But what if I meet one of your roommates?" he asked in mock fear.

"What about it?" I giggled.

"I'll be shy. And they'll, you know . . . *think* things about me."

He hung his head and went all coy and simpery.

"What kind of things?" I laughed.

"They'll wonder where I slept and my reputation will be ruined."

"Go on, I'll defend your honor if anyone says anything."

His voice and his accent were so beautiful, I could have listened to him forever.

"Great robe!" said Gus. It was a white terry cloth one with a hood and he put it on and put up the hood and shadow boxed around my bed.

"Are you in the Ku Klux Klan, Lucy Sullivan?" he asked, looking at himself in the mirror. "Have you any burning crosses hidden under the bed?"

"No."

"Well, if you ever decide to join, you won't have to buy the uniform, just throw on your robe!"

I lay back against my pillow and smiled at him. I was happy.

"Right," he said. "I'll be off."

Gus opened the bedroom door and immediately slammed it shut again.

I jumped.

"What's wrong?"

"That man!" said Gus, sounding horrified.

"What man?"

"The tall one, who stole your friend's beer and my bottle of wine. He's right outside this door!

So Daniel had stayed the night—how funny.

"No, no, listen to me," I wheezed.

"He *is* Lucy, I swear he is," insisted Gus. "Unless I'm having the visions again."

"You're not having any visions," I said.

"Well, then we have to get him out of here! You won't have a stick of furniture left in the place otherwise—

honestly! I've met his type before. Thorough professionals . . ."

"No, Gus, please listen to me," I said, trying to be serious. "He won't steal our furniture—he's my friend."

"Really? Do you mean it? Well, I know it's none of my business and I know we've just met and I've no right to comment, but, a common criminal—I wouldn't have expected it, that's all . . . and I can't see what you think is so funny. You won't think it's funny when you see your couch on sale at Camden Market and you have to sleep on the floor. *I* certainly don't think it's a laughing matter . . ."

"Please shut up and listen to me, Gus," I managed to sputter. "Daniel, that's the tall man, outside the door. He didn't steal anyone's beer."

"But, I saw him . . ."

"It was his beer, though."

"No, it was Donal's beer."

"But he is Donal and his name is Daniel."

A pause while Gus digested this fact.

"Oh God," he groaned.

He lurched over and threw himself on my bed, his face in his hands.

"Oh God, oh God, oh God," he moaned.

"It's okay," I said gently.

"Oh God, oh God, oh God."

Gus looked up at me from between his fingers.

"Oh God," he said, his face stricken.

"It's fine."

"It's not."

"It is."

"No, it isn't. I accused him of stealing his own beer and then I drank it all. And then I took his girlfriend's bottle of wine . . ."

"She's not his girlfriend . . ." I said irrelevantly. "Although maybe she is now . . ."

"The scary blonde?"

"Er, yes." Karen *could* be described that way.

"Believe me," insisted Gus. "She's his girlfriend, all right, at least if *she* has anything to do with it."

"I suppose you're right," I admitted.

How interesting, I thought. So Gus could be perceptive and clued-in? How much of his flighty, madcap carry-on was an act? Or was he both perceptive and flighty? Could it all be part of the same man? And did I have the energy for it?

"I'm not usually obnoxious like that, Lucy, honestly I'm not," he insisted. "It was the drugs. It must have been."

"Okay," I said, feeling almost disappointed.

"I must apologize to him," said Gus, jumping up off the bed.

"No," I said. "Come back here. It's too early in the morning for apologies. Later."

Gus lurked by the door for a while, looking stressed and anxious, then he opened it a crack. "He's gone," he said with relief. "It's safe for me to go and hose myself down." And off he went.

While he was gone I lay in bed feeling very pleased with myself. I had to admit that I was relieved that he was slightly ashamed of himself for running off with Daniel's Guinness. It showed that he was a decent person. And a smart one too—he'd figured out Karen fairly quickly.

He looked even cuter than I remembered—smiley and attractive and not half as bloodshot around the eyes.

What would happen, I wondered, when he came back from the bathroom? Would he get dressed and leave, awkwardly omitting to say anything about calling me? Somehow I thought not. I certainly *hoped* not.

There wasn't that awful sordid feeling that often goes with waking up on a Sunday morning, either with a complete stranger in your bed, or in a complete stranger's bed.

At least Gus had woken me up. He hadn't inched carefully out of the bed and silently dressed in the dark and bolted out of the apartment, his underpants in his pocket, his watch forgotten on my bedside table.

I hadn't awakened to the sound of the front door slamming behind him. And, with my history of relationships, that counted as a flying start.

Being with Gus felt natural and right. I wasn't even nervous. Well hardly even.

He was back from the bathroom, with a pink towel around his waist, his hair wet and shiny, all clean and fragrant.

Suspiciously fragrant, actually.

I had been right about his legs.

He wasn't very tall, but he was all man.

A shiver ran through me. I was looking forward to . . . er . . . getting to know him better.

"You're looking at a man who has been exfoliated to within an inch of his life, Lucy." He grinned, looking very pleased with himself.

"Exfoliated, defoliated, cleansed, conditioned, emolliated, moisturized, massaged, anointed! What! You name it, I've had it done to me in the last ten minutes. Can you remember the days when all we were expected to do was wash ourselves, Lucy? But not anymore. We must keep up with the times, mustn't we, Lucy Sullivan?"

"Yes," I giggled. He was so funny.

"Can't let the grass grow under our feet, can we Lucy Sullivan?"

"No."

"You'd be hard-pressed to find a cleaner man in the whole of London."

"I bet."

"Wonderful bathroom facilities, Lucy. You must pride yourself on them."

"Er, yes, I suppose . . ."

The state of my bathroom wasn't something that exactly occupied my thoughts much.

"Lucy, I hope it's okay, but I used some of Elizabeth's stuff."

"Who's Elizabeth?"

"Well, there's little enough point in asking me, you should know, you live here. Isn't she your roommate?"

"No, there's only me and Karen and Charlotte."

"Well, she has a nerve in that case, because the bathroom is full of her things."

"What on earth are you talking about?"

"Elizabeth, what was her surname? Began with *G*. Ardent, that's what it was, I think. Elizabeth Ardent—I remember now because I was thinking it was a good name for a romantic novel writer—anyway she's got a load of bottles and tubes in the bathroom with her name on them."

"Oh God," I started to laugh.

Gus had used Karen's very expensive jars of Elizabeth Arden shower gel and body lotion. Or Elizabeth Hard-on as Charlotte and I called them. That was because we were jealous and coveted them, but we were afraid to touch them.

In fact even Karen didn't use them—they were really just exhibition pieces that she kept for show, to impress the likes of Daniel, not that he noticed things like that, what with him being a man. Up to now I'd even suspected that there was only colored water in the bottles.

Heads would roll over this.

"Oh no," said Gus nervously. "I've done it again, haven't I? I've committed another *faux pas*—surely I'm well over my quota already?—I shouldn't have used that stuff, should I?"

"Don't worry," I said. There really was no point worrying now—it was done—if Karen kicked up a fuss . . . no . . . *when* Karen kicked up a fuss, I'd offer to replace them.

"But, Gus, I think it would be better if you didn't use Karen's things again."

"Who's Karen? Oh aye, I get you—Karen owns Elizabeth's things? Poor Karen, getting hand-me-down bottles and tubes with someone else's name on them. A bit like me really, all my school books had someone else's name on them because I have so many older brothers. . . . Anyway, I'll use your things in the bathroom the next time."

"Good," I smiled, delighted at the suggestion that there would be a next time.

"Lucy," he said. He came over and sat beside me on my bed and held my hand. His hand was smooth and warm. Mine looked tiny beside it. I liked to feel tiny beside men. A couple of the men that I had gone out with were really skinny and nothing demoralized me more than going to bed with a man who had a smaller butt and thinner thighs than me.

"I really am sorry," said Gus earnestly, making circles on the back of my hand with his thumb, sending little shivers of delight through me. I could barely concentrate on what he was saying.

"You're very nice and I really like you," he went on

awkwardly. "And I've done an awful lot of things wrong already and we've only just met. Sometimes I joke at the wrong time and when something is important to me I get it even more wrong. Sorry."

My heart dissolved. I hadn't been angry with him anyway, but after his little speech I felt so tender, so . . . so, *cherishing* toward him.

"And about the stuff in the bathroom, perhaps if I spoke to Elizabeth and explained . . . ?"

"Karen!" I insisted. "She's Karen! Not Elizabeth."

I trailed off when I saw the twinkle in his eye.

I'm joking, Lucy," he said. "I know she's called Karen and that there's no Elizabeth living here."

"Oh," I said, a bit embarrassed.

"You must think I'm a half-wit," he said. "But it's very kind of you to humor me, all the same."

"I just thought . . . you know . . ." I limply tried to explain.

"It's okay," he said.

We gave each other a knowing little smile, this would be our little joke.

Already we had shared secrets, in-jokes, verbal shorthand!

"It's fine," I said. "Everything's fine."

"If you say so. And now, Lucy, we'll go for a walk."

He had made me laugh with a lot of the things he had said, but that suggestion made me laugh most of all.

"What's so funny, Lucy?"

"Me? A walk? On a Sunday?"

"Aye."

"No."

"Why not?"

"Because it's freezing outside."

"But we'll wear warm clothes. And we'll walk briskly."

"But, Gus, I never leave the house on any Sunday from October to April, except to go to the Cash'n'Curry in the evening."

"Then it's about time you started. What's this Cash' n'Curry place?"

"It's the Indian restaurant around the corner."

"Great name."

"Well, it's not really called Cash'n'Curry, it's called something like The Star of Lahore or The Jewel of Bombay."

"And you go there every Sunday night?"

"Every Sunday night without fail, and we always have exactly the same thing."

"Okay, well we might go there later, Lucy, but right now we'll go to Holland Park, it's only down the road from here."

"Er, is it?"

"Aye. How long have you lived here, Lucy Sullivan?"

"A couple of years." I mumbled it and tried to make "years" sound like "weeks."

"And in all that time you've never been to the park? That's a disgrace, Lucy."

"I'm not really an outdoor creature, Gus."

"I am."

"Will they have a television there?"

"Aye."

"Really?"

"No. But I'll entertain you, don't worry."

"Okay."

I was really very pleased. Delighted, in fact. He wanted to spend the day with me.

"Can I wear this sweater?"

"Yes, in fact you can have it, I hate it."

Gus was rummaging around in my cupboards and had unearthed a revolting dark blue Aran sweater that my mother had knitted for me. I had never worn it precisely *because* she had knitted it for me.

"Wow, thanks, Lucy Sullivan."

 25

I went to take a shower and when I got back my room was empty—Gus was gone and I felt slightly panicky. I was afraid that he might have left the apartment completely but I was more afraid that he hadn't. He had an admirable capacity to create havoc and, despite his touching apology earlier, I wasn't yet convinced that it was safe to let him roam my place without a chaperone.

Visions of finding him lying in bed with Daniel and Karen, blithely chatting, while they put a reluctant and ill-tempered halt to their sexual activities, appeared before me.

But it was fine.

Gus was in the kitchen, sitting at the table with Daniel and Karen. They were all drinking tea and the newspapers were spread out. To my intense relief, everyone was getting along nicely and having a civilized Sunday morning chat, stolen Guinness and misappropriated Elizabeth Arden toiletries notwithstanding. Gus and Daniel seemed to have resolved their differences regarding Gus's unauthorized drinking of Daniel's Guinness. Gus and Karen appeared to be the best of friends.

"Lucy," smiled Gus when I appeared in the kitchen doorway, "come in and sit down and partake of some nourishment."

"Oh," I said faintly, a bit taken aback by all the camaraderie. I was a little bit, well, not *annoyed* exactly, but a bit put out, I suppose because all these people, who only knew one another because of me, were getting along fine without me.

"I explained to Karen about me using her Elizabeth Ardent things," sang Gus, his face a picture of innocence. "And she says it's okay."

"It's fine," said Karen, smiling at Gus, smiling at Daniel, smiling at me.

Gosh! I'm sure Karen wouldn't have been quite so reasonable if Charlotte or I had used said Elizabeth Arden toiletries.

She obviously liked Gus.

Or maybe Daniel had surpassed himself between the sheets the previous night. No doubt I'd find out later. She would tell everything, in the minutest possible detail, when the menfolk were gone.

I spent *hours* getting ready. It was the hardest thing in the world to look as if I was dressed sensibly and to look pretty and feminine and skinny at the same time. It was far harder to do that than getting ready for dinner with Daniel the previous evening had been. The trick with dressing for a visit to the great outdoors was to look as if I didn't care how I looked, as though I'd just grabbed anything that came to hand and slung it on me. I wore my jeans—I couldn't really see any way around it, even though I hated the way they made my thighs stick out.

I hated my thighs more than life itself and I would have given anything to have had skinny ones. I even used to pray for them. Well, I had once. It was one Christmas day at Mass (my mother insisted that we still go to Mass *en famille* and I had learned to go along with it). When the priest said that we should pray for our own special intentions, I prayed for thinner thighs. Afterward my mother asked me what my "special intention" was and when I told her she was furious and told me that that was a completely unworthy and inappropriate thing to pray for. So I shamefacedly slunk back into the church, piously bowed my head and prayed for thinner thighs for her, Dad, Chris, Pete, Granny Sullivan, the poor people in Africa and anyone else who might like them.

But God didn't reward my altruism by granting me slimmer thighs and I found that the only way to make them look small was to surround them with big things. So I put on my heavy, clumpy boots. But then I had to cancel out the trucker image that they conjured up by wearing a girly, pink angora sweater. And a big checked blue-and-black jacket, to make me look fragile and tiny.

I spent another hour or so trying to make it seem as if I had just loosely bundled my hair up on top of my head. It took forever to arrange my curls so that they looked as if they had just fallen down around my face at random.

Then a heavy application of makeup to achieve the Un-madeup Look, or Bare-faced chic, if you prefer. All pink cheeks and clear white skin and bright eyes and fresh lips.

I found Gus in the front room, obviously firmly bonded with Karen, Charlotte and Daniel. They looked as if they'd known each other all their lives and my heart lifted. I wanted my roommates and friends to like him. And I wanted him to like my roommates and friends.

Although not too much, obviously.

There's only one thing worse than your boyfriend and roommates not liking one another and that's when they like each other a bit too much. It can lead to all sorts of terrible complications and confusion over the sleeping arrangements.

Charlotte's Simon had called and Charlotte, all made-up and perfumed, was excitedly preparing for the lunch.

"Condoms," she said feverishly, sitting down and rummaging through her bag. "Condoms, condoms, have I got condoms?"

"But you're only meeting him for lunch," I said.

"Lucy, don't be ridiculous," she said scornfully. "Oh good . . . damn, there's only one—what flavor is it? Pina Colada—but it'll just have to do."

"You look lovely, Lucy," said Daniel admiringly.

"Aye, you do. Beautiful." Gus turned around to have a good look at me.

"Yes, you do," echoed Charlotte.

"Thanks."

"Are we ready?" Gus got up.

"We are," I said.

"Very nice meeting you all," said Gus to the general assembly, all rancor from the previous evening seemingly long forgotten. "And good luck with the . . . er . . . um . . ." he nodded to Charlotte.

"Thanks." She smiled nervously.

"Have fun." Daniel winked at me.

"You too." I winked back.

 26

At least it wasn't raining. It was cold, but the sky was blue and clear and the air was still.

"Do you have gloves, Lucy?"

"Yes."

"Well, give them to me."

"Oh." *Selfish bastard.*

"Och, no, not for me!" he laughed. "Look, one for your right hand and one for my left hand and then we'll hold hands with our two middle ones. See?"

"*I see.*"

That was great because it took care of the awkward question of hand-holding. A matter that wasn't a problem at all on the previous alcohol lubricated evening, but that could have become a bit of an issue in the cold sober light of day.

On we marched, swinging hands, the cold air reddening our faces.

We lolled on a bench and held hands and watched the squirrels running and jumping about.

Even though I felt a little bit shy, I couldn't take my eyes off Gus. He was something to look at—his hair so black and shiny, his jaw covered in stubble (he obviously hadn't found Karen's razor), and his eyes bright green in the cold winter light.

It was wonderful to be with him.

"This is lovely." I sighed. "I'm so glad you forced me to come."

"I'm glad you're glad, Lucy Sullivan."

"And the squirrels are so sweet," I said. "I love watching them running about, jumping, gambolling."

Gus quickly sat up and stared at me.

"Are you serious?" he demanded, looking very alarmed.

What *now,* I wondered, feeling anxious. Was he about to go off on another mad flight of fancy?

He was, apparently.

"Well," he sputtered. "I have to say that the barbarians are well and truly at the gates when the dumb beasts of the fields have to entertain themselves by illicit betting . . . but that's London for you, I suppose. Next they'll be smoking crack!"

Oh my God, I thought, he's *bonkers.* But I couldn't take it seriously, I was laughing so much that I could barely speak.

"Not gambling, *gambolling,*" I said.

"I heard you the first time, Lucy Sullivan," he said. "And what is it, Lucy?" he demanded. "The dogs? The horses? Bingo? Eyes down and two fat ladies for the little squirrels! Cards? Blackjack? Roulette? There's no innocence anymore, Lucy! None. There's nothing unspoiled. To think that the little squirrels are gambling, it breaks my heart—you wouldn't get that in Donegal. What was wrong with gathering nuts? No thrill left in it, I suppose. . . . The influence of television."

He stared at me, realization dawning.

"Oh," he said, shamefaced. "Oh. Oh no. You meant the gambolling type of gambling. Not the gambling type of gambling."

"Yes."

"Oh. Oh. Well, sorry about that. A misunderstanding. You must think I'm fit to be locked up. The padded room for Gus."

"No. I think you're hilarious."

"That's very decent of you, Lucy" he said. "Most people just say that I'm crazy."

"Why's that?" I asked, amused.

"Search me," he said, his pixie face a picture of assumed innocence.

I'd be delighted to, I thought.

"Anyway," he continued, "if they think *I'm* crazy, they should meet the rest of my family."

Oh oh! I sensed an unpleasant revelation hovering on the horizon. But I squared my shoulders and met it head on.

"Er, and what are they like, Gus?"

He gave me a sidelong grin and said, "Well now, insane isn't a word I care to bandy about, Lucy, but . . ."

I tried to hide my alarm, but it must have shown on my face because he burst out laughing.

"Poor Lucy. Would you look at the worried little face!"

I tried to smile gamely.

"But settle yourself, Lucy, I'm only teasing. They're not actually insane . . ."

I breathed a sigh of relief.

". . . *as such* . . ." he continued. "But very, very emotional, I suppose is the best way of describing it."

"How do you mean?" I might as well deal with it there and then, I decided.

"I'm kind of afraid to tell you, Lucy, in case I convince you that I'm stone crazy. When you hear the kind of background I come from, you'll probably run away screaming."

"Don't be silly," I said reassuringly. But I had a little

knot in my stomach. Please God, don't make this too awful. I like him too much.

"Are you sure you want to hear this, Lucy?"

"I'm sure. Nothing can be that bad. Have you parents?"

"Oh aye. The full complement. A matching pair. A complete set."

"You already mentioned that you had lots of brothers . . . ?"

"Five of them."

"That's a lot."

"Not really, not in the area I come from. I was always ashamed that my number of brothers didn't run to double digits."

"Older or younger?"

"Older. They're all older than me."

"So you're the baby."

"I am, although I'm the only one of the guys who doesn't still live at home."

"Five grown men all living at home—that must create a lot of problems."

"Jesus! You don't know the half of it. But they have to, really, because they work on the farm and in the pub."

"You own a pub?"

"We do."

"You must be loaded."

"Well, we're not."

"But I always thought owning a pub meant you could almost print your own money."

"Not our pub. It's my brothers, you see. Fond of the drink."

"Ah, I see, they drink the profits."

"No they don't," he laughed. "There aren't any profits to drink, because they drink the drink."

"Oh Gus."

"And we hardly ever have any stock because they drink it all and we owe money to every brewery in Ireland so almost none of them will deliver to us anymore. Our name is a hissing and a byword among the distillers of Ireland," he said, quoting P.G. Wodehouse. My, what a literary fellow this was.

"But don't you have customers, couldn't you make a profit from them?" I asked.

"Not really, because we're in such a remote area. Our only customers are my brothers and my da. And the local constabulary of course—and *they* only come after closing hours every night. And they can't be charged the full price—in fact they can't be charged any price—because they'd close us down for breaking the liquor laws, if we tried to."

"You're joking."

"I'm not."

My head was racing, trying to come up with money-spinners, profit-making schemes for Gus's family's pub, Karaoke evenings? Quiz nights? Special promotions? Food at lunchtime? And I said as much to him.

"No, Lucy." He shook his head and looked amused and sad at the same time. "They're not great organizers. Something would go wrong because they're forever getting drunk and fighting each other."

"Are you serious?"

"I am! Most nights in our house are conducted in a state of high drama. I'd come home in the evening and the brothers would be in the kitchen and a couple of them would be covered with blood and another would have his hand wrapped up in a shirt after putting his fist through a window and they'd be calling one another names and then they'd start crying and telling one another that they loved each other like a brother. I hate it."

"And what would they fight about?" I asked, intrigued, *fascinated.*

"Oh anything at all. They're not picky. A dirty look, an inflection in a voice, anything!"

"Really?"

"Yes. I was home at Christmas and the first night I was back we all had a huge feed of drink. And it was great for a while, until things went wrong, the way they usually do. At about midnight P.J. thought Paudi was looking at him funny so P.J. hit Paudi, then Mikey shouted at P.J. to leave Paudi alone and John Joe hit Mikey for shouting at P.J., then P.J. hit John Joe for hitting Mikey and Stevie started crying because of brother being set against brother. And then P.J. started crying because he was sorry for upsetting Stevie, then Stevie hit P.J. for starting it all, then Paudi hit Stevie for hitting P.J. because he had wanted to hit P.J. . . . And then my da came in and he tried to hit all of them."

Gus paused for breath. "It was terrible. It's the boredom, I'm sure of it. But the whole thing is fueled by alcohol. They calmed down a bit a few years ago when we got Sky Sports, but then the da wouldn't pay the bill for it, so the ruckus started up again."

I was spellbound. I could have listened forever to Gus's beautiful, lyrical accent, telling the story of his fascinatingly dysfunctional family.

"And where do you fit into it all? Who do you hit?"

"No one. I don't fit into it at all, at least I try my very best not to."

"The whole thing sounds hilarious," I said. "Like something out of a play."

"Really?" said Gus, sounding shocked, annoyed even. "Maybe I've told it wrong because it wasn't funny at all."

Immediately I felt ashamed.

"Sorry, Gus," I muttered. "I forgot for a moment that this is your life we're talking about. It's just that you tell it so well. . . . But I'm sure it was terrible really."

"Well, it was you know, Lucy," he said, indignantly. "It left terrible scars, it made me do awful things."

"Like what?"

"I used to walk the hills for hours and talk to the rabbits and write poetry. Of course it was only because I wanted to get away from the family and because I didn't know any better."

"But what's wrong with walking the hills and talking to the rabbits and writing poetry?" I thought it sounded wild and romantic and Irish.

"Plenty, Lucy, as I'm sure you'd agree if you ever read any of my poetry."

I laughed, but only a little bit, I didn't want him to think I was making fun of him.

"And rabbits make very poor conversationalists," he said. "Carrots and sex, that's all they talk about."

"Is that right?"

"So as soon as I got away from there, I dropped the poetry and the tortured soul image."

"Well, there's nothing wrong with being a tortured soul . . ." I protested, desperate to cling to the image of Gus as a poetic figure.

"Oh, there *is*, Lucy. It's embarrassing and boring."

"Oh, is it? I quite like tortured souls . . ."

"No, Lucy, you mustn't," he said firmly. "I insist."

"So what are your parents like?" I asked, changing the subject.

"My father is the worst of them all. A terrible man when he has drink taken. Which is most of the time."

And what about your mother?"

"She doesn't really do anything. Well, I mean she does

*plenty*—all the cooking and washing and stuff, but she doesn't try to keep them in line. I suppose she's too afraid. She prays a lot. And cries—we're a great family for crying, a very lachrymose crowd. She prays for my brothers and father to give up the drink."

"And do you have any sisters?"

"Two, but they escaped when they were very young. Eleanor got married when she was nineteen to a man who was old enough to be her grandfather, Francis Cassidy from Letterkenny."

Gus seemed to cheer up at the memory. "He only came up to the farm once and that was to ask the da for her hand, and maybe I shouldn't tell you this because you'll think that we're a crowd of savages, but we ran him out of the place. We tried to set the dogs on poor old Francis, but the dogs refused to bite him. Afraid they might catch something, probably."

Gus peered at me closely. "Should I bow my head in shame, Lucy?"

"No," I said. "It's funny."

"I know it wasn't very hospitable, Lucy, but we had little to amuse us and Francis Cassidy was awful, far worse than any of us. He was the most miserable-looking old stick you ever laid eyes on and he must have had the evil eye because the hens didn't lay for four days afterward and the cows had no milk."

"And what about your other sister?"

"Eileen? She just disappeared. None of the local boys came looking for her hand—I suppose Francis Cassidy had warned them off. We only noticed she was gone when the breakfast wasn't on the table one morning. It was summer and we were making the hay and had to get up at the crack of dawn and Eileen was supposed to make the food before we all went off to the fields."

"And where had she gone?"

"I don't know, Dublin, I think."

"And wasn't anyone worried about her?" I asked, appalled. "Didn't anyone try to go after her or to find her?"

"They were worried all right. They were worried that they'd have to make their own breakfasts from then on."

"But that's terrible," I said, feeling upset. The story of Eileen had upset me far more than the story of Francis Cassidy and the dogs. "Really, really terrible."

"Lucy," said Gus, squeezing my hand. "*I* wasn't worried about having to make my own breakfast. *I* wanted to go after her, but my da said he'd kill me."

"Fair enough," I said, feeling a bit better.

"I missed her, she was lovely, she used to talk to me. But I was glad for her that she was gone."

"Why?"

She was too bright to let my father marry her off to one of the old men who owned the neighboring farms. He wanted to get his hands on their land, you see."

"That's barbaric," I said in horror.

"Some people might call it good economics," said Gus. "But I wouldn't be one of them," he added hastily, when I gave him a glare.

"And what became of poor Eileen?" I asked, feeling as though my heart would break from the sadness of it all. "Did you ever hear from her again?"

"I *think* she went to Dublin, but she never wrote to me, so I don't know for sure."

"It's so sad," I breathed.

Then a thought struck me and I looked at him sharply. "You're not making any of this up, by any chance, are you? This isn't one of your inventions like the squirrels gambling and my roommate Elizabeth Ardent?"

"No," he protested. "Of course it's not. Honestly,

Lucy, I wouldn't joke or make things up about something important. Although I wish the story of my family *was* a fairy tale. I suppose it sounds very peculiar to a sophisticated city girl like yourself.''

Oddly enough, it didn't.

''But, you see, we were very isolated,'' Gus went on. ''The farm was remote and we didn't meet that many other people so I didn't know any better. I had nothing to compare my family to. For years I thought that the fights and the crying and the shouting and everything were perfectly normal and that everyone lived like us. It was a big relief, I can tell you, to find out that my suspicions were correct and that they were really as crazy as I had thought they were. So that's the story of my origins, Lucy.''

''Well, thank you for telling me.''

''Have I scared you away?''

''No.''

''Why not?''

''I don't know.''

''Your family must be crazy too.''

''They're not, sorry to disappoint you.''

''Then why are you so tolerant about my crowd?''

''Because you're you, not your family.''

''If only it was that simple, Lucy Sullivan.''

''But it can be, Gus . . . Gus *what?*''

''Gus Lavan.''

''Pleased to meet you, Gus Lavan,'' I said, shaking hands with him.

*Lucy Lavan,* I was thinking. *Lucy Lavan?* Yes, I liked it. Or how about it being double-barreled. *Lucy Sullivan Lavan?* That had a lovely ring too.

''And I'm very pleased to meet you, Lucy Sullivan,'' he said solemnly, clasping my hand. ''Although I've already said that, haven't I?''

"Yes, you said it last night."

"But it doesn't make it any less true, Lucy. Want to go for a pint, Lucy?"

"Er, yes, if you want. Have you walked enough?"

"I've walked enough to work up a thirst, ergo I've walked enough."

"Fine."

"What time is it, Lucy?"

"I don't know."

"Don't you have a watch?"

"No."

"Neither have I. It's a sign."

"Of what?" I asked warmly. That Gus and I were soul mates? That Gus and I were ideally matched?

"That we'll always be late."

"Oh. Um, what are you doing?"

Gus had leaned back almost horizontally on the bench and was staring at the sky, sucking his teeth and muttering things like "a hundred and eighty degrees" and "seven hours ahead in New York" and "or maybe that's Chicago."

"I'm looking at the sky, Lucy."

"Why?"

"To find out the time, of course."

"Of course."

A pause.

"Any conclusions?"

"Yes, I think so." He nodded his head thoughtfully. "I think so."

There was another pause.

"Lucy, I've made up my mind that it's almost definitely—of course there's always room for human error here, you understand—but I'm prepared to say that it's almost definitely daytime. Eighty-seven percent certain. Or maybe eighty-four."

"I'd say you're right."

"I'd be interested to hear your views on the matter, Lucy."

"I'd say it's about two o'clock."

"Oh god." He jumped up from the bench. "That late? Well come on then, we'll just have to do our best."

"What are you talking about?" I giggled, as he dragged me after him through the park.

"Closing time, Lucy Sullivan, closing time. A dirty word. Two dirty words, actually. Filthy, heinous words," he said, almost spitting them out. "Filthy! The pubs close at three o'clock today and they don't open again until seven—am I right?"

"Yes." I tried to keep up with him, "unless they've made changes to the liquor laws this morning."

"Do you think they might have?" asked Gus, stopping abruptly.

"No."

"Well, then, come on," he said, almost running. "We've only got an hour."

 27

We stopped at the first pub we came to when we got out of the park. It wasn't too awful, which was just as well because I sensed that Gus would have made me go in even if the roof had caved in and the walls were falling down.

He put his hand on my arm at the door.

"Lucy, I'm sorry about this but I'm afraid that you'll have to finance this mission. I get my unemployment on Tuesday so I'll pay you back then."

"Oh . . . oh . . . fine."

My heart sank, but I caught it before it hit the ground. After all it wasn't Gus's fault that I met him on a weekend when he was broke.

"What would you like to drink?" I asked him.

"I'll have a pint."

"Of what?"

"Guinness, of course . . ."

"Of course."

". . . and a small one," he added.

"A small one?"

"Jameson's whiskey, no ice."

"Er, right you are."

"But make it a big one," he suggested.

"Sorry?"

"A big small one."

"What . . . ?"

"A big Jameson. A *large* one."

"Oh, okay."

"I hope you don't mind, Lucy, but I don't see any point in doing things by half," he said apologetically.

"It's fine," I said faintly.

"And whatever you're having," he added.

"Um, thanks."

If I had been Karen, I would have said my "um, thanks" sarcastically, but seeing as I was only me I just said "um, thanks" like I really meant "um, thanks."

"There's a table just over here, Lucy. I'll guard it while you get the drinks."

I stood at the bar and I felt sad for just a moment. Then

I forced myself to stop. I was being silly. He'd have money on Tuesday.

"And maybe some potato chips," said Gus's voice in my ear.

"What flavor?"

"Salt and vinegar . . ."

"Okay."

"Good woman." I got myself a modest Diet Coke.

Gus had finished his pint and his large small one before I finished my drink. In fact he nearly had them finished by the time I sat down.

"We'll have another," announced Gus.

"I suppose we will."

"You stay where you are," he said kindly. "Just give me the money and I'll get them."

"Oh, okay," I said, fishing in my pocket for my purse which I had just replaced and pulled out a fiver.

"Five pounds?" he said doubtfully. "Are you sure that'll be enough, Lucy?"

"Yes," I said firmly.

"Don't you want one for yourself?"

"Yes!"

While he was gone I drank the rest of my drink quickly. I decided that if he didn't give me back my change without me having to ask I would . . . I would . . . I don't know . . .

"Here's your change, Lucy."

I looked up from where I had been staring gloomily into my empty glass. Gus was looking at me anxiously, a few pennies in his open palm.

"Thanks." I smiled and took all thirteen pence or whatever it was. I suddenly felt better.

After all, it was the principle as much as the money.

"Lucy," Gus said earnestly. "Thank you, for the drinks and all that . . . it's very good of you. I get my check on

Tuesday and I'll take you out that night and I'll see you right. I promise. Er . . . thanks.''

"You're welcome," I smiled, feeling a lot, lot better. He had redeemed himself, perhaps he had sensed how disappointed I had begun to feel.

He was good at that—redeeming himself, that is. At pulling himself back when he hovered on the brink of my disapproval, just at the last minute.

It wasn't that I minded spending money on him—or anyone for that matter—especially when it was for something as important as lunchtime drinks for them, but I minded very much feeling as if they thought I was an idiot, a soft touch.

He had several more drinks which I happily paid for ("I'll see you right on Tuesday, Lucy") in the next short hour.

"We've done marvelous things in the short time slot we had available to us, Lucy." Gus surveyed the table full of empty glasses as three o'clock approached and the bartender invited us to leave.

"Isn't it truly amazing what you can achieve when you set your mind to it?" He waved his remaining half-empty pint glass around to emphasize his point. "All it takes is a bit of effort.

"Although I'm disappointed in you, Lucy." He affectionately touched my face. "I'm sorry to have to tell you. But two Diet cokes and a gin and tonic? Are you sure you're Irish?"

"Yes," I said.

"Well, you'll just have to pull your weight more the next time, you can't just leave it all to me, you know."

"Gus," I giggled. "I've a bit of bad news for you."

"What is it?"

"I don't really drink all that much. And I never drink

during the day. . . . Usually," I added hastily as he looked accusingly at my gin glass.

"Really? But I thought . . . Didn't you say? . . . But you don't mind *other* people drinking lots, though, do you?" he asked hopefully.

"Not at all," I assured him. "Not at all."

"That's fine then." He sighed with relief. "Christ, you had me worried there for a moment. Would you say the bar really *is* closed?"

"Yes."

"Maybe I'll just go up and make sure," he suggested mischievously.

"Gus! It's closed!"

"But there's a barman there. They *must* still be serving."

"He's washing glasses."

"I'll just go and check."

"Gus!"

But he had hopped out of his seat and was up at the counter having a conversation with the bartender that involved Gus in a lot of energetic gesticulation. Then to my horror I heard slightly raised voices, which stopped abruptly when Gus slammed his hand down on the wooden counter with great finality. He made his way back over to me.

"They're closed," he murmured, subdued. He picked up his pint and wouldn't meet my eye.

I was aware that the few remaining customers were watching us with amused interest. I was slightly embarrassed, but it was funny.

"I don't know what was up with him at all, but that barman fella was a very unreasonable character," Gus muttered. "Unreasonable and unpleasant. There was no need for what he said to me. And whatever happened to 'the customer is always right'?"

I laughed and Gus glared at me.

"*Et tu*, Lucy?" he demanded.

I laughed again. I couldn't help it—it must have been the gin.

"We won't come here again, Lucy. Oh no! I don't come to a pub to be insulted, so I don't, Lucy. Indeed I do not!"

His good-looking, mobile face was grim with annoyance.

"I've plenty of other places I can go to be insulted," he added gloomily.

"What did he say to you?" I asked, trying to stop my mouth from twitching.

"Lucy, I wouldn't repeat it and certainly not in your presence," he said earnestly. "I would neither soil my own mouth nor pollute the fragrant air around your delicate ears by repeating what that . . . that . . . *lousy* bastard, that mean-spirited, bureaucratic, anal-retentive fucker, called me."

"Fair enough," I said, somehow keeping a straight face.

"I've too much respect for you, Lucy."

"I appreciate that."

"You're a lady, Lucy. And there are certain rules, certain personal restraints, that I apply when I'm in the presence of a lady."

"Thanks, Gus."

"And now," he said, standing up, and draining his glass, "our work here is done."

"What would you like to do now?" I asked.

"Well, it *is* Sunday afternoon and we've had a couple of drinks and it's cold and we have just met the previous evening, therefore it is written that we go back to your apartment and snuggle on the couch and watch a black-

and-white movie.'' Gus smiled meaningfully at me and slipped his arm around my pink angora waist. He pulled me slightly toward him and I felt light-headed with . . . well, it must have been lust, I suppose. It was lovely to be held by him. Even though he wasn't very tall, he was strong and manly.

"That sounds wonderful.'' A thrill ran through me. Although I was afraid that there might not be a black-and-white film on and that Daniel and Karen might be having sex on the living-room floor. We could always go see Adrian and get a video if there wasn't anything suitable on the TV, but I wasn't quite so sure how to deal with the Daniel and Karen problem.

And what if Adrian got upset when he saw me with a guy? How would I cope? It was a sorry state of affairs, but such was life, where every silver lining had a cloud, and every piece of happiness had its price in someone else's pain.

 28

That night, after Gus had gone home, my happiness was almost uncontainable. I was itching to talk about Gus, to go into minute detail of what I was wearing when I met him, what he said to me, what he looked like, and all that.

But my usual confidantes were unavailable—Karen and Charlotte were out and Daniel was with Karen and I was too mad at Megan and Meredia, so I called Dennis. And amazingly, he was in.

"I thought you'd be out," I said.

"Is that why you called?"

"Don't be so touchy."

"What do you want?"

"Dennis," I breathed dramatically. "I met a man."

He gasped. "Do tell." Sometimes he talked like that, even though he was from Cork.

"Come over, it's more exciting if I tell you in person," I said.

"I'm on my way."

I had to rush around and put on makeup and comb my hair because Dennis always scrutinized my appearance, telling me whether I had lost or gained weight, what my ideal weight should be, whether he liked or hated my hair and so on. He was worse than my mother, but at least he had an excuse—he was a gay man, he couldn't help himself.

He arrived in about ten minutes. Every time I saw him, he had cut his hair shorter and shorter and all he had now was a little cap of blond fuzz. Which, with his long skinny neck, made him look like a duckling.

"That was quick," I said as I opened the door. "Did you get a taxi?"

"Taxi, schmaxi! The journey I've had—stop! I'll tell you later, I want to hear your hot news."

Dennis sometimes overdid his flamboyant homosexual act, but I was too grateful to have found a confidante to tell him to stop.

Then he inspected my appearance and I passed, with a couple of recommendations. He demanded tea and complained about the pattern on the mug. "A cat, a CAT!— Really, Lucy, I don't know how you can live like this."

There were only about four things in Dennis's flat, but they were really beautiful and expensive.

"You're my para-girlfriend squad," I told him as we sat down.

"What's that?"

"In an emergency, when I need to girltalk and there's no girls available, you rush to my side," I explained. "I have visions of you pulling on a uniform and sliding down a pole."

He blushed so red his face was darker than his bleached hair.

"Do you mind?" he said haughtily. "My private life is my own affair."

"Assume gossiping positions," I said so we both sat on the sofa, facing each other.

I told him about going to the fortune-teller. "You should have told me," he grumbled. "I would have liked to come."

"Sorry." I quickly moved on to the awful rumor that I was getting married.

"Honestly, Dennis, I was *miserable.* Apart from the humiliation and all that, it made me feel so lonely. Like I really would never get married."

"I really will never get married," said Dennis. "I won't be *permitted* to." He sort of spat when he said "permitted."

"Sorry, that was insensitive of me," I said hurriedly. I didn't want Dennis to start going on and on about gay men being discriminated against and how they should be allowed to get married just like "breeders," as he insisted on calling heterosexuals.

"It made me feel old and left on the shelf, empty and pathetic. You know?"

"Ooooh, I do, my dear." He pursed his lips.

"Dennis, *please* don't go all poofy on me."

"What do you mean?"

"Don't call me 'my dear,' " I begged. "It's so affected. You're Irish and don't ever forget it."

He rolled his eyes.

"Now where was I?" I said. "Oh, yes, I can't believe that so much changed in twenty-four hours."

"It's always darkest just before the dawn," said Dennis sagely. "So you met this man on Saturday night?"

"Yes."

"He *must* be the one that was predicted for you," said Dennis, telling me exactly what I wanted to hear.

"I think he might be," I said shamefacedly. "I know I shouldn't believe it, and please don't tell anyone that I do, but wouldn't it be nice to think so?"

"Can I be your bridesmaid?"

"Of course."

"Except I can't POSSIBLY wear pink, it makes me look like DEATH!"

"Fine, fine, have whatever color you like." I wasn't interested in anything except keeping the discussion centered directly on Gus. "Oh Dennis, he's exactly what I want, he's so me. If I'd gone to God and described my perfect man, and God had been in a good mood, he would have given me Gus."

"Really? That good?"

"Yes. Dennis, I'm a bit ashamed to think this way, but he's too good for it just to be random. The fortune-teller must have been for real. I feel like it was meant to happen."

"This is fabulous," said Dennis, all excited.

"And I feel different about my whole life, my past," I said, waxing philosophical. "All those awful people that I went out with in the past were for a reason. You know the way I always seemed to lurch and drift from one awful relationship to the next?"

"Yes, only too well."

"Well, sorry about that, but it won't happen again. But, you see Dennis, all the time I had been moving one step closer to Gus. All those wasted years when I felt as if I was wandering in the wilderness, I had actually been on the right path."

"Do you think it's the same for me?" he asked hopefully.

"I'm *sure* of it. I have been led safely through the Minefield of Wrong Men," I went on, getting carried away, "sustaining mere flesh wounds, and I've reached the clearing on the other side and there, waiting for me, was Gus.

"Oh, Dennis, if only I had *known* that there would be an end to my loneliness."

"If only we both had known," said Dennis, no doubt thinking of all the nights spent listening to me going on and on.

"I should have had faith."

"You should have listened to *me*."

"We just have no idea what is out there for us, what life is leading us to," I said, getting misty-eyed. "I used to think that I was master of my own destiny, captain of my own ship. In fact, Dennis, I suspected that this was *why* my life was such a shambles—because I was directing things."

"Right, that's enough of that," said Dennis impatiently. "Knock off the philosophy, I see what you're getting at, but tell me about *him*. I want exact measurements!"

"Oh, Dennis, he's great, really great, everything about him feels right. I feel that this is a good one."

"Details," he said impatiently. "Has he muscles?"

"Well, sort of . . ."

"That means he hasn't."

"No, Dennis, really, he is very muscley."

"Is he tall?"

"No."

"What do you mean 'no'?"

"I mean he's not tall."

"You mean he's short."

"Okay, Dennis, he's short. But so am I," I added hurriedly.

"Lucy, you always had rotten taste in men."

"That's rich," I said. "Coming from the man who loves Michael Flatley."

Dennis hung his head in shame.

"The man who has watched the *Riverdance* video a hundred times," I taunted.

One night when he was drunk, Dennis had told me that. He regretted it bitterly.

"It's a big world," he said humbly. "There's room for all kinds of taste."

"*Exactly,*" I said. "So Gus might be short . . ."

"He *is* short."

". . . but he's really good-looking and he has a great body and . . ."

"Does he work out?" asked Dennis hopefully.

"Somehow I'd guess he doesn't." I was sorry to disappoint Dennis, but I couldn't lie to him. Anyway he'd notice when he met Gus.

"Does that mean that he drinks a lot?"

"It means he's a party animal."

"I see. He drinks a lot."

"Oh, Dennis, stop being so negative." I rolled my eyes in exasperation. "Wait until you meet him—you'll love him, honestly! He's wonderful, so funny and charming and intelligent and nice, and I swear to God, *really* sexy. And he mightn't be your type, but I think he's perfect!"

"So what's the catch?"

"What do you mean?"

"Well, there's always a catch, isn't there?"

"Get lost," I said, "I know I haven't exactly been lucky but . . ."

"I don't just mean with *your* men," he sighed. "With *every* man. Nobody knows that more than me."

"Dennis," I said. "I don't think there is a catch."

"Trust me," he said. "There's a catch. Is he rich?"

"No."

"Is he actively poor?"

"Well . . ."

"Oh, Lucy, not again! Why do you always pick these paupers that have horrible clothes?"

"Because I'm not shallow like you. You're far too concerned with boys' clothes and the way they cut their hair and the watch they have."

"Maybe I am," he said huffily. "But you're not concerned enough!"

"Anyway," I said, "I don't pick them, it just happens."

"I bet if you lived in California, you wouldn't get away with saying that. But never mind—so how come he's poor?"

"It's not what you think," I explained eagerly. "It's not as if he's lazy. He's a musician and work is hard to come by."

"A musician—again?"

"Yes, but this one's different, and I have the utmost respect for anyone willing to endure financial hardship for the sake of his art."

"I know."

"And I'd happily give up my own nine-to-five drudgery except that I'm not talented at anything."

"But don't you mind being with someone who never

has any money? And don't give me that line about love will conquer all, and that other things are more important. Let's be practical here.''

"I don't mind at all. It's just that I'm not sure I have enough money to keep both of us in the manner to which Gus seems to be accustomed.'' I felt awkward about admitting this.

"What manner is that? Does he take cocaine?''

"No.'' Then I thought about it. "Well, maybe he does, actually.''

"You'll have to get a second job, if that's the manner to which he's accustomed.''

"Shut up, I'm trying to tell you, earlier this evening, Gus and I went for a pizza, at Pizza My Mind . . .''

"But it's Sunday—why didn't you go to the Cash'n'Curry?''

"Because Daniel and Karen went there and they were looking deeply in love and I didn't want to disturb them.''

"Daniel and KAREN?!'' shrieked Dennis, blanching. "Karen and DANIEL?''

"Er, yes.'' I had forgotten that Dennis had a crush on Daniel. "Karen, from here? Karen McHaggis, or whatever her tartany, Scottish name is.'' Dennis didn't like Karen. He'd like her even less now.

"Yes, that Karen.''

"With Daniel, *my* Daniel?''

"If that's Daniel Watson you're talking about, then yes, *your* Daniel.''

"Oh dear, that's upset me now.'' He looked very shaky. "I need a drink.''

"There's a bottle of something over there.''

"Where?''

"Over there, on the bookcase.''

"You're such peasants, keeping your booze on your bookcase."

"Well, what can we do? We haven't any books, we have to keep something on it."

He rummaged around on the shelves, "I can't see it."

"I'm sure it was there earlier."

"It's not here now."

"Maybe Karen and Daniel drank it. Sorry, sorry!" I said hurriedly, as he winced again.

"You can take it from me, it won't last." His voice had a slight tremor. "He's gay, you know."

"But you say that about every man in the whole universe."

"Daniel really is. Sooner or later, he'll see the light. And when he does, *I'll* be there."

"Fine, fine, whatever you say." I didn't want to upset him, but really! Every gay man I knew insisted that every straight man they knew was really a closet gay.

 29

Dennis sat down again and placed his hand on his chest and breathed deeply for a long time while I wriggled with impatience. Finally he said, "It's all right now, I'm over it."

"Okay." I launched back into the story. "So at Pizza My Mind, Gus didn't have any money—well, obviously, because he didn't have any last night or earlier today and even though he's a talented man, I don't think that alchemy is one of his particular gifts . . ."

"So you had to pay for the two of you."

"Yes, which is fine because it's extremely reasonable . . ."

"And the waiter has a lovely butt . . ." Dennis was a gay man twenty-four hours a day, he never let up.

"Quite. But Gus drank about ten bottles of Peroni and . . ."

"Ten bottles of Peroni!"

"Relax," I said. "I've no problem with that in principle, especially because Peroni is weak, but it has to be paid for."

"You don't feel like he's taking advantage of you, do you?" said Dennis, looking levelly at me.

The thought *had* crossed my mind earlier in the day while we were in the pub, and that upset me because I lived in fear of being thought an idiot, taken for a fool.

But I absolutely hated arguments about money. It reminded me of my childhood. Memories of my mother shouting at Dad, her face red and distorted. I would never behave like that.

"No, really, Dennis, because then he said some really lovely things in the restaurant."

"Ten Peronis worth of loveliness?"

"Easily."

"Let's hear it."

"He took my hand," I said slowly, trying to build up effect, "and said, very seriously, 'I really appreciate this, Lucy.'

"And then he said, 'I hate not having money, Lucy,' and get this Dennis, *'especially when I meet someone like you.'* What do you think of that, eh?"

"What did he mean?"

"He said that I was lovely, and should be taken to beautiful places and have beautiful things given to me."

"Except that you won't be getting them from him." Dennis could be very blunt.

"Shut up," I said. "He said that he'd love to wine and

dine me and buy me flowers and chocolates and fur coats and fancy kitchens and electric carving knives and one of those little vacuum cleaners that you can use on the couch and everything my heart desires.''

"And what does your heart desire?'' asked Dennis.

"It desires Gus.''

"I don't think that's your heart we're talking about.''

"You're so vulgar, do you ever think of anything but sex?''

"No. Then what did he say?''

"He said that the little vacuum cleaners were great for getting fluff out of your coat pockets.''

"He sounds like he's a sugar bowl short of a Fornasetti dinner service to me,'' snorted Dennis. "Carving knives and vacuums and fur coats, honestly!''

But he didn't know the half of it and I felt reluctant to tell him. I didn't want negative comments, I wanted great rejoicing, to match my mood. Because the conversation with Gus had got a little bit tangled after that.

"Do you like flowers?'' he had asked.

And I had said, "Yes, Gus, they're lovely, but my life isn't incomplete without them.''

Then he said, "And chocolate?''

"Yes, I like chocolate an awful lot, but I'm not lacking for it.''

"Oh! You're not?'' Concern crossed his face, and he suddenly seemed to go into a deep slump. "Well, what did I expect?'' he said mournfully. "A beautiful woman like you. How could I have been so stupid to think that I might be the only man in your life?''

"Gus, please stop. What are you talking about? No, it's okay,'' I said to the waiter who had come running when he heard Gus's outburst. "No, really, everything is fine, thanks.''

"You might as well get me another of these, while you're at it," said Gus waving a Peroni bottle at the waiter. (That must have been his ninth.) "I'm talking about you, of course, Miss Lucy Goddess Sullivan—it *is* Miss, I presume . . . ?"

"Yes."

". . . And the suitors that bring you the chocolate."

"Gus, I don't have suitors bringing me chocolate."

"But didn't you say . . . ?"

"I said that I don't go without it. And I don't. But I buy it myself."

"Oh," he said slowly. "You buy it yourself. I see . . ."

"Good." I laughed. "I'm glad you see."

"An independent woman, Lucy. That's what you are. You don't want to be under an obligation to them, and you'd be right. To thine own self be true, as our friend Billy Shakespeare was forever telling me."

"Er, who don't I want to be under an obligation to?"

"The suitors."

"Gus, there aren't *any* suitors."

"No suitors?"

"No. Well not just at the moment." I didn't want him to think I was a total loser.

"Why not!!?"

"I don't know."

"But you're beautiful."

"Thank you."

"I never heard before that the English were a short-sighted race, but they must be. It's the only explanation I can come up with."

"Thank you."

"Stop saying 'thank you.' I mean it."

There was a pleased little pause where we sat smiling

at each other, Gus's eyes slightly glazed over, probably from the excess of Peronis.

There was no need to tell any of that to Dennis. I decided to pass over it and tell him the next good thing.

When Gus said, "Er, Lucy, can I ask you something?"

And I answered, "Of course."

"I couldn't help overhearing that you're currently without a suitor . . ."

"Yes."

". . . So would I be right in thinking that there's a vacancy?"

"Yes, I suppose that's one way of putting it."

"I know that this is going to sound outrageously forward of me, but is there any chance at all that you might consider me for the position?"

And I looked at the red-and-white checked tablecloth, too shy to meet his eyes and murmured "Yes."

Dennis was disappointed in me.

"Oh, Lucy." He sighed. "Haven't you listened to anything I've told you—you're not supposed to submit so easily. Make them work for it."

"No, Dennis," I explained firmly. "You've got to understand that I was afraid to play games with him—he was liable to get confused even when I was being totally straightforward. Introducing manipulation and feminine wiles—saying 'no' when I meant 'maybe,' saying 'maybe' when I meant 'yes'—could be the undoing of us."

"Okay, if you insist. So what happened then?"

"He said, 'I'm also unattached romantically; do you mind if I eat the last piece of pizza?' "

"The silver-tongued devil," muttered Dennis, clearly unimpressed.

"I was thrilled," I said.

"Isn't it going a bit far to be thrilled?" asked Dennis.

"I mean, it was paid for, so someone might as well eat it but, really, Lucy, thrilled?"

I let it pass.

"And what's he like in bed?" asked Dennis.

"I don't actually know."

"You wouldn't let him?"

"He didn't try."

"But you were together for nearly twenty-four hours. Aren't you worried?"

"No." I wasn't. Granted his restraint was unusual. But not unheard of.

"He's probably gay," said Dennis.

"He's not gay."

"But you don't seem upset that he didn't jump you?" said Dennis, sounding confused.

"That's because I'm not upset," I said. "I like men to take things *slowly,* men who want to get to know me before they sleep with me."

That really was true, it wasn't just bravado for Dennis's benefit—I was horrified by men who were upfront (as it were) about their need for sex, big grown-up men with huge sexual appetites. Men with come-to-bed eyes, men with big thighs and hairy chests and huge unshaven jaws, men who got erections six times an hour, men who smelled of sweat and salt and sex. Men who entered rooms by saying bodily, "Here's my hard-on, the rest of me will be along in about five minutes."

*Pelvo-centric* men put the fear of God in me. Probably because I thought that they'd be very demanding and critical of my performance. These men could pick and choose from any woman they wanted so they'd be used to the best. If I clambered into their bed with no chest, no long legs, no tan, they'd be bitterly disappointed.

"What's the meaning of this?" they'd demand when I

removed my clothes. "You're not like the one I slept with this afternoon. You're not a woman. Where are the tits?"

I hoped that, if a man got to know me before we went to bed together, I would have a better chance of his being nice and not laughing at me. That he would be more prepared to overlook my obvious physical shortcomings because I had a nice personality.

That's not to say that I *hadn't*, once or twice, slept with men I had just recently met. There were times when I felt that I had no choice. Times when I had liked a man and was afraid that if I repulsed his sexual advances he would run away and have nothing further to do with me. If Gus had insisted on sexual relations I probably would have complied. But I was a lot happier that he hadn't.

"You and your Catholic guilt," said Dennis, shaking his head sadly. I had to stop him before he launched an attack on the Catholic Church and the nuns and the Christian Brothers and how they damaged the psyche of every young boy or girl that came into contact with them, taking away their capacity for guilt-free sensuous pleasure. We could have been there all night.

"No, Dennis, it's not Catholic guilt that stops me from being promiscuous."

I suspected that if I had big bouncy breasts and long, slender, cellulite-free golden thighs, I could have overlooked my Catholic guilt. I would probably have been a lot more likely to confidently hop into bed with total strangers. Maybe sex would have been an activity that I could just enjoy, instead of it mostly being an exercise in damage control, trying to act like I was enjoying myself while at the same time managing to hide a butt that was too big, a chest that was too small, thighs that were too . . . etc., etc.

"Well, if you're sure." Dennis still sounded a bit doubtful.

"Really, Dennis, I'm very sure."

"Okay."

"So, all in all, to wrap up, to summarize, what do you make of the whole thing?" I asked gleefully. "Doesn't he sound great?"

"Well, I don't think that it would be what *I* want . . ."

I mouthed "Michael Flatley" at him.

". . . but," he said hurriedly, "he does sound cute. And if you will insist on choosing men that haven't any money, I hope you know what you're doing. I wouldn't recommend it but I seem to be talking to the wall."

"And isn't it amazing what the fortune-teller said?" I urged, steering him back onto the track of positive comment.

"I have to admit that the timing is uncanny," he agreed. "It must be a sign. I would normally advise caution, but this does seem to be written in the stars."

That was exactly what I wanted to be told.

"Apart from the money, is he nice to you?" asked Dennis.

"Very nice."

"Okay. I'll have to see him before I can fully endorse him, but at the moment, you have my provisional blessing."

"Thank you."

"Right then, it's twelve thirty, I'm off. I'm going out tonight."

"Are you going to take poppers and wear a check shirt and dance to The Pet Shop Boys?"

"God, Lucy." He was disgusted. "That's outrageous stereotyping."

"But are you?"

"Yes."

"Well, have a great time. I'm going to bed."

I went to sleep happy.

 30

Of course it was a different story the following morning when I woke up and realized that I was expected to get out of bed and go to work.

I felt like hiding, but then again it was Monday and it was hard to change the habit of a lifetime. Meeting a new guy, even someone as great as Gus, couldn't transform me overnight into someone who bounded out of bed before the alarm went off.

I pawed around until I found the snooze button, negotiating another five minutes of guilt-ridden dozing for myself. I would have given anything not to have had to get up. *Anything*.

Someone was in the bathroom, which was nice. There was no point in my getting up until it was free. A short reprieve.

Time for me to lie in bed, half asleep, idly contemplating the various suicide options available to me, because, naturally, they seemed a lot more inviting than getting to work.

I had toyed with the idea of suicide several times—most weekday mornings actually—and a long time ago I had realized how *badly* the modern apartment is equipped for the killing of oneself. Not a bottle of poison, not a noose, not a farm implement anywhere.

But I shouldn't have been so negative—they do say that

where there's a will there's a way. But then again, if I hadn't been so negative, I wouldn't have wanted to kill myself and the whole discussion would be moot anyway.

I ran through the list of possibilities available to me.

I could have taken an overdose of painkillers. But I was fairly sure that that didn't work, at least not for me, because a couple of times when I had a very bad hangover I had taken about twelve tablets and I didn't even feel sleepy, never mind like I was dying.

The idea of being smothered with a pillow didn't seem to be too awful. Quite a nice, peaceful way to go, with the added advantage of not having to leave your bed to do it. But it was a little bit like synchronized swimming—rather pointless if you tried to do it on your own.

Just then I heard someone coming out of the bathroom and I stiffened with horror but, quick as a flash, someone else went in. I breathed out with relief—no need to get up just yet. Although I was living on borrowed time and I knew it. But for the moment I could stay horizontal and contemplate doing myself in although I knew that I didn't really want to kill myself at all—the taking of one's own life is unnatural.

It is also an awful lot of trouble.

It was ironic, really—you want to die because you can't be bothered to go on living—but then you're expected to get all energetic and move furniture and stand on chairs and hoist ropes and do complicated knots and attach things to other things and kick stools from under you and mess around with hot baths and razor blades and extension cords and electrical appliances and weedkiller. Suicide was a complicated, demanding business, often involving visits to hardware shops.

And if you've managed to drag yourself from the bed and go down the road to the garden center or the drug store, by then the worst is over. At that point you might as well just go to work.

No, I didn't want to kill myself. But it was a long way from not wanting to kill myself to actually *wanting* to get up. I may have won the battle, but there was, as yet, no sign of me winning the war.

Karen burst into the room. She looked chic and efficient and her makeup was perfect. The effect was a bit scary at that hour of the morning. Karen always looked *groomed* and her hair never got frizzy, not even when it rained. Some people are like that. But I wasn't one of them.

"Lucy, Lucy, Lucy, wake up," she ordered. "I want to talk about Daniel. Has he ever been in love, I mean *really* in love?"

"Er . . ."

"Come on, you've known him for years."

"Well . . ."

"He hasn't really, has he?"

"But . . ."

"And wouldn't you say it's about time that he was?" she demanded.

"Yes," I said. It was easier to agree.

"Me too."

Karen slumped onto my bed. "Move over. I'm exhausted."

We lay in silence for a short time. We could hear Charlotte, in the bathroom, singing "Somewhere over the Rainbow."

"That Simon guy must have a big one," commented Karen.

I agreed.

"Oh, Lucy," she sighed dramatically. "I don't want to go to work."

"Me, either."

Then we played the Gas Explosion game.

"Wouldn't it be great if there was a gas explosion?" said Karen.

"Yes! Not a bad one but . . ."

"Well, bad enough to keep us at home . . ."

"But not bad enough to hurt anyone . . ."

"Exactly, but the house would collapse and we'd be stuck here for days with just the TV and the magazines and we'd have to eat all the stuff in the freezer and . . ."

Although the stuff in the freezer was nothing but a beautiful fantasy. We never had anything in it except a huge bag of peas that had been there when Karen moved into the flat four years before. Sometimes we bought big tubs of ice cream with the intention of having modest little amounts every so often and making it last for months, but they usually didn't even last the evening.

Sometimes, for variety, we played the Earthquake game instead. We wished for an earthquake that had our apartment at its epicenter. But we were always careful not to wish death or destruction on anyone other than ourselves. In fact, all we wished destruction on was the way out of our apartment. Magazines, televisions, beds, sofas, and food were miraculously saved.

Sometimes we used to wish for a broken leg or two, lured by the idea of several weeks solid, uninterrupted lying down. But the previous winter Charlotte had broken her little toe at her flamenco dancing class (at least that was the official story, the truth was that she had broken it jumping over a coffee table while under the considerable influence of alcohol) and she said the agony was beyond description. So we no longer wished for broken limbs, but sometimes we wished for a burst appendix.

"Okay," said Karen with determination. "I'm going to work."

She left and Charlotte arrived.

"Lucy, I've brought you a cup of coffee."

"Oh, er, thanks," I said grumpily, dragging myself upright.

In her work clothes and without any makeup, Charlotte looked about twelve. Only her enormous chest gave it away.

"Hurry up," she said, "and we'll walk to the tube together. I need to talk to you."

"About what?" I asked warily, wondering if it might be about the pros and cons of the morning-after pill.

"You see," she said, looking miserable, "I slept with Simon yesterday and do you think I'm awful to sleep with two people in the one weekend?"

"Nooooo . . ." I said soothingly.

"I am, I know I am, but I didn't *mean* to, Lucy," she said anxiously. "Well I meant to when I did it, but I didn't ever decide to sleep with two people. How was I to know on Friday night that I'd meet Simon on Saturday night?"

"Exactly," I fervently agreed.

"It's awful, Lucy, I keep breaking my own rules," said poor Charlotte, intent on chastising herself. "I always said that I'd never, ever sleep with someone on the first night— not that I *did* sleep with Simon on the first night, because I waited until the following afternoon—and it was evening really. After six."

"That's fine then," I said.

"And it *was* great," she added.

"Good," I said encouragingly.

"But what about the other guy, the Friday night one— god, I can't even remember his name—isn't that awful, Lucy? Imagine! I let someone see my butt and I can't even remember his name. Derek, I think it was Derek," she said, her face screwed up in concentration. "You saw him—did he look like a Derek to you?"

"Charlotte, please, stop being so hard on yourself. If you can't remember his name, you can't remember it. And does it really matter?"

"No, of course it doesn't really," she said, agitatedly. "Of course it doesn't. Or it might have been Jeff. Or Alex. Oh god! Come on, are you getting up?"

"Yes."

"Do you want me to iron something for you?"

"Yes, *please.*"

"What?"

"Anything."

Charlotte left to get the iron and I dragged myself up to sit on the edge of my bed. Charlotte called to me from the kitchen, something about having read somewhere about an operation you can have in Japan where you can get your hymen sewn back up and thereby have your virginity restored. Did I think she should have it done?

Poor Charlotte. Poor all of us.

It was very nice and we were very grateful to get the beautifully wrapped (albeit reluctantly given) gift of sexual liberation, but who was the out-of-touch, aged great-aunt that gave us the hand-crocheted coordinating packages of guilt?

*She* wouldn't be getting a thank-you card.

It was like being given a present of a beautiful, short, tight, sexy, shiny, red dress on the condition that you wear flat brown loafers and no makeup with it. Giving with one hand and taking away with the other.

Work wasn't too awful. I certainly felt a lot better than when I had left on Friday.

Megan and Meredia were very contrite and sweet. They

weren't speaking to each other, but that was nothing unusual. Except from time to time when Megan said casually to Meredia, "Would you like a cookie, Eleanor?" or "Pass me the stapler, Fiona," and Meredia would hiss in reply, "My name is Meredia."

They were very nice to me. True, I was still getting the occasional amused look from some of the other employees, but I no longer felt so raw and vulnerable and embarrassed. I could see things differently—I realized that everyone must think that Megan and Meredia were the dumb ones, not me. After all they had started the stupid story.

And, of course, there had been one major change in my life since Friday. I had met Gus. Every time I thought of him I felt as though I'd been wrapped in a protective armor, that no one could now think of me as a sad pathetic loser because, well . . . I *wasn't,* was I?

It was kind of ironic that on Friday everyone had thought that I was getting married, when I didn't even have a boyfriend and now, on Monday, when I had met someone very special, no one would dare to bring up the subject of marriage in my presence.

I was bursting to tell Meredia and Megan about Gus, but it was too soon to forgive them, so I had to keep my mouth shut until the correct annoyance period had been observed.

Another reason that I no longer felt the center of attention at work was because I really wasn't—I was yesterday's news.

The story had broken about Hetty and the big crush that Poison Ivor had on her. Apparently he had gone out on Friday night and gotten plastered and told the entire company, from the managing director to the mailroom and everyone in between, that he was in love with Hetty and that he was distraught that she had left her husband, although strictly speaking he wasn't distraught that she had left her husband, he was only distraught that she hadn't left her husband for him.

As for Hetty, there was no word from her.

"Is Hetty coming in today, or is she still unwell?" I asked Ivor, all innocence. That was the pretense that we seemed to have decided to observe.

"I don't know," he said, his eyes watering. "But seeing as you're so concerned, you can take over her work until she gets back," he hissed at me.

The bastard!

"Certainly, Mr. Simmonds."

*In your dreams, pal.*

"What's happening with Hetty?" I asked Meredia and Megan when Ivor had gone into his own office and shut the door, doubtless to put his head down on his desk and sob like a child. "Have either of you heard from her?"

"Yes, yes, I have," said Meredia, eager for a chance to rebond with me. "I stopped by her house yesterday . . ."

"You *vulture!*" I exclaimed.

"Look, do you want to hear or don't you?" she asked sourly.

I wanted to hear.

". . . and she doesn't seem at all happy."

"At all happy," repeated Meredia, heavily and gloomily, *thrilled* with the drama of it all.

The phone rang, interrupting her. She grabbed it and listened impatiently for a few moments, then she barked, "Yes, I see, but unfortunately our systems are down at present and I'm unable to check your account. Let me take down your number and I'll call you back. Um," she nodded, writing nothing down. "Yes, got that. I'll call you back as soon as I can." She slammed down the phone. "Christ! Bloody customers!"

"*Are* our systems down?" I asked.

"How should I know?" said Meredia, sounding surprised. "I haven't turned anything on yet. I wouldn't have thought so, though. Now, where was I? Oh yes, Hetty . . ."

We did that kind of thing a lot in the office. Sometimes we said our systems were down, sometimes we answered the phone and said that we were only the cleaner, sometimes we pretended that the line was very bad and that we couldn't hear the customers, sometimes we hung up and pretended that we'd been cut off, sometimes we pretended that we couldn't speak English very well ("I am not spigging Engrish"). Customers got very annoyed with us and often demanded to speak to our managers and when that happened we put them on hold for a few minutes and then we came back on the line, all unctuous and soothing, reassuring the furious customer that the offending employee was in the process of cleaning out her desk.

Meredia told me at length how miserable Hetty was, how thin and gaunt she looked.

"But she always looks thin and gaunt," I protested.

"No," she said, annoyed. "You can tell that she's suffering a great deal, that she's involved in a very traumatic . . . traumatic . . . er, trauma."

"I can't really see what she's miserable about," commented Megan. "She's got two men, instead of just one. Two heads—and not just heads—are better than one, I always say."

"Oh, God, honestly!" spluttered Meredia in disgust. "How like you to reduce everything to . . . to . . . *base* animal lusts."

"There's a lot to be said for it, Gretel," said Megan vaguely, a secret little smile playing about her luscious, ripe mouth.

She murmured something else before gliding from the room. I think it might have been "threesome."

"My name is Meredia," Meredia roared after her.

"Stupid bitch," she muttered. "Now, where was I. Oh yes."

She cleared her throat.

"She's torn between two lovers." Meredia was passionate. "On the one hand there's Dick, dependable, reliable Dick, the father of her children. And on the other hand there's Roger, exciting, unpredictable, passionate . . ."

On and on she went until eventually it was lunchtime. Which of course was the time when I stopped work and left the office and went shopping for an hour.

The fact that I hadn't actually started work yet wasn't of any real importance.

I went out to get Daniel a card and a birthday present, which was always a bit of an ordeal.

I never knew what to get him.

What do you buy for the man who has everything? I wondered. I could get him a book, I thought—but he already had one.

I must remember to tell him that, he'd enjoy it.

I always ended up getting him something awful and unimaginative like socks or a tie or hankies.

And it was made worse by the fact that he always got me something lovely and thoughtful. For my last birthday he gave me a gift certificate for a day at a spa, which was total and absolute bliss. A guilt-free day, lying around by a pool, being massaged and pampered.

Anyhow, I got him a tie. I hadn't got him one of those for a couple of years, so I thought I might get away with it.

But I got him a nice card, a nice, funny, affectionate card and signed it "love, Lucy" and hoped that Karen wouldn't see it and accuse me of trying to steal her man.

The wrapping paper cost nearly as much as the tie. It must have been made out of spun gold.

I did the wrapping of the tie in the office but I had to go back out to the post office to mail the package. I *could* have put it through the office mail but I would have liked Daniel's present to reach him sometime this century and the two Neanderthals that worked in the mailroom couldn't necessarily guarantee that. It's not that they weren't nice— they were very nice, in fact, their congratulations on my bogus marriage had been sincere and effusive—but they didn't seem too bright, somehow. Ready, willing, but not overly able, would be the best way to describe them.

Eventually five o'clock rolled around and, like a bullet departing the barrel of a gun, I left for home.

 31

I loved Monday evenings. I was still at that stage in my life when I thought that weekdays were for recovering from the weekend. I couldn't understand the rest of the world who seemed to be under the impression that it was the other way around.

Monday night was usually the only night in the week when Karen, Charlotte and I were all at home in the apartment, worn out from the rigors of the preceding weekend.

On Tuesday night Charlotte had her flamenco dancing class. (Or her flamingo dancing, as she thought it was. No one had the heart to correct her.) A couple of us were often to be found missing in action on Wednesday night.

And very often on Thursday night all of us would be out, in a warm-up session for the full-blown socializing that the weekend entailed, when we'd all be out, all the time. (My depression permitting, of course.)

Monday night was the night when we went to the supermarket and bought enough apples and grapes and low-fat yogurt to last us the week. It was the night that we ate steamed vegetables and said that we really must cut out the pizzas, that we would never drink again, at least not until the following Saturday night.

(By Tuesday we were back on the pasta and wine, by Wednesday the ice cream and chocolate cookies and a couple of pints at the local pub, by Thursday the drinking session after work and the Chinese takeout and there was never any restraint to speak of between Friday and Sunday. Until Monday rolled around and we bought apples and grapes and low-fat yogurt again.)

Charlotte was already in when I got home, unpacking groceries and throwing out vast tracts, *acres*, of very-past-their-use-by-date, uneaten, low-fat yogurts that were dancing jigs with each other in the fridge.

I put my bag down next to her bag, so that they could chat with each other.

"Show me, show me, what did you get? Anything good?" asked Charlotte.

"Apples . . ."

"Oh. Me too."

". . . and grapes . . ."

"Me too."

". . . and low-fat yogurts . . ."

"Me too."

"So, no, sorry, nothing good."

"Oh dear, but it's just as well because I'm going to eat sensibly from now on."

"Me too."

"And the less temptation the better."

"Exactly."

"Karen's gone up to the corner shop. Let's hope she doesn't buy anything good there."

"Mr. Papadopoulos's?"

"Yes."

"She won't."

"Why not?"

"Because there isn't anything good there to buy."

"I suppose you're right," said Charlotte. "Everything there looks a bit . . . well, dusty, doesn't it? Even things like the chocolate looks like it's been there since before the war."

"Yes," I agreed. "We're very lucky, really. Can you imagine what we'd look like if we lived near a nice store, that sold delicious things."

"Huge," agreed Charlotte. "We'd be enormous."

"In fact, if you think about it," I said, "it's really one of the amenities of the place. It should've been in the ad—'three-bedroom apartment, fully furnished, zone two, close to tubes and buses, miles from a shop that sells chocolate.' "

"Absolutely!" said Charlotte.

"Oh, here's Karen now."

Karen marched in with a face like thunder and banged her shopping down on the kitchen table. She was clearly annoyed.

"What's up, Karen?" I asked.

"Look, who the hell put some pesetas in the change jar? I'm so embarrassed. Mr. Papadopoulos thinks I tried to cheat him and you know what everyone says about Scottish people and money!"

"What do they say?" asked Charlotte. "Oh yes, that you're really cheap."

She stopped when she saw the expression on Karen's face.

"*Who* put them there?" Karen demanded. As previously noted, she could be very scary.

I toyed with the idea of lying and blaming, say, the guy whom Charlotte had brought home Friday night. He called on Sunday evening to speak to Charlotte, only to be told that there was no one of that name living here.

I thought about denying all knowledge.

"Er . . ."

And then thought better of it.

Karen would find out eventually. Karen would break me down. My guilty conscience would eat away at me until I confessed.

"Sorry, Karen, it was probably my fault . . . I didn't put them into the change jar *as such,* but it's my fault that they're in the house at all."

"But you haven't even been to Spain."

"I know, but Gus gave them to me and I didn't want to take them and I must have left them on the table and someone else must have put them in thinking that they were real money . . ."

"Oh well, if it was **Gus, that's** okay."

"Really?" chorused **Charlotte** and I, in surprise. Karen was rarely so compassionate and merciful.

"Yes, he's a sweetie. So cute. Crazy as a loon, of course, but in such a cute way . . . Elizabeth Ardent . . ." she chuckled to herself. "He makes me laugh."

Charlotte and I exchanged alarmed looks.

"But, don't you want to smack him?" I asked anxiously. "And make him go to Mr. Papadopoulos and explain that you're not a dishonest Scottish skinflint and . . ."

"No, no, no," she said, waving her hand dismissively.

I was touched by the change in Karen; she seemed so much less aggressive, so much *nicer*.

"No," she continued. "You'll do. You can go. You can go up to Mr. Papadopoulous and apologize."

"Er . . ."

"But you needn't go right now. Wait until you've had your dinner, but don't forget he closes at eight."

I stared at her, unable to figure out if she was serious or not. I had to be sure because I didn't want to go to all the trouble of feeling nervous, just to find out that I didn't need to.

"You are joking, aren't you?" I asked hopefully.

There was a tense little pause and then she said, "Okay, I'm joking. I'd better be nice to you now, what with you being Daniel's friend and all."

She gave me a charming, disarming, I'm-so-brazen-but-you-can't-help-liking-me-for-it grin, and I grinned back weakly.

I was all for bluntness. Well, actually that's a complete lie, I thought it was one of the most overrated things I had ever heard of. But Karen behaved as if being blunt was a great virtue, the kindest act she could do for you. Whereas I felt there were some things that didn't need to be said or shouldn't be said. And that sometimes people used "I'm just being honest" as an opportunity to be malicious. That they opened the nastiness floodgates, were viciously cruel, completely trashed a life and then absolved themselves with an innocent face and a plaintive, "But I was only being honest."

But I had no right to complain about these people—

Karen may have been too fond of confrontation, but I was phobically frightened of it.

"Just make sure you keep telling him what a fabulous person I am," she said. "And tell him that millions of guys are in love with me."

"Er, okay," I agreed.

"I'm steaming some broccoli," said Charlotte, turning the conversation to matters domestic. "Would either of you like some?"

"Well, I'm steaming some carrots," I said, "so would either of you like some of them?"

We hammered out a tripartite agreement concerning the equable sharing out of our steamed vegetable assets.

"Oh, Lucy," said Karen casually. Too casually. I braced myself. "Daniel called."

"Oh, er, good . . . did he?"

Was that noncommittal enough for her?

"For *me*," she said triumphantly. "He called to talk to me."

"Great."

"Not you. Me."

"Great, Karen," I laughed. "So you two must be an item, then?"

"Certainly looks that way," she said smugly.

"Good for you."

"You'd better believe it."

We had our steamed vegetables, we watched the soaps and a harrowing documentary about natural childbirth that had us all squirming in our seats. Women with contorted faces, covered in sweat, panting and gasping and groaning.

And that was only me, Charlotte and Karen.

"Jesus," said Charlotte, staring at the screen transfixed, her face rigid with shock. "I'm never having a baby."

"Me neither," I agreed fervently, suddenly aware of all the advantages of *not* having a boyfriend.

"But you can have an epidural," said Karen. "And then you wouldn't feel anything."

"But it doesn't always work," I reminded her.

"Really? How would you know?" she demanded.

"She's right," said Charlotte. "My sister-in-law said that it didn't work for her and that she was in absolute *agony* and that they could hear her screams three streets away."

Karen didn't look terribly convinced by Charlotte's bloodthirsty tale. The sheer force of Karen's will would ensure that her epidural would work; it wouldn't dare not to.

"Oh dear," I said faintly. "Oh dear. Can we watch something else?"

At about nine-forty the short-term fix of the steamed vegetables wore off and real hunger kicked in.

Who would crack first?

The tension built and built until finally Charlotte said casually, "Does anyone feel like coming for a walk?"

Karen and I breathed surreptitious sighs of gratitude.

"What kind of walk?" I asked carefully.

I wasn't signing up for anything that didn't involve food, but Charlotte didn't let me down.

"A walk to the chip shop," she said shamefacedly.

"Charlotte!" chorused Karen and I in outrage. "For shame. What about all our good intentions?"

"But I'm hungry," she said in a little voice.

"Eat a carrot," said Karen.

"I'd rather eat nothing than eat a carrot," admitted Charlotte.

I knew how she felt. I'd have preferred to eat a piece of the mantelpiece than eat a carrot.

"Well," I sighed. "If you're really starving, I'll come with you." I was delighted. I was dying for chips.

"And," sighed Karen, as if it was a real hardship, "just to make you feel better you may as well buy me a bag of chips too."

"You mustn't if it's just to make me feel less guilty," said Charlotte sweetly. "Just because I've no willpower doesn't mean you have to break your diet."

"It's no trouble," protested Karen.

"No honestly," insisted Charlotte. "There's really no need for you to have any. I can live with my guilt."

"Just shut up and buy me chips!" shouted Karen.

"Large or small?"

"Large!"

 32

Gus was taking me out on Tuesday after work. He had said so on Sunday night.

But spirits had been very high on Sunday night, particularly in Gus's blood-to-alcohol ratio, the ten-minute walk from the pizza place to my flat took over half an hour because he was so skittish and playful and I was a little bit concerned that he might have got the arrangements confused for Tuesday night. I was afraid he might get the place wrong or the time wrong or even the day wrong.

Trying to finalize the details had turned into a bit of a confused nightmare. When he walked me home on Sunday night, he politely shook my hand and said, "Lucy, I'll see you tomorrow."

"No, Gus," I corrected gently. "You won't see me tomorrow. Tomorrow's Monday. You're meeting me on Tuesday."

"No, Lucy," he corrected back, just as gently. "When I go home tonight I'll make some, er . . . certain pharmaceutical arrangements and when I wake up it'll be Tuesday. So to all intents and purposes, Lucy Sullivan, I'll see you tomorrow. At least I'll see you on *my* tomorrow."

"Oh, I see," I said doubtfully. "Where will I meet you?"

"I'll pick you up from work, Lucy. I'll rescue you from the administration mines, from down Credit Control pit."

"Good."

"Remind me again," he said, holding my upper arms and pulling me to him, "it's Fifty-four Cavendish Crescent and you're liberated at five-thirty?"

He gave me a sweet, slightly unfocused grin.

"No, Gus, it's not Cavendish Crescent, it's Newcastle Square, and it's number Six," I told him.

In fact I had told him several times and even written it down for him, but it had been a long day and he had had an awful lot to drink.

"Oh really?" asked Gus. "I wonder why I thought it was Cavendish Crescent?"

"No idea, Gus," I said briskly. I was *not* going to indulge in conjecture about what went on in 54 Cavendish Crescent, if indeed such a place existed—I was busy, hanging on by my fingertips to control the conversation, trying to ensure that Gus knew where, when and how to meet me.

"Where's the piece of paper I gave you with the address on it?" I asked, aware that I sounded like a mother or a schoolteacher, but if it had to be done, then it had to be done.

"I don't know," he said, letting go of my arms and

feeling around in his pockets and patting his jacket. "Oh no, Lucy, I think I've lost it."

I wrote it out for him again.

"Try and remember," I smiled nervously, handing him the piece of paper. "It's Six Newcastle Square, at five o'clock."

"*Five* o'clock? I thought you said five-thirty."

"No, Gus, five o'clock."

"Sorry, Lucy, I can never remember anything. I'd forget my own name—in fact I often do. Many's the conversation I've had where I've had to say to the other person, 'Sorry, I didn't catch my name.' I've a head like a . . . like a, you know, one of those round things, lots of holes in it?"

"Sieve." Anxiety made me abrupt.

"Oh Lucy, don't be angry." He laughed softly. "It was only a little joke."

"Okay."

"I think I've got it right finally," he promised, giving me a slow smile that made my stomach flip. "It's five o'clock at Fifty-six Newcastle Crescent . . ."

". . . No, Gus . . ."

". . . No, no, no, sorry, Cavendish Square . . ."

It wasn't his fault, I thought, trying to calm myself. In a way it was very sweet. And anyone would be confused and mixed up if they had drunk as much as Gus had.

". . . No, no, no, don't be angry with me, Lucy, Fifty-six Newcastle Square, at five o'clock."

"Six."

Confusion passed over his harassed face.

"You just said five o'clock!" he complained. "But it's no problem, Lucy—isn't it a woman's prerogative to change her mind?—so change it if you must."

"No, Gus, I haven't changed my mind. I meant five o'clock, at number Six."

"Okay, I have it now, I think," he smiled. "Five

o'clock at number Six. Five o'clock at number Six. Five o'clock at number Six."

"I'll see you then, Gus."

"Not six o'clock at number five?" he asked.

"No!" I said in alarm. "Oh I see, you're only joking . . ."

He raised a hand in farewell to me and said, parrotlike, "Five o'clock at number Six, five o'clock at number Six, sorry, Lucy, but I can't stop to say goodbye to you because I'll forget five o'clock at number Six, five o'clock at number Six, but I'll see you then, five o'clo . . ."

And off he went up the road still saying ". . . at number Six, five o'clock at number Six . . ."

I stood in the gateway, staring up the dark road after him. I was disappointed that he hadn't tried to kiss me. Never mind, I told myself. It was far more important that he remembered where he was supposed to be meeting me on Tuesday. Assuming he made it to the correct building on the right day at the appointed time, there would be plenty of time for kissing then.

". . . five o'clock at number Six, five o'clock at number Six . . ." floated back to me on the cold night air, as he marched in time to his mantra.

I shivered, partly from the cold, partly from delight and went inside.

So the anxiety I was feeling on Tuesday morning was as much fear that he wouldn't turn up at all, as pleasurable anticipation.

Nevertheless, I put on a very nice pair of underwear, because it was always better to be prepared. I tried on my green little thing that looked like a jacket with a nipped-in waist but was really a very short flared dress and then I pulled on my boots. I admired myself in the mirror. Not bad, at all, I thought.

Then a little thrill of panic ran through me—what if he didn't turn up? Oh, why couldn't I have gotten his phone number from him, I thought in anguish. I should have asked for it, but I was afraid if I did that I'd seem too eager.

And I knew I would arouse the suspicions of everyone at work by wearing something to the office where you could see my butt if I lifted my arms. They were like that at work—you couldn't even comb your hair without a rumor starting that you liked someone, you couldn't get your bangs trimmed without everyone concluding that you had some new guy. There were three hundred employees spread across five floors of office space and they all had a keen interest in the affairs of their co-workers. It said a lot about how interesting they found their workloads.

It was like working in a goldfish bowl. Nothing happened that didn't cause some comment. Even speculation about the fillings of people's sandwiches could take up the best part of an afternoon. ("She never used to eat egg salad sandwiches, it was always ham. And she's had egg salad twice this week. I'd say she's pregnant.")

Caroline, the receptionist, was the source of most of the gossip. She missed *nothing* and, if there was nothing to miss, she just made it up. She was always stopping people and saying things like "Ooh, that Jackie from accounts is looking a bit pale today. Romantic trouble, eh?" And before you knew it the entire building would be buzzing with the rumor that Jackie was getting divorced. And all because she had got up too late that morning to apply her foundation before coming to work.

So I could hardly bear to think of the utter humiliation of spending the day avoiding doing my office chores half-naked, and then no man turning up at five o'clock to account for it.

I *could* have brought my going-out clothes into the office in a separate bag and changed after work, but that would probably have created even more of a scandal. ("Did you see that Lucy Sullivan? Coming in with an overnight bag? On a Tuesday?")

As it was, there was utter mayhem in the office when I unwrapped myself from my horrible brown winter coat and revealed myself in all my short-skirted glory.

"Jeez," declared Megan, "you're looking a bit breezy today!"

"Who is he?" demanded Meredia.

"Er," I blushed. I tried to pretend that I didn't know what they were talking about, but it was no good. I was a hopeless liar.

"I, er, met a guy this weekend."

Meredia and Megan threw each other triumphant looks. Smug, "I knew this was going to happen" kind of looks.

"Well, we can see that," said Meredia scornfully. "And you're meeting him this evening . . ."

"Yes." Well, I certainly *hoped* that I would be.

"So tell us about him."

I hesitated for a moment. I was still supposed to be mad at the two of them, but the desire to talk about Gus was overwhelming.

"Okay." I smiled, giving in. I pulled up a chair to Megan's desk, settling in for a long one, and off I went with Gus's résumé. "Well, his name is Gus and he's twenty-four . . ."

Megan and Meredia listened intently and oohed and aahed appreciatively and squirmed with delight when they heard about the nice things Gus had said to me.

". . . And he said he'd like to give you one of those little vacuum cleaner things for the couch?" asked Meredia, impressed.

"Yes, isn't that so sweet?"

"Christ," muttered Megan, throwing her eyes to

heaven. "Never mind that. How's he equipped? Is it short and fat? Long and skinny? Or my own personal favorite, long and fat?"

"Er, um . . . it was nice," I said vaguely.

Before I was forced to admit that I hadn't actually seen it yet, Poison Ivor marched in and caught us sitting around doing nothing. He shouted a bit and we all slunk shamefacedly back to our desks.

"Miss Sullivan," he barked, "you appear to have forgotten the bottom half of your suit this morning."

Heartbreak was turning him mean and ugly. Not that he hadn't been mean and ugly before Hetty ran off with her brother-in-law.

"It's a dress, actually," I said brazenly, Gus-induced happiness making me bold.

"Not the kind of dress that I'm familiar with," he shouted. "Not the kind of dress that I want in this office. Wear something decent tomorrow." And he slammed into his office and banged the door.

 33

At about twenty to five, I departed the office to go to the ladies room to apply my makeup in anticipation of Gus's estimated time of arrival of seventeen hundred hours.

I was sick with anxiety. Almost as soon as I had finished telling Meredia and Megan about Gus, I was so, so sorry that I had spilt the Gus beans. I had been dying to boast about him, but now I was sure I had jinxed the whole thing. By talking about him I had tempted fate and he wasn't going to arrive.

I'll never see him again, I thought.

But I'll put my makeup on just in case.

On the way to the ladies room I saw a couple of the security guards out by the front desk tussling with someone. Winos and homeless men were always trying to come into the building out of the cold, and the guards had the unpleasant task of having to eject them. The saddest thing of all was that I often *envied* the homeless people. If I had had a choice between sitting in my office and sitting on some cardboard in a freezing doorway, I think I'd have chosen the freezing doorway option.

The security guards were supposed to police the building, only admitting people who were expected and who signed in and got a visitor's pass. But these guys weren't great at defending themselves and occasionally, when they tried to throw someone out, it could turn nasty, especially if the trespasser was drunk.

That was always good fun and, if Caroline was in a good mood with us, she would call our office and we would all rush up to have a ringside view.

I craned my neck to get a good look. A foreign body was being marched to the door, but he was putting up a good fight, struggling hard, and I smiled as I saw him kick Harry. I always sympathized with the underdog.

I turned away, thinking vaguely that there was something very *familiar* about the intruder who was being ejected, when I suddenly heard my name being called. "There she is, Lucy Sullivan, Lucy, Lucy, Lucy!"

"Lucy, Lucy," called the voice frantically. "Tell them who I am."

I slowly turned around, with a horrible feeling of impending doom.

It was Gus. The struggling, flailing, kicking person in the arms of Harry and Winston was Gus.

He twisted around and turned wild eyes upon me. "Lucy," he beseeched, "save me."

Harry and Winston paused, poised on the brink of flinging Gus bodily into the street. "Do you know this man?" asked Winston disbelievingly.

"Yes, I do," I said calmly. "Perhaps you could tell me what's going on here."

I was trying to speak with quiet authority, trying not to show that I was *dying* with embarrassment and it seemed to work.

"We found him on the fourth floor and he didn't have a pass and . . ."

*The fourth floor,* I thought in shock.

"I was looking for you, Lucy," declared Gus passionately. "I had every right to be there."

"No, you bloody well did not, sunshine," said Harry threateningly. You could tell he was itching to pull Gus along by the ear, to treat him like an urchin chimney sweep from a Dickens novel. "Up on the fourth floor, 'e was, no less. Acting like he owned the bloomin' place, sitting in Mr. Balfour's chair, 'e was. I've worked here for thirty-eight years and it's the first time . . ."

The fourth floor was where the high-ranking managerial staff had their quarters, and it was treated with as much reverence as if it were heaven. The fourth floor was Wholesale Metals and Plastics' version of the Oval Office.

I had never been there myself, because I was far too insignificant, but Meredia had been hauled up there once for some offense or other and from what she said it was a cosseted wonderland of thick, beautiful carpets; thick, beautiful secretaries; mahogany paneling; works of art; leather chaise-longues; globes that opened out to be drinks cabinets and lots of fat, bald men taking Zantac.

Horrified though I was, I had to marvel at Gus's daring. But Harry and Winston seemed to be badly shaken by his profane, irreverent behavior.

I decided I had better take charge.

"Thanks, guys," I said, trying to make light of things. "But it's all right. I'll take care of this."

"But he still doesn't have a pass," said Harry stubbornly. "You know the rules, love. No pass, no entry." Harry was a nice man but he liked to do things by the book.

"Okay," I sighed. "Gus, would you mind waiting over here by the front door for a little while? At five o'clock I'll come and get you."

"Where?"

"Just here," I said, gritting my teeth and steering him to the row of seats by the entrance.

"And I'll be all right here, Lucy?" he asked anxiously. "They won't come and try to throw me out again, will they?"

"Just sit there, Gus."

I went to the ladies room, burning with anger. I was furious. Furious with Gus for making a spectacle of me at work and even more furious that he had made the spectacle of me before I had put on my makeup.

"Fuckit!" I hissed, almost in tears I was so angry. I kicked the trash can. "Fuckit, fuckit, fuckit!"

I could have died.

Caroline had witnessed the whole thing, so the entire building would know in five minutes. It was only a few days since I had last been a laughingstock in my workplace and I wasn't sure if I was ready for it to happen again. And worse than that, Gus had seen me without my makeup.

I had known Gus was a little bit eccentric and I had liked it, but I wasn't at all happy about the scene I had just witnessed. My faith in Gus was shaken and it felt horrible. Could I be wrong about Gus? Was this relationship going to be another disaster? Was Gus more trouble than he was worth? Should I just get out now?

But I didn't want to feel that way about Gus.

Please God, don't let me become disillusioned with him. I couldn't bear it. I liked him so much and I had so much hope for us.

But a little voice whispered to me that I could leave him sitting at the front door and exit out the back way. And the notion momentarily filled me with huge relief until I realized that he'd probably wait all night and then come back again the next morning and wait for all eternity until I eventually showed up.

What should I do? I wondered.

I decided to tough things out.

I would go up to the front door and be nice to him and act like he had done nothing wrong.

By the time I applied my fourth and final coat of mascara I had calmed down considerably. There is obviously something very soothing about putting on lipstick and foundation and eyeliner.

I reminded myself of Saturday night and the joy I had felt at meeting him. I reminded myself of the lovely day we had had on Sunday, how we had so much in common, how he was everything I had ever wanted, how he made me laugh, how he seemed to understand me.

How could I possibly have considered abandoning him? I wondered.

Especially when—against all the odds—he had managed

to arrive at the right time (roughly), on the right day in the right place? I started to feel compassionate and forgiving. Poor Gus, I thought. It wasn't his fault. He was like a child in his innocence—how was he to know about the rules and regulations of Wholesale Metals and Plastics?

The whole thing had probably been awful for him too. He must have had a terrible shock. Harry and Winston were big, burly men. Gus was probably terrified.

When I finally collected Gus, not only was I a lot calmer, but a change seemed to have come over him also. He seemed much more normal, more sensible, more grown-up, more in control.

He stood up as he saw me approaching.

I was aware of the shortness of my skirt and the interested glances I got from the other employees. Gus's eyes briefly flickered appreciatively over me before he assumed a funereal expression, white, grim, anxious.

"Lucy," he said quietly, gently. "So you came back? I was afraid that you might escape out the back door."

"It did occur to me," I admitted.

"I can't say I blame you," he said, looking tense and miserable.

Then he cleared his throat and launched into a speech of apology, which he had obviously rehearsed while I was in the ladies room.

"Lucy, I can only apologize from the bottom of my heart," he said rapidly. "I had no intention of doing anything wrong and I hope you can find it in your heart to forgive me and . . .

On and on he went, saying that even if I forgave him, that he wasn't sure he could ever forgive himself etc., etc.

I waited for him to stop, for his apology to run its course. His self-denigration became more and more outrageous, his demeanor more and more abject, his expression just slightly too sheepish and humble. Suddenly the entire episode struck me as hilarious.

What the hell did it matter? I wondered, unable to stop a smile spreading across my face as I realized how *silly* the whole thing was.

"Here!" said Gus, suddenly pausing in his overblown prostration. "What's so funny?"

"Nothing." I laughed. "Just, you, you know, and the look on your face, like you were going off to be executed and Harry and Winston and the way they were acting like you were some sort of dangerous criminal and . . ."

"Well, it wasn't very funny for me, Lucy," said Gus huffily. "It was like *Midnight Express.* I thought I'd be thrown in the slammer and I feared for my bodily integrity."

"But Harry and Winston wouldn't hurt a fly," I reassured him.

"What Harry and Winston do with insects is no concern of mine," said Gus, all indignation. "Their private lives are their own affair, but, Lucy, I was sure they were going to kill me."

"But they didn't kill you, did they?" I asked nicely.

"No, I suppose not . . ."

He suddenly relaxed.

"You're right." He grinned. "Jesus, I thought you were never going to speak to me again. I'm so embarrassed . . ."

"*You're* embarrassed . . ." I snorted.

Then I laughed and he laughed and I realized that this would be one of those little incidents that we would tell to our grandchildren. ("Grandad, Grandad, tell us about the day you got thrown out of Grandma's office . . .") This was history in the making.

"I hope I haven't gotten you into trouble," said Gus anxiously. "There's no danger that you'll lose your job?"

"No," I said. "No danger."

"Are you sure?"

"I'm certain."

"How can you be so sure?"

"Because nothing good ever happens to me."

We both laughed a bit at that.

"Come on." He smiled and put his arm around my waist and steered me down the steps. "Let me take you somewhere nice and spend lots of money on you."

 34

It was a wonderful evening.

First he took me to a pub and bought me a drink. He even paid for it.

Then, when he was back from the bar and sitting next to me, he fished around in his bag and presented me with a small bunch of squashed flowers. But, squashed and all as they were, they looked as if they'd been bought in a shop and not stolen from someone's garden, so I was delighted.

"Thank you, Gus," I said. "They're beautiful." Because they were, in a kind of disheveled way. "But you shouldn't have," I protested. "There was no need."

"Of course I should have, Lucy," he insisted. "What else could I do? A wonderful woman like you?"

He smiled at me and he looked so handsome that my heart flipped over. Happiness rushed through me and everything suddenly seemed right.

I was so *glad* that I hadn't given him the slip and escaped out the back way.

"And that's not all," continued Gus, putting his hand back into his bag and, like Santa Claus, pulling out a parcel wrapped in paper that had pictures of babies and storks on it.

"Oh God, sorry about the paper, Lucy," he said, looking at it in disappointment. "I didn't notice in the store that it was wedding paper."

"Er . . . well, don't worry," I reassured him, tearing off the offending paper.

It was a box of chocolates.

"Thank you," I said, delighted, *thrilled* that he had gone to such trouble for me.

"And there's more," he announced, starting the fishing process again, his arm in his bag up to his shoulder. If it's the small vacuum cleaner thing for the couch, I'll die laughing, I decided, absolutely charmed by Gus's thoughtful parade of presents, which he had based on our conversation in the pizza place on Sunday night.

He must like me, I thought. He must *really* like me to go to so much trouble. I was soaring with happiness.

Eventually he pulled out a small package, also wrapped in the stork paper. It was about the size of a box of matches so it couldn't have been the vacuum cleaner.

"I couldn't afford the entire coat," he said, as if that was some kind of explanation. "So instead I'm buying it in installments for you."

"Open it." He laughed, when I stared at him in confusion.

So I opened it and it was a little fur key ring.

How sweet! Gus had remembered about the fur coat.

"May the furs be with you," he said. "I think it's mint."

"Or maybe you mean mink," I said nicely.

"Oh, maybe I do," he said. "Or it could be stable. But, Lucy, you're not to worry, I know how some people get upset about fur and the killing of animals and all that—I don't myself because I'm a country boy, but I know that others do—but no animals died to make this little key ring for you."

"I see."

That would mean that it wasn't mink. Or mint. Or even stable. But it didn't matter. At least I would be safe from the animal rights activists and their buckets of red paint.

"Thank you very much, Gus," I said, slightly overwhelmed. "Thank you for all the nice things you've given me."

"You're welcome, Lucy," he said.

Then he gave me a knowing wink. "And that mightn't be all you're getting—you mustn't forget that the night is still young," he grinned.

"Er, yes," I muttered, blushing.

Perhaps tonight would be the night, I thought, nervous excitement fluttering about in the pit of my stomach.

"And, tell me," I giggled, eager to change the subject, "what on earth were you doing sitting in Mr. Balfour's chair?"

"Sitting in it, like the man said," said Gus. "Not desecrating a sacred shrine."

"But Mr. Balfour is our managing director," I tried to explain.

"But so what?" said Gus. "It was only a chair, and Mr. Balfour—whoever he is—is only a man. I really can't see what all the fuss was about."

Gus was absolutely right, I thought. What a really great attitude he had.

"Send those two security guards to Bosnia for a couple

of weeks and we'll see how concerned they'll be about Mr. Balfour's chair when they get back," he added. "And send Mr. Balfour too while you're at it. Now, drink up your drink there, Lucy, so I can take you somewhere and feed you."

"Oh, Gus, I can't let you spend all your unemployment check on me," I wailed. "I couldn't. The guilt would kill me."

"Lucy, hush yourself, you're going to eat your dinner and I'm going to pay for it and let that be the end of it."

"No, Gus, I can't, really I can't. You've bought me all these presents and a drink, let me pay for the dinner, please."

"No, Lucy, I won't hear of it."

"I insist, Gus, I absolutely insist."

"Insist away, Lucy," said Gus. "But it won't do you any good."

"Shut up, Gus," I said. "I'm paying and that's that."

"But Lucy . . ."

"No," I said. "I won't hear another word about it."

"Well, if you're sure," he said reluctantly.

"I'm sure," I said, firmly. "Where would you like to go?"

"Anywhere, really, Lucy. I'm easy to please. So long as it's food, I'm happy to eat it . . ."

"Good," I said, delighted, my head racing with the possibilities available to us. There was this terrific Malaysian place down by . . .

". . . especially pizzas, Lucy," continued Gus. "I'm fond of pizzas."

"Oh," I said, reeling my imagination back from Southeast Asia. ("Come back, come back, there's been a change of plan.")

"Okay, Gus, then a pizza it is."

It was one of those perfect nights. We fell over ourselves in our attempts to talk to each other, we had so much to tell each other about ourselves. Neither of us could get our words out quickly enough to keep pace with our enthusiasm and excitement.

Every second sentence was one of us saying, "*Exactly, that's exactly* what I think," and "I don't believe it—do you feel like that about it, too?" and "I couldn't agree more with you, I really couldn't."

Gus told me about his music, about all the instruments he could play, about the type of things he liked to write.

It was all wonderful. I know that we had talked a lot on Saturday night and we had spent all day Sunday together, but this was different. This was our first date.

We stayed in the restaurant for hours and hours and talked and held hands across the garlic bread.

We talked about ourselves as children, we talked about ourselves now, and I felt that no matter what I said to Gus, no matter what I told him about myself, that he would understand. Understand like no one else ever had, or could.

I allowed myself to daydream a little about what it would be like to be married to Gus. It wouldn't be the most conventional of marriages, but so what? The days of the little woman staying at home and doing the housework in a little cottage with roses around the door, while the man went out and toiled from dawn to dusk, were long gone.

Gus and I would be each other's best friends. I would encourage him in his music and I would work and support both of us and then, when he was discovered and was famous, he'd tell Oprah that he couldn't have done it without me and that he owed all his success to me.

Our house would be full of music and laughter and

great conversation and everyone would envy us and say what a wonderful marriage we had. And, even when we were really rich, we would still take pleasure in the simple things in life and would each be the other's favorite person. Lots of interesting and talented people would drop by without being invited and I'd be able to throw together wonderful dinners for them, out of leftovers, while discussing the early films of Jim Jarmusch in a thought-provoking and incisive way.

Gus would be totally supportive of me and I wouldn't feel so . . . so *lacking* when I was married to him. I would feel whole and normal, as if I belonged just like everyone else.

Gus would never be tempted by the glamorous groupies that he might meet on tour because none of them would give him the same feeling of total love and security and belonging that he'd get from me.

After the dinner Gus said, "Are you in a hurry to get home, Lucy, or would you like to go somewhere else?"

"I'm in no hurry," I said. I wasn't. I was, by then, *certain* that our relationship would be consummated later on that evening and, while I was delighted, I was also petrified. I wanted it, yet I was afraid of it.

Any delay of the moment of truth was something I rejected, yet welcomed.

"Okay," said Gus, "I'd like to take you someplace."

"Where?"

"It's a surprise."

"Great."

"We'll have to get a bus, Lucy, do you mind?"

"Not at all."

We got the number 24 and Gus paid my fare. The gesture delighted me. It was such a sweet, teenagery thing to do.

When the bus reached the delights of Camden Town, Gus and I got off.

Gus held my hand and led me through the carpet of empty Special Brew cans and past the people, lying on cardboard, asleep in doorways, the young men and women sitting on the filthy street asking for any spare change. I was appalled—because I worked in central London, I knew about the homelessness problem in the city, but there were so *many* homeless people here that I felt as if I had stumbled into another world, a medieval world where people were forced to live in dirt and die from hunger.

Some of the people were drunk, but lots more of them weren't. Not that that was a yardstick.

"Stop, Gus!" I said, as I got my purse out of my bag.

The awful dilemma—should I give all my change to one person so that he could do something decent with it, like get something to eat or drink, or should I try and share it among as many people as possible so that lots of people got a few pennies? But what can you do with pennies? I anguished. It wouldn't even buy a bar of chocolate.

I stood on the street, people passing and bumping into me, as I tried to make up my mind.

"What do you think I should do, Gus?" I beseeched.

"Actually, I think you should toughen up, Lucy," he said. "Learn to close your eyes to it. Even if you gave away every penny you have, it wouldn't make any difference."

He was right—every penny I had didn't exactly amount to very much, but that didn't matter.

"I can't close my eyes to it," I said. "At least let me give away my loose change."

"Well, give it all to one person then," said Gus.

"Do you think that's the right thing to do?"

"If you try to visit every down-and-out in Camden, sharing your money among them, the pub I'm taking you to will be closed by the time you finish, so, yes, I think that giving it all to one person is the right thing to do," he said good-humoredly.

"Gus! How can you be so heartless?" I exclaimed.

"Because I have to be, Lucy, we all have to be," he said.

"Okay, who should I give it to, then?"

"Anyone you like."

"Anyone?"

"Well maybe not just anyone, it might be better if you gave it to someone who is actually poor and homeless—don't go accosting people in the wine bars or the restaurants, trying to get them to take your money."

"But I want to give it to the person who deserves it the most," I explained. "How will I know who that is?"

"You won't, Lucy."

"Oh."

"You're meant to be committing a selfless act of charity, Lucy. Not making a moral judgment."

"But, I'm not . . ."

"Aye, you are. You want to feel that you're getting value for your money by giving it to the person whom you think deserves it the most," he said. "Would you feel bad if your money went to a drunken, thieving, wife beater?"

"Well, yes . . ."

"Then you've got it all wrong, Lucy," said Gus. "The giving should be the important bit, not the receiving, or rather the receivee."

"Oh," I said faintly. Maybe he was right. I was humbled.

"Right," I said, making up my mind. "I'll give it to that guy sitting down over there."

"Oh no, don't, Lucy," said Gus, pulling me back by my arm. "Not him. He's a bastard."

I stared at Gus in annoyance for a moment and then the pair of us exploded with laughter.

"Are you joking?" I finally asked.

"No, Lucy," he laughed apologetically. "I'm not. Give your money to anyone in the whole of Camden, except him. Him and his brothers are a crowd of shysters. *And* he's not even homeless—he has a subsidized apartment in Kentish Town."

"How do you know all this?" I asked, intrigued, but not certain whether to believe him.

"I just do," said Gus darkly.

"Well, what about that man over there?" indicating another poor unfortunate, sitting in a doorway.

"Go to it."

"He's not a bastard?" I asked.

"Not that I know of."

"What about his brothers?"

"I've heard nothing but good things about them."

After I unloaded my pathetic handful of coins, I turned around and bumped into an older man who was lurching along the street.

"Oh hello, good evening to you," he said to me, in a very friendly way, as if we knew each other. He had an Irish accent.

"Hello." I smiled back.

"Do you know him?" asked Gus.

"No," I said doubtfully. "At least, I don't think so, but he said 'hello' so it was only polite to say 'hello' back."

Gus led me across the road and down a side street and into a brightly lit, warm, noisy pub.

It was completely packed with people, laughing and talking and drinking. Gus seemed to know absolutely everyone there. In a corner were three musicians, a man with a bodhrán, a woman with a tin whistle and someone of indeterminate sex playing a fiddle.

I recognized the tune—it was one of my dad's favorites. All around me were the sounds of Irish accents.

I felt as if I had come home.

"Sit here," said Gus, guiding me through the throngs of red-faced, happy people and indicating a barrel. "I'll be as quick as I can getting the drinks."

He was gone forever, while I sat perched uncomfortably on the barrel, the rim of it gouging a furrow in my butt.

What time was it? I wondered. I was sure it was well past eleven, yet the bartenders were still serving.

A thought suddenly struck me—could this be an illegal bar—the type my dad often waxed lyrical about?

Perhaps it was, I thought in excitement.

I didn't have a watch and neither did the woman beside me and neither did her friends, but one of them knew someone on the far side of the pub who had one and she insisted on fighting her way through the throng to locate the person and ascertain the time for me.

She was back a while later.

"Twenty to twelve," she said, returning to her pint of lager.

"Thanks," I said, a thrill of excitement running through me. So I had been right—this *was* an illegal bar.

How wonderful. Daring, decadent, dangerous. Maybe it was wrong of Gus to bring me here and put me in danger of being arrested, but I didn't care. I felt as if I was walking on the wild side, as if I was truly living.

Gus finally came back with the drinks.

"Sorry I was so long, Lucy," he apologized. "I ran into a crowd of Cavan men and . . ."

"Fine, fine," I interrupted, clambering down from the barrel. I was too eager to discuss our breaking of the law to be bothered with his apologies.

"Gus, aren't you worried about the police?" I breathed, my eyes round with delighted horror.

"No," he said. "I think they're well able to look after themselves."

"No," I giggled, "I mean, aren't you worried that they might arrest us?"

He felt around his jacket pockets, then sighed with relief and said, "No, Lucy, not at this particular moment, I'm not."

He wasn't taking me seriously and I was annoyed.

"No, Gus," I protested. "Aren't you afraid that they might raid here and beat us all up and arrest everyone?"

"But why would they do that?" asked Gus, puzzled. "Haven't they got plenty of people out on the street to arrest when they feel the need for a punching bag? Weren't they given the Vagrancy Act especially for that reason?"

"But, Gus," I said in exasperation, "what if they hear the music? What if they realize that we're all in here drinking when it's way past eleven?"

"But we're not doing anything wrong," said Gus. "Although that's never stopped them in the past," he added.

"But we *are*," I insisted. "This is illegal. Closing time is eleven o'clock. We're breaking the law."

"No, we're not." He laughed.

"Yes, we are."

"Lucy, Lucy, listen to me! This pub has a special license until twelve. No one's doing anything wrong!"

"Oh."

I was terribly disappointed.

"You mean this is all legal and aboveboard?" I asked, subdued.

"Yes, Lucy, of course it is." He laughed. "You don't think I'd bring you somewhere where you might get into trouble, do you?"

"Well, er, you know . . . I just thought . . ."

At the end of the evening Gus came home with me. There was no question about it, no awkwardness, it seemed like the most natural thing in the world. Nothing was said, it just happened. When we finally escaped from the pub and all the people Gus knew, we both just assumed that we would get a taxi back to Ladbroke Grove. And so we did.

Gus didn't suggest that we go back to his house and it never occurred to me to suggest it either. I didn't think there was anything odd about that.

Maybe I should have.

 35

On Thursday there were two blots on my otherwise pristine landscape of happiness.

The news broke that Hetty had officially handed in her notice. And it made me sad. Not just because she was the only one of us who ever really did any work, but because I would miss her. I hated change and I wondered with trepidation what we would get in her place.

Second, I had agreed to visit my mother on Thursday when I finished work.

I was at that phase of the relationship with Gus when my every waking thought was of him. I was delightfully happy nearly all of the time (except for the hours between seven-thirty and ten o'clock). If I wasn't actually *with* Gus, I wanted to talk about him, to anyone, to everyone. To describe how gorgeous he looked, to tell how smooth his skin was or how sexy he smelled or how green his eyes were or how silky his hair was or how beautiful his accent was or how fascinating his conversation was, or how nice his teeth were for someone who'd been brought up on a remote farm, or how his butt was the size of a stamp. Or to recount, in great detail, stories of the nice things that he'd said to me and given to me as gifts.

I was buzzing with happiness and adrenaline and it never occurred to me that I might be the most boring person in the world. I felt that everyone else was surely as happy for me as I was. Of course they weren't, and they consoled themselves by saying to each other, "It'll never last," and "If I hear once more about how he opened her bra and took it off with his teeth, I'll scream."

Not, of course, that Gus did remove my bra with his teeth. Although we did indeed consummate our relationship on Tuesday night, *Nine and a Half Weeks* it wasn't. Which was fine with me—being blindfolded and fed pickled onions wasn't my idea of pleasant sex. Because I had such an inferiority complex and wasn't very sexually confident, I liked things straightforward in bed. Men who expected lots of different positions scared the lust out of me.

Even without the different positions, I was still a ball of nerves when Gus and I got back to my flat. Luckily, I was a very drunk ball of nerves and that removed most of the potential awkwardness. In fact we were both roaring with laughter and fell into the bedroom right away.

Gus pulled off his clothes at high speed and then jumped onto the bed with me.

I fully intended not to look at his erect penis—I thought I was far too shy. But, as though against my will, my eyes kept being drawn to it. And drawn to it. And drawn to it. I couldn't stop. I was mesmerized by it.

Very attractive it was too, for a six-inch lump of throbbing, veiny purpleness. It never ceased to amaze me how something so intrinsically, well . . . weird looking, I suppose, could be so erotic.

Then it was my turn to disrobe.

"What's going on here?" Gus plucked at my clothes in mock alarm. "You're still dressed. Come on, get them off, quick, quick."

It was great fun. It reminded me of when I was a little girl being undressed by my mother.

"Legs out straight," he ordered, as he stood at the foot of the bed and held the toes of my tights and pulled. When I heard the sound of them ripping, all I could do was laugh and laugh.

"Arms up," he barked, as he tugged off my top. "Jesus! Where's your face gone?"

"In here." I muffled through my top. "You've got to do the neck hole as well as the arm ones."

"Thank God for that—I thought I'd decapitated you with my passion."

I was undressed in record time, but, for once, I wasn't shy and embarrassed and ashamed of my body. There was no chance to be modest and coy because Gus was so matter-of-fact about it all.

"You're not a medical student, are you?" I asked suspiciously.

"No."

Of course he wasn't. I'd forgotten that medical students were the very ones to snigger uncontrollably every time they heard the word *bottom*.

Gus didn't bother much with foreplay. Unless him asking me, "Are you on the pill?" counted. He was really frenzied and eager. Of course, I was delighted with his enthusiasm; it showed that he really liked me.

"You're not to come in three seconds," I admonished. And when he did come in three seconds, the pair of us fell onto the bed laughing.

Then Gus practically fell asleep on top of me. But I wasn't disappointed or annoyed. I didn't scream at him and demand that he get it up again immediately and service me until I had had ten orgasms—as was my right as a nineties woman. I was relieved that he wasn't very sexually sophisticated, because it meant that there was nothing for me to live up to. For me, sex was more about warmth and affection than orgasms. And he was good at the warmth and affection bit.

With Gus, I had bypassed all that gentle, getting-to-know-you nonsense and gone straight for the falling-in-love jugular.

Which is why I bitterly resented having to go and see my mother. It was a waste of time that could have been better spent with Gus, or at the very least telling people about Gus.

The only thing that made it remotely bearable was the fact that Daniel was coming with me. I couldn't talk about Gus while I was actually with my mother, but on the train journey both there and back I could bend Daniel's ear.

\*     \*     \*

After work on Thursday I met Daniel and we caught the tube to the far reaches of the Piccadilly Line.

"I can think of far better things to do this evening than going hundreds of miles to see my mother," I muttered, as we stood swaying on a packed train, the air thick with the smell of damp overcoats, the floor awash with brief-cases. "Like mining salt in Siberia."

"Don't forget your dad," reminded Daniel. "You're going to see your dad also. Doesn't that make you happy?"

"Well, yes, but I can't talk to him when she's around. And I hate leaving him; I feel so guilty."

"Oh, Lucy, you make life so difficult for yourself," sighed Daniel. "It doesn't have to be that bad, you know."

"I know," I smiled, "but maybe I enjoy it."

I didn't want Daniel to start counseling me, because I knew it wouldn't do any good, but he was the type of person who, once he got the bit between his teeth, wouldn't give up easily. And many a friendship has come aground on the rocks of misguided help.

"Maybe you do actually enjoy it," he admitted, looking a bit surprised at the discovery.

"Good." I smiled. "I'm glad we agree. Now I don't have to put up with you worrying about me."

When we came out of the tube it was dark and cold and there was a fifteen-minute walk to my house.

Daniel insisted on carrying my bag.

"My God, Lucy, this weighs a ton. What's in here?"

"A bottle of whiskey."

"Who's that for then?"

"Not for you." I giggled.

"I might have known. You never give me anything except abuse."

"That's not true! Didn't I give you a beautiful tie for your birthday?"

"Yes, you did, thank you. At least it was one step up from last year."

"What did I give you then?"

"Socks."

"Oh yes."

"You always get me 'Dad' presents."

"What do you mean?"

"You know—ties, socks, hankies—they're the type of thing everyone gives to their dad."

"I don't."

"Don't you? What do you give him?"

"Money, mostly. And sometimes a bottle of nice brandy."

"Oh."

"Anyway, this year I was going to get you something different. This year I was going to get you a book . . ."

"But I have one already, yes, I know, I know, Lucy," he interrupted briskly.

"Oh," I laughed. "Have I said that to you before?"

"You could say that, Lucy. Once or twice, maybe."

"Whoops, how embarrassing. Sorry."

"Sorry for what? Sorry for repeating your crappy joke for the hundredth time? Or sorry for calling me an uncultured philistine?"

"Palestine," I said vaguely.

"Filipino," he countered.

"Sorry for repeating my crappy joke—hey, it's not crappy anyway—for the hundredth time. I'm certainly not sorry for implying that you're not very bright. Look at the women you go out with!"

"Lucy!" he barked. I looked at him in alarm—he

sounded like he was really annoyed. Then he laughed, shaking his head in disbelief.

"Lucy Sullivan, I let you get away with so much, I really don't know why I haven't killed you before now."

"Actually, neither do I," I said thoughtfully. "I am very unkind to you. And the thing is I don't really mean it. I don't really think you're thick at all. I *do* think you have awful taste in women and I *do* think you treat them very badly, but apart from that you're quite all right really."

"Jesus, praise indeed," grinned Daniel. "Can I have that in writing?"

"No."

We marched on in silence, past rows and rows of boxy little suburban houses. It was freezing.

Daniel spoke after a while.

"So who's it for then?"

"Who's what for?"

"The whiskey. Who's it for?"

"Dad, of course. Who else?"

"Is he still on the sauce?"

"Daniel! Don't say it like that."

"Like what?"

"You're making it sound like he's a wino or something awful."

"But it's just that Chris said he'd given up."

"Who, Dad?" I said scornfully. "Given up drinking? Don't be ridiculous. What would he want to do that for?"

"I don't know," said Daniel, ultramildly. "That's just what Chris told me. He must have got it wrong."

We trudged on in silence.

"So what did you get your mum?"

"Mum?" I asked in surprise. "Nothing."

"That's a bit mean."

"No, it's not. I never get her anything."

"Why not?"

"Because she works. She has money. Dad doesn't work, Dad doesn't have any money."

"So you wouldn't ever think of bringing her a little present?"

I stopped walking and stood in front of Daniel, forcing him to stop also.

"Look, you big rat," I said angrily. "I get her presents on her birthday, at Christmas and on Mother's Day and that's enough for her. *You* might get *your* mother presents every time you see her, but I don't. Stop trying to make me feel like a bad daughter!"

"I only meant . . . oh never mind." He looked so woebegone that I couldn't stay angry with him.

"Okay," I said, touching his arm, "if it makes you feel any better, I'll get her a cake when we get to the shops."

"Don't bother."

"Daniel! Why are you so sulky?"

"I'm not."

"Yes, you are. You said 'don't bother.' "

"Yes," he laughed, sounding exasperated. "I said don't bother, because I've got a cake for her."

I tried to look disgusted.

"It's good manners. Your mum is giving me my dinner, I'm just being polite."

"You might call it politeness. I call it kissing up."

"Okay, Lucy." He laughed. "Call it what you want."

We rounded the corner and I saw my house and my heart sank. I hated my house. I hated coming out here.

I thought of something.

"Daniel," I said urgently.

"What?"

"Mention Gus to my mother and you die."

"As if I would." He looked hurt.

"Good, I'm glad we understand each other."

"You don't think she'll be pleased, then?" asked Daniel archly.

"Shut up."

 36

I saw a curtain twitching in the front room. Mum had the front door open before we even had a chance to ring the bell.

For a moment I felt a little bit ·sad.

Doesn't she have anything better to do? I wondered.

"Welcome," she said gaily, all hospitality and good cheer. "Come in out of the cold night. How are you, Daniel? Aren't you very good to come all this way to visit us? Are you frozen?" she asked, grabbing Daniel's hands. "No, you're not too bad. Take off the coats and come on in, I've just made a pot."

"I didn't know you'd taken up pottery." Daniel smiled at Mum flirtatiously.

"Stop!" She laughed and rolled her eyes at him. "You're a terrible man."

I stuck my fingers down my throat and made gagging noises.

"Stop it," muttered Daniel.

"Why are you being mean to me?" I said in surprise. "You never usually are."

"Because sometimes you're childish and horrible."

That annoyed and upset me, so as we took off our coats in the tiny hall and left them on the bottom of the banisters, I mimicked "childish and horrible" about fifty times in a stupid voice.

Daniel looked at me with raised eyebrows but I knew he was trying not to laugh.

"If you say to me 'that's very mature behavior,' I'll hit you," I warned him.

"That's very mature behavior."

So we had a little skirmish. I tried to hit him but he grabbed my wrists and held them tightly. And then he laughed at me while I pushed and twisted against him, trying to get free. But I couldn't budge, not even an inch, while he looked totally unconcerned and grinned down at me.

I was disturbed by his macho act. In fact, if it had been anyone other than Daniel, it would have been quite erotic.

"You big bully." I knew that would upset him. I was right, he let go immediately. And then, perversely, I felt disappointed.

We went into the warm kitchen where Mum was messing around with cookies and sugar and pints of milk.

Dad was in an armchair, snoring quietly, his hair white and wispy and sticking up from his head. I patted it down tenderly. His glasses were all askew, and with a painful twist in my stomach, I realized that he was starting to look old. Not middle-aged or even elderly, but like a little old man.

"You'll be grand now when you have a nice warm cup inside you," Mum said. "Did you get a new skirt, Lucy?"

"No."

"Where's it from?"

"It's not new."

"I heard you the first time. Where's it from?"

"You won't know it."

"Try me—I'm not the old fuddy-duddy she thinks I am," she said, smiling at Daniel, shoving platefuls of cookies across the table at him.

"Kookai," I said, between gritted teeth.

"What kind of name for a shop is that, at all?" she asked, pretending to laugh.

"I told you you wouldn't know it."

"I don't. And I don't want to know it. What's it made of?" She grabbed the fabric.

"How do I know?" I said, annoyed, trying to pull my skirt back from her claw. "I buy things because I like them, not because of what they're made from."

"I'd say it's only synthetic," she said, rubbing it.

"Stop it."

"And the hem—a child could sew that hem better. What did you say you paid for it?"

"I didn't."

"Well, how much did you pay for it?"

I wanted to say that I wasn't going to tell her, but I knew how childish that would sound.

"I can't remember."

"I'd say you can remember, all right. But you're too ashamed to tell me. Much more than it's worth."

I said nothing.

"You were always hopeless with money, Lucy."

Still I said nothing.

The three of us sat in silence, me sullenly refusing to drink my tea, because she had made it.

She always brought out the worst in me.

Daniel broke the tension by going out into the hall and coming back with the cake he had bought for her.

Naturally she was delighted, and was all over him like a skin disease.

"You're so sweet! There was no need for you to do that. Although it's a sorry state of affairs that my own flesh and blood brings me nothing."

"Oh, it's from the two of us, not just me," said Daniel quickly.

"Kiss-up," I mouthed across the table at him.

"Oh," said Mum. "Well, thanks, Lucy. Except you know I've given up chocolate for Lent."

"But cake isn't chocolate," I said weakly.

"Chocolate cake is chocolate," she said.

"You could freeze it to have after Lent is over," I suggested.

"It'd never keep."

"It would."

"Anyway that would be contrary to the whole spirit of Lent."

"All right then! *Don't* eat it. Daniel and I will."

The offending cake sat in the middle of the table; it had suddenly become something frightening, like a bomb. If I hadn't known better I would have sworn that it was almost pulsating. I knew that it would never be eaten.

"What have you given up for Lent, Lucy?"

"Nothing! I have enough misery in my life," I added cryptically, hoping that she would realize that I was talking about visiting her, "I don't need to give up anything."

·And to my surprise she didn't retaliate. She looked at me, almost . . . *tenderly* . . . for a moment.

"I've made your favorite dinner," she said.

"Have you?" I wasn't even aware that I had a favorite dinner. But just to be mean I said, "Oh great, Mum. I didn't know you could cook Thai."

Mum made a kind of a "let's humor her" face at Daniel. "What's she talking about? Cooking ties? You were always a bit peculiar, Lucy, but just to please you we'll get a few of your father's old ties from upstairs.''

I made a face.

"He won't be needing them," Mum added bitterly. "He hasn't worn a tie since his wedding day.''

"Not so," slurred a voice from the corner. "Didn't I wear a tie to Mattie Burke's funeral?" Dad had opened his eyes and was looking confusedly around the room.

"Dad!" I said, delighted, "you're awake.''

"Oh, the dead arose and appeared to many," called Mum sarcastically as Dad struggled to sit up straight.

"They did not!" said Dad. "That wasn't Mattie Burke, that was Laurence Molloy. Did I ever tell you about that, Lucy? A great couple of days when Laurence Molloy pretended to be dead so we could have a right good oul' wake for ourselves. Except Laurence wasn't too happy when it dawned on him that he had to lie there, stretched out on some hard plank of wood, getting nothing to drink, save the fumes from our breath, so up he jumps out of the coffin and grabs a bottle out of someone's hand. 'Gimme that' he says . . .''

"Shut up, Jamsie," barked my mother. "We have a visitor and I'm sure he doesn't want to hear stories about your misspent youth.''

"I wasn't telling him stories about my misspent youth," grumbled Dad. "Laurence Molloy's wake was only a couple of years ago . . . oh hello, son," he said, spotting Daniel, "I remember you. You used to come around to play with Christopher Patrick. A big, long, lanky article you were then, stand up so I can see if you've got any shorter!''

Daniel stood up awkwardly, amid much scraping of chairs.

"Longer, if anything!" declared Dad, "and I wouldn't have thought it was possible."

Daniel gratefully sat down again.

"Lucy," said Dad, turning his attention to me, "my darling girl, my little sweetheart, I didn't know you were coming. Why didn't you tell me she was coming?" he demanded of my mother.

"I did tell you."

"You did not tell me."

"I did tell you."

"You most certainly did not tell me!"

"I di . . . oh what's the use. I might as well be talking to the wall."

"Lucy," said Dad, "I'll go and smarten myself up a bit and I'll be back before you know it, in two shakes of a lamb's tail."

He shuffled out of the room and I smiled affectionately after him.

"He's looking great," I said.

"Is he?" said Mum coldly.

An awkward little pause followed.

"More tea?" Mum asked Daniel, following the great Irish tradition of filling any conversational gaps by pressing nourishment on people.

"Thanks."

"Another cookie?"

"No thanks."

"A little piece of the cake?"

"No, really, I'd better not. I must leave room for my dinner."

"Go on, you're a growing lad."

"No, honestly."

"Are you certain now?"

"Mum, leave him!" I laughed, remembering what Gus

had said about Irish mothers. "So what *have* you made for our dinner?"

"Fish fingers, beans and chips."

"Er, nice, Mum."

True, it had been my favorite dinner well over half a lifetime ago, until I moved up to London and became acquainted with such exotica as tandoori noodles and Peking duck flavored potato chips.

"Great," grinned Daniel. "I love fish fingers, beans and chips."

He sounded as though he really meant it.

"You'd say that no matter what you were being given, wouldn't you, Dan?" I said. "Even if Mum said 'Oh Daniel, I thought we'd serve up your testicles in a white wine sauce' you'd say 'mmmmh, lovely, Mrs. Sullivan, that sounds delicious.' Wouldn't you?"

I giggled at his horrified expression.

"Lucy," he winced, "you really must be more careful."

"Sorry," I laughed. "I forgot I was talking about your most prized possessions. Where would Daniel Watson be without his genitalia? Your life would be over, wouldn't it?"

"No, Lucy, that's not why. Any man would find that suggestion upsetting, not just me."

My mother had finally found her voice.

"Lucy—Carmel—Sullivan!" she gasped, apoplectic with horror. "*What on earth* are you talking about?"

"Nothing, Mrs. Sullivan," said Daniel hastily. "Nothing at all. Nothing, honestly."

"Nothing, Daniel? Well that's not what Karen says." I winked at him, while Daniel began a frenzied conversation with Mum. How was she? Was she working? What was it like at the dry cleaners?

Mum's head jerked from me to Daniel and back again. She was torn between delight at being the center of Daniel's attention and the suspicion that she was letting me get away with something totally heinous and unforgivable.

But her vanity won. Soon she was regaling Daniel with stories of the spoiled rich bastards whom she had to serve in the dry cleaners, how they wanted everything done yesterday, how they never said thanks, how they parked their cars, "big flashy BMXs or BLTs or whatever they are," so that they blocked the traffic, how critical they were. "In fact only today one of them arrived in—a right young pup— and threw—yes! *threw*—a shirt at me and shoved it in my face and said 'What the hell have you done to this?' Well, Daniel, first and foremost, there was no need to swear at me and I said as much to him and I looked at the shirt and there wasn't a speck on it . . ." and so on and so on.

Daniel had the patience of a saint. I was so glad he had come with me. I simply couldn't have borne it on my own.

". . . and I said, 'It's as white as snow' and he said 'Exactly, it was blue when I brought it in' . . ."

On and on droned my mother. On and on smiled and nodded Daniel sympathetically. It was wonderful, I barely needed to be there, just the occasional nod or "mmm" was all my mother required from me. All her attention was focused on Daniel.

Finally, the dry cleaning saga came to an end.

". . . So he says to me 'See you in court' and I says to him 'See you in court yourself' and he says 'You'll be hearing from my solicitor' and I says 'Well, I hope he can shout good and loud because I'm nearly deaf in one ear.'"

"And how are you, Daniel?" asked Mum finally.

"Fine, Mrs. Sullivan, thanks."

"He's better than fine, aren't you, Daniel? Tell Mum about your new girlfriend."

I was delighted. I *knew* that that would upset her. She still held out hopes that I might somehow get Daniel to fall for me.

"Stop, Lucy," muttered Daniel, looking embarrassed.

"Oh, don't be shy, Daniel." I knew I was being annoying but I was enjoying it tremendously.

"Anyone we know?" asked Mum, hopefully.

"Yes," I said happily.

"Oh?" She was trying, rather badly, to hide her excitement.

"Yes, it's my roommate Karen."

"Karen?"

"Yes."

"The Scottish one?"

"Yes. And they're mad about each other. Isn't it great? Well, isn't it?" I asked again, when she didn't answer.

"I always thought she was a bit unladylike . . ." said Mum and then clapped her hand over her mouth in pretend horror. "Oh, Daniel, can you believe I just said that? I'm so sorry. Sacred Heart of Jesus, how could I be so tactless? Would you ever please forget I said anything, Daniel—it was a long time ago when I saw her."

"Consider it forgotten," said Daniel, smiling slightly. He was so *good*.

"Bad and all as Lucy is," my mother said, in a pretend vague fashion, as if she was just talking to herself, "at least you'd never catch her going out with her bosom on display."

"That's because I haven't *got* a bosom to have on display. If I had you can be bloody sure that I'd display it."

"Language, Lucy," she said, hitting me on the arm.

"Language?" I sputtered. "You think *that's* language. I could show you language . . ."

I stopped and inwardly cursed Daniel for being there. I

couldn't fight with her properly while we had a visitor. Not that Daniel counted as a visitor, as such, but all the same.

"Excuse me a moment," I said and left the room. I got the bottle of whiskey from my bag in the hall and went upstairs. I wanted to talk to Dad alone.

 37

Dad was in his bedroom, sitting on the bed, putting on his shoes.

"Lucy," he said. "I was just on my way back down to you."

"Let's just stay here a minute," I said, hugging him.

"Grand," he said. "We'll have a little chat all on our own."

I gave him the bottle of whiskey and he hugged me again. "You're very, very good to me, Lucy," he said.

"How are you, Dad?" I asked, tears in my eyes.

"Grand, Lucy, grand. Why the tears?"

"I hate to think of you stuck here, all on your own, with . . . with *her*," I said, nodding toward downstairs.

"But I'm fine, Lucy, so I am," he protested, laughing. She's not the worst. We get along together all right."

"I know you're only saying that so I won't worry about you," I sniffed, "but thanks."

"Oh, Lucy, Lucy, Lucy," he said, squeezing my hand, "you mustn't take it all so seriously. Try and enjoy yourself, because we'll be dead soon enough."

"Oh no," I wailed and then I *really* started to cry.

"Don't talk about dying. I don't want you to die. Promise me you won't die!"

"Er . . . well . . . if it makes you happy, I won't die, Lucy."

"And if you have to die, promise me that we can die at the same time."

"I promise."

"Oh, Dad, isn't it awful?"

"What, love?"

"Everything. Being alive, loving people, being afraid that they'll die."

"Is it?"

"Yes, of course it is."

"Where did you ever get such terrible notions from, Lucy?"

"But . . . but . . . from *you*, Dad."

Dad hugged me awkwardly and said that I must have misheard him, that surely he never said anything of the sort and that I was young and had a life to live and that I should try and enjoy it.

"But why, Dad?" I asked. "You never tried to enjoy your life."

"Lucy," he sighed, "it was different for me. It *is* different for me—I'm an old man now. You're a young woman. Young, beautiful, educated—never forget the benefits of an education, Lucy," he insisted fiercely.

"I won't."

"Promise me."

"I promise."

"You have all these things going for you; you should be happy."

"How can I be?" I pleaded. "And how can you expect me to be? We're the same, Dad, you and I. We can't help seeing the futility, the waste, the darkness."

"What is it, Lucy?" Dad searched my face for some sort of clue. "Is it a fella, is it? Some youngster is after leading you up the garden path? Is that what it is?"

"No, Dad," I laughed even though I was still crying.

"It's not that lanky one in the kitchen, is it?"

"Wha . . . oh Daniel? No."

"He didn't, er, you know . . . take liberties with you, Lucy, did he? Because if he did, so help me God, as long as there's breath in my body, I'll get your two brothers to knock him into the middle of next week. A kick in the arse and a map of the world, that's what that fella needs and that's what that fella will get. He's a bigger fool than he looks if he thinks he can interfere with the daughter of Jamsie Sullivan and live to tell the tale . . ."

"Dad," I wailed. "Daniel hasn't done anything."

"I've seen the way he looks at you," Dad said darkly.

"He doesn't look at me *any* way. You're imagining things."

"Am I? Sure, maybe I am. It wouldn't be the first time, I suppose."

"Dad, this isn't about a fella *at all*."

"But then why are you so lonesome?"

"Because I just am, Dad. The same way as you are."

"But I'm fine, Lucy, honest to God so I am. Never better."

"Thanks, Dad," I sighed, leaning against him. "I know you're only saying it to make me feel better, but I appreciate it all the same."

"But . . . ," he said, looking a bit bewildered. He looked like he was searching for something to say, but couldn't think of anything. "Come on," he said eventually, "till we go down for our chips."

Down we went.

The evening was rather grim, what with my mother and

I at loggerheads and Dad staring suspiciously at Daniel, convinced that he had improper intentions toward me.

Our spirits lifted slightly when dinner was banged down in front of us.

"A rhapsody in orange," declared Dad, looking at his plate. "That's what it is. Orange fish fingers, orange beans and orange chips and, to wash it all down, a glass of the finest Irish malt, which as luck would have it, also happens to be orange!"

"The chips aren't orange," said Mum. "And have you offered Daniel a drink?"

"They are *so* orange," protested Dad hotly. "And no I haven't."

"Daniel, would you like a drink?" asked Mum, standing up.

"Well, if they're not orange, what color would you say they are?" demanded Dad of the table in general. "Pink? Green?"

"No thanks, Mrs. Sullivan," said Daniel nervously. "I wouldn't like a drink."

"You're not getting one," said Dad belligerently. "Unless you say the chips are orange."

Mum and Dad stared at Daniel, both willing him to be on their side.

"They're more a kind of a golden color," he finally suggested, ever the diplomat.

"They're orange!"

"Golden," said Mum.

Daniel said nothing. He just looked embarrassed.

"All right then." Dad roared and slammed his hand down on the table, causing all the plates and cutlery to jump and rattle. "You drive a hard bargain. Goldeny orange, and that's my final offer. Take it or leave it. But you can't say I'm not a fair man. Give him a drink."

After that, Dad cheered up again in no time. The dinner worked wonders on his lugubrious mood.

"There's only one thing to beat a fish finger," he said, delightedly, smiling around the table. "And that's six more of them."

"Look at that," he said admiringly, lifting the entire fish finger up onto his fork and twiddling it around so that he could view it from all angles. "Beautiful. That's craftsmanship, you know. You'd need a university schooling to know how to make one of these lads properly."

"Jamsie, stop making an exhibition piece of your dinner," Mum said, ruining the fun.

"I'd like to meet this Captain Birds Eye character and shake him by the hand and congratulate him on a job well done," declared Dad, ignoring her. "So I would. Maybe they'll have him on *This Is Your Life.* What do you think, Lucy?"

"I don't think he's a real person, Dad," I giggled.

"Not real?" asked Dad. "But I've seen him on the TV. Big white whiskers on his face and he lives on a ship."

"But . . ."

I wasn't sure whether Dad was joking or not. I thought he was—I certainly hoped he was.

"He should be given the Nobel prize, so he should," declared Dad.

"The Nobel prize for what?" asked Mum, sarcastically.

"The Nobel prize for fish fingers, of course," said Dad, sounding surprised. "What kind of Nobel prize did you think I meant, Connie? The prize for literature? Sure, that wouldn't make any sense at all!"

Then Mum gave a little laugh and the two of them looked at each other in a funny way.

After the dinner plates were cleared away, Dad retreated

to his armchair in the corner while Daniel, Mum and I stayed at the kitchen table and drank oceans of tea.

"I suppose we'd better go," I said idly, at about half past ten. I had spent the previous half hour trying to pluck up the courage to make the suggestion. I knew it wouldn't go down too well with my mother.

"Already?" she shrieked. "But you just got here."

"It's late, Mum, and it'll be later still by the time I get home. I need my sleep."

"I don't know what's wrong with you at all, Lucy. When I was your age I could stay up dancing until the sun rose."

"Iron supplements, Lucy," shouted Dad from the corner. "That's what you need. Or what's that other thing all the youngsters take to give them energy?"

"I don't know, Dad. Caffeine?"

"No," he muttered. "It had a different name."

"We really must go. Mustn't we, Daniel?" I said firmly.

"Er, yes."

"Cocaine! That's what it is," shouted Dad, delighted that he had remembered. "Go down to the Medical Hall and get yourself a dose of cocaine and you'll be leaping around the place in no time."

"I don't think so, Dad," I giggled.

"Why not?" he demanded. "Or is cocaine one of those illegal ones?"

"Yes, Dad."

"That's a bloody outrage," he declared. "Them legislators go and ruin everything on us, with their taxes and 'this is illegal,' 'that is illegal.' What harm would a drop of cocaine do you now and then? They've no bit of fun in them, at all, so they haven't."

"Yes, Dad."

"Why don't you stay the night, Lucy?" suggested Mum. "The bed is made up in your old room."

I was filled with horror at the idea. Stay under her roof? Feel like I was trapped here again? Like I'd never escaped?

"Er, no, Mum, Daniel has to get home so I may as well go back up to town with him . . ."

"But Daniel can stay, too," said Mum excitedly. "He can stay in the boys' old room."

"Thanks very much, Mrs. Sullivan . . ."

"Connie," she said, leaning across the table and placing her hand on his sleeve. "Call me Connie, it seems a bit silly for you to call me 'Mrs. Sullivan' now that you're all grown up."

Good god! She was acting, as though . . . as though, she was *flirting* with him. I could have thrown up.

"Thanks very much, *Connie*," repeated Daniel, "but I'd really better get back. I've got a very early meeting in the morning . . ."

"Well if you're sure. Far be it from me to interrupt the wheels of industry. But you'll come and see us again soon?"

"Certainly, I'd love to."

"And maybe you'll both stay the next time?"

"Oh, I'm invited too, am I?" I asked.

"Lucy," tisked Mum. "You don't need an invitation. How do you put up with her?" she asked Daniel. "She's very touchy."

"She's not too bad," mumbled Daniel. His innate politeness made him want to agree with Mum, his innate sense of survival reminded him that he would be foolhardy to annoy me.

It must be hard being Daniel, I thought, and feeling like you had to try and please everyone all of the time. Being charming and amenable twenty-four hours a day must take it out of a body.

"You could have fooled me," said Mum sharply.

"Er, can we call for a taxi?" asked Daniel, eager to change the subject.

"What's wrong with getting the tube?" I asked.

"It's late."

"So?"

"It's wet."

"So?"

"I'll pay."

"Fine."

"There's a cab company down the road," said Mum. "If you're that eager to get going, I'll give them a call."

My heart sank. The cab company down the road was staffed by an ever-changing assortment of Afghani refugees, Indonesian asylum seekers and exiled Algerians, none of whom could speak a word of English and who, to judge by their sense of direction, had just arrived in Europe. I had every sympathy with their various causes, but I wanted to get home without having to go via Oslo.

Mum called them.

"Fifteen minutes," she said.

We sat around the table and waited. The atmosphere was awkward, as we tried to pretend that our ears weren't straining to hear the sound of a car's brakes outside the front door. None of us spoke. I certainly couldn't think of anything lighthearted to say that might dispel the tension.

Mum sighed and said stupid things like "well." She was the only person I knew who could say "well" and "another cup of tea?" bitterly.

After what seemed like ten hours I thought I heard a car outside the house so I ran out to have a look.

Sure enough, an ancient filthy Ford Escort had pulled

up, and even through the gloom I could see that it was covered in rust.

"Here's our cab," I said. I grabbed my coat, hugged Dad and hopped into the car.

"Hello, I'm Lucy," I said to the driver. As we would be spending a lot of time together, I thought we might as well be on first-name terms.

"Hassan," he smiled.

"Can we first go to Ladbroke Grove?" I asked.

"Not much English," said Hassan apologetically.

"Oh."

"*Parlez-vous français?*" he asked.

"*Un peu,*" I replied. "And do you *parlez* any *français?*" I asked Daniel as he got into the car.

"*Un peu,*" he replied.

"Daniel, this is Hassan. Hassan, Daniel."

They shook hands and Daniel patiently tried to negotiate directions.

"*Savez-vous* the Westway?"

"Er . . ."

"Well, *savez-vous* the center of London?"

A blank look.

"Have you *heard* of London?" Daniel asked gently.

"Ah, yes, London." Understanding dawned on Hassan's face.

"*Bien!*" said Daniel, pleased.

"It is the capital city of the United Kingdom."

"That's the one."

"It has a population of . . ." Hassan went on.

"Can you take us there, please?" asked Daniel. He had begun to sound anxious. "I'll give you directions. And lots of money."

And off we went, Daniel occasionally shouting "*A droit,*" or "*A gauche.*"

"Thank God that's over," I sighed, as we drove away, Mum waving down the darkened road after us.

"I thought it was a nice evening," said Daniel.

"Don't be ridiculous," I said scornfully.

"I *did.*"

"How could you? With that . . . that . . . mean old woman there?"

"I presume you're talking about your mother. And I don't think she's mean."

"Daniel! She never misses a chance to put me down."

"And you never miss a chance to rile her up."

"What? How dare you? I am such a good and dutiful daughter and I let her get away with so many insults."

"Lucy," Daniel laughed. "You don't. You wind her up and you say things to deliberately upset her."

"I really don't know what you're talking about. And anyway, it's none of your business."

"Fine."

"And isn't she *boring?*" I continued almost immediately. "Going on and on about the bloody dry cleaners. What do we care about it?"

"But . . ."

"What?"

"I don't know . . . I think she's lonely. She must not have anyone to talk to . . ."

"If she's lonely, it's her own fault."

". . . stuck in that house with only your dad to talk to. Does she ever get out? Apart from going to work?"

"I don't know. I don't think so. And most important, I don't care."

"There's an awful lot of fun in her, you know?"

"I don't know."

"No, really, Lucy, there is. She's still a youngish woman."

"She's an old hag."

"You're unbelievable!" said Daniel. "You are *so* un-reasonable. She's not an old hag. She's very pretty. You look a lot like her."

"Daniel," I hissed, "that is the worst thing you've ever said to me. It's the worst thing anyone has ever said to me."

He just laughed.

"You're crazy."

"It was lovely to see Dad, though."

"Yes, he was quite nice to me," said Daniel.

"He's always nice."

"The last time I met him he wasn't."

"Wasn't he?"

"No. He called me an English bastard and accused me of stealing Ireland and oppressing him for seven hundred years."

"He didn't mean you personally," I said soothingly. "You were just a symbol to him."

"It still wasn't nice," said Daniel stiffly. "I've never stolen anything in my life."

"Never?"

"Never."

"Not even when you were a little boy?"

"Er, no."

"Are you sure?"

"Yes."

"*Really* sure?"

"Well, *fairly* sure."

"Not even candy from a shop?"

"No."

"Sorry, I didn't catch that?"

"*No!*"

"There's no need to shout."

"All right then! Yes! I suppose you're thinking about that time in Woolworth's when Chris and I stole those knives and forks."

"Er . . ."

This was all news to me, but Daniel was racing ahead.

"You never let me get away with anything, do you?" he demanded angrily. "You just ferret everything out of me. I can't have any secrets from you . . ."

"Why knives and forks," I interrupted, puzzled.

"Why not?"

"But . . . what did you want with them? Why did you steal them?"

"Because we could."

"I don't understand."

"Because we could. We took them *because* we *could.* Not because we wanted them," he explained to me. "The prize wasn't what we acquired, it was the acquiring itself. The act of acquisition was the important part.

"Oh."

"Do you understand?"

"Yes, I think so. And what did you do with them?"

"I gave them to my mother for her birthday."

"You mean pig!"

"But I got her something else also," he said hurriedly. "An egg timer. No, no, I *paid* for the egg timer. Don't look at me like that, Lucy!"

"It's not because I thought you stole the egg timer. It's because it's an egg timer at all! What kind of present is that for a woman?"

"I was young, Lucy. Too young to know better."

"What age were you? Twenty-seven?"

"No," he laughed. "I was about six."

"You haven't changed much, have you, Daniel?"

"How do you mean? That I still steal cutlery from Woolworth's to give to my mother for her birthday?"

"No."

"How then?"

"By taking things just because you can."

"I don't know what you're talking about?" he said huffily.

"Oh yes, you do," I sang, happily.

"I don't."

"You do. Am I annoying you?"

"Yes."

"I'm talking about women, Daniel. Women and you, Daniel. You and women, Daniel."

"I thought you might be," he said, trying to hide a little smile.

"The way you take them just because you can."

"I don't."

"Yes, you do."

"Lucy, I bloody well *don't.*"

"Well, what about Karen?"

"What about her?"

"How much do you like her? Or are you just amusing yourself with her?"

"I really like her," he said earnestly. "Lucy, I do. She's smart and great company and pretty."

"Honestly?" I asked sternly.

"Honestly."

"Are you serious about her?"

"Yes."

"God."

A little pause.

"Er, are you, you know . . . *in love* with her?" I asked cautiously.

"Lucy, I haven't known her long enough to be in love with her."

"Fine."

"But I'm trying to be."

"I see."

Another peculiar little pause.

I really couldn't think of one thing to say. And that had never happened with me and Daniel before.

"Dad was quiet tonight," I said eventually. "Very well behaved."

"Yes, he didn't even sing anything."

"Sing?"

"He usually treats me to several rousing choruses of 'Carrickfergus' or 'Four Green Fields' and makes me sing along with him."

I had an uncomfortable feeling that Daniel was laughing at Dad, but I didn't want to find out for certain, so I said nothing.

A long time later we arrived at my apartment.

"Thanks for coming with me," I said to Daniel.

"Don't be silly. I enjoyed it."

"Well, er, good night."

"Good night, Lucy."

"I'll see you soon. You'll probably be around to see Karen."

"Probably." He smiled.

I felt an unexpected rush of annoyance, the childish feeling of "He's supposed to be *my friend*."

"Bye," I said shortly, turning to get out of the car.

"Lucy," said Daniel.

There was something unusual, something new in his tone, *urgency* perhaps, that made me turn and look at him.

"What?" I asked.

"Nothing . . . just . . . good night."

"Yes, good night," I said, trying to sound exasperated. But I didn't get out of the car. There was a funny tension that told me I was waiting for something, but I didn't know what it was.

We must be having a fight, I decided, one of the silent but deadly types.

"Lucy," said Daniel, again in that funny, urgent voice.

But I didn't say anything, I didn't sigh and demand "what?" like I usually would have.

I just looked up at him and, for the first time in my whole life, I felt *shy* with Daniel. I didn't want to look at him, but I couldn't stop myself.

He put his hand up and touched my face and I watched him, like a rabbit caught in a car's headlights. What the hell was he doing?

He gently pushed my hair back out of my eyes while I sat rigid, staring at him.

Then I came to life again.

"Good night," I yelled cheerfully, gathering my bag and moving toward the car door. "Thanks for the lift. See you soon."

"Oh, and *bonsoir*," I called to Hassan. "*Bon chance* with the Home Office."

"*Salut*," he called back.

I ran toward the house and put my key in the door. My hands shook. I couldn't get inside fast enough. I just wanted to get to my room and be safe. I felt really scared. What was the sudden tension between Daniel and me? There were so few people that I felt comfortable with, so few people that I considered to be friends. I couldn't bear it if things went wrong with Daniel.

But something *was* wrong, things had taken a turn for the very weird. Maybe he was mad at me for being mean about his girlfriends. Maybe he'd fallen in love with Karen and was feeling all protective about her.

Maybe he wouldn't need me anymore if he had fallen in love and found a soul mate—because that was what happened sometimes. How many friendships end when one of the parties fell in love? Hundreds, probably. I shouldn't be surprised if it happened with Daniel and me.

Anyway, I had Gus. I had other friends. I would be fine.

 38

It was about six weeks later, on a Sunday night, *late* on Sunday night.

We had been back from the Cash'n'Curry for a while, Gus had left about an hour before. Karen, Charlotte and I were limply draped over various pieces of the living-room furniture, eating potato chips, watching TV and recuperating from the weekend. Karen suddenly sat up straight, looking as though she had come to a major decision.

"I'm having a dinner party on Friday," she declared, "and you two and Simon and Gus are invited."

"Gosh, thanks, Karen," I said, nervously.

I had known she was plotting something. She'd been staring at the fire for the last half hour with a funny, determined look on her face.

"Is Daniel coming?" asked Charlotte, naïve to a fault.

Of course Daniel was coming. Daniel was the reason that Karen was *having* it.

"Of course Daniel is coming," said Karen. "Daniel is the bloody reason I'm *having* it."

"I see," nodded Charlotte.

I saw too.

Karen was going to cook a very elaborate, multicourse dinner, serve it stylishly, graciously and without spilling anything on her dress or getting a red, shiny face. She would look beautiful, be witty and entertaining company, all in an attempt to show Daniel how indispensable she was to him.

"We'll have a lovely dinner," she said. "And you'll all have to dress up."

"That sounds like fun," said Charlotte. "I can wear my cowgirl outfit."

"Not that kind of dressing up," said Karen in alarm. "I mean glamorous dressing up, nice dresses, jewelry, high heels."

"I'm not sure if Gus has a nice dress," I said.

"Ha, ha," said Karen, unamused. "Very funny. But make sure he turns up in something decent and not in his usual Salvation Army rejects.

"And now," continued Karen, "I'll need, let's say . . . ooh . . . thirty pounds from each of you now and we'll sort out the final sum later."

"Wha-at?" I asked, flooded with alarm.

I hadn't been expecting that. Neither had Charlotte, judging by the way her jaw had fallen open.

Oh no! I had partied hard with Gus all weekend and I felt far too fragile to have a "discussion" with Karen.

"Yes," she said, annoyed. "You don't expect me to pay for all the food, do you? I'm masterminding the whole thing and I'm doing all the cooking."

"Oh, well, fair enough," said Charlotte, trying to sound cheerful and giving me a "let's try and look on the bright side of this" look. "We can't expect her to feed us and our boyfriends out of the goodness of her heart."

How right she was.

"Good, that's settled," said Karen firmly. "And I'll need the money now, if you don't mind."

There was a stricken pause.

"Now," repeated Karen.

There was a half-hearted reach for purses, followed by half-hearted excuses.

"I don't think I have it just now."

"Can I give you a check?"

"Will tomorrow evening be okay?"

"Honestly, Karen," I said, "how can you possibly expect us to have any money left on a Sunday night? Especially after the weekend we've just had. And for that matter, *why* do you need it now? I don't think the grocery store is open at ten-thirty on Sunday night."

"Not for tonight, stupid. For tomorrow. I'll do the shopping on the way home from work tomorrow, so I need the money now."

"Oh."

"We'll all walk down to the cash machine now," said Karen in a voice that brooked no argument.

Charlotte attempted a brave protest, but she was doomed to failure.

"But it's raining and it's Sunday night and I'm in my nightgown . . ."

"You don't have to get dressed," said Karen kindly.

"Thanks," sighed Charlotte.

"Just put a coat on over your nightgown," continued Karen. "And a pair of leggings and boots, and you'll be fine. It's dark, no one will see."

"Okay," said Charlotte, meekly.

"And both of you don't have to go," continued Karen.

"Lucy, give your card to Charlotte and tell her your PIN number."

"You mean you're not coming?" I said faintly.

"Lucy, *honestly* at times you can be so dumb. Why would I need to go?"

"But, I thought . . ."

"You *didn't* think, that's your problem. Anyway, Charlotte is going, there's no need for you to go."

I didn't bother getting annoyed with her. One of the features of successful apartment sharing is the ability to let other people act completely horrible from time to time. So that when you feel like behaving like an antichrist, they'll return the favor.

"I can't let Charlotte go alone," I said.

"You're damn right. Charlotte isn't going alone," called Charlotte from her bedroom.

Karen shrugged. "If you're going to be noble about it . . ."

I put on my coat over my pajamas and tucked my pajama bottoms into my boots.

"My umbrella's in the hall," sang Karen.

"You can stick your umbrella where the sun doesn't shine," I said from the safety of the far side of the closed front door.

Of course, another feature of successful apartment sharing is recognizing an opportunity to let off steam.

Charlotte and I battled through the rain to the bank.

"Bitch!" said Charlotte.

"She's not a bitch," I said grimly.

"Isn't she?" asked Charlotte, sounding surprised.

"No! She's a *fucking* bitch," I corrected.

Charlotte stamped along through the puddles. "Bitch, bitch, bitch, bitch, bitch, bitch, bitch, bitch, *bitch!*" she shouted.

A man out walking his dog crossed the road when he saw this pair of foul-mouthed lunatics, marching along, the frills of Charlotte's pink nightgown flouncing wildly beneath her coat with each stride she took, the legs of my powder-blue pajamas flapping in the wind.

"I hope she gets the clap from Daniel," I said. "Or herpes, or genital warts or something really horrible."

"Or crabs," agreed Charlotte, viciously. "And I hope she gets pregnant. And the next time Daniel is over, I'm going to walk around the apartment with no clothes on, so that he can see that I've got bigger tits than her. She'd hate that, the bossy old bitch."

"Do!" I said fervently. "In fact, you should try to seduce him."

"Yes," she agreed, enthusiastically. "I'd love to."

"In fact, you should try and have sex with him in her bed, if you could possibly manage it," I suggested with malicious pleasure.

"Great idea!" squealed Charlotte.

"And then tell her that he said that she was no good in bed and that you were much better."

"I don't know, though," said Charlotte doubtfully. "It might not be that easy, you know, he seems to really like her. Why don't *you* try?"

"Me?"

"Yes, you'd have a better chance," she said. "I think Daniel has a soft spot for you."

"Maybe he does," I said gloomily. "But this is sex we're talking about, Charlotte. It's no good if Daniel's spot for me is soft."

We both laughed and felt better. Except that it made me think of Daniel—Daniel, who was barely speaking to me. Or maybe I was barely speaking to Daniel. Something odd was going on, at any rate.

We got the money and returned home, wet and resentful, and handed it over to Karen in surly fashion.

"So where can I stick my umbrella?" she asked archly, from her supine position on the couch.

I reddened with embarrassment. But when I looked at her she was grinning.

I laughed, the tension dispelled.

"I'm going to bed. Good night," I said.

"Good night," called Karen to my back. "Oh and, Lucy, I'll need you and Charlotte to be here on Thursday night for the cleaning and the preparations."

I paused in the doorway and realized that another feature of successful apartment sharing is the ability to imagine your roommate being beaten on the head with a stick.

"Okay," I mumbled, without turning around.

I spent the night fantasizing about putting all Karen's clothes in black trash bags and leaving them out for the garbage men.

On Thursday night, the Night of the Long Preparations, I thought I had died and gone to hell.

Karen had decided to prepare most of the food the night before, so that on the actual night of the dinner she would have very little to do, other than look beautiful and cool and calm and in control.

Except that Karen was so nervous and so determined to impress Daniel that she seemed to be more—how would I put it?—difficult, than usual. She had always been dynamic and strong-willed, but there was a fine line between being dynamic and strong-willed and being a bossy bitch. Karen seemed to have successfully made that leap.

She had decided that Charlotte and I would do the actual hands-on preparation and she, herself, would be more in the role of an Artistic Director, overseeing us, advising, guiding and managing us.

In other words, if there were potatoes to be peeled, she had no intention of doing them.

Charlotte and I were barely in the door from work before she set about organizing us.

"You," she shouted at Charlotte, pointing a pen and reading from a list, "are on carrot, pepper, zucchini, and eggplant preparation; coriander and lemongrass soup; and asparagus soufflé duty."

"And you," she shouted at me, "are on duchesse potato, kiwi fruit purée, cranberry jelly, whipped cream, stuffing mushroom and Viennese cookie duty."

Charlotte and I were terrified. We had barely heard of most of these things, let alone knew how to cook them. Charlotte's culinary specialty was toast, mine was pasta, and anytime we tried to make anything more complicated than that, we ended in tears and fights and recriminations. Outside incineration, inner rawness, raised voices, hurt feelings, spillages and slippages. You can't make an omelet without breaking legs—or at least *I* had certainly never managed it.

That evening the kitchen was a scene from Dante's Inferno. The circle where sinners were tormented with fruit and vegetables. All four rings and the oven were in constant use, steam billowing, lids rattling and hopping, water boiling over. There were mounds of grapes, asparagus, cauliflower, potatoes, carrots and kiwi fruit everywhere. The heat was intense and Charlotte and I were the color of tomatoes. Karen wasn't.

There was no room for anything, because Karen had made us move the kitchen table into the living room.

"Just put them down over there. No, no, not on the meringue base, for Christ's sake!" she screeched, when I had to empty the fridge of its normal contents to make room for the twenty or thirty desserts she seemed to be expecting us to make.

Everywhere there was food. On the top of the fridge, on the draining board, most of the floor was covered in bowls of pork that was marinating and gelatin that was setting and garlic bread that was wrapped in tinfoil. I was afraid to move my foot half an inch in case I ended up ankle-deep in olive oil, red wine, juniper, vanilla, cumin and "Karen's secret ingredient" marinade. And as far as I could see Karen's secret ingredient was nothing other than ordinary brown sugar. I was itching to slap her.

I peeled fourteen million potatoes. I sliced seventeen thousand kiwi fruit. Then I chopped them. And then I had to shove them through a sieve—whatever that was all about. I skinned my knuckles carrying the kitchen table down the hall. I cut my thumb when I sliced the fruit. Chili got into the cut. Karen said I should be more careful, that she didn't want blood in the food.

Every so often she came around and "jokingly inspected" what we were doing and, even though I knew it was ridiculous, I felt nervous. She was like a sergeant-major examining the young soldiers on parade.

"No, no, no," she said, and to my disbelief, she rapped me on the knuckles with a wooden spoon! "That's not the way to peel potatoes. You're taking half the potato off with the skin. It's wasteful, Lucy."

"Fuck off with the wooden spoon," I said angrily, wishing my peeler was a knife.

The bossy bitch had gone too far and the wooden spoon had hurt.

"Oooooh, we *are* grouchy this evening," she laughed. "You'll have to learn how to accept constructive criticism, Lucy. You'll never succeed with that attitude."

I could taste fury in my mouth. But I was trying—I had to understand that she was crazy about a man. Even if he was Daniel. It wasn't my place to judge.

"And what on earth is this?" she demanded. She had moved on to where Charlotte was peeling carrots, and held up a carrot from the "done" pile.

"It's a carrot," said Charlotte. Surly. Defensive.

"What kind of a carrot?" asked Karen slowly and meaningfully.

"A peeled carrot."

"A *peeled* carrot!" said Karen in triumph. "A *peeled* carrot, she tells me. Might I just ask you, Lucy Sullivan, does this carrot look peeled to you?"

"Yes," I said loyally.

"Oh no, it does not! If this is a peeled carrot it's a very badly peeled one. Start again, Charlotte, and get it right this time."

"Knock it off, Karen," I blurted out, too angry to care. "We're doing you a favor."

"Excuse me?" said Karen archly. "But run that one by me again—*you're* doing *me* a favor? I think not, Lucy. But, by all means stop if you want, just don't expect a place set at the table for Gus and yourself tomorrow night."

That shut me up.

Gus had been very excited when I had told him about the dinner, especially the dressing up part. He'd be bitterly disappointed if he couldn't come. So I swallowed my rage. Another installment on my road to ulcerdom.

"I'm having a glass of wine," I said, angrily, reaching for one of the bottles that were in the fridge. "How about you, Charlotte?"

"No, you are not!" declared Karen. They're for tomorrow ni— Oh go ahead. I'll have one while you're at it."

On and on into the night we worked, peeling, scraping, slicing, grating, stuffing, whipping, piping, baking.

We did so much work that Karen was almost grateful, but only for about two seconds.

"Thanks, both of you," she said, bending down to take something out of the oven.

"Sorry?" I asked, so tired that I thought I was hearing things.

"I said 'thanks,' " she said. "You're both very goo . . . Oh Christ! Move, move," she yelled, kicking me out of the way, throwing down a tray of what must have been the Viennese cookies, sending them skittering into the bowl of ratatouille. "I'm burned to a crisp!" she gasped. "These bloody oven gloves are useless."

I finally got to bed at about two o'clock, my hands raw and cut, stinking of garlic and Drambuie. My prize nail, that I'd nurtured since it was tiny, was snagged and broken.

 39

It was a good thing I got a seat on the tube the next morning, because I was so tired that I would have lain down on the floor otherwise. Charlotte and I spent our journey wearily discussing how much of a stupid bitch we thought Karen was.

"I mean, who does she think she is?" asked Charlotte, yawning.

"Exactly!" I yawned back, slumped in my seat. I noticed that my shoes were filthy and scuffed and that made me feel depressed. I sat up straight so that I wouldn't see them, but then I had to look at the horrible man in a suit, sitting opposite me, who had his eyes trained on Charlotte's breasts, his eyes glazing with lust every time she yawned and her chest expanded. I wanted to hit him, to batter him around the head and neck with his *Daily Mail*.

I thought I had better close my eyes for the rest of the journey, it was safer.

"And it won't last with Karen and Daniel," declared Charlotte, uncertainly. "He'll get sick of her."

"Ummm," I agreed, opening my eyes for a moment. I clamped them shut again, but not before I had seen an ad on the wall asking for donations for animals that had been mistreated, and a heart-rending picture of a skinny, miserable-looking dog.

It was almost a relief to get to work, where I had to endure taunts from Meredia and Megan who insisted that I'd been out drinking the night before.

"I *haven't*," I protested feebly.

"Course you have," snorted Megan. "Just look at you."

The moment I put my key in the door on Friday evening, Karen was in the hall. She had taken Friday afternoon off work so that she could get her hair done and clean the apartment. She immediately set about organizing me.

"Wash yourself and get dressed *now*, Lucy. I need to run through the arrangements with you."

In fairness to her, the place looked beautiful.

There were fresh flowers everywhere. She had laid a crisp white tablecloth on the nasty Formica kitchen table and placed an exquisite candelabra, with eight red candles, in the middle of it.

"I didn't know we had that candelabra," I said, thinking how nice it would look in my bedroom.

"We don't," she said shortly. "I borrowed it."

While I was in the bathroom she hammered on the door and shouted, "I've put clean towels on the rail, don't even *think* of using them."

It was eight o'clock. The three of us were ready.

The table was laid, the candles were lit, the lights turned down low, the white wine was in the fridge, the red wine was opened and ready in the kitchen, and pots and pans and containers of food stood on the stove, poised.

Karen switched on the stereo and strange noises came from it.

"What's that?" demanded Charlotte in shock.

"Jazz." Karen sounded slightly embarrassed.

"Jazz?" snorted Charlotte derisively. "But we hate jazz. Don't we, Lucy?"

"Yes." I was happy to confirm.

"What do we call people who like jazz, Lucy?" asked Charlotte.

"Goateed, beatnik art students?" I suggested.

"That's it," she said in glee. "Guys who wear black French polos and ski pants."

"Maybe, but we like **jazz now**," said Karen firmly.

"You mean, Daniel does," muttered Charlotte.

Karen looked exquisite—or ridiculous, depending on your point of view. She wore a pale green, off-the-shoulder, Grecian type of dress. Her hair was up, but lots of it was falling down in little curls and tendrils. She shone; she looked so much more glamorous and soignée than Charlotte or I. I was wearing my gold dress, the one I had worn the night I had met Gus, because it was the only dressy-up dress I had, but it looked tatty and bedraggled compared to Karen's splendor.

Charlotte, to be frank, looked a bit of a mess, even worse than me. She wore the only formal dress that she had, the one she had worn when she was her sister's bridesmaid, a huge red taffeta meringue. I think she must have put on some weight since the wedding, because her chest fairly exploded from the strapless bodice. Karen looked very doubtful when Charlotte rustled out from her bedroom, said, "Da, daaah!" and did a little pirouette. She probably wished she had allowed Charlotte to wear her cowgirl outfit after all.

Karen had given frantic instructions. "Now when they arrive, I'll keep them talking in the front room, Lucy, you turn on the oven at a very low heat to warm the potatoes and Charlotte, you stir the . . ."

She paused suddenly, a horrified look on her face.

"The bread, the bread, the bread," shrieked Karen. "I forgot to buy the bread. Everything's ruined! Totally ruined. They'll all have to go home."

"Karen, calm down. It's on the table," said Charlotte.

"Oh. Oh. Oh, thank God. Is it really?" She sounded close to tears. Charlotte and I exchanged long-suffering looks.

Karen was quiet for a moment, then she looked at the clock.

"Where the fuck are they?" she demanded, lighting a cigarette. Her hand shook.

"Give them a chance," I said soothingly. "It's just eight."

"I said eight o'clock on the dot," said Karen aggressively.

"But no one takes that seriously," I murmured. "It's considered bad manners to arrive on time."

It was on the tip of my tongue to remind her that it was only a dinner party and that the guest of honor was just Daniel, but I stopped myself in time. Waves of aggression came from her.

We sat in tense silence.

"No one's coming," said Karen tearfully, gulping back a glass of wine. "We may as well throw it all out. Come on, let's go to the kitchen and fling it all in the garbage."

She banged her glass down on the table and stood up.

"Well, come on," she ordered.

"No!" said Charlotte. "Why should we throw it out? After all the trouble we've gone to? We can eat it ourselves and we'll freeze what we don't eat."

"Oh, I see," said Karen, nastily. "We can eat it ourselves, can we? What makes you so certain that no one's coming? What do you know that I don't?"

"Nothing," declared Charlotte in exasperation. "But you said . . ."

The doorbell rang. It was Daniel. Relief was written all over Karen's beautifully made-up face. My God, I thought with a little jump, she really is bonkers about him.

Daniel was wearing a dark suit and a dazzling white shirt, which set off the faint tan he still had from his vacation in Jamaica in February. He looked tall and dark and handsome, he smiled a lot, his hair flopped over his forehead and he had brought two bottles of chilled champagne—the ideal guest. I couldn't help smiling. Perfectly dressed, beautifully behaved, and just ever so slightly clichéd.

He said all the things that nice polite people say when they come to dinner at your house, like, "Mmmm, something smells delicious," and, "You look wonderful, Karen. And you, Charlotte."

Only when he got to me did his impeccable manners

slip a little. "What are you laughing at, Sullivan?" he demanded. "My suit? My hair? What is it?"

"Nothing," I protested. "Nothing at all. Why should I laugh at you?"

"Why change the habit of a lifetime?" he muttered. Then he moved away from me and said more of those polite guest things like "Can I do anything to help?" knowing that the answer would be an avalanche of "Nos" and "Not at alls" and slightly hysterical "Everything's under controls!"

"Have a drink, Daniel," said Karen graciously, as she swept him into the living room. Charlotte and I attempted to follow them but Karen stuck her head back out at us. "Get stirring," she hissed, blocking our entrance, as I ran into the back of Charlotte.

The doorbell rang again. Simon this time. As always he was dressed to kill, wearing a dinner suit and a red satin cummerbund that looked really stupid. He had brought a bottle of champagne also.

Oh dear, I thought. Gus is going to be the odd man out—more than usual, that was. Gus wouldn't bring champagne. Gus probably wouldn't bring anything.

Not that it would embarrass me, but I was worried that it might embarrass him.

I wondered if I could run out to the liquor store to buy some champagne and slip it to Gus when he arrived, but I was on potato-heating duty so I was confined to barracks.

Simon said, as Daniel had moments earlier, "Mmmm, something smells delicious."

Gus wouldn't. Gus would say, "Where's the spuds, I'm starving."

"How's it all going?" asked Karen, appearing at the kitchen door. She had obviously left Daniel and Simon to do some awkward male bonding in the front room.

"Fine," I said.

"Watch that sauce, Lucy," she said anxiously. "If there are lumps in it, I'll kill you."

I said nothing. I felt like throwing the saucepan across the kitchen at her.

"And where's your crazy Irishman?"

"On his way."

"He'd better hurry up."

"Don't worry."

"What time did you tell him?"

"Eight o'clock."

"It's a quarter past now."

"Karen—he'll be here."

"He'd better."

Karen swished back to the front room, with a bottle of something under her arm.

I kept stirring the sauce, a tiny little flutter of anxiety coming to life in my stomach.

He *would* be here.

But I hadn't spoken to him since Tuesday and I hadn't seen him since Sunday. That suddenly seemed like an awfully long time. Time for him to have forgotten me?

A little while later Karen was back.

"Lucy," she yelled. "It's half past eight!"

"So?"

"So where the hell is Gus?"

"I don't know, Karen."

"Well," she sputtered. "Don't you think you had better find out?"

"Why don't you call him?" suggested Charlotte. "Just to make sure that he hasn't forgotten. He might have gotten the day wrong."

"He might have got the *year* wrong," said Karen, nastily.

"I'm sure he's on his way," I said, "but I'll give him a call just in case."

I sounded a lot more confident than I felt. I wasn't at all sure that he was on his way. Anything could have happened to Gus. He could have forgotten, he could have got delayed, he could have fallen under a bus. But I wasn't going to let anyone know how worried I was.

I was embarrassed. I felt ashamed. Both their boyfriends had arrived on time. *With* bottles of champagne. My boyfriend was already half an hour late and he wouldn't even have a bottle of *tap water* with him when he did eventually turn up.

*If he turns up,* said a little voice in my head.

Panic rushed through me. What if he didn't arrive? What if he didn't come and didn't call and I never heard from him again? What would I do?

I tried to calm myself down. Of course he would come. He was probably outside right now. He really liked me and he obviously cared about me, of course he wouldn't abandon me.

I didn't want to call him, I had never called him. He had given me his phone number when I had asked for it, but I had gotten the feeling that he wasn't that eager for me to call him. He said that he hated phones, that they were a necessary evil. And there had never been any need for me to call him because he always called me, and now that I thought of it, they always seemed to be brief calls from a pay phone somewhere noisy. Or else he stopped by my apartment or picked me up from work.

We certainly didn't spend hours and hours on the phone whispering and giggling to each other, the way Charlotte and Simon did.

I found his number in my purse and dialed it. His phone rang and rang forever and no one answered.

"No answer," I said in relief. "He must be on his way."

Just then someone picked up the phone at the other end. A man's voice said "Hello."

"Er, hello, can I speak to Gus?"

"Who?"

"Gus. Gus Lavan."

"Oh, him. No, he's not here."

I put my hand over the mouthpiece. "He's on his way." I smiled at Karen.

"When did he leave?" she asked.

"How long ago did he leave?" I parroted.

"Let's see, ooh, about two weeks ago, I suppose."

"Wha . . . at?"

My horror must have shown on my face because Karen burst out, "I don't believe it! I bet the little bastard just left five minutes ago. Well, tough for him because we're going to start without him . . ."

Her voice trailed away as she marched down the hall, no doubt to galvanize Charlotte into finalizing the appetizers.

"Two weeks?" I asked quietly. Horrified and all as I was, I knew that this was something best kept to myself. It would be far, far too humiliating to broadcast it to my roommates and their boyfriends.

"About two weeks," said the voice, considering. "Ten days, something like that."

"Oh, well, er, thanks."

"Who's calling anyway? Is it Mandy?"

"No," I said, feeling as if I was going to burst into tears. "It's not Mandy."

*Who the fuck was Mandy?*

"Can I give him a message if I happen to see him again?"

"No. Thank you. Goodbye."

I hung up. Something was wrong. I knew it. This was not normal behavior. Why hadn't Gus mentioned that he was leaving his apartment? Why hadn't he given me his new phone number? And where on earth was he now?

Daniel had come out to the hall. "Christ, what's wrong with you?" he asked.

"Nothing," I said, attempting a smile.

Karen came back down the hall.

"Sorry, Lucy, we'll wait a little bit longer for him."

Oh no. No, no, *no*. I didn't want any waiting to be done. I had a horrible feeling that he wasn't going to come. I didn't want us all to sit watching the door because then it would be so *obvious* when he didn't arrive. I wanted the evening to proceed without him. And then, if he arrived, it would be a bonus.

"Er, no, Karen, we may as well start."

"No, honestly, another half hour won't matter that much."

It was typical. Karen was being nice—which didn't happen very often—and for once I didn't want her to be.

"Come in and sit down and have a glass of wine," suggested Daniel. "You're as white as a ghost, you look exhausted."

We trooped into the front room and I took a glass of wine from someone's hand and tried to act normal.

The others were acting relaxed and happy, chatting, lolling about, sipping wine, but I was rigid with tension, white-faced, silent, straining to hear the sound of the doorbell, praying to hear the phone.

Oh, please, Gus, don't do this to me, I begged silently. Please God, please God, make him come.

In what seemed like thirty seconds later, it was nine o'clock.

Time was such a contrary bastard. When I wanted it to

gallop along, it slowed to a standstill. It could take up to twenty-four hours for an hour to pass.

And now that I wanted time to stop, it was racing.

Whenever there was a lull in the conversation—and there were a few, because we were all slightly uncomfortable with so much formality in our own home and enough wine hadn't yet been drunk—someone would say, "What's keeping Gus?" or "Where's he coming from? Camden? He might have trouble on the tube," or "I'm sure he didn't realize that you meant eight o'clock so literally."

Nobody seemed terribly worried. But I was.

I was scared.

It wasn't just the fact that he was late—although that was deeply embarrassing after all the fuss Karen had made about the dinner—but his lateness, taken in conjunction with his having moved out of his apartment without telling me. Now *that* was ominous. No matter what way I looked at it, I felt it was not A Good Thing.

I kept having little stabs of despair.

What if he didn't come?

What if I never saw him again?

And who was Mandy?

I made attempts to join in with the slightly self-conscious camaraderie in the living room, tried to listen to what they were saying, to force a smile onto my rigid, white face.

But I was so agitated, I could hardly sit still for a moment.

And then the pendulum swung back in the other direction and I calmed down. After all he was only an hour, well an hour and a quarter—damn, was it an hour and a quarter already?—late. He would probably arrive in a moment, a little bit drunk, with some hilarious, outlandish excuse. I was always overreacting to things, I told myself sternly. I was certain that he would come and I was slightly amused at how easy it was for me to think the worst.

Gus was my friend. We'd become close over the past couple of months, I knew he cared about me and that he wouldn't let me down.

 40

By ten o'clock the potato chip bowls were all emptied and everyone seemed to be drunk.

"I'm not listening to any more of this," announced Charlotte, turning off the stereo. "Jazz, my ass."

Karen allowed Charlotte to change the tape, which meant that she too must have had enough of John Coltrane's later meanderings.

"Okay then," announced Karen, changing the subject. "Gus or no Gus, it's time to eat. I want you to have the delicious food before you're all too drunk to appreciate it.

"Dinner is served. Charlotte, Lucy." She motioned us toward the door.

That was our cue to become serving wenches.

I couldn't eat anything. I was still hoping desperately that Gus would show up. Just arrive along with some fantastic, outrageous excuse. I won't be mad at you, Gus, I promised fervently. Honestly, just get here and I won't say a thing.

After a while everyone stopped saying things like "I

wonder what's keeping Gus," and "What could have happened to Gus," and looking out the window to see if a taxi was coming up the road with Gus inside it.

In fact, everyone took great care not to mention Gus at all. It had become clear that Gus wasn't merely late, but that he wasn't coming.

They all knew that I'd been stood up and, in their awkward, embarrassed way, they were trying to pretend that I hadn't been and if I had, that they certainly hadn't noticed. I knew they were just trying to be kind, but their kindness was humiliating.

The evening was interminable. There was so much food, so many courses, I thought it would never end. I would have given anything to go to bed, but pride forbade me.

It was only much, much later when everyone was *really* drunk—as opposed to just very drunk—that the subject of Gus was brought up again.

"Dump the fucker," slurred Karen. Her hairdo was keeling over to one side. "How dare he treat you like this? I'd kill him."

"Let's give him a chance." I smiled tensely. "Anything could have happened to him."

"Oh come *on*, Lucy," scoffed Karen. "How can you be such an idiot? It's *obvious* that he's stood you up."

Of *course* it was obvious that he'd stood me up, but I was hoping to hang on to a remnant of my dignity by pretending that he hadn't.

Daniel and Simon looked uncomfortable. Simon said heartily to Daniel, "Well, how's work?"

"He could have called," said Charlotte.

"Maybe he forgot," I said miserably.

"Well, he shouldn't have," slurred Karen.

"Have you checked the phone?" Charlotte shouted suddenly. "I bet the phone is broken, the lines are down or something, that's why he hasn't called."

"I doubt it," said Karen.

"Maybe you didn't hang it up right," suggested Daniel. "Maybe it's off the hook and he hasn't been able to get through."

Because Daniel had suggested it, the idea was given a bit of credibility. There was a surge toward the hall, me at the head of it, hoping against hope that Daniel was right. Of course he wasn't. There was nothing wrong with the phone and the receiver had been replaced perfectly.

How embarrassing.

"Maybe something's happened to him," I suggested hopefully. "Maybe he's had an accident. He could have been knocked down and killed," I said, fresh hope surging through me. Far better for Gus to be lying broken and bloodied beneath the wheels of a truck than for him to have decided that he didn't like me anymore.

Karen was having a passionate but hard-to-follow argument with Simon about Scottish nationalism when the knock on the door finally came.

"Quiet," shouted Daniel. "I think someone's at the door."

We fell silent—surprise, rather than the desire to hear, robbed us of the power of speech.

We held our breath and listened. Daniel was right.

Someone *was* knocking on the door.

*Thank God,* I thought fervently, relief making me dizzy.

*Thank you God, thank you God, thank you God!* Pencil me in for charitable work, kindness to the poor, contributions to church funds, bad skin, anything you like, but thank you God for giving me back Gus.

"I'll answer it, Lucy." Charlotte swayed to her feet.

"You don't want him to think you've been worried. Just look casual."

"Thanks," I said, rushing to the mirror in panic. "Do I look okay? Is my hair all right? Oh no, look at how red my face is! Quick, quick, someone give me lipstick!"

I ran my fingers through my hair and flung myself onto the couch, trying to look unconcerned, and waited for Gus to roll into the room. I was so *happy* I couldn't sit still. I was looking forward to hearing whatever elaborate and imaginative excuse he might make. No doubt it would be hilarious.

But a while passed and he didn't appear. I could hear voices in the hall.

"What's keeping him?" I hissed, anxiously perched on the edge of my seat.

"Just relax." Daniel rubbed my knee. He stopped abruptly when Karen stared pointedly at his hand, then at him, then at his hand again. She had a peculiar expression, which kind of slid off her face. I realized that she had been trying to arch her eyebrows quizzically, but it had lost something in the inebriation.

More time passed and still Gus didn't appear. I realized that something was wrong—perhaps he hadn't come in because he was injured—and after a few minutes I couldn't bear it anymore and, throwing my veneer of unconcernedness to the wind, I went out to have a look.

There was no Gus.

Just Neil from downstairs.

Neil was in a bad mood, complaining about the music and wearing a very short robe.

I had been certain that Gus was on the premises and it took a great leap of imagination for me to grasp that, he actually wasn't. I squinted drunkenly past Neil, wondering why I couldn't see Gus hovering behind him. And when it hit me that Gus hadn't arrived after all, I could hardly believe it.

The disappointment was so intense that the ground literally rocked beneath my feet. (Then again, it might have been all the wine I'd drunk.)

". . . You don't have to turn the music down," Neil was saying. "But for pity's sake, change the tape. If you have any compassion, any feeling for a fellow human being, you'll change the tape."

"But I *like* Simply Red," said Charlotte.

"I *know*!" said Neil. "Why else would you play it for eight weeks nonstop? *Please*, Charlotte."

"Okay," she agreed sulkily.

"And would you mind playing this instead?" he asked, handing her a tape.

"Get lost!" spluttered Charlotte. "The nerve of you, this is *our* apartment, we'll play *our* music."

"But I have to listen to it too, you know . . ." whined Neil.

I lurched back into the front room.

"Where's Gus?" asked Daniel.

"Don't know," I muttered.

I got very drunk, and at some late hour, I think it was about half past two, I decided that I would find Gus. Maybe I could get his new number from the man I had spoken to in his old apartment.

I sneaked out to the hall to the phone. If Karen and Charlotte knew what I was doing they would have tried to stop me. Luckily they were all really drunk. They had stopped playing strip Trivial Pursuit because Charlotte had insisted on putting on some Spanish music. Then she demonstrated the steps that she had learned at her flamingo dancing lessons and made them all join in.

I knew what I was doing had desperation stamped all

over it, but I was drunk, I had no willpower. I had no idea what I would say if I did get through to him. How could I explain that I'd found his new number and tracked him down without seeming like a woman obsessed? But I didn't care.

Surely I had every right to find him and speak to him, I reasoned drunkenly. I *deserved* an explanation.

But I wouldn't be angry with him, I decided. I would be friendly and would calmly ask why he hadn't come.

There was a tiny sober little part of me that said I shouldn't call him, that I was behaving like a crazy person, that I was compounding my humiliation by trying to trace him, but I didn't listen. I was in the grip of a compulsion and I couldn't stop myself.

But no one answered the phone. I sat on the hall floor and let it ring until I got the recorded message telling me that my number wasn't being answered—hey, thanks, I would never have noticed otherwise—and in frustration I slammed the phone back on the cradle. I was barely aware of the tumbling and commotion in the front room.

"No answer?" asked someone. I jumped.

Damn! It was Daniel, en route to the kitchen, probably looking for more wine.

"No," I said, angry that I'd been caught.

"Who were you calling?" asked Daniel.

"Who do you think?"

"Poor Lucy."

I felt terrible. It wasn't like the old days when Daniel laughed at me and made fun of my misfortunes. Things had changed and I didn't feel as if Daniel was my friend anymore. I had to hide my feelings from him.

"You poor little thing," he said again.

"Oh shut up," I said sulkily, looking up at him from my position on the floor.

We had somehow crossed a line. All that light-hearted sparring had become real and nasty.

"What's wrong, Lucy?" Daniel crouched down to where I was slumped on the floor.

"Oh, don't start," I spat. "You know what's wrong."

"No," he said. "I mean, what's wrong with us?"

"There is no 'us,' " I said, partly to hurt him and partly to avoid the confrontation that I felt was imminent.

"Yes, there is." He gently put his hand on my neck and began stroking the area under my ear with little circles of his thumb.

"There is," he said again. His thumb sent odd shivers through my neck and down into my chest. Suddenly I couldn't breathe too well and then, to my disbelief, I felt my nipples begin to harden.

"What the fuck are you doing?" I whispered, staring up into his handsome familiar face.

But I didn't pull away. I was drunk, I was rejected and someone was being nice to me.

"I don't know," he said, sounding shocked. I could feel his breath on my face. Oh Christ, I thought in horror, as Daniel's face came closer to mine. He's going to kiss me. Daniel! *Daniel*'s going to kiss me, even though his girlfriend is only two yards away and I'm so drunk or upset or whatever that I'm going to let him.

"What's keeping Dan?" said Karen's voice, as she flounced out into the hall.

Saved by the belle!

"What are the pair of you doing down there?" she screeched.

"Nothing," said Daniel, getting to his feet.

"Nothing," I gasped, clambering to mine.

"You were supposed to be getting ice for Charlotte's ankle," said Karen in a fury.

"Why, what's happened?" I asked, glad of the diversion, *any* diversion, as Daniel made for the kitchen.

"She tripped doing her flamingo dancing," said Karen coldly. "And she's sprained her ankle. But it would appear that Daniel would rather sit on the floor and chat to you than help poor Charlotte."

I went back into the front room. Charlotte was stretched out on the couch, giggling and saying "ouch" as Simon massaged her foot and looked up her dress.

There was almost no wine left, just dribs and drabs in the bottom of bottles, but I made my way around the table drinking everything in my path, until it all ran out. I was desperate for something to drink and suddenly there seemed to be nothing.

An argument broke out because Charlotte insisted that her ankle was broken and that she should go to the hospital, and Simon said that it definitely wasn't broken, it was only sprained. Then Karen said that Charlotte should stop whining and then Simon intervened and told Karen to shut up and not to say nasty things to his girlfriend, and if Charlotte wanted to go to the hospital then to the hospital she would go. Karen asked Simon who had made his dinner for him that evening and Simon replied that he had heard all about Karen and the work she had made Charlotte do and that if anyone deserved thanks for the food that evening it was Charlotte . . . and on and on.

I sat, gulping a half-bottle of red wine that I had found abandoned behind the couch, swinging my legs, enjoying the argument.

Karen shouted at Charlotte for telling Simon that she had done all the cooking. Charlotte had done nothing! Nothing! Just peeled a few carrots and that was all . . .

I smiled over at Daniel, forgetting for a moment what had happened, or nearly happened, in the hall. He grinned back, then I remembered what had happened, or nearly happened, in the hall, so I blushed and looked away.

I found some gin and finished that. And I still wasn't drunk enough. I was sure that I had a bottle of rum in the cupboard in the front room but search as I might, I couldn't find it.

"Gus probably stole it," suggested Karen.

"He probably did," I said grimly.

Eventually I admitted defeat, went to bed, alone, and passed out.

 41

I jerked awake at about seven o'clock—it *was* Saturday, after all—and immediately knew that something was wrong. What was it?

Oh yes! I remembered.

Oh no! I wished I hadn't.

Luckily I was badly hung over, so I was able to go back to sleep.

I woke again at ten and the realization that I had lost Gus hit me like a clunk on the head from a frying pan. I got up and dragged myself down the hall and found Charlotte and Karen in the kitchen cleaning up. There was so much leftover food that I could have cried, but I didn't because they would have thought that I was crying about Gus.

"Morning," I said.

"Morning," they replied.

I waited. I held my breath, hoping that one of them would say, "Oh, Gus called."

But they didn't.

I knew there was no point in asking if he had called. They both knew how important it was to me. If Gus had called they would have excitedly told me immediately. In fact, they would have come to me with the news, they would have awakened me.

But even knowing that, I still found myself asking tentatively,

"Did anyone call for me while I was asleep?"

I couldn't stop myself. In for a penny, in for a pound. I was hurt—why stop now?

"Er, no," muttered Karen, not meeting my eye.

"No," agreed Charlotte. "No one."

I had known that was the case, so why did I still feel so disappointed?

"How's your ankle?" I asked Charlotte.

"Fine," she said, looking sheepish.

"I'm just running out to buy the paper," I said. "And then I'll be back to help with the cleaning. Does anyone want anything?"

"No thanks."

I didn't even want the paper. But a watched pot never boils and if I did a vigil around my phone, Gus wouldn't call. I knew that if I was out of the house there was a better chance he might call me.

When I let myself back in, I held my breath, waiting for Karen or Charlotte to run down the hall and say, breathlessly, "Guess what? Gus rang," or "Guess what? Gus is *here*. He was kidnapped last night and they just let him go a few moments ago."

But no one ran down the hall and breathlessly told me

anything. I was forced to go, cap-in-hand, to the kitchen, where I was handed a tea towel.

"Did anyone call for me?" I found myself asking, hollowly.

Again, Karen and Charlotte shook their heads. I shut my mouth grimly. I'm not going to ask again, I decided. I was tearing myself apart with disappointment and I was embarrassing them.

I followed the advice of thousands of women's magazines and Kept Busy. Keeping Busy is supposed to be very good for taking your mind off runaway men and, as luck would have it, there was an alarming amount of cleaning up to be done after the excesses of the previous evening—although I hadn't expected that *I'd* have to do any of it. I thought that I'd be given compassionate leave, that because Gus had dumped me, everyone would be nice to me, that I'd be given a special dispensation and Karen would let me off my chores.

Not a chance.

Karen wasted no time in setting me straight.

"Keep busy," she said cheerfully, as she loaded me up with filthy plates. "It'll take your mind off him."

That made me feel even more upset—I wanted sympathy, I wanted kid-glove treatment, I wanted to be treated like a convalescent invalid. What I didn't want was to do the cleaning up.

And anyone who says that Keeping Busy is a distraction from heartbreak is mistaken, because I Kept *very* Busy that day, and I thought about Gus constantly—how cleaning the bathroom was supposed to make me feel better about Gus disappearing had me baffled. All that happened was the one form of misery was temporarily exchanged for another.

I vacuumed the entire flat, I washed the unbroken plates

and glasses, I put the broken plates and glasses into a trashbag and attached a nice little note for the garbagemen so that they wouldn't cut themselves. I emptied mountains of ashtrays, I covered bowls of untouched food and put them in the fridge, where they would take up valuable low-fat yogurt space for three weeks and grow mold before they would eventually be thrown out. I tried to get the candle wax out of the carpet and couldn't, so I moved the couch to cover it. And I thought continually about Gus.

My nerves were *shot*. The phone rang all day long and every single time I jumped and twitched and frantically prayed, Please God, let it be Gus. I didn't dare pick it up, just in case it was Gus. Answering the phone was tantamount to admitting I cared and that would have been unforgivable. Karen or Charlotte had to leave their pot scrubbing (in Charlotte's case) or their dancing around spraying air freshener (in Karen's case) and do it for me.

And, as befitted a rejected woman, I insisted that they observe a five-ring interval before answering.

"Not yet, not yet!" I begged, time after time. "Let it ring a bit longer. We can't let him think that we're waiting for him to call."

"But, we are." Charlotte looked puzzled. "At least you are."

It made no difference. Only one of the calls was for me, and that was from—of all people—my mother.

"What took you so long to answer?" she demanded when Charlotte sadly handed me the receiver.

And suddenly it was Saturday night.

Saturday night had always played a starring role in my life. It had been a thing of beauty, a bright spot in a dark world, but an *empty* Saturday night, a Gus-free Saturday night—well, I was shocked to find that I was almost *frightened* of it.

Every Saturday night for the previous—had it only been six weeks?—had been taken care of because I had been with Gus. Sometimes we had gone out, and other times we stayed in, but whatever we had done, we had done it together. And now I felt as if I had never, ever had a free Saturday night before in my life, so alien did it feel to me.

It had taken on a certain malevolence, as though someone had flung a snake at me and told me to amuse it for a few hours.

What was I supposed to *do* with it? And with whom? All my friends were paired up with someone. Charlotte was with Simon, Karen was with Daniel, Daniel was with Karen and anyway Daniel wasn't my friend anymore.

I could have called Dennis but that was a ridiculous idea. It was a Saturday night, he was a gay man, he would be at home shaving his head and revving up for a night of unbridled hedonism.

Charlotte and Simon invited me to go to the movies with them—as Charlotte said, the movies were about all she could stomach after the imbibing of the previous evening—but I didn't want to go.

It wasn't that I was afraid of being a third wheel—I had no problem with that, after all I'd done it many times in the past, and the first ten thousand times are the worst—but I'm ashamed to say I was afraid to leave the apartment in case Gus arrived.

Like a fool, I was still hoping that I might hear from him. In fact, what I actually hoped for was that, at around eight, he would arrive in a borrowed, too-big jacket and a badly knotted tie, having made the mistake of thinking that Saturday night was the night for the dinner and not Friday.

It was possible, I told myself weakly.

Things like that happened sometimes. Maybe it would happen to me and I would be saved. I could draw back from the edge of the abyss laughing because I hadn't needed to be there at all.

Karen and Daniel didn't invite me to join them in what-ever they were doing. Somehow I hadn't expected them to. Anyhow I didn't want them to. I felt so uncomfortable around Daniel that we were barely speaking to each other. And I blushed when I remembered how I had thought that he was going to kiss me the previous evening, when it was obvious, in hindsight, that he was only being nice because Gus had stood me up. How could I have thought such a thing? I asked myself in mortification. And worse again, how could I have thought that it was a nice idea? It was Daniel, after all. It would have been like thinking that kissing my brother was a nice idea.

Everyone left and I was alone in the flat on a bright Saturday evening in April.

Somewhere in between Gus entering and exiting my life, winter had changed into spring, but I had been too busy enjoying myself and falling in love to notice.

I found rejection that much harder to cope with when the evenings were bright.

At least when it was dark I could draw that curtains and light the fire and snuggle and hide and feel quite cozy in my aloneness. But the brightness of the spring evening was embarrassing. It highlighted what a failure I was— my rejection was too visible. I felt as if I was the only person in the whole world sitting in, alone, on a Satur-day night.

After eight o'clock came and Gus didn't, I moved down one more step on the stairs of misery. Why couldn't I have just tumbled straight to the bottom and gotten it over and done with? I understood the wisdom of pulling a

Band-Aid off a cut with a single, flamboyant, eye-watering rip, but when it came to matters of the heart, I removed things from me with painful slowness.

I decided to go out to get a video. And a bottle of wine, because there was no way I'd get through the evening without a drink.

"Gus won't call anyway, Gus will be out with Mandy," I said, playing "it really doesn't matter" with the gods. If you can play that well, if you can convince the gods that you really don't want what you really do want, then you'll probably get lucky.

At the video shop Adrian greeted me like a long-lost sister. "Lucy! Where've you been?" he roared the length of the shop. "I haven't seen you in *so long*!"

"Hi, Adrian," I mouthed at him, hoping to lower his volume slightly by setting a good example.

"To what do we owe this pleasure?" he yelled. "Alone on a Saturday night? He must have dumped you!"

I smiled tightly and picked up *Reservoir Dogs*.

When Adrian had turned around to find my video, I gave him a halfhearted vetting. I owed it to myself, I told myself. Now that I was single again I had to keep my eyes peeled for the potential husband that Mrs. Nolan had predicted for me. He wasn't bad, I thought wearily. Nice butt, nothing wrong with it, couldn't fault it except for one thing, it wasn't Gus's butt. Nice smile, but it wasn't Gus's smile.

It was a total waste of time, my head was filled with Gus and I couldn't look at another man.

Anyway I didn't really believe that it was over with Gus—it was too soon. I needed to be hit over the head with proof, battered into the ground by it, before I could truly believe it. Giving up didn't come easily to me. Letting go was not one of my strong points.

On the one hand I knew for certain that I'd never see

Gus again, and on the other hand I just couldn't stop hoping that there would be some explanation, no matter how unlikely, and that we could start over again.

I went next door to the liquor store. It was full of young, happy people, buying bottles of wine and cans of beer and hundreds of cigarettes. I was suddenly pierced with the old familiar feeling that life was a party to which I hadn't been invited. A feeling of belonging had made a guest appearance in my life while I'd been with Gus, but now I was back to feeling like an uninvited guest at life's feast.

As I walked slowly back to the apartment, trying to waste time, I was suddenly overcome with panic, convinced that Gus was calling me at that instant. I rushed up the road and back into the apartment and breathlessly ran to see if the little red light on the answering machine was blinking. But it wasn't. It stared and stared and stared at me and didn't blink once.

It took forever for the evening to inch painfully, slowly toward darkness, for other people to come home from their nights out, for other people to go to bed, for the gap between me and everyone else to narrow, for me to stop feeling like the *only one* . . .

I got drunk and once again I called the number that Gus had given me. Nobody answered—luckily. Although I didn't feel that it was lucky at the time, I was furious, beside myself with frustration and loneliness. I just wanted to talk to him, if I could have spoken to him I knew he would make it all right.

I even, in my drunken state, thought about getting a taxi to Camden and walking around and seeing if I could find him but thankfully, something stopped me—maybe the idea of stumbling across him with the mysterious Mandy. A little bit of sanity pierced my armor of obsession.

*     *     *

I woke to the stillness of Sunday morning. I knew, even before I got out of bed, that I was the only person in the flat, that Karen and Charlotte hadn't come home the previous night. It was only seven o'clock and I was completely awake and completely alone.

How was I supposed to fill my head to keep the loneliness away? How was I supposed to stop myself from going mad thinking about Gus?

I could have read but I didn't want to, there was nothing I wanted to read. I could have watched TV but I knew I wouldn't be able to concentrate. I could have gone for a run, that might have taken away some of the terrible anxiety, but I could barely get out of bed. I was buzzing with nervy adrenaline but I couldn't face getting up. It wasn't just Gus that had deserted me, but my dreams of marrying him had also evaporated. Letting go of the fantasy was almost as hard as letting go of the man.

Of course, it was my own fault. I should never have taken Mrs. Nolan's predictions seriously. I was the one who had berated Meredia and Megan for believing her. No sooner were their backs turned, than I had believed her also.

So instead of treating it like a casual fling, I had thought that Gus was the one for me and that we'd be together forever.

It wasn't *really* my fault, I tried to persuade myself. Mrs. Nolan had sensed my insecurity and loneliness and told me what I wanted to hear. And, while I could take or leave the actual getting married part—you know, the white dress, arguments with my mother, cake, all that—I was very pleased with the promise of a soul mate.

How had I coped before I met Gus? I wondered. How had I filled all that empty space? I didn't remember it ever feeling quite this empty, but it must have, because I had lived for Sunday after Sunday without Gus.

Then I realized what had happened. He had come, filled the gap and, when he left, he took more than he had arrived with. He had charmed his way into my heart, made me trust him and then, when I wasn't looking, had stolen my emotional fixtures and fittings, leaving my interior living room stripped bare.

I had been suckered and not for the first time.

Sunday took an eternity to pass. Charlotte and Karen didn't come home. The phone never rang. At about nine o'clock I brought back the video, got another one and a bottle of wine. I drank the wine, I got drunk, I went to sleep.

And then it was Monday morning. The weekend was over and he hadn't called.

 42

Hetty's replacement started work with us that morning.

It had been six weeks since she had left, a long time for three people to spend trying to do the work of one.

But Ivor had begged Personnel for a stay of execution, a couple of weeks grace before they advertised for a new person. The poor fool had held out hope that Hetty might return to his short, pudgy, pink, freckled arms.

But she was now living in Edinburgh with her brother-in-law—very happily, by all accounts—so he had finally come to terms with it.

Our new colleague happened to be a young man. That wasn't the random stroke of luck that it might, at first glance, appear to be. Oh no!

Meredia had arranged it that way. And the only reason that I knew about it was because I had caught her at her machinations.

A couple of Mondays before, because of a series of unfortunate accidents—my train rushed in as I reached the platform, my connecting train was actually waiting for me, etc., etc.—I had arrived early for work.

Meredia was actually in *before* me. That was surprising in itself, but what was more surprising was that she was already working, feverishly sorting through a pile of papers, discarding some and feeding others into the paper shredder.

"Morning," I said.

"Shut up, I'm busy," she muttered.

"Meredia, what are you doing?"

"Nothing," she said, continuing to cram documents into the shredder.

I was intrigued, because she was obviously up to something. I should have known that there was no way that she'd be working at a quarter to nine on a Monday morning on *work* work.

I took a closer look at the pile of papers on her desk. They were job applications.

"Meredia, what are these and where did you get them?"

"They're the applications for Hetty's replacement. Personnel sent them down for Smelly Simmonds to look at."

"But why are you shredding them? Don't you want a new person in?"

"I'm not getting rid of them all."

"I see." I didn't.

"Just the married women," she continued.

"Might I ask why?"

"Why should they have a husband *and* a job?" asked Meredia, bitterly.

"You're joking?" I said weakly. "Are you trying to tell me that you're destroying all the applications from the married women just because they're married?"

"Yes," she said grimly. "I'm simply evening up the good fortune in the world. You can't depend on karma to work properly. So, if you want something done right, you have to do it yourself."

"But Meredia," I protested, "just because they're married doesn't mean that they're happy. They could be married to a man who hits them or who has affairs or who's really boring. Or they could be widowed or separated or divorced."

"I don't care," sniffed Meredia. "They've still had their big day, they've still had their waltz up the aisle wearing their fancy dress."

"But if you don't want them to be happy, surely the best possible thing you could do is ensure that one of them gets this job. Look at how miserable we all are!"

"Don't try and get around me, Lucy," she said scrutinizing another. "What do you think this Ms. L. Rogers is? Married or not married?"

"I don't know. You're not *supposed* to know. That's why she put 'Ms.' "

"Not married, I bet," continued Meredia, ignoring me. "She's only put 'Ms.' to hide the fact that she doesn't have a man. Okay, she gets an interview."

"Well, look at it another way," I suggested. "What if we get a single woman in here? Doesn't that just increase the competition for the few available men out there?"

I had only been joking, but a spasm of horror wobbled across Meredia's face.

"Christ, you're right, you know," she said, "I never thought of that."

"In fact," I said, feeling a bout of mischief making coming on, "you'd be much better off getting rid of the applications from all the women and just keeping the men's."

She liked the sound of that.

"Brilliant!" she exclaimed, hugging me. "Brilliant, brilliant, brilliant!"

I was pleased—any kind of subversion in the workplace lessened the tedium.

So she frantically flicked through the bundle of applications, and set about weeding out *all* the women before Ivor came in.

But the purge didn't end there. Having the power of life and death over people had gone to her head.

"Why should we put up with some old man?" she demanded. And then proceeded to cull all of the men over thirty-five.

The once fat pile was emaciated by then and she whittled it down even more by checking under their hobbies and interests section.

"Hmmm, this one likes gardening. Say 'bye bye,' " she said, flinging it to one side.

By the time she was finished there were only four left. Four men, between the ages of twenty-one and twenty-seven, who listed their hobbies variously as "partying," "working out," "socializing," "vacationing in Ios" and "drinking."

I had to say, it looked promising. If I hadn't been living in a fool's paradise at the time thinking everything was blissfully wonderful with Gus, I would have been quite excited myself.

All four of them came for interviews over the course of that week. As each one arrived, Meredia, Megan and I loitered by reception to get a good look at them before they were whisked away to Personnel so that Blandina could ask them where they saw themselves in five years time. ("Swinging from a noose if I'm still working here," was the correct answer, although they didn't know. Never mind—if they got the job, they'd find out quick enough.)

We'd rate them on a scale of ten for good-lookingness, niceness of butt, etc., not, of course, that Meredia, Megan and I actually had any say in the final outcome. But that didn't stop us from discussing them with passionate interest. "I liked number two," said Megan. "What do you think, Louise?"

"My name is Meredia" said Meredia hotly. "And number three was by far the cutest."

"I preferred two," I said. "He looked really *nice*."

Megan liked the sound of number four, the one who put "working out" as one of his hobbies, but when he arrived, we were all saddened to observe that he was terminally homosexual. And naturally he wasn't picked because Ivor was about as homophobic as you could get. When he came back to the office after interviewing him, he told us many jokes along the lines of, "If I had dropped fifty pence on the floor, I wouldn't have bent down to pick it up," and, "Backs to the wall, eh? Guffaw, guffaw."

"But seriously, girls," he continued, "we couldn't have a gay man in here."

"Why not?" I demanded.

He went all coy. "What if he . . . er . . . *liked* . . . me."

"You!" I sputtered.

"Yes, me," said Ivor, smoothing back what remained of his hair.

"But he didn't *look* mentally retarded," I said, while Megan and Meredia sniggered. Ivor narrowed his eyes at me but I didn't care, I was furious.

"What do you mean, Miss Sullivan?" he asked coldly.

"I mean that just because he's gay and just because you're a man doesn't mean that he'll be attracted to you."

The cheek of him to think that *anyone*, man, woman, child or farmyard animal, might find him attractive.

"Of course he'd be attracted to me," muttered Ivor. "You know what they're like. Promiscuous."

There was a chorus of outrage from Meredia, Megan and me.

"How dare you!" and "You fascist!" and "How the hell would you know?"

"What if he already has a boyfriend?" demanded Megan. "What if he's in love with someone?"

"Don't be ridiculous," stuttered Ivor. "And you can all shut up because we're not hiring him. He can go off and get himself a job hairdressing, or waiting tables. He'll be much better suited to that."

He went into his office and slammed the door, and left the three of us positively seething.

Number two, the nice, smiley, twenty-seven-year-old, drew the short straw. He was offered the job, and he compounded his misfortune by accepting it.

His name was Jed and, although he hadn't been the best looking of the bunch, I had a good feeling about him. He never stopped smiling, lovely big smiles. The corners of his mouth disappeared into his hairline and his eyes were nowhere to be seen—it would be interesting to see how quickly the job wiped the smile off his face.

Mr. Simmonds was very excited. "It'll be great to have

another man around the place," he kept saying, sloughing his hands together with glee, visualizing lunchtime pints and manly chats about cars and being able to throw his eyes to heaven and snort "Women!" and get an empathetic response.

Jed started work the Monday after Gus had disappeared on me.

I surprised myself by my resilience that morning. I got up, showered, dressed myself, went to work, wondered where I had gone wrong with Gus, but mostly felt not too bad, although in a dead kind of a way.

Megan was in the office before me, just back from a weekend in Scotland. She had been all Australian about it—why fly when you can spend twelve hours in a rattley old bus and save a little money? She had taken in about ten cities in the course of her forty-eight hours and climbed a few mountains and met a couple of guys and gotten plastered in a Glasgow pub with them and slept on the floor at their hostel and found time to send postcards to everyone she had ever met and hadn't slept a wink and still looked beautiful and raring to go. She even brought us back a present, a slab of Scottish toffee, the good old-fashioned type that's harder than diamond and glues your teeth together and renders you speechless.

Next to arrive was Meredia. She bustled in wearing her best curtain in honor of our new employee and pounced on the toffee, ripping off the tartan cellophane. We all dug in.

Then Jed arrived, looking shy and nervous, but still grinning like a loon. He was wearing a suit and shirt and tie, but we'd soon knock that out of him.

Poison Ivor arrived hot on his heels and did his Important Businessman routine. He shouted and made lots of manly physical contact and threw his head back a lot and barked with laugher. He'd copied it from the bosses upstairs. He loved to do it but didn't often get the chance.

"Jed!" he barked, sticking out his hand and shaking Jed's. "Good to see you! Glad you could make it! Sorry I wasn't here to greet you—got caught up in something, you know how it is? I hope this lot of reprobates, ha ha, have been looking after you, ha ha." He slung his arm paternally across Jed's shoulder, and steered him over to my desk. "Ladies, ha ha, I'd like you to meet the latest addition to our team, ha, ha, Mr. Davies."

"Jed, please," murmured Jed.

A silence followed. None of us could speak because our jaws were glued together with toffee. But we smiled and nodded in an enthusiastic way. I think we made him feel welcome.

Ivor talked on and on about the importance of his office in the structure of the company, and about the career opportunities for Jed, "if you work hard." He flashed the rest of us a bitter look when he said that. "Someday," he said, "you could even end up at my level."

Then he finished by saying, "Well, I can't stand here all day chatting. I'm a very busy man." He gave Jed a rueful, I-work-so-hard, one-man-to-another smile, and self-importantly sailed into his office.

There was a moment of silence. We all smiled awkwardly at one another.

Then Jed spoke.

"Asshole," he said to the closed door.

The relief—Jed was one of us! Megan, Meredia and I exchanged proud, delighted smiles. Such promise! And he had only been in the office ten minutes. We would painstakingly mold him and guide him until he was as sarcastic and cynical as, well, maybe even, *Meredia*.

 43

I tried very hard not to think about Gus, and it worked. Apart from a constant feeling of slight nausea, I would barely have known how miserable I was. The sensation of having swallowed a lump of lead and not having the energy to drag the extra weight around with me was another little clue.

But that was all.

I didn't cry, or anything like that. I didn't even tell the girls at work. I just couldn't be *bothered* to, I was too disappointed.

It was only when the phone rang that I wasn't quite in control. Renegade Hope managed to give me the slip and escape from its container to play hopscotch on my nerve endings. But never for long. By the third ring I'd usually caught up with it, forced it back into the container, and sat on the lid.

The only phone call of note that I got that week wasn't. It was from my brother, Peter.

I couldn't for the life of me understand why he was calling me. He was my brother and I loved him, I suppose, but it wasn't as if we *liked* each other very much.

"Have you been out home recently?" he asked.

"A few weeks ago," I admitted, hoping that his question wouldn't be followed with, "Well, don't you bloody well think it's time that you went?"

"I'm worried about Mammy," he said. "She's gotten a bit funny, strange."

"In what way?" I sighed, trying to be interested.

"Forgetting things."

"Maybe she has Alzheimer's."

"Oh, you have to make a joke about everything, don't you, Lucy?"

"I wasn't joking, Peter. Maybe she does have Alzheimer's. What kind of things has she started forgetting?"

"Well, you know the way I hate mushrooms?"

"Um, do you?"

"Yes! You know I do. *Everyone* knows I do!"

"All right, all right, calm down."

"Well, when I was out there the other night she gave me mushrooms on toast for dinner."

"And . . . ?"

"What do you mean 'and?' Isn't that enough! And I said it to her. I said, 'Mammy, I hate mushrooms' and she just said, 'Oh, I must be mixing you up with Christopher.' "

"That's shocking, Pete," I said dryly. "We'll be lucky if she lives to see the end of the month."

"Jeer all you like," he said, sounding hurt. "But there's more."

"Do tell."

"She's done something funny to her hair."

"Anything would be an improvement."

"No, Lucy, it's funny. It's all kind of curly and blond, she doesn't look like Mammy anymore."

"Ah! Now it all makes sense," I said solemnly. "There's no need to worry, Peter, I know exactly what's up."

"Well, what is it?"

"She's got a boyfriend, silly."

Poor Peter got very upset. He thought that our mother was like The Blessed Virgin, only more chaste and saintly. But at least I got rid of him and hopefully he wouldn't bother me with any more ridiculous phone calls. God knows, I had enough real things to worry about.

 44

Megan and her housemates were having a party that Saturday night.

She shared a three-bedroom house with twenty-eight other Australians, all of whom did shift work, so there were actually enough beds to sleep whoever needed to sleep at any given time. It just meant that the beds were used on a time-share basis, around the clock, twenty-four hours a day.

Apparently Megan shared a single bed with a roofer called Donnie and a night porter called Shane, neither of whom she ever saw. In fact, she liked to make it sound as if they had never actually met.

She promised me that there would be thousands of single men at the party. (On Thursday, I had sheepishly come clean to my colleagues about Gus's disappearance.)

I was miserable on Saturday. Without Gus, and Mrs. Nolan's promise of imminent marriage, my life was so, so, *nothingy*. There were no added extras, no human accessories, no soft-focus future, no soaring magic, nothing at all to enhance me. I, on my own, was colorless, dull, earthbound, unadorned. I had become the Amish frock of personalities and even *I* had lost interest in myself.

I didn't want to go to the party because I was too busy feeling sorry for myself, but I had to, because I'd arranged to meet Jed there. I couldn't stand him up because he wouldn't know anyone else. Meredia had other plans.

Of course, Megan would be there, but she was the hostess, and she'd be too busy breaking up fights and having beer guzzling competitions to look after Jed.

Jed and I met at the tube station at Earls Court, or Little Sydney, as it should have been called.

Now, going for drinks with work people after work is one thing, but I always drew the line at having them spill over into my weekend.

But Jed was different—he was wonderful, *exceptional*. By the end of his first week he'd already coined the name "Mr. Semens" for Mr. Simmonds, been late once, called a friend long distance in Madrid twice and could fit a whole chocolate cookie into his mouth at once. He was much more fun than Hetty had ever been. I think Ivor had already begun to feel as let down and betrayed by Jed as he had once been by Hetty.

As Megan had promised, the party was packed with men—huge, drunk, boisterous men. It was like being in a forest. Jed and I got separated when we arrived and I didn't see him again for the rest of the night. He was just too short to find.

The giants were called things like Kevin O'Leary and Kevin McAllister and shouted drunkenly at one another about the time they'd gotten drunk and gone white-water rafting in the Zambia. Or when they'd gotten drunk and gone sky-diving in Jo'burg. Or when they'd gotten drunk and gone bungee jumping off some Aztec ruins in Mexico City.

They were very foreign to me, a different breed of man from what I was used to. They were too big, too sun-bleached, too enthusiastic.

And worst of all they all wore strange jeans—they were made of blue denim, but the resemblance ended there. (They're jeans, Jim, but not as we know them.) There were no recognizable brand names and I think Jed was the only man in the house who had a button-fly, all the others had zippers. One guy had a parrot embroidered onto his back pocket, another one had a seam sewn down the center of his legs, a kind of built-in crease. Another one had pockets all down the side of his legs and yet another one had jeans that were made up entirely of little squares of denim. It was horrible. There were even a couple of *stone-washed* pairs. These guys didn't seem to care.

I had thought that I didn't mind how a man dressed, but I realized that night that I did care a lot. I liked a man to look like he hadn't given a thought to how he dressed but it had to be a very specific type of not having given it a thought.

All of them tried to get me into bed—some of them tried twice and three times—using the same lines.

"Do you sleep on your stomach?"

"No."

"Well, do you mind if I do?"

After I had been thus approached for about the fifth time, I said, "Kevin, ask me how I like my eggs in the morning."

"Lucy, how do you like your eggs in the morning?"

"Unfertilized!" I shouted. "Now fuck off!"

They were impossible to offend.

"Okay," they shrugged. "No hard feelings." They just moved on to the next woman who strayed into their line of vision, propositioning her in the same charming way.

By about one-thirty I had drunk four million cans of beer and I was stone cold sober. I hadn't seen one attractive man and I knew that things wouldn't get any better. If I stayed any longer I'd be throwing good time after bad. I decided to quit while I wasn't ahead.

No one noticed me leave.

I stood alone on the road, trying to flag down a taxi, and wondered in despair—was that it? Was that all I could expect from life? Was that the best I could expect from being a single woman in London?

Another Saturday night over and nothing to show for it.

My apartment was silent when I got in. I felt so depressed that I vaguely contemplated suicide, but couldn't muster the enthusiasm for it. Maybe in the morning, I promised myself, maybe I'll feel more energetic when I'm not so depressed.

You rotten bastard, Gus, was my last thought before I went to sleep. This is all your fault.

 45

*A couple of* weeks had passed and Gus still hadn't phoned me.

Every morning I thought I had come to terms with it and every evening when I went to bed I realized that I had been holding my breath all day, hoping, almost *expecting*, to hear from him.

I discovered that I had become an embarrassment.

By allowing myself to be dropped by Gus I had upset

the delicate tripartite balance that had existed between my roommates and me. When the three of us had had boyfriends, things had been fine. If one couple wanted to have the living room to themselves—for whatever reason—all the other couples had to do was go to their respective bedrooms and make their own entertainment.

But now that I was on my own, the couple who wanted the living room would feel guilty about banishing me to the sensory deprivation of my bedroom and then they'd feel annoyed with me, because annoyance is much more pleasant than guilt. Being dropped by Gus was regarded as being my own fault, a result of careless, slipshod behavior.

Charlotte decided that it was time for me to get a new boyfriend. She had a childish desire to help and a not-so-childish desire to get me out of the house once in a while so that she and Simon could play doctors and nurses, or whatever it was they got up to.

"You really should forget about Gus and try and meet someone else," she said, encouragingly, one evening when just the two of us were in.

"Give it time," I said. Surely *she* was supposed to say that to *me* and not the other way around, I thought in confusion.

"But you'll never meet anyone if you never go out," she said.

And, of course, she would never get to have sex with Simon on the hall floor, either, if I never went out. But she was nice enough not to say it quite so directly.

"But I do go out," I said. "I went to a party on Saturday night."

"We could put an ad in the paper for you," suggested Charlotte.

"What kind of an ad?"

"An ad in the personal columns."

"No!" I was horrified at the suggestion. "I may be in a bad way, all right, I *am* in a bad way, but I hope I'll never sink that low."

"No, Lucy," protested Charlotte, "you've got it all wrong. Lots of people do it."

"You must be out of your mind," I said firmly. "I am not about to enter that twilight world of singles bars, singles laundromats, men who say on the phone that they look like Keanu Reeves and then when they turn up they're more like Van Morrison without the dress sense, men who say they want an equal loving partnership when they are really serial killers who want to bludgeon you to death. No way. Absolutely not."

Charlotte found that hilarious.

"You've got it all wrong," she wheezed, wiping her eyes. "It's not like that anymore. It used to be sleazy . . ."

"Would you do it?" I asked, cutting to the heart of the matter.

"Well, it's hard to say," she stuttered. "I mean, I *have* a boyfriend . . ."

"Anyway, it's not just the sleaze that I object to," I interjected angrily, "it's being tarred with the 'Sad and Lonely' brush that upsets me. Don't you understand Charlotte—my hope will die with my few remaining ounces of self-esteem."

"Don't be silly," said Charlotte, sitting up straight on the couch and reaching for the nearest pen and a piece of paper, which turned out to be the Chinese takeout menu.

"Come on," she said happily. "Let's make up a lovely description of you and lots of great guys will answer and you'll have a great time!"

"No!"

"Yes," she said nicely, but firmly. "Now let's see, how

will we describe you? . . . Hmmm, how about 'short'? . . . no, maybe not 'short.' "

"Definitely not 'short,' " I found myself agreeing. "That makes me sound like a dwarf."

"You're not allowed to saw 'dwarf' anymore."

"Vertically challenged, then."

"What's that?"

"A dwarf."

"Why didn't you just say that?"

"Bu . . ."

"Okay, how about 'petite'?"

"No, I hate 'petite.' It sounds so . . . so . . . girly and pathetic. Like I can't change a lightbulb without breaking a fingernail."

"Fair enough. Maybe I'll ask Simon to write an ad for you—after all he's in advertising."

"But, Charlotte, he's a graphic designer."

She looked blankly at me.

"What do you mean?"

"I mean that he does the, er, drawings, for the ads. Not the writing."

"So *that's* what a graphic designer does," she said, as if she'd just found out the earth was round.

Sometimes Charlotte really scared me. I wouldn't have liked to live in her head, it must have been a dark, lonely, frightening place. You could walk for miles and miles without meeting a single intelligent thought.

"Please forget it," I pleaded.

"Well, why don't we just run through the ones here in *Time Out* and see if there's anyone nice for you."

"No!" I said in despair.

"Oh listen, here's a good one," squeaked Charlotte. "Tall, muscular, hirsute, oh . . . oh dear . . ."

"Yuk," I squirmed. "That's not my type at all."

"Just as well," said Charlotte, a bit deflated looking. "She's a lesbian. Such a pity. I was starting to like the sound of her myself. Oh well."

Charlotte continued reading. Every now and then she'd make an inquiry of me.

"What does it mean when they say they've got a *s-o-h*?"

"That they've got a sense of humor?"

"So what's *g-s-o-h* then?"

"Good sense of humor, I suppose."

"Oh, that's nice."

"No, it's not, Charlotte," I said annoyed. "It just means that they think they're hilarious and they laugh at their own jokes."

"What does *w-slash-e* mean?"

"Well endowed."

"No!"

"Yes."

"Gosh! That sounds really sort of show-offy, doesn't it? That would put you off, wouldn't it?"

"It depends. It would certainly put me off. But maybe not everyone."

"You wouldn't be interested in weekday afternoon romps in Hampstead with a married couple?"

"Charlotte!" I said outraged. "How could you make such a suggestion? You know I can't get the time off work," I added grumpily, and the pair of us cackled a bit at that.

"How about 'caring, affectionate man with so much love in his heart to give to the right girl'?"

"No way! He sounds like a *total* loser. A male version of me."

"Yes, he does sound a bit wet," agreed Charlotte.

"Well, how about 'virile, demanding hunk seeks classy, athletic, supple woman for adventures'?"

"Supple?" I shrieked. "Athletic? Adventures? How vile and awful. Could he be a bit more *overt* about what he wants from a relationship? Jesus!"

I was getting upset. It was terribly depressing. Sordid and sad. For as long as I lived, I would never go out with a man that I'd met through the personal ads.

"You look lovely," said Charlotte, adjusting my collar.

"Is that supposed to make me feel better?" I asked bitterly.

"I bet you'll have a great time," she said, tentatively.

"I know for a fact I'll have a horrible time."

"Think positive."

"Think positive indeed! Why the hell don't you go?"

"I don't need to go. I already *have* a boyfriend."

"Rub it in, why don't you?"

"But he might be nice," suggested Charlotte.

"He *won't* be nice."

"No, really, he might."

"I can't believe you're doing this to me, Charlotte," I said, still stunned.

I really couldn't believe it—Charlotte had betrayed me. She'd set me up with some man she had found in the personal ads. Without even consulting me, she had arranged a date for me and some American man. And of course when I found out, I was outraged.

Although my reaction wasn't as extreme as Karen's. When she heard about "my blind date"—as Charlotte insisted on calling it—she laughed until she cried. She managed to stop laughing just long enough to call Daniel to tell him all about it, and then she convulsed for another twenty minutes.

"Christ, you really *are* desperate," she said as she hung up the phone and wiped tears from her cheeks.

"It has nothing to do with me," I protested angrily. "And I'm not going."

"But you have to go," said Charlotte. "It wouldn't be fair to him."

"You're out of your crazy little mind," I said.

She stared at me, her big blue eyes filling with tears.

"Sorry, Charlotte," I said awkwardly. "You're not crazy."

Simon had called her crazy a few days before and her boss called her crazy quite a bit, so she was a bit sensitive about craziness allegations.

"But, Charlotte, really," I blustered, trying to be strong, "I'm not going out with him. I don't care how nice or normal he sounds."

"I was only trying to help," she sniffed, tears trickling out of the corners of her eyes. "I thought it would be nice for you to meet a sweet man."

"I know," I stretched up and guiltily put my arm around her. "I know, Charlotte."

"Don't be mad at me, please, Lucy," she sobbed.

"I'm not mad," I said, hugging her. "Oh, Charlotte, please don't cry."

I hated to see anyone cry—with the possible exception of my mother—but I promised myself, no matter what happened, no matter how much she cried, I was not giving in to Charlotte, I was not going to meet this man Chuck.

I gave in to Charlotte and agreed to meet Chuck. I'm not really sure how or why, but I agreed. Although I retained a small remnant of self-esteem by complaining bitterly about it.

"He'll be completely vile," I assured Charlotte as I prepared to leave. "Do I look all right?"

"I keep telling you, you look lovely. Doesn't she, Si?"

"What? Oh yes, yes, lovely," agreed Simon, heartily. He was just dying for me to leave, so he could have sex with Charlotte.

"And, Lucy, he might be nice," she said.

"He'll be awful," I promised.

"You never know," said Charlotte darkly and wagged a finger at me, "he could be The One."

And to my horror, I found myself agreeing with her, or at least hoping that she was right. She had a point—he *might* be nice, he could be the exception that proved the rule, he might not be an anal-retentive, ax-murdering, astonishingly ugly, emotional cripple.

*Hope,* that fickle foolish creature, that emotional prodigal son, was making a guest appearance in my life. In spite of all the times hope had let me down in the past, I had decided to give it one more chance.

Would I ever learn? Am I addicted to disappointment? I wondered.

But then there was a surge of excitement through me— what if he was great? What if he was like Gus, only more normal and not so dippy and without the minimalist approach to phone calls? Wouldn't it be wonderful? And, just supposing that I did like him and it all worked out, I could still be within Mrs. Nolan's timeframe. I would have time to go to America to meet his family and organize a wedding within six months.

 46

I was meeting him at eight o'clock outside one of those boring steakhouse restaurants that proliferate in central London, to cater to the masses and masses of Americans who visit the city every year.

Chuck had said—for a moment my head swam because I could hardly believe I was having dinner with a man called Chuck—Chuck had said I would recognize him by his navy raincoat and a copy of *Time Out*. By his navy raincoat and copy of *Time Out* so shall he be known!

I had no intention of loitering outside the restaurant waiting for him to arrive, thus leaving myself at his mercy if he turned out to be a total horror. Instead I cased the joint from across the road and pretended to be waiting for a bus. With the collar of my coat up I kept my eyes trained on the doorway opposite.

I had butterflies in my stomach because, while I fully expected him to be untouchable, there was always a small chance that he might be nice.

At five to eight my subject arrived, navy raincoat and copy of *Time Out* all present and correct.

From my lookout perch he seemed fine. Well, at least he *looked* normal enough. Only one head, no obvious disfigurements, no extra limbs, no missing limbs—at least none that I could see. I couldn't speak for his toes or his penis on such short acquaintanceship.

I crossed the road for a closer look.

Not bad, not bad at all.

In fact, he could even have been described as handsome. Medium height, tan, dark hair, dark eyes, nice bones, a *strong* face. There was something about him that reminded me of someone . . . who could it be? It would come to me later.

Hope buzzed around in my chest. He wasn't my usual type, but things had never worked out with any of my usual types, so what the hell, I might as well give this a chance.

Maybe I owe you one, Charlotte, I thought.

He had seen me; had noted my matching copy of *Time Out*. He spoke. No spit landed on my face. This was looking good.

"You must be Lucy," he said. Nil points for originality, minus several million for ugly pants and ten out of ten for no hare lip or stutter or dribble.

Yet.

"And you must be Chuck?" I asked, not exactly breaking any new conversational ground myself.

"Chuck Thaddeus Mullerbraun the Second, all the way from Redridge, Tucson, Arizona," he grinned. He stuck out his hand and gave me a hefty, hearty handshake.

Oh--oh, I thought.

Quickly I pulled myself up short. It wasn't his fault-- Americans always did that. Ask them anything, *anything*, from "is there a god?" to "Can you pass the salt, please?" and the first thing they do is tell you their full name and address. As if they're afraid that, if they don't keep reminding themselves who they are and where they come from, they'll just disappear.

I *did* find it a bit odd. What if someone stopped me in the street and asked me the time and I replied, "Lucy

Carmel Sullivan the First, all the way from the top floor apartment, 43D Bassett Crescent, Ladbroke Grove, London W10, UK. Sorry I don't have a watch, but I think it's about one-fifteen.''

It was just a different custom, I reminded myself, like Spaniards having their dinner at two in the morning. I should be embracing this contact with a different culture. *Vive la difference!*

But wait.

*Lucy Mullerbraun?*

I think I liked Lucy Lavan better, I thought wistfully, but there was no point pursuing that line of inquiry at this particular juncture.

Or at any juncture, ever.

"Shall we?" he suggested politely, indicating the door into the restaurant.

"Why not?"

We went into the vast restaurant where a small Puerto Rican man showed us to a window table.

I sat down.

Chuck sat down opposite me.

We gave each other halting, nervous smiles.

I started to speak, and he started to speak at the same time. Then we both stopped and neither of us said anything, then at the same time we both said, "You first, no really," then we both laughed, then we both said "Please, you go first."

It was kind of endearing. It broke the ice.

"Please," I said, taking charge, afraid that the double act could continue all night, "You go first, really, I insist."

"Okay." He smiled. "I was just going to tell you that you've got beautiful eyes."

"Thank you." I smiled back, flushed with pleasure.

"I love brown eyes," he said.

"So do I," I agreed. So far so good. We'd obviously got a couple of things in common.

"My wife has brown eyes," he said.

*What?*

"Your wife?" I asked faintly.

"Well, ex-wife," he corrected. "We're divorced now, but I keep forgetting."

What was I supposed to say to *that*? I didn't know he'd been married. But so what, I decided, getting a firm grip on myself, everyone has a past and anyway he never said he *hadn't* been married either.

"I'm over it now," he said.

"Er . . . good, good," I said, trying to sound encouraging.

"I wish her well."

"Marvelous," I said, heartily.

A little pause.

"I'm not bitter," he said bitterly, staring bitterly at the tablecloth.

Another little pause.

"Meg," he said.

"S . . . sorry?" I said.

"Meg," he said again. "That's her name. Well, it's actually Margaret, but I always called her Meg. A little nickname, I suppose."

"That's nice," I said weakly.

"Yes," he said, giving a very whimsical, faraway smile. "Yes, it was."

An awkward silence followed.

I was aware of a faint sinking noise. It took me a moment or two to realize that it was the sound of my heart. The sound of it on an express elevator, no-stops-allowed, one-way-ticket, to my boots.

But perhaps I was being negative.

Maybe we could help mend each other's broken hearts. Perhaps all he needed was the love of a good woman. Perhaps all I needed was the love of Chuck Thaddeus Mullerbraun from—where was it—somewhere in Arizona.

The waitress came to take our drinks order.

"A glass of your finest English tap water for me," said Chuck, leaning back in his chair and slapping his stomach. I had a horrible feeling that his shirt was nylon. And what was that about tap water? He was *drinking* tap water? Did he have a death wish?

The waitress gave Chuck a filthy look. She knew a cheapskate when she saw one.

Surely he wasn't expecting me to have tap water also?

Well, I was sorry, but he could go to hell, because I wanted a drink. A real drink.

Start as you mean to go on.

"A Bacardi and Diet Coke," I said, trying to sound like it was a reasonable request.

The woman went away and Chuck leaned across the table. "I didn't know you drank *alcohol*," he said.

*Maybe we wouldn't be mending each other's broken hearts, after all.*

He might as well have told me he didn't know I had sex with small children, he said it with so much distaste and disgust.

"Yes," I said a little defiantly. "Why not? I enjoy a drink now and again."

"Okay," he said slowly. "Okay. Okay. That's cool with me. That's okay."

"Don't you drink yourself?" I asked.

"Yeah, I drink," he said.

*Thank God.*

"I drink water," he continued. "I drink sodas. That's

all I need to drink. The best goddam drink in the world—a glass of ice-cold water. I don't need alcohol.''

I braced myself. If he tells me he's just high on life, I'm leaving, I promised myself.

But, alas, it was not to be.

And on with the conversation, such as it was.

"Your . . . er . . . Meg doesn't drink?" I asked. "Alcohol," I added hurriedly, before he started playing semantics with me again.

"Never touched alcohol, never needed to," he bellowed.

"Well, it's not as if I need to," I said, wondering why I was bothering to try and defend myself.

"Hey." He stared at me intently. "You gotta ask yourself—who are you trying to convince? Me? Or you?"

You know, now that I looked at him properly, he wasn't so much bronzed as *orange*. Not so much tanned, as tangerine.

Our drinks arrived. Chuck's glass of water and my Instrument of the Devil and Diet Coke.

"Are you ready to order?" asked the waitress.

"Hey, we just got here," said Chuck rudely.

The woman slunk away. I wanted to run after her and apologize, but Chuck engaged me in what could laughingly be called conversation.

"Have you ever been married, Lindy?" he asked.

"Lucy," I corrected him.

"What?" he asked.

"Lucy," I said. "My name's Lucy."

A blank stare from Chuck.

"Not Lindy," I said, by way of explanation.

"Oh, I *see*," he said, with a big, jovial burst of laughter. "Excuse me, excuse me. I gotcha. Yeah, yeah, *Lucy*."

He laughed again. A big, thigh-slapping bellow.

It took him quite a while to stop laughing, actually.

He kept shaking his head in disbelief and saying things like "Lindy! Well how about that?" and "Ha, ha, ha. Lindy! Can you truly believe it?"

Then he put on a down-South red-neck accent and said something that sounded like "Waall, tie me down you hog and whup ma hide with molasses!"

At least I *think* that was what he said.

And the face that looked so *strong* on first meeting was actually *immobile,* unmoving, rigid. I sat with a fixed smile on my face and waited for him to calm down and then said, "In answer to your question, Brad, no, I've never been married."

"Hey, hey, *hey,*" he said, his face darkening with annoyance. "The name's Chuck. Who's this Brad guy?"

"It was a joke," I explained quickly. "You know . . . you called me Lindy. I called you Brad."

"Yeah, right." He stared at me as if I was completely crazy. His face was like a slide show—one static image after another, with little gaps of nothingness while he cleared one emotion and waited for the new one to arrive.

"Hey, lady," he demanded. "Are you some kind of wacko? Because I got no room for wackos in my life right now."

I clamped my mouth shut to stop myself from asking him just *when* he might have room for wackos in his life, but it was difficult.

"It was a joke," I said nicely. I thought I had better appease him because I was just a little bit alarmed at his abrupt change of mood.

He probably belonged to a gun club. There was a slightly odd, kind of manic look in his eyes that I hadn't spotted when I first met him. And there was something weird about his hair . . . what was it?

He stared at me and nodded his head slowly (I couldn't help noticing that while his head moved, his hair seemed to stay in the same place) and said, "Right, I get it. This is humor, right?"

He flashed a mouthful of teeth at me. To let me know he appreciated my humor.

*. . . It wasn't just that it was obviously blow-dried and flicked . . .*

"That was an example of humor, hey? Yeah, pretty good."

*. . . And of course it was thick with hairspray . . .*

"I like it, yeah, yeah, I like it. You're one funny little lady, arencha?"

*. . . Could it be a wig? . . .*

"Mmmm," I murmured, I was afraid to open my mouth to speak in case I spewed all over him, right into his brushed-denim lap.

*. . . Although it was more like a helmet, actually, all rigid and sticky . . .*

He picked up a bread roll and shoved it into his mouth in one bite and chewed and chewed and chewed, like a cow chewing the cud. It was disgusting.

I could hardly believe what he did next.

It was not so much that he broke wind. It was more like he took a hammer to it and shattered it into a million pieces.

Yes, he broke wind, long and loud and unapologetically.

While I was still reeling from the shock of that, the poor waitress came back to take our order, although I was sure I would vomit if I was required to eat anything. But there was nothing wrong with Chuck's appetite. He ordered the biggest steak on the menu and asked for it rare.

"Why don't you just get the entire cow brought along to the table and you can get it to climb up onto your plate?'' I suggested. I had nothing against people eating red meat, but it was so nice to be mean to him that I wasn't able to pass up the chance. But unfortunately he just laughed.

Such a pity, a waste of good nastiness.

Then he decided that it was time that we got to know each other better, time to share life experiences.

''Hey, ya ever go to the Caribbean?'' he barked at me. And, without waiting for my answer, launched straight into a description of the white sands, the friendly natives, the great tax-free shopping, the wonderful cuisine, the cut-price all-inclusive deals he could get because his brother-in-law worked for a travel agent . . .

''Well, he's not technically your brother-in-law anymore, now that Meg has divorced you, is he?'' I interrupted, but he elected not to hear me. All his attention was focused on himself.

On and on went the lyrical description. The beautiful cabana he had stayed in, the phosphorescence from the tropical fish. I was patient for as long as I could, until I couldn't take anymore. I very rudely interrupted a description of the clean, clear, blue water on which he went sailing in a glass-bottomed boat.

''Let me guess,'' I said sarcastically, ''you went there with Meg.''

He looked up at me quickly, as suspicion clanked onto his immobile face.

Then I gave him a dazzling smile, just to confuse him.

''Hey, how d'ya guess?'' He grinned at me.

I sat on my hand to stop myself from punching him in the face.

''Oh, feminine intuition, I guess.'' I giggled daintily, certain I could feel vomit lapping at the back of my teeth.

. . . *And speaking of teeth, what was wrong with his?*

"So you'd like to have a relationship with me, Lisa?"

"Er . . ." How could I tell him I'd rather have a relationship with a leper without offending him?

The leper, that is.

"Cos I gotta warn you," he grinned, "I'm a pretty choosy guy."

Where was my dinner?

I no longer cared.

"But you're kinda cute."

"Thanks," I muttered. Don't bother, please.

"Yeah, on a scale of one to ten, I'd give you a . . . let's see, yeah, I'd give you a seven. No, let's say a six point five. I gotta deduct a half a percent because you drank alcohol on the first date."

"I think you must mean half a point, not half a percent, you're talking about tens, not hundreds, and what's wrong with drinking it on the first date, as opposed to any other time?" I demanded coldly.

He frowned slowly at me. "You got a big mouth on you. You ask a whole lot of questions, ya know that?"

"No, really Chuck, I'm very interested in knowing why I've lost half a point with you."

"Okay. Okay. I'll tell ya, I'll tell ya. Sure, I'll tell ya. You realize the signals that drinking alcohol on a first date gives out, Lisa? You see the kind of statement you're making about yourself?"

I stared blankly at him.

"No," I said sweetly. "But please do enlighten me."

"Huh?"

"Enligh . . . er, please do *tell* me."

"A, V, A, I, L, A, B, L, E," he spelt out slowly.

"Sorry?" I said, confused.

"Available," he said impatiently. "It says to me that you're available."

"Oh, *available*," I said, understanding. "Well, perhaps if you had spelled it properly I might have realized what you were trying to say."

His eyes narrowed.

"Hey, what are you trying to say here? That you're smarter'n me or something?"

"Nothing of the sort," I said politely. "I was just letting you know that there are three *A*s in available." God! He was nasty!

"No man has any respect for a woman who is a drunk," he said, looking with narrowed eyes at my Bacardi and then at me.

This had to be a joke. It had to be some kind of setup. That was the only explanation. I looked around the room, half expecting to see Daniel sitting at one of the other tables laughing hysterically.

But I recognized no one.

Oh dear, I sighed to myself, I wish this was over. What a waste of an evening. Especially a Friday evening, when there were such good things on TV.

"You know, you don't actually have to put up with this," a rebellious little voice whispered in my head.

"But of course I do," a dutiful little voice whispered back.

"No, honestly, you don't," replied the first voice.

"But, but . . . I agreed to meet him, I have to stay the allotted time. I can't leave. It wouldn't be *polite*," protested my dutiful part.

"*Polite*," spluttered the rebellious voice, "*polite!* Is he polite?"

"Yes, but, I hardly ever meet men and I shouldn't look a gift horse in the mouth and . . ." explained my dutiful part.

"I don't believe what you're saying," said the rebellious part, sounding genuinely shocked. "Do you really have such a low opinion of yourself that you'd rather be with a man like this than alone?"

"But I'm so lonely," said the dutiful voice.

"Desperate, you mean," snorted the rebellious voice.

"Now that you put it like that . . ." said the dutiful part reluctantly, loath to turn away a man, *any* man, even a truly awful man.

"I *do* put it like that," said the rebellious part firmly.

"Well, okay then, I suppose I could pretend to be sick," said the dutiful voice. "I could fake a broken leg or a burst appendix, or something."

"No, you damn well won't," said the rebellious part. "Why spare him? If you're leaving, do it properly. Let him know how objectionable he is, how obnoxious you find him. Stand up for yourself—make a statement."

"Oh, I couldn't . . ." protested the dutiful part.

The rebellious voice was silent.

". . . Could I?"

"Of course you could," said my rebellious voice warmly.

"But . . . but . . . what am I to do?" asked the dutiful part, excitement beginning to burn in the pit of its stomach.

"I'm sure you'll think of something."

Chuck was droning on again.

"I was on the tube today and no kiddin' here, Lizzie, I was the only white guy on it . . ."

Right! Enough! No more.

"But I'm afraid of him," realized my dutiful part. "What if he tracks me down and tortures me and kills me—let's face it, that's the kind he seems to be."

"Don't be afraid," said the rebellious voice. "He doesn't know where you live, he doesn't even have your phone number. All he has is a P.O. box number. Go on! You've nothing to worry about.''

Feeling light-headed with unaccustomed power I stood up, gathering my coat and my bag.

"Excuse me." I smiled sweetly, interrupting Chuck's speech about how there should be tighter controls on emigration and how only white people should have a vote. "I'm just going to the little girls' room."

"You gotta take your coat to the rest room?" inquired Chuck.

"Yes, Chuck," I said sweetly. Dickhead!

I walked away from him, my legs shaking. I was afraid but I was also happy.

I passed our waitress clearing a table and I had so much adrenaline throbbing through me I could barely speak properly.

"Excuse me," I said, my words tripping over each other, my tongue far too big for my mouth. "I'm at the table by the window and the gentleman would like a bottle of your most expensive champagne sent over, please."

"Certainly," said the woman.

"Thank you," I smiled, and moved past her.

As soon as I got home I would call the restaurant to make sure that the waitress didn't end up having to pay for it herself, I decided.

I reached the Ladies, hesitated for only a moment, then kept on walking. I felt as if I were dreaming. It was only when I crossed over the threshold from the restaurant into the rainy street that I really believed that I had done it, that I had left.

My initial plan had been to just leave and go home, letting the passage of time be Chuck's indicator that I was never to return. But that would be a mean thing to do.

His dinner would get cold while he was waiting for me to get back. And waiting, and waiting . . .

Always assuming the revolting man would have the manners to wait for me to get back before tucking into his meal. Nevertheless I decided to give him the benefit of the doubt. I pulled my coat on, and even though it was a wet, Friday evening, I got a taxi immediately.

The gods were smiling on me. That was the kind of sign I needed to feel that I had done the right thing.

"Ladbroke Grove," I told the driver excitedly, as I clambered in. "But before that can you do me a favor?"

"Depends," he said suspiciously. But that's London cab drivers for you.

"I've just said goodbye to my boyfriend. He's going away forever and he's sitting by the window in this restaurant here and I wonder if you could drive slowly by until he sees me so that I can wave farewell one last time."

The taxi man seemed genuinely moved by my request.

"Just like Frank Sinatra and Ava Gardner. And I thought that romance was dead," he said hoarsely, a catch in his voice. "No problem, darling. Just tell me which one he is."

"That, er, tanned, handsome man just up there," I said, pointing to where Chuck was sitting, admiring his reflection in his knife.

The taxi driver drove up right beside Chuck's table and I rolled down my window.

"I'll turn the light on, love, so he can see you better," said the driver.

"Thank you."

Chuck twiddled the knife backward and forward, catching his reflection in different lights.

"Likes 'imself," commented my driver.

"He certainly does."

"You sure that's 'im, love?" asked the driver doubtfully.

"Certain."

Chuck was starting to look annoyed now. I had obviously spent more time than Meg used to in the Ladies and he didn't approve.

"Should I toot the horn, love?" asked my faithful driver.

"Why not?"

The driver beeped the horn and Chuck looked out into the street to see what all the commotion was about. I leaned out of the taxi window and waved energetically.

He smiled in cheery recognition when he saw me and raised his hand to wave back at me.

But then confusion began to inch its way painfully slowly across his stupid face when he noticed that the familiar looking person he was waving to was actually his date for the evening, the woman he was supposed to be having dinner with, the woman whose scampi-in-the-basket was, as we speak, being placed reverently in front of her empty chair, and that she was sitting in a taxi about to depart the scene. The fledgling cheery wave halted abruptly in its tracks.

He wrinkled his orange forehead. He didn't understand. This does not compute.

And then the penny dropped.

The look that appeared on his face was worth it all. When he realized that I was not in the little girls' room but was in fact escaping in a taxi, it was nothing short of beautiful. It had been worth the whole vile evening just to see the disbelief and rage and fury on his smug, weird, tanned face. He leaped up from his chair, and dropped the knife that he had so admired himself in.

I couldn't stop laughing.

"What the . . . ?" he mouthed out the window, his face contorted with fury. He looked almost animated.

"Fuck you!" I mouthed back in at him. Then I thrust both my hands out into the wet night and raised the first two fingers of each hand in a 'V' gesture at him, just in case his lip reading wasn't too good. I made short, sharp upward motions with both my hands for about ten seconds while he stared at me in an impotent fury from the window.

"Drive," I ordered.

The driver put his foot on the accelerator just as two waiters appeared behind Chuck, one with an ice bucket and a white napkin, the other with a bottle of champagne.

In the cab I realized who Chuck had reminded me of. It was *Donny Osmond*!

Donny Osmond singing "Puppy Love."

Orange, sincere, soulful Donny Osmond with puppy dog eyes to match his puppy love. But a Donny Osmond for whom the glitter had faded, who had had a hard life, a Donny Osmond who things hadn't worked out for, a bitter, humorless, right-wing Donny.

Long before I reached home, I felt guilty about Chuck and the bottle of champagne. It wasn't fair that he should have to pay for it. Just because he was a nasty, horrible person didn't mean that I had to behave like one too. So the minute I got into the apartment I called the restaurant.

"Er, hello," I said nervously. "I wonder if you can help me. I was in your restaurant earlier and I had to leave suddenly, and before I left I ordered a bottle of champagne for my companion. It was an . . . er . . . surprise, and I don't think he would have wanted to pay. And I want to be sure that the waitress didn't have it docked from her wages or anything . . ."

"An American gentleman?" a man's voice asked.

"Yes," I reluctantly confirmed. Gentleman, my foot!

"And you must be the woman with the mental illness?" inquired the voice.

The cheek of him! How dare the voice imply that I was crazy.

"The American man explained how you often do this kind of thing, that you can't help yourself."

I swallowed my rage.

"I'll pay for the champagne," I muttered.

"There's no need," said the voice. "We have agreed to overlook the damage he's caused to the furniture if he pays for the champagne."

"But it hardly seems fair for him to have to pay for it when he didn't drink it," I said.

"But he did drink it," said the voice.

"But he doesn't drink," I protested.

"Yes, he does," said the voice. "Come and look for yourself, if you don't believe me."

"You mean he's still there?"

"Oh, yes! And that's not alcohol-free tequila he's drinking."

Oh God! So now I had turning Chuck into a drunkard on my conscience. But what the hell—it might be the best thing that ever happened to him.

Now for the TV!

To my great dismay, Karen and Daniel were in the front room. They were sharing a bottle of wine and were sickeningly holdy-handy, watching *my* shows on *my* TV.

"You're home early," said Karen, annoyed.

"Mmmmmm," I said noncommittally.

I was annoyed also. That means no TV for me. I couldn't stay in the same room as Karen and Daniel while they were cuddling.

I would have to go and sit in my bedroom while they stretched out on the couch and Karen put her head in

Daniel's lap and Daniel stroked Karen's hair, and Karen stroked Daniel's . . . well, whatever else they got up to, which I didn't really want to think about.

They were so lovey-dovey, they were disgusting.

Charlotte and Simon never made me feel awkward, I just didn't know what it was about Daniel and Karen.

"How are you?" asked Daniel, looking all smug and superior.

"Fine," I said airily.

"And how was your blind American?" asked Daniel.

"Crazy."

"Really?"

"Really."

"Oh Lucy, not again," sighed Karen. "You're beginning to make a habit of this kind of thing."

"I'm going to bed," I said.

"Good," said Karen, winking lasciviously at Daniel.

"Ha, ha," I said, keen to seem like a good sport. "Good night."

"Lucy, don't feel you have to leave just because we're here," said Daniel, polite as ever.

"*Do,*" corrected Karen.

"Stay," urged Daniel.

"Don't," laughed Karen.

"Karen, don't be so rude," said Daniel, looking embarrassed.

"I'm not being rude," smiled Karen. "I'm just being honest. I'm letting Lucy know where she stands."

I went, feeling inexplicably tearful.

"Oh, by the way, Lucy," called Karen after me.

"What?" I asked, standing by the door.

"There was a phone call for you."

"Who was it?"

"Gus."

 47

*A great load* tumbled from me and I breathed out, a long, delicious sigh—I'd been waiting to do that for three weeks.

"Well, what did he say?" I demanded, excitedly.

"That he'd call again in an hour and that if you weren't back then he'd call every hour until you got home."

Happiness flooded through me. He hadn't abandoned me, I hadn't done anything wrong, my position hadn't been usurped by Mandy.

A thought struck me.

"Where did you say I was?" I asked breathlessly.

"Out."

"Out with a man?"

"Yes."

"Great! That might worry him. What time is he calling back at?"

Karen sat up straight and stared at me.

"Why?" she asked. "Surely you're not going to *speak* to him?"

"Er, yes, I am," I said sheepishly, shifting from one foot to the other.

Daniel shook his head in a "will she ever learn" kind of way and gave an exasperated little smile. The gall! What would he know of the agonies of unrequited or semi-requited love?

"Haven't you any self-respect?" asked Karen disbelievingly.

"No," I said absently, wondering what tone I should adopt with Gus—amused? cross? stern?

I knew I was going to forgive him—it was only a question of how hard I was going to make him work for it.

"Well, it's your funeral," said Karen, turning away from me. "He should call in about twenty minutes."

I went to my room and jumped up and down with delight. Twenty minutes—how could I contain myself?

But I had to be calm, I couldn't let him know how thrilled I was so I forced myself to take deep breaths.

But I couldn't stop smiling—at five to ten, I'd be speaking to Gus, Gus whom I thought I'd lost forever, and I could barely wait.

When my digital alarm clock said nine-fifty-five, I placed my feet in the starting blocks and waited for the starter gun.

And waited. And waited . . .

He didn't call. Of course, he didn't call.

How could I have possibly thought he might?

So that I wouldn't cry, I fed myself all the usual excuses. My clock could be fast. Gus couldn't tell the difference between five minutes and an hour, he was probably in a pub where, if there was a phone at all, it was probably broken and if it wasn't broken it was probably being hogged by some young woman from Galway on a marathon tearful call home.

But after eleven I admitted defeat and went to bed.

"The little bastard," I thought angrily. "He had his chance and he blew it. When he does ring, I'm not going to speak to him. And if I do speak to him, it'll only be to tell him that I'm not speaking to him."

Some time later I heard the doorbell ring and I sat up

in bed in horror. Oh no! He was here, on the premises and I'd taken my makeup off! Christ, what a disaster. I leaped out of bed and heard Karen or Daniel pressing the buzzer.

"You keep him talking," I hissed at Karen, sticking my head out of my bedroom door. "I'll be ready in five minutes."

"Keep who talking?" she asked.

"Gus, of course."

"Why, where is he?"

"On his way up—you've just buzzed him in."

"No, I haven't," she said.

"Yes, you have," I insisted. "Just now."

She was behaving very oddly, but she didn't *look* drunk.

"No, I haven't," she insisted. She looked at me closely. "Are you all right, Lucy?"

"I'm fine," I said. "It's you I'm worried about. If it wasn't Gus, then *who* did you open the door for?"

"The pizza man."

"*What* pizza man?"

"The pizza man delivering the pizza for me and Daniel."

"But, *where?*"

"Here," she said, flinging open the front door, revealing a man in a red plastic suit and a bike helmet, with a cardboard box in his hands.

"Daniel," she shouted. "Get out the plates and napkins."

"I see," I whispered, and slunk back to bed.

Why had Gus ever bothered phoning at all, I wondered tearfully. What good had it done me? None whatsoever. Just caused upset and upheaval.

Hours later, when everyone was in bed and the flat was in darkness, the phone rang. I woke immediately—even in my sleep my nerves were still on full alert, hoping for Gus's call. I stumbled out into the hall to answer it because I knew it had to be Gus—no one else would call at such an hour, but I was too asleep to be happy about it.

Gus sounded drunk.

"Can I come over, Lucy?" was the first thing he said.

"No," I said, as I wondered, "Whatever happened to 'Hello'?"

"But I must see you, Lucy," he shouted passionately.

"And I must get my sleep."

"Lucy, Lucy, where's your fire, your passion? Sleep indeed. You can sleep anytime. But it's not every day we get the chance to be together."

I knew that only too well.

"Lucy, please," he said. "You're angry at me, is that it?"

"Yes, I'm angry at you," I said evenly, trying not to sound so angry to frighten him away.

"But please, Lucy, I've got an excuse," he promised.

"Let's hear it."

"The dog ate my homework, my alarm clock didn't go off, my bike got a flat."

I didn't think it was funny.

"Oh-oh," he sang. "She's gone all quiet on me, that must mean that she's mad again," he said. "Seriously, Lucy, I do have an excuse."

"Please tell me it."

"Not over the phone. I'd rather come and see you."

"You won't see me until I hear your excuse," I said.

"You're a hard woman, Lucy Sullivan," he shouted sadly. "Hard! Cruel!"

"The excuse?" I asked politely.

"It's really better if I explain it in my full three dimensions. Disembodied voices aren't half as good," he said wheedlingly. "Please, Lucy, I hate the phone."

I was well aware of that.

"Come over tomorrow, then. It's far too late now."

"Late! Lucy Sullivan, when did the time ever matter to the both of us? You're like me—a free spirit who is not bound by time, as issued to us by that crowd of meanies in Greenwich. What's happened to you? Has your soul been stolen by the goblins of clock watching?"

He paused for a second and then said in tones of hushed horror, "Jesus, Lucy—you haven't gone and bought a *watch!?*"

I laughed—the little swine. How could I scare him if he made me laugh?

"Come over tomorrow morning, Gus." I tried to sound crisp and authoritative, "and we'll talk then."

"No time like the present," he said cheerfully.

"No, Gus. Tomorrow."

"Who knows what tomorrow will bring, Lucy? Tomorrow is another day and who knows where we might be?"

Whether or not he meant it as one, I knew a threat when I heard it—he might not call me tomorrow, I might never hear from him again, but right then, at that very moment, he wanted to see me. He was *mine,* and I would be well advised not to look a gift horse in the mouth, to catch the ball on the hop, and to learn the difference between birds in the hand and birds in the bush.

*Do you really want him on these terms?* asked a little voice in my head.

*Yes,* I replied wearily.

*But, haven't you any self-respe . . . ?*

*No, I haven't! How many times do I have to tell you?*

"Okay, Gus." I sighed, pretending that I had just given

in, although, of course, the outcome had never been in doubt. "Come over."

"I'm on my way," he said.

That could have meant anything from fifteen minutes to four months, and my dilemma was should I put my makeup on or should I just stay as I was.

I knew about the dangers of tempting fate—if I put my makeup on, he wouldn't come. If I *didn't* put my makeup on, he would come, but would be so shocked at what I looked like that he would immediately leave.

"What's going on?" whispered a voice. It was Karen. "Was that Gus?"

I nodded, "Sorry for waking you."

"Did you tell him to go and fuck himself?"

"Er, no, you see I haven't heard the full story yet. He's, er, coming over now to tell me it."

"Now!? At two-thirty in the morning?"

"No time like the present," I said weakly.

"In other words, he was at a party and didn't score with anyone and he's in the mood for sex. Nice one, Lucy, you certainly put a high price on yourself."

"It's not like that. . . ." I said, my stomach lurching.

"Good night, Lucy," she sighed, ignoring me. "I'm going back to bed.

"With Daniel," she added smugly.

I knew she was going to tell Daniel all about it, because she told him *everything* about me, well, all the embarrassing and shameful stuff, at any rate. I had no privacy, and I hated him knowing so much about me and being smug and judgmental.

He was always in the apartment, I almost felt like we lived together. Why couldn't the pair of them go to *his* place and leave me alone in peace?

"I wish they'd split up," I thought fiercely.

I decided that I'd hoodwink Fate; I was sick of it having all the power. So, while I did put on some makeup, I didn't get dressed.

And, in no time at all, the sound of the buzzer boomed through the flat in a manner that would wake the dead. It stopped and gave some welcome peace for a few seconds before starting again and continuing for what seemed like hours—Gus had arrived.

I opened the door of the flat and waited for him to appear, but he didn't. And then I could hear raised voices from a few floors below. Eventually he stumbled up the stairs, looking cute, sexy, disheveled and drunk.

I was lost, hopelessly, completely lost. It was only when I saw him that I realized how much I had missed him.

"Jesus, Lucy," he grumbled, as he wriggled past me and into the flat, "that neighbor of yours has a ferocious bad temper. It was a mistake anyone could make."

"What have you done, Gus?" I asked.

"I rang the wrong bell," he said sulkily, clumping straight into my bedroom.

Now, now, wait a minute, I thought. He's being too forward altogether. He can't just waltz up here after no contact for three weeks and expect to jump straight into bed with me.

Apparently he could. He was already sitting on my bed, taking off his boots.

"Gus . . ." I said tentatively, about to embark on my lecture. You know, the usual—how dare you treat me like this, who do you think you are, who do you think I am, I've too much respect for myself (a lie), I'm not putting up with this (another lie), etc., etc.

"And I said to him, Lucy, I said, 'I only woke you up, it's not like I invaded Poland.' Ha, ha, I knew that'd give him something to think about. German, isn't he?"

"Sorry, Gus, no. He's Austrian."

"Sure, it's all the one. Aren't they all big and blond and always eating sausages?"

Then he focused his bloodshot eyes on me, seeing me for the first time since he had barged in.

"Lucy! My darling Lucy, you're looking beautiful."

He jumped up and ran over to me and the scent of him triggered a longing and lust that surprised me with its intensity.

"Mmmmmmm, Lucy, I've missed you." He nuzzled my neck and slid his hand under my pajama top. The touch of his hand on my bare skin made me shiver with lust that had slumbered undisturbed for three weeks, but with supreme self-control I pushed him away.

Get off! I thought—I haven't given you my lecture yet.

"Oh, Lucy, Lucy," he murmured, as he relaunched his attack. "We must never be apart again."

He slid one arm tightly around my waist and opened the top button of my pajamas with the other. I fumbled with it, trying to close it again, but it was merely a symbolic gesture.

I couldn't help myself—he was too sexy. Beautiful and dangerous and roguish. And he *smelled* so nice, so like Gus.

"Gus!" I wrestled with him as he tried to get my top off, "you didn't call me for three wee—"

"I know, Lucy, I'm sorry Lucy," he said, tugging hard. "But I never wanted it to be that way. Jesus, you're beautiful."

"I deserve an explanation, you know," resisting hard as he pushed me toward the bed.

"Indeed you do, Lucy, indeed you do," he agreed vaguely, as he pushed down on my shoulder, trying to get me to buckle at the knees. "But can I do it in the morning?"

"Gus, do you solemnly promise that you have a good excuse and that you'll tell it to me in the morning?"

"I do," he said, staring sincerely into my eyes and at the same time tugging hard, trying to get my pajama bottoms down.

"And you can give me hell. You can even make me cry," he promised.

So we went to bed.

I remembered what Karen had said, but I disagreed with her—I didn't feel used. I *wanted* Gus to want to have sex with me. That would prove that he still liked me. But I had forgotten that Gus was a bit of a wham, bam, thank you ma'am kind of guy—the sex was over almost as soon as it started. As in the past, Gus came in a matter of minutes. Which left plenty of time to hear his excuses. But he fell sound asleep immediately afterward.

And eventually I fell asleep too.

 48

The following morning Gus wasn't any easier to pin down for his lecture.

Considering how drunk he had been the previous night, he was surprisingly full of energy. By rights he should have been flat on his back, begging for a bucket and swearing never to drink again, like any normal person. Instead he was awake at the crack of dawn, eating cookies.

And when the mail arrived, he bounced out to the hall to get it, and then, with much rustling of paper and ripping of envelopes, opened mine and told me what was in it.

"Oh, good girl, Lucy." He sounded proud. "I'm glad to see that you owe those Visa lads lots more money. Now all you have to do is move and not tell them."

I lay in bed and wished bleakly that he would calm down. Or at least stop reminding me how much money I owed.

"What's going on at Russell and Bromley?" he asked. "Is it your old trouble again?"

"Yes." A pair of black suede knee boots and a pair of sexy, snakeskin sandals, to be precise. "Now, Gus!" I tried to be firm and get his attention. "We really must—"

"What about this one, Lucy?" He waved an envelope at me. "It looks like Karen's bank statement. Should we . . . ?"

God, it was tempting. Charlotte and I suspected that Karen had thousands salted away and I would have *loved* to know.

But I had work to do.

"Never mind Karen's bank statement, Gus." I tried again. "You said last night that you had an excuse and that . . ."

"Can I have a shower, Lucy?" He interrupted. "I think I smell a bit."

He lifted up his arm and put his nose to his armpit.

"Pooh," he said, making a disgusted face. "I stink, therefore I am."

He smelled fine to me.

"You can have a shower in a little while. Give me that envelope."

"But we could steam it and she'd never know . . ."

It was obvious that, despite his passionate promises the

previous night, he had no intention of explaining anything to me.

And I was so delighted he was back that I didn't want to scare him away by pushing for explanations and apologies.

But, at the same time, he had to realize that he couldn't get away with treating me badly.

Of course, he *could* get away with treating me badly, in fact, he just had. But I had to, at least, lodge my protest, go through the motions of acting as if I had self-respect. In the hope that, even though I couldn't fool myself, perhaps I could fool him.

I would have to trick him into having the Serious Talk. It would have to be coaxed out of him, wheedled out of him, so that he wasn't even aware that he was doing it. He wouldn't cooperate if he was approached full-frontal, as it were. I would have to be very, very pleasant, but with an undercurrent of firmness. I turned to Gus who was stretched out on the bed, reading a pension offer thing from my bank.

"Gus, I'd like to talk to you," I said, striving to sound pleasantly firm, or failing that, firmly pleasant.

I must have overdone the firmness because he said, "Oh-oh," and made an "Oh-oh" face. And he jumped off the bed and huddled, cringing, in the space between the dresser and the wall. "I'm scared."

"Come on now, Gus, there's no need to be afraid."

But he wasn't taking it seriously at all. He kept poking his head of black curls out and I'd catch a glimpse of his bright eyes, before he'd whisk his head back in and I would hear him muttering, "Oh, no, I'm done for, she's going to make mincemeat of me."

"Gus, come out, please, there isn't anything to be afraid of."

I tried to laugh to show how good-humored I was, but

it was hard work being patient. It would have been great to shout at him.

"Come on, Gus, I'm not scary, you know that."

"The only thing I have to fear, is fear itself, is that it?" asked his disembodied voice.

"Exactly." I nodded to the wardrobe.

"But, the thing is, Lucy," it continued, "I actually fear fear an awful lot."

"Well, you must stop. There's nothing to be afraid of with me."

He slunk out, looking cute. "You won't shout at me?"

"No." I was forced to agree with him. "I won't shout at you. But I do want to know where you've been for the last three weeks."

"Has it been that long?" he asked innocently.

"Come on now, Gus. The last time I heard from you was the Tuesday night before Karen's party. What have you been up to?"

"This and that." He was vague.

"You can't just disappear for three weeks, you know?" But I said it very gently so that he wouldn't get annoyed and tell me to get lost and that he could disappear for as long as he liked and there wasn't anything I could do about it.

"All right then," he said. I leaned toward him eagerly, hoping to hear stories of natural disasters and acts of God. That neither I nor Gus were responsible for the three-week severance.

"The brother came over from th'Emerald Isle and we had a bit of a drinking spree."

"A spree that lasted three weeks?" I asked disbe-lievingly. I didn't like the fact that I kept calling it three weeks, I should have been vaguer about it. I didn't want him to think that I'd counted the days since he'd been gone, which is of course, exactly what I *had* done.

"Yes, a session that lasted three weeks," he said sounding surprised. "What's wrong with that?"

"What's wrong with that?" I echoed mockingly.

"I've often been missing in action for lots longer than three weeks," he said, sounding confused.

"You're trying to tell me that you've been out drinking for three weeks?"

And suddenly I was appalled at myself. I sounded just like my mother, the tone of voice, the accusation, even the words.

"Och, I'm sorry, Lucy," said Gus. "It's not as bad as it sounds. I forgot about Karen's party and by the time I remembered I was too afraid to call you, because I knew you'd be furious."

"But why didn't you call the next day?" I asked, cringing with pain as I remembered the agony of waiting that I had endured.

"Because I was in a state about missing the party and annoying you, so Stevie said to me, 'There's only one thing that'll straighten you out, and that's . . .'"

". . . Another drink, I'm sure," I finished for him.

"Exactly! And the next day . . ."

". . . You felt so bad about not ringing me the previous day that you had to go and get drunk to feel all right about it . . ."

"No," he said, sounding surprised. "The next day there was a big party in Kentish Town that started at eleven in the morning and we went along to that and got good and hammered, Lucy. Hammered! You never saw anyone so drunk, I hardly knew my own name."

"That's no excuse!" I exclaimed, and then shut up abruptly as, once again, I heard my mother. "You know

I don't mind you getting drunk." I tried to sound calm. "But it's not okay to simply disappear and then come back and act like nothing is wrong."

"Sorry," he exclaimed. "Sorry, sorry, sorry."

Then I braced myself for the hardest question of all.

"Gus, who's Mandy?" I stared hard into his face so that I could draw conclusions from his reaction.

Was it my imagination or did he look alarmed? It *could* just have been my imagination. After all, his jaw didn't drop open and he didn't bury his face in his hands and sob, "I knew this day would come."

In fact all he did was look sulky and say "No one."

"She can't be no one. She's someone." I smiled tightly to convey that I wasn't accusing him of anything, that my fire was strictly friendly.

"She's no one special. She's just a friend."

"Gus," I said, my heart beating fast. "There's no need to lie to me."

"I'm *not*." Aggrieved, pained.

"I'm not saying you are. But if you're seeing someone else, I'd rather know."

I didn't say, if you're seeing someone else you can go and fuck yourself, which is what I *should* have said. But I didn't want to commit the cardinal sin of seeming to care. Popular myth has it that women are desperate to trap men, that men are afraid of being trapped, so the best way to trap them is to pretend that you don't want to trap them. However, that had backfired more times than I'd care to mention, with me saying, "I don't own you. But if you are seeing someone else, I'd like to know." And then meeting my so-called boyfriend at a party wrapped around another woman and wanting to throw a drink at the two of them. And then being told, "But you *said* you didn't mind.

"Lucy, I'm not seeing any other girls," said Gus. He

had lost the defensive look and there was the light of sincerity in his green eyes.

He looked as if he cared about me. And although I was afraid of seeming ungrateful, I pushed ahead.

"Gus, *were* you seeing someone else, you know, before, when we were, er, you know, seeing each other?"

He looked puzzled for a moment while he translated my question into his vernacular. Then he got it.

"Was I two-timing you?" He sounded horrified. "I was NOT."

There was always the chance that he was telling the truth. In fact he probably was because he didn't have the organizational skills to live a double life. As it was, it was a triumph that he remembered to keep breathing when he woke up every morning.

"How dare you?" he demanded. "What kind of person do you think I am?"

The combination of his passionate denials and my desperate desire to believe him, meant that I did. Relief made me joyous and slightly light-headed.

Then he kissed me and I felt even more light-headed.

"Lucy," he said. "I would never do anything to hurt you."

I believed him. It would have been churlish to bring up the fact that he *had* hurt me. The important thing was that he hadn't meant to.

"Now can I hose myself down?" He asked meekly.

He went and had his shower and I thought about my mother. It had scared me a lot to hear me sounding like her. I would try even harder to be more and more liberal, I promised myself.

I heard Daniel and Karen greet Gus, as Gus came out of the bathroom.

"Morning, Gus," said Daniel. Was there something amused in his tone, I wondered defensively.

"Morning, Danny Boy," said Gus jovially, as if he'd never been away.

"Morning, Paddy O'Paddy," said Karen to Gus.

"Morning, Heather McShortbread," said Gus to Karen.

"Morning, Pisshead O'Bricklayer," said Karen to Gus.

"Morning, Skinflint McSeanConnery," said Gus to Karen.

I heard roars of laughter. Outside the bathroom door was obviously the place to be.

Roommates and boyfriend had successfully rebonded, and no one seemed embarrassed except me.

 49

So Gus and I became an item again. And I tried to relax and give him a longer leash. Gus was a free spirit, I constantly reminded myself. Normal rules didn't apply to him. Just because he was late, or talked for hours to someone else at a party where I knew no one, didn't mean that he didn't care about me. I wasn't lowering my expectations, I decided. I was simply changing my perspective.

I knew he cared about me because he had come back, after the three-week hiatus. He hadn't had to do that, no one forced him. And with my new attitude Gus and I got on beautifully. He behaved impeccably. Well, as impeccably as he could without ceasing to be Gus.

It was summer and for once it acted like it.

The weather in London was so unusually warm and

sunny that many people took it as a sign that the world was about to end.

Day followed day of golden, blue-skied heat, but the population of London had been betrayed by the weather so many times that they expected the heat wave to disappear at any moment.

Everyone shook their heads and said gloomily, "It won't last, you know." But it did last and it seemed that the sun would shine forever.

I remember the time as idyllic.

Weeks and weeks where life seemed heavenly, where I felt as if I were living in a little golden cocoon. My bedroom was flooded with yellow light every morning, so that it was nearly a pleasure to get up and live my life.

My depression always abated in the summer, and even work didn't seem so grueling. Especially after we had the minimutiny and the maintenance department had to buy us a fan.

Most lunchtimes, Jed and I went to Soho Square where we scrambled with several thousand other office workers for a square inch of grass on which to lounge and read our books.

Jed was the best person to do that with because if he tried to talk to me, I could just tell him to shut up and he would. We could lie there in companionable silence.

At least, I found it companionable.

Meredia wouldn't come with us because she hated the sun. She spent her lunchtimes hidden in the office, with the blinds down, trying to cast a spell on the weather, so that it would rain. Every day, she anxiously read the forecast, hoping for news of a drop in the temperature, raging as big black clouds that were coming from Ireland bypassed the UK and made straight for France.

Throughout the day, she treated us to the sight of her

hiking up her skirt to shake containers of talcum powder between her gargantuan thighs. "Warm weather isn't kind to the larger woman," she would say bitterly, and then ask if we wanted to see her red chafe marks.

The only thing that cheered her up was reading the temperatures of places in the world that were hotter than London. "At least I'm not in Mecca," she often sighed. And, "Think of what it must be like in Cairo," was another.

Megan wouldn't come to the park either.

Like a true Australian, she reveled in the warm weather, and took her sunbathing seriously. Far more seriously than Jed and I did.

She laughed at me and all the other girls who sat on the grass and pulled our skirts up above our knees and thought that we were daring and unfettered. She was in a different league—she went to the open-air pool and sunbathed topless.

Her contempt for Meredia was even more energetic than usual. "Listen, Pauline," she hissed. "If you don't stop whining about your thighs, I'm going to show you my tanned nipples."

"Keep talking, keep talking," said Jed eagerly to Meredia. She bestowed a sour look upon him and muttered, "My name is Meredia."

Megan blossomed in the heat. She was totally at home with it. She wore cut-off jeans to work—it wasn't her fault she looked like something out of *Baywatch*. She didn't mean to be provocative, she couldn't help being beautiful.

But I was very glad I wasn't Australian. I would have been far too self-conscious to walk around half-naked. I thanked God that I had been born in a cold country.

Most afternoons we had an ice cream run and even Ivor joined us. Like the soldiers that played football in no-man's-land at Christmas, the unusual weather made us suspend our usual hostilities. Although it was far from pleasant to watch Ivor nibbling all the chocolate off his Dove Bar and then seeing his fat red tongue swirling around the ice cream bit.

Megan was eventually dragged up to Personnel because there had been complaints about her shorts. The complaints must have been lodged by some of our female employees, because they certainly weren't made by the hordes of men who came to our office on the flimsiest of pretexts, to inspect her long, golden thighs.

Meredia was thrilled. She hoped that Megan would be fired. But Megan came back with a mysterious, yet satisfied smile.

"Should we help you clear out your desk?" asked Meredia hopefully.

"Maybe, Rosemary, maybe," smirked Megan.

"What are you looking so pleased about?" Meredia was confused and suspicious. "And it's Meredia," she added vaguely.

"I may be moving *up*." Megan punctuated this with a point of her finger toward the ceiling. "Up, in the world."

Meredia looked stricken. "What do you mean?" she gasped. Then she rallied. "Up to the welfare line?"

"Oh no," said Megan. That mysterious, satisfied, sphinxlike smile again. "Just up a few floors."

Meredia looked as if she was going to pass away.

"How many?" she managed to ask hoarsely. "One?"

Megan smiled and shook her head.

"Two?"

Another smile and another shake of the head.

Meredia barely managed to squeak "Three?"

And Megan, cruel, cruel Megan, waited a few, breathless, unbearable seconds before once again shaking her head.

"Not . . . *not* the fourth floor?" whispered poor Meredia.

"Yes, the fourth floor."

It appeared that Megan in her shorts had appealed to Frank Erskine, one of the flabby, bald, soft old men in Management. And in the godlike way that these men seemed to have, Frank had promised to create a position for her.

"What position might that be?" asked Meredia, with bitter innuendo. "The flat-on-your-back position?"

The news spread like headlice in an elementary school because Megan's shorts-to-riches story captured the imagination of the entire staff. It was everyone's fantasy to be plucked from the ignominy of Credit Control on the ground floor and suddenly elevated to the heights of the fourth floor. With the commensurate elevation of pay, of course.

People sighed and said, "And to think I didn't believe in fairy tales."

Meredia took it bad, she was a broken woman. Eight years she'd been there, she moaned, eight years. And that Australian slut was barely off the plane. And she was probably the direct descendant of a sheep thief.

Whenever anyone said to Meredia, "I hear Megan's going up in the world," she said, "She's going up because she goes down, if you follow me." Then she would purse her lips and nod her head self-righteously.

It wasn't long before word of Meredia's scurrilous allegations made its way back to Megan.

Megan, flint-eyed with rage, took Meredia aside. I'm not sure what she said to her, but it was enough to ensure that Meredia looked pale and terrified for a couple of days. And, thereafter, she energetically stressed that Megan had got the promotion entirely on her professional merits.

At least that's what she said in public.

 50

Thinking back to that summer, I remember that Gus would pick me up after work, just as the burning heat of the day was starting to abate. And we would sit outside pubs on balmy evenings, drinking cold beer, talking, laughing.

Sometimes there were lots of us, sometimes just me and Gus. But always there was the still, warm air, the clink of glasses, the hum of conversation.

The sun didn't set until late and the sky never really became night. The blueness just intensified and changed to a darker shade, then only a few hours later, the sun rose again on another dazzling day. And the heat changed people, it made them so much nicer.

London was full of chatty, friendly people, the same people who slunk around miserably the rest of the year. Their mood was rendered open and Mediterranean by being able to sit in the street at eleven o'clock at night wearing a T-shirt and not freezing to death.

And when you looked around at a beer garden full of people, it was obvious who had a job and who was unemployed. Not just because the unemployed ones never bought a round, but because they had great tans.

It was always too warm to even think about eating until ten or eleven in the evening, when we would wander languidly along to some restaurant that had all its doors and windows opened onto the street, and drink cheap wine and pretend that we were abroad.

Every night we went to bed with the windows open, covered only by a sheet and it was *still* too hot to sleep.

It was impossible to imagine ever being cold again. One night I was so warm that, in desperation, I poured a glass of water over myself in bed. Which was very pleasant. And the height of passion that it incited Gus to was even more pleasant.

There was always too much to do. Life was a nonstop parade of barbecues, parties and nights out, or at least that's how I remembered it. There must have been *some* nights when I stayed in and watched TV and went to bed early but, if there were, I can't recall them.

And not only was there lots to do, but there were lots of people to do it with. There was always someone to go out with. Quite apart from Gus, that is, who was available for outings every night.

There was never any danger of wanting to go for a drink and having no one to go with.

The people from my office often came out with Gus and me. Even poor Meredia lumbered along and sat and gasped and fanned herself and talked about how faint she felt.

Jed and Gus got along very well—at least after a while. When they first met they were like two shy little boys who wanted to play with each other but didn't know how to go about it. But eventually they both emerged from behind the folds of my skirt and made overtures. Gus might have offered to show Jed his new lump of hash, something like that. Then there was no stopping them. I barely got to speak to Gus on the nights that Jed came out. The pair of them had long, heads together, sotto voce conversations that I suspected had something to do with music. Boys often talked about that kind of thing. Where they tried to outdo each other by remembering the name of some obscure group that someone played guitar with before he left and played guitar for another. It could keep them occupied for *days*.

But whenever anyone asked Jed and Gus what they were talking about they would just say mysteriously, "It's a guy thing, you wouldn't understand."

Which earned them indulgent smiles until the night they said it to Charlotte's Simon.

The two of them constantly bitched about Simon and his ever-changing array of slick, fashionable clothes and his electronic personal organizer and the copy of *GQ* he always had about his person. But there was no need for them to be so obvious about it.

They never missed a chance to upset poor Simon.

"Is that a new T-shirt?" Gus asked Simon one night. Gus had a butter-wouldn't-melt-in-his-mouth expression that signaled trouble.

"Yeah, it's from Paul Smith," said Simon proudly, holding out his arms for us all to get a good look at it.

"We're twins!" said Gus engagingly. "It's just like the ones I got in Chapel Street market, five for five pounds. But I don't think the fella who sold it to me was one of the Smiths, I thought they were all arrested last month for receiving stolen goods. Are you sure it was a Smith?"

"Yes," said Simon, tightly. "I'm sure."

"Maybe they're out already," said Gus vaguely. And then moved on to something else, happy that he had ruined Simon's enjoyment of his new T-shirt.

The long-awaited evening rolled around when Dennis finally met Gus. Dennis shook hands with Gus and smiled politely. Then he turned to me and made an anguished face and put his knuckles in his mouth. "A word in private," he said and dragged me across the pub.

"Oh Lucy," he moaned.

"What?"

He put his hands on his face in distraught manner and whispered dramatically, "He's an angel, an absolute *angel*."

"You like the look of him?" I was suffused with pride.

"Lucy, he's DIVINE!"

I had to agree.

"It's so rare to come across a good-looking Irishman," went on Dennis, "but when they get it right, they *really* get it right."

Dennis commandeered Gus that evening, which made me quite edgy. Dennis constantly insisted that all was fair in love and war. At least when he liked someone else's boyfriend, he did. And later that night, when Gus and I were going home on the bus, Gus said, "That Dennis is a friendly fellow."

Could Gus really be that innocent?

"Does he have a girlfriend?"

"No."

"That's a shame, a nice guy like him."

I braced myself for Gus to tell me that he was meeting Dennis for a boys-only drink later in the week, but thankfully he didn't.

"We must fix him up with someone," said Gus. "Have you any single friends?"

"Only Meredia and Megan."

"Well, it can't be that poor Meredia," said Gus sympathetically.

"Why not?" I asked, all defensive.

"Well, isn't it obvious?" said Gus.

"Isn't what obvious?" I sneered, getting ready to push him out of the seat and onto the floor of the bus.

"Come on now, Lucy, don't tell me you haven't noticed," he said reasonably.

"That she's overweight?" I demanded hotly. "That's a lovely attit . . ."

"No, you big idiot," he said. "I don't mean that. Jesus, Lucy, that's a shocking thing to say, I wouldn't have expected that from you."

"What are you talking about?"

"Meredia and Jed, of course."

"Gus," I said earnestly. "You're fucking crazy."

"Maybe," he agreed.

"What do you mean 'Meredia and Jed'?"

"I mean that Meredia is very fond of Jed."

"We're all very fond of Jed," I said.

"No, Lucy," said Gus. "I mean she's fond of the idea of Jed in his birthday suit."

"No, she's not," I scoffed.

"Yes, she is."

"But how do you know?" I asked.

"Isn't it obvious?"

"Not to me."

"Well, it is to me," said Gus. "And you're the woman, you're the one who's supposed to have the intuition."

"But, but . . . she's too old for him."

"Well, you're older than me."

"Only by a couple of years."

"Anyway, love knows no age," said Gus wisely. "I read that in a fortune cookie."

Well, well, well. How thrilling. The romance! The intrigue! Love among the threatening letters.

"And does *he* like her?" I asked eagerly, suddenly very interested.

"How would I know?"

"Well, you must find out. You talk to him, he talks to you."

"Yes, but we're men, we don't talk about that kind of thing."

"Promise me that you'll try, Gus," I pleaded.

"I promise," he said. "But it still doesn't solve the problem of Dennis not having a girl."

"What about Megan?"

Gus made a face and shook his head. "She has notions, that one. She thinks she's it. She'd think she was too good-looking for Dennis, even though he's a handsome guy."

"Gus! Megan isn't a bit like that."

"She is," he muttered.

"She isn't," I insisted.

"She is," he insisted back.

"Have it your way," I said.

"That'd make a welcome change," he said gloomily.

When I debriefed Dennis afterward, first of all he told me that Gus was gorgeous, then he told me that Gus was gay. No surprises there. But then he defused the celebratory tone of the conversation by asking about Gus and his money situation.

"Oh that," I said dismissively. "It's not a problem."

"But does he have any money?"

"Not much."

"But you two go out all the time."

"So what?"

"Have you been to any of his gigs?"

"No."

"Why not?"

"Because he gets most of his work in the winter."

"Just be careful, Lucy," warned Dennis. "He's a heart-breaker, that one."

"Thanks for the advice, Dennis, but I'm able to look after myself."

"No, you're not."

I saw a lot of Charlotte and Simon over the summer. When the usual suspects were rounded up for a postwork drink, they were nearly always to be found in the thick of things.

Then they went to Portugal for a week. They asked Gus and me to go with them. Or rather, Charlotte asked me to come and said that I could bring Gus along, if I wanted. And not to worry about him and Simon squabbling.

But Gus and I didn't have enough money to go—not that I minded, because my life felt like a holiday anyway.

Gus, Jed, Megan, Meredia, Dennis and I went out to the airport to see them off, because we all had become so attached that we couldn't bear to be parted.

For the week they were away, we had lots of conversations like "What do you think Simon and Charlotte are doing now?" and "Do you think they're thinking about us?"

Even Gus missed Simon. "I've no one to make fun of," he complained.

The night that they came back, everyone was so ecstatic that there was a wild celebration. We drank all the duty-free vinho verde that they had brought home. The evening was deemed to be a great success when Charlotte vomited and had to be put to bed.

During that summer, the only people who didn't come out and play were Karen and Daniel.

I barely saw them.

Karen spent most of her time in Daniel's apartment. She stopped by at our place occasionally to pick up a change of clothes, just running in and out while Daniel waited in the car.

Daniel and I *never* saw each other on our own anymore. In fact we didn't even call each other.

Which gave me a sense of regret, because that was the kind of sentimental, emotional fool I was. But I didn't know what to do about it; there was no road back.

So I tried to focus on the good things in my life— namely Gus.

I realized just how serious Daniel and Karen had become when the news broke that they were going to Scotland together in September. From the gleam in Karen's eye, she thought she was home free with Daniel. It was only a matter of time before she could start fighting with her mother about the inviting of fifth cousins four times removed and comparing the respective merits of lemon meringue pie and baked Alaska.

I wondered if she would ask me to be her bridesmaid. Somehow I thought not.

One Saturday night, all of us—me, Charlotte, Simon, Gus, Dennis, Jed, Megan, even Karen and Daniel—went to an open-air concert in the grounds of a stately home in north London.

Even though it was classical music, we had a wonderful time. Stretched out on the warm grass, listening to the rustle of the leaves in the still evening air, sipping champagne, eating sausage rolls and mini-eclairs.

After the concert was over, we decided we had had enough of behaving like adults and we hadn't yet wrung enough debauched enjoyment out of the evening. It was only midnight and going to bed before the sun rose was regarded as a wasted night.

So we bought lots of wine from a twenty-four-hour shop

that was happy to break the law and piled into several taxis and went back to our apartment.

Where there were no clean glasses, so Karen volunteered me to wash some.

While I was in the kitchen dashing cups under the running tap, resenting every moment that I was away from the fun in the front room, Daniel came in searching for the corkscrew.

"How are you?" I asked. Before I knew what had happened I'd smiled; old habits die hard.

"Fine," he said, looking bleak. "And you?"

"Fine."

An awkward pause.

"I haven't seen you for ages," I said.

"No," he agreed.

Another pause. Talking to him was like trying to get blood out of a turnip.

"So you're off to Scotland?" I said.

"Yes."

"Looking forward to it?"

"Yes, I've never been to Scotland before," he said tersely.

"And it's not just that, is it?" I teased gently.

"What do you mean?" He stared coldly at me.

"Well, you know, meeting Karen's family and all that." I nodded eagerly. "So what's next?"

"What are you talking about?" he said, tight-lipped.

"You *know*," I said, smiling uncertainly.

"No, I don't," he snapped. "It's just a bloody holiday, okay?"

"Christ," I muttered. "I remember when you used to have a sense of humor."

"Sorry, Lucy." He tried to grab my arm, but I shook it off and walked out of the kitchen.

My eyes filled with tears, which was really scary because I *never* cried. Except when I had PMS, and that didn't count.

Or whenever there was a program about Siamese twins who had been separated and one of them died. Or whenever I saw an old person hobbling down the road on their own. Or whenever I went into the living room and everyone yelled at me for coming back without the clean glasses. The bastards.

But despite the high-profile presence of Meredia, Jed, Megan, Dennis, Charlotte and Simon in my life, there was no denying that it was The Summer of Gus.

From the moment he returned from the three-week absence, we were hardly ever apart.

I made occasional perfunctory attempts to spend evenings on my own—not because I wanted to, but because I felt that it was expected of me.

I had to pretend that I was independent, that I had a life of my own, but the truth of it was that anything I enjoyed without Gus, I enjoyed even more with Gus.

And he was just as bad.

"We won't see each other tonight," I said a few times. "I have to do my wash and take care of some errands."

"But, Lucy," he wailed, "I'll miss you."

"But I'll see you tomorrow," I said, pretending to be exasperated, but, of course, I was delighted. "Surely you can survive without me for one night."

But each time, Gus arrived at my flat by nine o'clock, trying to look shamefaced, but not pulling it off.

"Sorry, Lucy." He grinned. "I know you want to be alone. But I had to see you, just for five minutes. I'll be off, now that I've had my fix."

"No, don't go," I said every time, as he must have

known I would. It was alarming to find that I considered any time away from Gus a waste.

Although I tried not to be obvious about it, I was crazy about him. And he seemed to be crazy about me, too, if the amount of time that he spent with me was any indication.

The only trouble—if trouble it was—was that he hadn't told me that he loved me. He hadn't actually said the words, "I love you, Lucy." Not that I worried—well, not much anyway—because I knew that normal rules didn't apply to Gus. He probably did love me but it might have slipped his mind to mention it. After all, that was the kind of man he was. But nevertheless, I thought it was best that I didn't tell him that I loved *him*—even though I did—until he told me.

No point in any premature jumpings of guns.

Besides, there was always a small chance that he *didn't* love me, and there is *nothing* more embarrassing.

I would have liked to talk to him about our relationship, like where we were going and our future. But he never brought it up and I felt too awkward to.

I had to be patient, but it was hard to play the waiting game. The few times that I had any fears or doubts, I referred myself to Mrs. Nolan's prediction, and remembered that I had seen the future and it was Gus. (Or that I had seen the future and it drank, as smug Daniel put it.)

I consoled myself that patience is a virtue, that all things come to he—or she—who waits. And ignored the adages that urged me to strike when the iron is hot, not to let the grass grow under my feet, and that to stand still is to die.

I don't remember having great concern about my future with Gus throughout the magical, golden summer. At the time I *thought* I was happy, and that was good enough for me.

 51

The twelfth morning in August didn't seem any different from all the other golden mornings that had preceded it.

Except for one important detail—Gus got up before me.

It was impossible to stress just how unusual that was. Every morning when I left for work, Gus was still sound asleep. And at some stage, much, *much* later in the day he let himself out, closing and locking the door behind him. (After first eating anything in the fridge that wasn't actually moving, then making a couple of phone calls to Donegal.) This meant that the flat wasn't actually deadbolt locked and was thereby at the mercy of roving burglars, which caused several arguments between Karen and me, on the rare occasions when Karen came home.

But I couldn't bring myself to give Gus a set of keys because I didn't want to scare him with a "Let's live together" message.

And I consoled Karen that the flat was so messy that if any burglars *did* break in, they'd think a rival gang had gone over the place just a few minutes previously. We might even come home to find a *new* TV and stereo in the front room, I suggested enthusiastically to a skeptical raise of Karen's eyebrows.

That morning Gus got up before me, which started distant alarm bells ringing in my brain. He sat on the bed and, as he put on his shoes, he commented casually, "D'you know, this is getting a bit heavy, Lucy."

"Mmmm, I s'pose," I said, still too sleepy to notice that I was alarmed.

But it took only a second for me to realize that he wasn't just making idle conversation when he said, "I think we should slow down a bit."

The "this is getting a bit heavy"—particularly his use of the word *heavy*—had started Alsatian dogs barking by the perimeter fence. But the "I think we should slow down a bit" had the sirens whining and the searchlights swooping back and forth over the grounds.

While I scrambled around in the bed, trying to sit up, a voice in my head announced, *This is an emergency, boyfriend trying to escape, repeat, boyfriend trying to escape.*

I had the sensation of being in an elevator that was dropping dangerously quickly, because every woman knows that talk of slowing down or seeing less of each other is actually guyspeak for, "Take a good, long look at me; you will never see me again."

I hoped that I would be able to tell what was going on from the expression on his face. But he wouldn't look at me, his black curly head was bent over his feet as he laced his shoes with unprecedented diligence.

"Gus, are you trying to tell me something?"

"Maybe we should take a little break from each other," he muttered.

It sounded as if he'd been coached, as if he was clumsily reading from a teleprompter. In fact, it looked as if he was reading his lines from his shoe. But at the time I was so shocked by what he was saying that I couldn't be bothered worrying that these weren't the kind of things he normally said.

I should have noticed that the very fact that Gus had

even bothered to tell me that he was ending things was wildly out of character.

"But why?" I asked, in horror. "What's happened? What's gone wrong? What's changed?"

"Nothing."

Finally and nervously he lifted his head. He must have laced and unlaced his shoes forty times.

When his sidelong glance found my face, he looked guilty for a split second, then burst out, "It's your fault, Lucy, you shouldn't have got so involved, you shouldn't have let it get so serious."

I hadn't realized that Gus was from the attack-is-the-best-form-of-defense school of ending relationships. I had thought that hit-and-run was more his style.

I was too stunned to remind him that he hadn't left me alone for a single night, that I hadn't even been able to shave my legs without having him camped outside the bathroom door, roaring that he missed me, asking me to sing to him, demanding to know how much longer I was going to be.

But I couldn't afford the luxury of being angry with him. That would have to wait until later.

As I stuttered and stumbled and tried to get out of bed, Gus backed toward the door and raised a hand in farewell.

"I'm going now, Lucy. Good luck! May the road rise with me." He sounded upbeat and cheerful. And more so with every inch he moved away from me.

"No, Gus, wait, please. Let's talk about this. Please, Gus."

"No, I've got to go now."

"Why, why in such a hurry?"

"I just do."

"Well, could we meet later? I don't understand this, please talk to me, Gus."

He looked sulky and surly.

"Will you meet me after work?" I asked, trying to sound calm, striving to keep the edge of hysteria out of my voice.

Still he said nothing.

"Please, Gus," I said again.

"Okay," he muttered, sliding out of the room.

Then there was the bang of the front door. He was gone and I was still half asleep, wondering if it was all a nightmare.

It wasn't even eight o'clock.

I had been too dazed to think of throwing myself in front of the door in an attempt to stop him from leaving. And when it occurred to me, instead of being grateful, I was furious.

Somehow I got to work, not that I was much use when I got there. I felt as if I were wading around under water—everything was muffled, fuzzy, happening in slow motion. Voices came from a long way away, stretched and distorted. I couldn't really hear them and I couldn't concentrate on what they wanted from me.

The day was a slow agony of inching toward five o'clock.

Now and then, like the sun breaking through the clouds, I could think clearly. When that happened, waves of panic swept over me. What if he didn't come, I asked myself in appalled horror? What would I do?

But he *had* to come, I reasoned desperately. I *had* to talk to him, to find out what was wrong.

The worst part was that I couldn't tell anyone at work what was wrong. Because Gus wasn't leaving just me, he was leaving Jed, Meredia and Megan too, and I was afraid that they'd be hurt. I was also afraid that I'd get the blame.

I spent the day in a daze.

When I should have been calling customers and threatening to sue them if they didn't pay us soon, I was in another world, where the only thing that meant anything was Gus.

*Why* did he think we were getting too serious, I wondered. Apart from the obvious fact that we were. But what was wrong with that? I struggled to do some work, but it mattered so little.

Who cared if Spare Tires had exceeded their ninety-day credit period by about two years? I didn't give a damn. I had bigger, more important things to worry about. So what if Wheel Meet Again had gone out of business owing us thousands of pounds? What did any of it matter when my heart was aching?

The pointlessness of my job was always highlighted when my heart was broken. Being abandoned brought out the nihilist in me.

I miserably made phone calls, wishy-washily threatened to sue people and take them for every penny they had, and thought, In a hundred years, *none* of this will matter.

Several millennia later the day finally dragged itself to its sluggish close.

And when five o'clock came, Gus didn't.

I hung on desperately until half past six, because I was at a complete loss about what I should do with me, my time, my life.

Waiting for Gus was all I was good for.

But he didn't come.

Of course he didn't come.

And as I wondered what my next move should be, something that had been shimmering ominously at the back of my mind crystallized into a conscious fear.

*I didn't know where Gus lived.*

If he didn't come to me, I couldn't go to him. I had no phone number, no address for him.

He had never taken me to his house, everything we did together—from sleeping to sex to TV watching—happened at my apartment. I had known it wasn't right, but whenever I suggested going home with him, he fobbed me off with a selection of surreal excuses. Which were so bizarre that I shuddered at the ease with which I had swallowed them.

I shouldn't have been so pliant, I thought in despair. I should have *insisted*. If I had been more demanding, I wouldn't be in such a mess. At least I'd know where to find him. I couldn't believe how docile I had been—hadn't I even been *suspicious?*

In fact, as I remembered it, I *had* been suspicious. But because it threatened to ruffle the calm surface of my happiness, I forced myself not to be. I had let Gus get away with an awful lot, with the vague, catch-all explanation that he was unusual and eccentric. And now that he had disappeared, I could hardly credit my naïveté.

If I had read about me in the newspaper—about a girl who had been going out with a guy for five months (nearly), (if you count the three weeks in May that he'd been missing), and that she didn't even know where he lived—I would have dismissed her as a half-wit who deserved everything she got.

Or didn't get.

But the reality had been so different. I had been afraid to force anything because I didn't want to drive him away. And anyway, I had thought there was no need to force anything because he behaved as if he *cared* about me.

But the frustration of not being able to contact him was unbearable. Especially because it was all my fault.

Over the next few interminable, hellish days, Gus didn't reappear, and I didn't hold out any hope that he would.

Because I had realized something awful—I had been *expecting* him to leave me. All the time that I'd been with him, I had been waiting for it.

My idyllic summer had been nothing but a sham. Although it was only in retrospect that I could see tensions beneath the balmy, sunny surface.

I had never felt safe after his three-week disappearance. I *pretended* that I did, because it felt nicer that way. But things had never been the same. It had tipped the balance of power completely in Gus's favor—he had treated me with a lack of respect and I had told him that it was perfectly all right to do so. I had given him *carte blanche* to treat me badly.

He had been quite gallant about it, never openly reminding me just how much of a hostage I was. But it was always there in the subtext—he had left me once and he could do it again, anytime he liked. He wielded his ability to disappear like a weapon.

A covert power struggle had gone on between Gus and me. He played brinkmanship, and I played stoicism. How long could he abandon me at a party before I got angry? How much money could he "borrow" from me before I refused to "loan" him any more? How flirtatious could he get with Megan, how many times did he have to touch her hair, before it wiped the fixed smile off my face?

All that fear had burned up so much of my energy I was continually nervy around him. Edgy. Every time he said he'd pick me up or meet me, my nerves were zinging until he turned up.

But I had stuffed all my questions beneath the surface, I couldn't let them pop their heads up and ruin things. I had papered over cracks, suppressed fears and swallowed insults, because I thought it was worth it. And it had seemed to be, because—at least on the outside—Gus and I were happy.

But now that he had gone, I realized that anytime I had been with him there was a fear that it might be the last. There was a kind of desperation in me, a need to get my money's worth. A need to cram as much Gus into my life as I possibly could, to store against the time when he would run away again.

 52

I eventually had to tell the others in the office that Gus and I were no more. It was horrible. Jed and Meredia were distraught—they looked like children who had just found out that there was no Santa Claus.

"Doesn't Gus like us anymore?" asked Meredia in a small voice, her head bent, plucking at her marquee of a skirt.

"Of course he does," I assured her warmly.

"Is it our fault?" asked Jed, looking as woebegone as a four-year-old. "Have we done something wrong?"

"Of course it's not your fault," I said heartily. "Gus and I can't be together anymore, but . . ."

I almost sat down and put my arms around the two of them and gently explained, "Sometimes grown-up people stop loving each other and it's very sad, but it doesn't mean that Gus doesn't love both of you very much, still . . ."

Instead I exclaimed tearfully, "Oh for God's sake. You're

not the children of a divorcing couple, so stop acting it! This is *my* tragedy," I reminded them, in more reasoned tones.

"Maybe we can still see him." Jed turned to Meredia. "Lucy doesn't have to be there."

"Thanks, you mean pigs," I said. "Next you'll be asking me to talk to him about visitation rights."

Megan was abrupt and unsympathetic. "You're better off without that loser," she said, with a dismissive wave of her hand.

She was right of course. But it was hard to feel grateful. I was punch-drunk, reeling from the sudden loss.

The unexpectedness of his departure had thrown me into a state of shock, especially because there had been no warning that his interest in me was waning—right up to the last few minutes he had certainly *acted* happy.

And well he might, I thought with a tinge of self-righteousness—I had put enough effort into making it all wonderful for him. Naturally, because I had the double handicap of being a woman, and having low self-esteem, I sought to blame myself. Why had he left? What had I done? What hadn't I done? If only I had known, I thought helplessly. Then I could have tried harder. Although, quite frankly, that was debatable.

The worst thing about Gus exiting from my life—the thing I *always* found hardest about rejection—was the amount of time I suddenly had on my hands. An entire fourth dimension had been handed to me, a bottomless pit of never-ending evenings, and I couldn't get rid of them fast enough.

I didn't remember it ever being so bad before. But I supposed I thought that every time my heart was broken.

To try to offload some of my surplus hours and minutes, I went out all the time, trying to party away my misery, to burn it off. I *had* to—I was too agitated not to. Just to do *nothing* was impossible.

But it didn't work, the awfulness never left me. Even as I sat in pubs with lots of happy, laughing people, I still felt the frantic, panicky fear racing around in my veins.

There was almost no escape from it. I could only sleep for a few hours a night. The falling asleep part wasn't hard, but I awoke really early in the morning, at four or five, and stayed awake. I couldn't stand to be alone. But there was no one that I wanted to be with. And no matter where I was, I wanted to be somewhere else. No matter who I was with, no matter what I was doing, no matter where I was, it was wrong, I didn't want it. Every night, I sat with crowds of people and I felt totally alone.

A couple of weeks passed, and perhaps I had gotten slightly better, but the change was too small for me to see.

"You'll get over him," everyone said sympathetically.

But I didn't want to get over him. I still thought he was the funniest, smartest, sexiest man I had ever met, or would ever meet. He was my ideal. And if I got over him—if I didn't want him anymore—I would have lost part of myself. I didn't want to let the wound heal. Anyway, despite what everyone said, I *knew* that I'd never get over him. I was in so much pain that I couldn't imagine not feeling it.

Besides, Mrs. Nolan and her bloody prediction were still on my mind. I found it hard to accept all the signs that were *screaming* that Gus wasn't the man for me, because it was nicer to believe that it was written in the stars that we'd be together.

"That Gus—what a bastard, eh?" Megan cheerfully remarked, one day at work.

"I suppose," I agreed politely.

"You're not going to tell me that you don't hate him?" Megan sounded outraged.

"I don't hate him," I said. "Maybe I should, but I don't."

"But why not?" she demanded.

"Because that's the way Gus is," I tried to explain. "If you love him, you've got to accept that you love the unreliable part of him also."

I waited for Megan to scoff and mock and call me a wimp and a girl. And she did.

"Don't be such an idiot, Lucy." She laughed. "It was your fault, you shouldn't have stood for any nonsense from him. With animals like Gus, you have to show them who's boss, you've got to *break* them.

"I always do," she added.

It was all right for Megan, she'd been brought up on a farm, an *Australian* farm, at that. She knew all about tethering and breaking spirits.

"I didn't want to *break* him," I said. "If he'd been well behaved, he wouldn't have been Gus."

"You can't have it both ways, Lucy," said Megan.

"I haven't got it *any* way," I reminded her.

"Come on, cheer up. You don't really care, do you?" she asked brightly.

"I do," I said humbly, because such lack of self-respect is not something to be proud of.

"No, you don't," she scoffed.

"I do."

"Do you really?" She looked at me anxiously.

"Yes."

"But why?" she asked.

"Because . . . because," I floundered. "Because he's so special. I've never met anyone like him. And I'll never meet anyone like him . . . *sniff* . . . ever again."

My voice wobbled dangerously when I said, "ever again," but I managed not to fling myself on my desk and sob bitterly.

"So if he arrived on your doorstep, begging you to take him back, you'd forgive him?" asked Megan, continuing to press me.

I didn't like the sound of that. I had a vague picture in my head of a terribly unfortunate woman, whose man beat her up and stole her money and had affairs with her friends.

"Megan," I said, anxiously, "I'm not one of those women who get treated badly by their man, but still take them back time after time after time."

"That's funny," said Megan. "Because you certainly act just like one."

"Only for Gus," I explained. "Only for Gus. I wouldn't do it for every man I ever met. Gus is worth breaking rules for," I added.

"So it seems," she said.

I felt a strange desire to hit her.

"But so what?" she boomed, determinedly upbeat. "You'll get over him. In two weeks time you won't even remember his name; you won't even know what all the fuss was about!"

 53

I could hear the screaming from three floors below, the dreadful sounds of an animal in pain or a woman giving birth or a child being scalded.

Something terrible had happened and as I ran up the stairs, I realized that the wails were coming from our apartment.

"Oh, Lucy," gasped Charlotte, as I fell in the front door. "I'm so glad you're here."

She was lucky. I was only home because there was no one to go for a drink with after work, except Barney and Slayer, the two Neanderthals from the mailroom.

"What's wrong?" I asked in horror.

"It's Karen," she said.

"Where is she? Is she hurt? What is it?"

Karen burst out of her bedroom, her clothes askew, her face red and blotchy with tears and threw a glass at the wall which shattered around the hall.

"The bastard, the bastard, the bastard!" she shrieked.

Something was very wrong with Karen, but at least there didn't seem to be anything wrong with her physically, although her hair could have done with a comb. There was a strong smell of alcohol coming from her.

Then she noticed me.

"And it's all your fault, you stupid bitch, Sullivan," she shouted.

"What's my fault? I haven't done anything," I protested, feeling guilty and frightened.

"Yes, it is. You introduced me to him. If I'd never met him, I'd never have fallen in love with him. Not that I *am* in love with him, I hate his guts!" she roared, running back into her room and flinging herself face-downward on her bed.

Charlotte and I followed.

"Is this something to do with Daniel?" I muttered to Charlotte.

"Don't say his name!" screeched Karen. "I never want to hear his name spoken in this apartment ever again."

"You know the way you've been the Spinster of this Parish?" muttered Charlotte to me.

I nodded.

"Well, you're not the only one now," she said.

So there had been a breakdown in the Daniel-Karen alliance.

"What's happened?" I asked Karen, gently.

"I broke up with him," she gulped, reaching for a bottle of brandy on her nightstand and swigging from it. Over half of it was already gone.

"Why did you break up?" I asked, intrigued. I had thought she really liked him.

"Just never forget it, Sullivan. *I* broke up with *him,* not the other way round."

"Fine," I said nervously. "But why?"

"Because . . . because . . ." Tears began rolling down her face again.

"Because . . . I asked him if he loved me and he said, he said . . . he . . . he . . . he . . ."

Charlotte and I waited politely for her to get to the point.

". . . he . . . DIDN'T," she finally managed and started that awful wailing again.

"He doesn't love me," she said, staring at me with unfocused, miserable eyes. "Can you believe it? He said he doesn't love me."

"If it's any help, Karen, I know what it's like. Gus broke up with me only two weeks ago, remember?"

"Don't be so fucking stupid," she said thickly, through her tears. "Gus and you weren't serious, Daniel and I were."

"I took Gus very seriously," I said stiffly.

"Then you were a fool," said Karen. "Anyone can see that he's crazy and unreliable and flighty. But Daniel has a, a . . . a GOOD JOB!"

She became incoherent with sobbing again and I couldn't really make out what she was saying. Something about Daniel owning his own apartment and having an expensive . . . *yard,* was it? No, no, sorry, an expensive *car.*

"Things like this don't happen to me," she sobbed. "It wasn't part of the plan."

"They happen to everyone," I said gently.

"No, they don't. They don't happen to me."

"Karen, really, they happen to everyone," I insisted. "Look at me and Gus . . ."

"*Don't* compare me to you," she screamed. "I'm nothing like you. Men break up with you, and you," she said nodding at Charlotte. "But they don't break up with me. I don't permit it to happen."

That shut Charlotte and me up.

"Oh God." Karen commenced a fresh bout of weeping. "How can I go to Scotland now? I've told everyone about Daniel and how rich he is. And we were going to drive up and now I'll have to pay my own fare and I was going to buy that jacket in Morgans and now I won't be able to. The bastard!"

She reached for the brandy bottle again.

It was a very old, rare brandy, the type that rich businessmen give to each other at Christmas, the type that you're not really supposed to drink. It's meant to be a decoration piece, more an ostentatious display of wealth than something you mix with ginger ale.

"Where did you get this?" I asked Karen.

"Took it from that bastard's apartment when I was leaving," she said viciously. "Only sorry that I didn't take more."

Then came more tears.

"And it's such a lovely apartment," she howled. "And I was going to decorate it, I was going to make him buy this wrought iron bed that I saw in *Elle Dècor*. He's such a bastard.''

Yes, yes, yes, quite.

"We must sober her up," I said.

"We could make her eat something," suggested Charlotte. "I'm hungry."

But as always, there was nothing in the apartment except some old low-fat yogurt.

So we went to the Cash'n'Curry. Because until that day, we'd only ever gone there on Sundays, our appearance caused consternation and confusion among the staff.

"Here, I could have sworn that today was Monday," said Pavel, in Bangladeshi, to Karim when the three of us walked in.

"Christ, me too," agreed Karim. "But it must only be Sunday. That's great, we close an hour earlier tonight. Right, you get their wine and I'll tell the chef they're here and he can get the chicken tikka masalas going."

"Can we have a bottle of house white, please?" I asked Mahmood, but Pavel was already behind the bar opening it for us. We always had exactly the same thing at the restaurant—they no longer even brought us menus. It was always one vegetable biryani, two chicken tikka masalas, pilau rice and white wine. Only the number of bottles of wine varied, but it was always at least two.

While we waited for the food we managed to piece together exactly what had happened with Karen and Daniel.

It seemed that Karen had been certain that Daniel had fallen in love with her and decided she was ready for a declaration to that effect. That would have given them enough time to buy an engagement ring before they went to Scotland, where they would break the happy news to Karen's parents. But Daniel was annoyingly reticent with his declaration, so Karen decided that she had better take events into her own hands, what with the date of their departure for Scotland drawing nearer. So, fully certain that the answer would be in the affirmative, she asked Daniel if he loved her. And Daniel put the cat among the pigeons, good and proper, by telling her that he was very fond of her.

And Karen said, very good, but did he *love* her?

And Daniel said that she was a joy to be with and a very beautiful woman.

I know all that, Karen had said scornfully, but do you love me?

Who's to say what love is? asked Daniel, no doubt getting increasingly desperate.

Answer me, yes or no, demanded Karen, DO-YOU-LOVE-ME?

I'm afraid that my answer would have to be no, said Daniel.

Cue shattered dreams, violent argument, theft of bottle of expensive brandy, calling of a taxi, hope by Karen that Daniel would burn in hell, departure of Karen from Daniel's apartment and arrival at ours.

"He's a bastard," sobbed Karen.

Mahmood, Karim, Pavel and the one who said his name was Michael all nodded in sympathy. They had been hanging on Karen's every word. Pavel looked close to tears.

Karen gulped back a glass of wine, spilling some of it down her chin and immediately filled up her glass again.

"'Nother bottle," she called, waving the empty one at the cluster of waiters.

Charlotte and I exchanged a glance that said "She's had quite enough to drink already," but neither of us dared say it to her.

Karim brought us more wine and, as he placed the bottle

on the table he murmured, "This one's on us, with our commiserations."

Charlotte and I ended up getting drunk also, because we were trying to save Karen from getting any drunker by drinking as much of the wine as we possibly could. Not that it worked, because Karen yelled for another bottle as soon as the second was finished and the whole process began all over again.

Although by then I was starting to enjoy myself.

Karen got drunker and drunker. She lit the wrong end of her cigarette twice, rested the cuffs of her jacket in her dinner, knocked a glass of water into my vegetable biryani and slurred "Looked disgustin', anyway."

And then, to my absolute horror, her eyes glazed over and she slowly keeled forward until she was face downward in her plate of chicken tikka masala and pilau rice.

"Quick, quick, Charlotte," I said in panic. "Lift her up, get her face out of her dinner, she'll drown!"

Charlotte yanked Karen's head up by the hair and Karen turned a drunken, confused face to Charlotte.

"Whatta fucker you doin'?" she demanded. She had some red masala sauce on her forehead and grains of rice in her hair.

"Karen, you passed out," I gasped. "You just collapsed into your meal. We'd better get you home."

"Fuck off," she slurred. "No, I didn't. I just dropped my cigarette and I had to pick it up off the floor."

"Oh," I said, both relieved and embarrassed.

"Stupid fuck," muttered Karen aggressively. "Are you trying to say I can't hold my drink?"

"C'mere you," she beckoned Mahmood. "D'you think I'm attractive? Eh, well?"

"Most attractive," he agreed warmly, thinking for a second that his luck was in.

" 'Course I am," said Karen. " 'Course I am."

"You're not," she added as an afterthought.

He looked hurt so I gave him a bigger than usual tip when we left. I had to pay because Charlotte had forgotten her purse in the excitement and although Karen tried to write a check, she was too drunk to even hold the pen.

We carried Karen home, undressed her and put her to bed.

"Drink some water, Karen, good girl, so you won't feel so bad when you wake up in the morning," said Charlotte, shoving a glass under Karen's nose. Charlotte was far from sober herself.

"I nevr, nevr want to wake up again," said Karen.

She made some funny, little whiney noises and I realized after a while that she was singing. Sort of.

"You're so vain . . . bet y'think thissongs aboucha. Doancha, doancha . . ." she whined.

"Come on, Karen, *please*," begged Charlotte, advancing again with the glass of water.

"Doan interrupme whem singin'. Singin' 'bout Daniel. Join in! You're so vain . . . betcha . . . think . . . thissongs . . . Come on," she said aggressively, "Sing with me."

"Karen, please," I murmured soothingly.

"Doan patronize me," she said. "Sing the fuckin' song. You're so va . . . come on, everybody!"

"Er, you're so vain," sang Charlotte and I, feeling very foolish. "Ahem, I, er, bet, you, um, think this song is about, ah, you . . ."

She passed out before we got to the second verse.

We tiptoed out of her room, shutting the door behind us.

"Oh Lucy," wailed Charlotte. "I'm so worried."

"Don't be," I said soothingly, with a confidence that I

didn't feel. "I'm sure she'll be fine. She'll bounce back in no time."

"Not about her!" said Charlotte. "I'm worried about me."

"Why?"

"First Gus goes, then Daniel, what if Simon is next?"

"But why on earth should he? It's not a contagious disease."

"But bad things always happen in threes," said Charlotte, her soft pink face crumpled with anxiety.

"Maybe they do in Yorkshire," I said kindly. "But you're in London now, so don't worry."

"You're right," she said, cheering up. "Anyway, Gus has dumped you twice, so with Daniel breaking up with Karen, that's three already."

"Well, what a pity that I didn't arrange for Gus to break up with me one more time. I could have saved Karen all this upset," I said a little tartly.

"Don't worry, Lucy," said Charlotte. "You couldn't have known."

 54

*And then there were three.*

Slow as she usually was, Charlotte's instinct had been entirely correct. Simon did not call her at work on Tuesday, and he normally called her every day, sometimes twice a day.

When she called him on Tuesday evening he wasn't in

and his normally friendly roommate was awkward and uncommunicative as to Simon's whereabouts.

"Lucy, I have a very bad feeling about this," Charlotte said.

She called him at work on Wednesday and Simon didn't answer his phone. Instead a woman did, and asked Charlotte, "Who's calling?" When Charlotte said "Charlotte," the woman immediately said, "Simon's in a meeting."

Charlotte called back about an hour later and exactly the same thing happened.

So, right away, Charlotte got her friend Jennifer to call and Simon was suddenly available to take the call from "Jennifer Morris."

Jennifer handed the phone to Charlotte when Simon said "Hello," and Charlotte said "Simon, what's going on? Are you trying to avoid me?"

And Simon laughed nervously and jovially and said, "Indeed not, indeed not, indeed not!"

Charlotte said that was when she really knew something was wrong because Simon would normally never say "Indeed not."

"Meet me for lunch, Simon," said Charlotte.

"Would love to, would love to," said Simon. "But no can do."

"Why are you talking like that?" asked Charlotte.

"Like what?" asked Simon.

"Like a dickhead with a mobile phone," said Charlotte.

(Which I thought was quite ironic because I had *always* thought that Simon was like a dickhead with a mobile phone. But I didn't say so because I didn't want to upset Charlotte any further.)

"No idea what you're talking about," said Simon.

Charlotte sighed. "Okay, tonight then."

" 'Fraid that's impossible," said Simon.

"Why?"

"Business, Charlotte, business," he drawled.

"But you've never had to do that before," said Charlotte.

"First time for everything," said Simon smoothly.

"Well, when *can* I see you?" asked Charlotte.

"Bad news, Charlie," said Simon, "but you can't."

"Until when?" she asked.

"You're not making this easy for either of us, are you?" he asked lightly.

"What are you talking about?"

"I mean, Charlotte, that you can't see me."

"Why not?"

"Because it's *o-v-e-r*, over."

"Over? Us? You mean *we're* over?" she asked.

"Bravo," he laughed. "The message finally hits home."

"And when were you going to tell me?" she asked.

"I've just told you, haven't I?" he said in a reasonable voice.

"But only because I called you. Were you going to call me? Or were you just going to let me find out myself?"

"You would have gotten the message soon enough," he said.

"But why?" asked Charlotte, her voice wobbling. "Don't you, don't you . . . *like* me anymore?"

"Oh, Charlotte, don't make a fool of yourself," he said. "It was fun, we both enjoyed ourselves and now I've found someone else to have fun with."

"But what about me?" asked Charlotte. "Who will I have fun with?"

"That's not my problem," said Simon. "But, anyway, you'll meet someone else. You're bound to, with those tits."

"I don't want to have fun with anyone else," pleaded Charlotte. "I want to have fun with you."

"Tough!" he said cheerfully. "Your time is up. Don't be selfish, Charlie, let some of the other girls have a turn."

"But I thought you cared about me," she said.

"Well, you shouldn't have taken it so seriously," he answered.

"So this is it?" she asked tearfully.

"This is it," he agreed.

"Lucy, he was like a total stranger," she said later. "I thought I *knew* him. I thought he cared about me, I just can't believe he could drop me so suddenly."

"I just don't understand *why!*" she said over and over again. "What did I do wrong? Why did he stop loving me? Maybe I've put on some weight? Have I, Lucy? Or did I go on too much about the bad time I was having at work? If only I knew."

She shook her head in bewilderment. "There's nothing so weird as men," she sighed.

At least she wasn't tortured by the images of that boyfriend-stealing mythical woman who colored the imaginations of us small-breasted, rejected women—A Girl with Bigger Tits, because Charlotte was That Girl with Bigger Tits.

But she doubted herself in every other area.

She forced him to see her. She stalked him with a tenacity and a determination that you wouldn't have believed she was capable of when you first saw her round, innocent face. She waited outside his office for a couple of days at his going-home time, then he finally agreed to have a drink with her, in the hope that she might leave him alone.

One drink led to several more and they both got very drunk and went back to Simon's and had sex.

Then in the morning Simon said, "That was very pleasant, Charlotte. Now stop hanging around outside my office. You're embarrassing yourself."

Charlotte was rather taken aback by all of this. She was inexperienced enough in the arena of love to assume that because he had slept with her, it meant that their romance was back on track.

"But . . . but," she said. "What about last night? Didn't it . . . ?"

"*No*, Charlotte," interrupted Simon impatiently. "It didn't mean a thing to me. Sex is sex. Now please get dressed and leave."

"And the worst thing is, Lucy," she complained afterward. "I *still* don't know why he ended it with me."

"But why not?" I asked.

"I forgot to ask."

"What were you *doing* all that time?" I asked in surprise. "No, no, don't tell me, I can guess."

"I'm too young to be a Spinster of this Parish," said Charlotte gloomily.

"You're never too young," I said wisely.

 55

Megan was due to start her new job that week, but there were complications. Well, only one actually.

To wit: Frank Erskine's mental health.

The MD wasn't too pleased with the behavior of one of his Directors.

Frank's offer to create a new job for an attractive, tanned young woman, who wore shorts, was regarded as the embarrassing act of a middle-aged man who should have known better. The company buzzed with the rumor that he was having a combination of midlife crisis and a nervous breakdown and wasn't capable of rational thought.

He was persuaded—quite forcibly, according to my sources in Personnel—to take an extended period of sick leave. Luckily his wife agreed to stand by him, and the press was kept out of it.

When he returned—although no one really thought he would—then Management would be only too happy to talk to Megan about her promotion.

But until then, Megan was condemned to fester in Credit Control. Meredia nearly vomited with glee.

 56

Three hearts were heavy.

It was as if we had all been struck down by the plague. The apartment should have been draped in black crêpe. All about us was an air of terrible gloom, sickness and death.

Whenever I came home I expected to hear the sounds of a funeral dirge being played on an organ, coming from the attic.

"There is a blight upon this house," I said, and the other two miserably agreed.

Then Charlotte asked what a blight was.

Even though it was still high summer, once you crossed the threshold into our apartment, it was loveless, bleak winter.

One Sunday lunchtime Karen and Charlotte went to the

pub to get drunk and hiss venomously at each other about how small Simon's and Daniel's penises had been really. And how the sex had been terrible and that they had never actually had any orgasms, but had faked every single one of them.

I would have loved to go with them but I had placed myself under voluntary house arrest.

I was slightly worried about how much I had been drinking, both during and especially post Gus, so I was seeking to escape by another route.

I was reading a great book about women who love too much. I was amazed that our paths had never crossed until now, but it had been published a good ten years earlier when I was a mere novice at being neurotic, only barely getting the hang of things.

The phone rang.

"Daniel," I said—for it was he. "And what do you want, you philandering fucker?"

"Lucy," he said in a low, urgent tone. "Is she there?"

"Is who here?" I asked coldly.

"Karen?"

"No, she's not, I'll tell her you called. Although don't hold your breath if you're expecting her to call back."

"No, Lucy." He sounded frightened. "Don't tell her I called. I want to talk to you."

"Well, I don't want to talk to you," I said.

"Please, Lucy!"

"No, get lost," I sputtered. "I've got my loyalties, you know. You can't just mess my friend around, break her heart, and still expect me to be your bosom buddy."

I expected him to say something about my bosoms, but he didn't.

"But, Lucy, you were *my* friend first," he said.

"Tough," I said simply. "You know the rules—boy

meets girl, boy breaks up with girl, boy has contract on life put out by girl's roommates.''

"Lucy," said Daniel, sounding very serious. "I've got something to say to you."

"Say it then, but be quick about it."

"Well, I never thought I'd hear myself saying this, but . . . well . . . I *miss* you, Lucy."

I felt a stab of sadness. But that was nothing unusual.

"You didn't call me all summer," I reminded him.

"You didn't call me either."

"Well, how could I? You were going out with someone and she would have killed me."

"You were going out with someone also," Daniel pointed out.

"Hah! Gus was hardly a threat, was he?"

"I wouldn't have said that."

"I know what you mean," I said, going all dewy-eyed at the memory of Gus. "Even though he's not very tall, I bet he can stand his own in hand-to-hand combat."

"I didn't mean that," said Daniel. "He doesn't need to hit anyone. He could have paralyzed me with five minutes of his boring conversation."

I was outraged. The idea of *Daniel* calling *Gus* boring. It was too ludicrous to even bother arguing about.

"Sorry," said Daniel. "I shouldn't have said that. He's a great laugh, really."

"Do you mean it?"

"No. But I'm afraid that you'll slam the phone down and refuse to see me."

"You're quite right to be afraid," I said. "Because I've no intention of seeing you."

"Please, Lucy?" he asked.

"What for? You're so pathetic—you're momentarily

without a woman and your ego can't handle it, so you call up good old Lucy and . . ."

"Jesus," he complained, "if I needed an ego boost, you'd be the last person I'd go to."

"Then why do you want to see me?"

"Because I miss you."

I'd momentarily run out of insults for him, and Daniel saw his opening.

"I'm not bored," he said earnestly, "I'm not lonely, I don't just want female company, I don't need an ego boost. I want to see you. No one else but you."

There was a pause. The air reverberated with his sincerity and for a moment I nearly believed him.

"Listen to you," I said with a little laugh. "You think you can charm every girl who crosses your path, don't you?"

But despite my bluster, there was a small flicker of something else. Relief, maybe? Although I couldn't give in just yet, it would disappoint him.

"You know that your usual smooth, slick lines don't work on me," I reminded Daniel.

"I know," he agreed, "And I know that if you do meet me, you'll be horrible."

"Oh yes?"

"You're going to call me a flirt and a . . a . . ."

"A slimebucket?" I supplied helpfully.

"Yes, a slimebucket. And a womanizer?"

"Of course—you can't even imagine what I have in store for you."

"That's okay."

"You're a sick man, Daniel Watson."

"But you'll meet me?"

"But . . . but, I like it here."

"What are you doing?"

"Lying down . . ."

"You can lie down here."

"Eating chocolate . . ."

"I'll buy you as much chocolate as you want."

"But I'm reading a great book and you'll want me to talk to you . . ."

"I won't. I promise."

"And I've no makeup on and I look horrible."

"So what?"

And when I asked, "How will I get over to your apartment?", my capitulation was complete.

"I'll drive over and get you," offered Daniel.

At that I threw back my head and laughed mirthlessly.

"What's so funny?" he asked.

"Daniel," I said. "Be realistic. How do you think Karen's going to feel if she sees your car outside our apartment?"

"Oh yes, of course," muttered Daniel, sounding ashamed. "How could I have been so insensitive?"

"Don't be stupid," I scoffed. "We all know that you're insensitive—after all, you're a man, aren't you? No, I mean if she finds out that you've come to see me and not her she'll kill you. And me," I added, suddenly touched by the cold hand of fear.

"Well, we'll have to think of something else then," said Daniel.

I waited for him to acknowledge that we couldn't see each other.

"I know!" he said eagerly. "I'll pick you up down by the traffic lights. She'll never see me there."

"Daniel!" I shouted, outraged. "How could you . . . ? Oh all right then."

As I got ready, I was aware of a feeling of subterfuge that I found both frightening and exciting.

Karen hadn't forbidden me to see Daniel. Not forbidden, as *such*. But I knew that she expected me to hate him for what he had done to her. That female roommate solidarity dictated a "One out, all out" stance whenever our guys dumped us. If they broke up with one of us, they had to forgo the pleasure of the company of all three.

But, once I had spoken to Daniel, I realized how much I had missed him. Now that we seemed to be friends again, it was safe to admit it. I had that bittersweet feeling that happens after you make up with someone.

He was fun and fun was a commodity that had been fairly thin on the ground of late.

I'd had enough of Karen, Charlotte and I going around with pinched faces and almost never eating—picking up a cracker, nibbling a tiny corner of it and then putting it down again and completely forgetting about it.

And I was worn down by the violent films that Karen kept renting. *Carrie* and *Dirty Weekend* and anything else that she could lay her hands on about women extracting revenge in a bloody and brutal fashion.

And Charlotte had regressed badly—we thought that we had said goodbye forever to Christopher Plummer and his thighs. But no, she had relapsed with a vengeance, watching *The Sound of Music* whenever Karen wasn't filling the screen with images of blood and pain. *Men's* blood and pain, if at all possible.

I was tired of living in a house of mourning. I wanted to put on a red dress and go out and party.

But I wasn't being fair. It was only sheer good fortune that my boyfriend had tired of me sooner than Karen's or Charlotte's, which meant that I was a couple of weeks further along the recovery process than they were.

How quickly we forget.

In fact it was only ten days since I had sat sniffing on

the couch, the remote control in my hand, and watched the part in *Terminator* where he says "I traveled through time for you." Then rewound it and watched it again. Then rewound it and watched it again. Then rewound it and . . .

It's scary, the things heartbreak makes us do.

But at least it meant that business was booming for Adrian.

Daniel looked shifty and nervous as he waited in his car by the traffic lights.

"Don't expect me to talk to you," I said, as I clambered in.

I had to admit that Daniel was looking quite attractive, if you liked that kind of thing.

I thanked God I didn't.

Instead of the work suits that I normally saw him in, he was wearing faded jeans and a really nice gray sweater. A *really* nice gray sweater, I thought, maybe he'd let me borrow it.

And I'd never noticed before how long and thick his eyelashes were—like the gray sweater they would have looked much nicer on me.

I felt a bit shy and awkward. It had been so long since I had seen him like this, on our own, that I'd forgotten how I was supposed to behave.

But by the warm rush of affection I felt for him, I must have been glad to see him.

"Do you want to drive?" he asked. The rush of affection intensified.

"Can I?" I breathed with excitement.

I had taken driving lessons and passed my test about a year before, even though I didn't have a car, couldn't afford a car and didn't need a car.

I had done it to feel empowered—yet another thing that I had done to try and make me satisfied with my life. Of course it hadn't worked. But one of its side effects was that I loved driving. And Daniel had a gorgeous car, sporty and sexy. I didn't know what *kind* of car it was, because, after all, I was a girl. But I knew the important things— that it looked great and went really fast.

Women loved it.

So we got out and swapped sides and he threw me the keys over the roof of the car. I drove through the London traffic to Daniel's flat, and had the best time I'd had since the last night I had sex with Gus.

Although I didn't mean to, I drove like a maniac. It had been a long time since I'd been behind the wheel of a car. Too long, probably. I did all kinds of reckless things that look great if you're driving a fast car. I pulled away from traffic lights with a roar, leaving the other drivers staring bitterly after me—that was called "burning them up" said Daniel. I drove out in front of other cars—Daniel said that was called "cutting them up" and while we were stuck in a traffic jam, I winked and smiled at attractive men in other cars—Daniel said that was called "acting like a brazen trollop."

I was slightly shocked when other drivers called me names and gesticulated angrily at me, when I burned them up and cut them up—at least at first. But I soon got the hang of the driving etiquette. So when one man cut in front of me, I furiously yelled "Asshole!" and tried to roll down the window so I could make rude gestures at him, but I couldn't find the handle.

He drove away with a look of fear on his face. And suddenly, like a mist clearing, I saw myself as I must have appeared to others. I was shocked—I hadn't realized that

I could be so aggressive. Worse, I hadn't realized that I'd enjoy it so much.

I was afraid that Daniel would be mad at me. "Sorry about that, Daniel," I muttered, and flicked a nervous, sidelong look at him, but he was laughing. "The look on that man's face," he wheezed. "He couldn't *believe* it." He laughed until tears ran down his face and finally managed to say, "And by the way, the switch for the electric windows is over there."

When we got to Daniel's road and I had parked about four feet from the curb, I said, "Thank you, Daniel. That's the best fun I've had in weeks."

I wasn't a bad driver but I wasn't too good at parking.

"You're welcome," he said. "You look good in it. You and the car suit each other."

I blushed and smiled, feeling happy and embarrassed.

"But it wasn't long enough," I complained.

"Well, if you like," he said, "next weekend, I'll take you out into the country and you can burn up everyone else on the highway."

"Mmmmm," I said noncommittally. There was something about the way he said "I'll take you" rather than "We can go" that made me feel funny. Not exactly nervous . . . well, maybe not *just* nervous.

"Er, Lucy . . ."

"What?"

"Would you be very offended if I parked the car a bit, um, closer to the curb?"

"No." I suddenly felt the need to smile at him. "No, not at all."

 57

I hadn't been to Daniel's apartment in forever. The last time I'd been there it had looked like a building site, because Daniel had been trying to put up shelves and most of the wall had fallen off onto the floor. You could hardly see the carpet because there was so much plaster on it.

But this time you'd barely have known it was a boy's apartment—it didn't look like a scrapyard or the inside of a sports bag. There were no broken motorcycle engines on the kitchen table, no stray pieces of chipboard cluttering up the hall, no badminton rackets on the sofa.

Having said that, I don't want to give the impression that Daniel's apartment was *nice*. The furniture was a bit weird because he had gotten some of it from his older brother Paul when his marriage broke up and he went to work in Saudi Arabia, and some of it from his granny when she shuffled off her mortal coil. I suppose the best thing that could be said about Daniel's furniture was that it hadn't enough character to be offensive.

Here and there, like oases in the desert, were a couple of things that were actively *nice*—a red giraffe compact disc holder, a free-standing candlestick—the sort of things that Simon's flat was packed with. But if you said to Simon, "nice shelf," he wouldn't just say "Thanks," he'd reel off, "Conran shop, Ron Arad, limited edition, be worth a fortune one day soon." Which was all probably

true, but it somehow struck me as, well, *unmanly*. All
Simon's inanimate articles had pedigrees and lineages, he
liked to be able to trace them right back to Le Corbusier
or the Bauhaus.

Simon never said, "Put on the teakettle." Instead he
said, "Gently flick the turquoise enamel genuine fifties
reproduction switch on my stainless steel Alessi pyramid
kettle. If you damage a hair on its sleek, silver head, I'll
kill you with the largest from my full set of Sabatier
knives."

Daniel's Nice Things were an odd mixture—some
looked like antiques and others were shiny and new and
modern.

"Oh, I love this clock," I said, picking it up off a
disgusting sideboard that had been part of his inheritance.
"I'd love one like this, where did you get it?"

"Er, Ruth gave it to me."

"Oh." And then I saw something else I liked.

"Look at this lovely mirror," I breathed, and ran to
touch the green wooden frame with covetous desire.
"Where did you get this?"

"Um, Karen gave it to me," he said sheepishly.

That explained the hodge-podge of different styles in
the flat—Daniel's women must have each sought to make
their mark on his furnishings but they seemed to all have
had different tastes.

"I'm surprised Karen hasn't asked for it back," I said.

"Actually she has," admitted Daniel quietly.

"So why is it still here?"

"She hung up on me after she told me she wanted it
and she's refused to take my calls since, so I don't know
when I should deliver it to her."

"*I* could take it home this evening," I suggested eagerly, as a vision of the mirror hanging in my bedroom

appeared before me. "But, no . . . I can't. She'd know I'd been here and I don't think she'd be too pleased."

"Lucy, you have every right to be here. . . ." said Daniel. But I ignored him. *I* knew I had every right to be there, but I knew that Karen would see it differently.

"Let's see the most important room in the house," I said, making for his bedroom. "What new things have you bought?"

I flung myself on Daniel's bed and bounced around a bit. "So this is where it all happens?" I asked.

"I don't know what you're talking about," he muttered. "Unless you mean sleep."

"But what's this?" I demanded, plucking at his duvet cover. "This looks suspiciously like it came from Habitat—I thought *lurve* machines like you had fur coverlets on your beds. Not that I know the difference between a cover and a coverlet."

"We do, but I took off the fur coverlet when you said you'd come over. And I unscrewed the mirror off the ceiling. But I didn't have time to turn off the video camera."

"You're disgusting," I said idly.

He smiled slightly.

"Imagine," I said, looking up at him, from where I was stretched out on his bed. "I'm in Daniel Watson's bed, well, *on* it, which will have to do. I'm the envy of hundreds of women."

He smiled more broadly.

"*Two,* anyway," I said, thinking of Karen and Charlotte.

Then I did what I always did when I was in Daniel's bedroom.

"Guess who I am, Daniel," I said. Then I wriggled around on his bed and made pretend noises of ecstasy.

"Oh Daniel, Daniel," I moaned.

I waited for him to laugh like he normally would, but he didn't.

"Have you guessed?" I demanded.

"No."

"Dennis," I said triumphantly.

He gave a weak smile. Maybe I'd done it once too often.

"So, who's your current bed mate?" I asked, changing the subject.

"Never you mind."

"*Is* there a current?"

"Not exactly."

"What? You mean you've liked a new woman for more than four hours and you haven't managed to seduce her with your 'I'm so innocent, I'm not a lech, I'm a really nice guy,' brand of charm? You must be losing your touch," I exclaimed.

"I must be."

He didn't smile the way he always did. He just walked out of the room. That was alarming so I jumped off the bed and ran after him.

"And how come your apartment is so clean?" I asked suspiciously, when we got back to his living room.

I felt ashamed because despite our best efforts, our apartment was always a mess. We always started off full of good intentions but after a day or so our resolve slackened and we said things like, "Charlotte, if you do my bathroom duty, you can borrow my suede dress for that thing you're going to on Friday night," and "Fuck off, Karen, I *did* clean it . . . yes, well, how could I use a Brillo pad?—Charlotte used them all on herself after sleeping with that Danish guy . . . well it's not my fault that it didn't all come off, it's not for lack of trying," and "I know it's Sunday evening and we're stretched out watching TV and we're all so relaxed that we're nearly comatose, but I have to do the vacuuming so I'm sorry but you're all going to have to move and you'll have to turn off the TV because I need the electrical socket. . . . Hey, don't shout! Don't shout! If it's that much of a disruption, I suppose I could leave it, I don't want to, but if you're certain that you'd rather I didn't . . ."

What we really needed was to pay someone to come in and clean for a couple of hours a week, but Karen vetoed the suggestion every time. "Why should we pay someone to do something that we can do ourselves?" she demanded. "We're young and fit and well able to do it."

Except that we didn't.

"Have you got some poor Filipina child-bride slave that you pay way under the minimum wage, coming in and 'doing' for you," I asked Daniel.

"I have not," he said, all affronted.

"Not even a bit player from *Eastenders,* with an apron and a headscarf and a bad back and red knees, coming in to dust and drink tea and complain?"

"No," said Daniel, "I do all my own cleaning, actually."

"Sure," I said disbelievingly. "Well I bet you get your current victim of a girlfriend to iron your shirts and clean the bathroom."

"I don't."

"Well, why not?" I asked. "I'm sure they'd love to. If someone offered to do my ironing in return for sexual favors, I wouldn't be able to turn it down."

"Lucy, I'll do your ironing in return for sexual favors," said Daniel, deadpan.

"Anyone apart from you, I think I must have forgotten to mention," I corrected.

"But, Lucy, I actually like doing housework," he said. I threw him a scornful look. "And you say *I'm* weird."

"I don't actually, Lucy," he said, looking hurt.

"Don't you?" I asked surprised. "Well, you should . . . Now me—I absolutely *hate* doing housework. If there's a hell being prepared for me—and I see no reason to think that there isn't—it'll involve me having to do all of Satan's ironing. And vacuuming—that's the worst, that's my room one-oh-one of housework, I'll be forced to vacuum all of hell every day. . . . I'm like Nature," I added.

"How so?" asked Daniel.

"Nature abhors a vacuum."

Daniel laughed. Thank God for that, I thought. He had been uncharacteristically mirthless.

"Now come over here, Lucy," said Daniel, and put his arm around me. I felt a little leap of fear, until I realized that he was only steering me across the room to the sofa.

"You wanted to be horizontal?" he inquired.

"Yes."

"Here's the very place to do it."

"What about the chocolate you promised me?" I demanded. Lying down was no good without the chocolate. And chocolate is at its best when eaten lying down.

"Consider it done." He left the room to get it.

That was the day that the weather broke.

It was the end of August and although it was no longer sweltering, it was still warm enough for all the windows to be open in Daniel's front room.

Suddenly, like a switch being flicked, the breeze picked up, the rustling of the leaves intensified, the sky darkened and we heard the first ominous growl of the storm.

"Was that thunder?" I asked hopefully.

"It sounded like it."

I raced to the window, and leaned out. An empty potato chip bag that had probably lain undisturbed all summer skittered along the pavement, whipped by the breeze. And in seconds the rain had started and the world was transformed.

The roads and gardens changed from beige and dry and dusty to dark and sleek, the bright green of the trees was instantly almost black.

It was beautiful.

The air smelled green and fragrant and cool. The scent of the wet grass rushed up to me as I leaned precariously out of the window. Now and then my face got splashed with raindrops so big that they nearly concussed me. I loved thunderstorms—the only time I ever really felt at peace with myself was during a storm. All the turmoil and exuberance seemed to calm me.

Apparently that wasn't just because I was weird—there was a scientific explanation for it. Thunderstorms filled the air with negative ions; although I'm not sure what they are, I know they're supposed to make you feel good. When I had found that out, I had even *bought* an ionizer to try to re-create the effect of a storm all the time.

But nothing compared to the real thing.

There was another rumble of thunder and the room was zapped by silver light. In the momentary flash of silver, Daniel's table and chairs and things looked startled, like people who had been unexpectedly awakened by the bedroom light being switched on.

The rain cascaded down and I could feel the bumping of the thunder deep within me.

"Isn't it amazing?" I said, and turned, smiling to Daniel.

He was standing a couple of feet away from me, watching me. Staring at me with hard intensity, curiosity on his face. I immediately felt awkward. He thought I was nuts

to enjoy the downpour. Then the funny, intense look disappeared and he smiled.

"I forgot that you always loved the rain," he said.
"You told me once that when it rains you feel that your
insides match your outsides."

"Did I?" I was embarrassed. "No wonder you think
I'm certifiable."

"But I don't," he said.

I smiled at him. He smiled back, a funny little twist of
a smile.

"I think you're incredible," he said.

That threw me.

There was a long pause. I tried to think of something light
and insulting—either to him or to me—to say. Anything to
dispel the tension. But I couldn't say a thing. I was mute. I
was pretty sure that he had meant "incredible" in a compli-
mentary way but I didn't know how I should respond.

"Come away from the window," he eventually said. "I
don't want you getting struck by lightning."

"Let's face it, if it could happen to anyone, it could
happen to me," I said, and we both laughed extra heartily.

Although we kept well out of each other's way.

He closed the windows, muffling the sounds of the
storm. And still the thunder complained and roared and
bumped above us. The rain torrented down and by five
o'clock in the afternoon, it was almost as dark as night.
Except for when there was a flash of lightning and the
room was lit up for a dazzling second. Water cascaded
down the windows.

"That looks like the end of summer," said Daniel.

I felt sad for only a moment. I always knew that it
wouldn't last forever and it was time to move on.

Anyway I liked autumn. Autumn—the season of new boots.
Eventually all the emotion of the storm was spent and

the rain settled down into a steady beating, calming, hyp-
notizing, cozy. I lay on the couch under a duvet, luxuriat-
ing in feeling snug, comfortable and safe.

I read my book and ate chocolate.

Daniel sat on the armchair, reading the papers and
watching the TV with the sound turned down.

I don't think we spoke one word to each other in two hours.

Now and then I would sigh and wriggle and say "God,
this is gorgeous," or "Peel me another grape, Coperni-
cus." And Daniel would smile at me when I said these
things, but I don't think they counted as conversation.

It was only hunger that eventually forced us to
communicate.

"Daniel, I'm starving."

"Well . . ."

"And don't tell me that I've been eating chocolate all
afternoon and that I can't be hungry."

"I wasn't going to." He sounded surprised. "I know
that you have a different stomach for cookies and sweets.
Would you like me to take you out for something to eat?"

"Does it mean I have to get off the couch?"

"Oh, I see the problem," he said. "Would you like
a pizza?"

"And garlic bread?" I asked hopefully.

"With cheese?" he asked smoothly.

What a man!

He opened a drawer on one of his fancy shelf units and
took out mounds of pizza leaflets and brochures.

"Have a look through these and decide what you want."

"Do I have to?"

"Not if you don't want to."

"But then how will I know about the different types?"

So he read aloud to me of pizzas.

"Thin crust or deep crust?"

"Thin crust."

"Normal or whole wheat?"

"*Normal!* Whole wheat—what a disgusting idea."

"Small, medium or large?"

"Small."

He was silent.

"All right then, medium."

Once the food order was established, conversation stopped again.

We watched TV, we ate, we barely spoke. I couldn't remember feeling as happy in ages. Not that this was saying much, considering that I'd been suicidal for weeks.

During the evening the phone rang twice, but when Daniel answered it, the person hung up. I suspected that it was probably one of his hundreds of ex-girlfriends. Which made me feel uncomfortable, because it reminded me of when *I* used to do that to men who had broken *my* heart. If Gus had had a phone I'd probably have done it about ten times a day.

Later, Daniel drove me home. I insisted that he drop me at the traffic lights.

"No," he said. "You'll get soaked."

"Please, Daniel," I begged. "I'm afraid that Karen will see your car."

"And what's wrong with that?"

"She'll make my life a misery."

"We have every right to see each other."

"Maybe," I agreed. "But I'm the one who has to live with her. You wouldn't be so brave if she was *your* roommate."

"I'll come in with you and *I'll* deal with her," he threatened.

"Oh no!" I exclaimed. "That would be awful. Look," I said, more calmly. "I'll talk to her, it'll be okay."

 58

As I ran along the puddled road, the rain pelting down on me, I agonized about what I would say to Karen when she asked me where I'd been. The easiest thing would be to lie, of course, except that she was bound to know I was lying.

And, anyway, why should I lie? I hadn't done anything wrong, I told myself. I had every right to see Daniel, he was my friend, he had been my friend for years, long before he had ever met Karen, long before I met Karen, for that matter. It all sounded terribly reasonable when I said it like that.

But as soon as I put my key in the door, my courage deserted me.

"Where the fuck have you been?"

Karen was waiting for me, her face like thunder, an ashtray a yard high on the table in front of her.

"Er . . ."

I would have quite happily lied but it was obvious that she knew.

How did she know? Who told her?

I found out later from Charlotte that it was Adrian. After the pub had shut, Karen and Charlotte decided to get a video to kill a couple of Sunday afternoon hours and Adrian asked them about "the guy in the expensive car" who had picked me up.

"Adrian looked like he was going to cry," said Charlotte. "I think he likes you."

My fault of course. If I had met Daniel at my apartment, instead of engaging in subterfuge, I wouldn't have been found out. Honesty was the best policy. Either that or covering my tracks properly.

"So what's going on?" she demanded, in a shrill voice. Her face was really pale except for two red blotchy patches on her cheeks. She looked *demented* with fury or nerves or something.

"Nothing's going on," I said, anxious to reassure her. Not just out of concern for my personal safety, but because I knew what a living hell it is when you suspect that the man you love has found someone else.

"Don't give me that."

"Really, Karen, I just went over to his flat. It was totally innocent."

"Innocent! Nothing that man does is innocent. And do you know who told me that—it was *you*, Lucy Sullivan."

"It's different with me . . ."

She laughed bitterly. "Oh no, it's not, Lucy, don't flatter yourself."

"I'm not . . ."

"Yes, you are. That's the way he operates—he made *me* feel like the only girl in the world."

"I don't mean that, Karen. I mean, it's different because he doesn't like me that way and I don't like him that way. We're just friends."

"Don't be so naïve. Anyway, I've always been suspicious of how you've always made far too much of a point of how you didn't think of him as gorgeous."

"I was only being the voice of reason . . ."

". . . and he wouldn't be bothered spending time with you if he didn't intend to get you into the sack—he can't resist a challenge. He'll try to seduce you just because you act like you don't want to.''

I opened my mouth but nothing came out.

''And is it true that he let you drive his car?''

''Yes.''

''The bastard—he never let me. In six months he never once let me.''

''But you can't drive.''

''Well, he could have taught me, couldn't he? If he had any decency he would have given me driving lessons.''

''Er . . .''

''So is he going out with someone else yet?'' she asked, her face twisting as she tried to smile.

''I don't think so,'' I said soothingly. ''Don't worry.''

''I'm not worried,'' she sneered. ''Why would I be worried? After all, I broke up with him.''

''Of course.'' It was hard to figure out the right thing to say.

''How can you be so pathetic?'' she demanded. ''Find your own guy, stop satisfying yourself with my leavings.''

Before I could defend myself against that she moved on to a different accusation.

''And how could you be so disloyal, how would you feel if I went out with Gus?''

''I'm sorry.'' I was humbled. She was right and I felt ashamed, a traitor.

''You're *not* to see him again, you're not to bring my ex-boyfriend into my own home.''

''But I wouldn't.'' I had thought I was being sensitive and mindful of her feelings, but she made me sound callous and selfish.

''And I suppose he talked all about me . . .''

I didn't know what to say—I was afraid I would hurt her if I said that he hadn't.

". . . Well, I don't want him to know anything. How can I have any privacy, with my roommate going out with my ex?"

"It isn't like that."

I felt torn apart with guilt and remorse. I hated myself for causing her pain, and I couldn't understand how it had ever seemed justifiable to do it.

Then came the thunderbolt.

"I forbid you to see him." She stared me right in the eye.

That was my cue to square my shoulders and swallow hard and tell her that she had no right to forbid me to see anyone.

But I didn't.

I felt too guilty to stand up to her. I had no right to. I was a bad friend, a bad roommate, a bad human being. I wanted to make it all right. I didn't think what it would be like if I didn't see Daniel because I wanted to make things up to Karen.

"Okay." I bowed my head and left the room.

 59

I went out with Daniel the following night—I couldn't understand what was happening to me. I knew I was for-bidden to see Daniel, and I was *terrified* of Karen, petrified.

But when he called and asked if he could take me for something to eat after work, for some reason I decided to say yes. Probably just because it had been so long since someone had taken me out and fed me. Although perhaps it was a form of rebellion, I thought, albeit a secretive, private form.

Just before Daniel arrived at my office I decided to reapply my makeup—even though it was only him I was going out with, a night out was a night out and I never knew who I might meet. But as I wobbled on my eyeliner I was alarmed to discover that I felt a bit fluttery and shaky. Surely to God I wasn't attracted to Daniel, I thought in horror. Then I realized that it was just good plain old-fashioned fear. Fear of Karen and what she'd do to me if she ever found out. What a relief! How much better it was to feel sick with terror, not sick with anticipation.

When Daniel walked into my office at five o'clock (wearing his Visitor's pass; Daniel would never do a Gus) I was so pleased to see him, even though he was wearing his suit, that I felt a lurch of self-righteous anger toward Karen. I even toyed with the idea that I might confront her. Although not seriously.

"We're going to the pub before our dinner," I said to Meredia, Megan and Jed. "You're welcome to join us."

But they declined. Meredia and Jed wore their "He's not Gus" faces, and watched me with narrowed, judgmental eyes as I put on my coat. Mummy had a new boyfriend; they wanted Mummy to be with Daddy.

Stupid fuckers.

Mummy wanted to be with Daddy also, but what could Mummy do about it? Would refusing a free meal from Daniel bring Gus rushing back?

Megan declined by cheerfully telling Daniel, "Thanks for the offer, and I hope you *will* be offended if I decline—

I'm not in the mood for a smoothie like you. I've got a date with a *real* man.''

Like me, Megan felt the need to punish Daniel for being good-looking and turning intelligent women to mush. All the same, that sounded a bit harsh. And who was this *real* man of whom she boasted? Probably one of the giant sheep shearers, who hadn't shaved for days or changed his underpants in as long.

So Daniel and I went to the pub alone.

"Karen called me," he said, as we sat down.

"Oh." I felt a belly-flop of alarm. "What did she want?"

*Were they going to get back together?*

"She told me to keep away from you," he said.

I exploded in relief. "And what did you say?"

"I said that we're both adults and we can do what we like."

"What did you have to go and say that for?" I wailed.

"But why not?"

"It's okay for *you* to be an adult and to do what you like—you don't have to live with her. If I try to be an adult and do what I like, she'll kill me."

"But . . ."

"So what did she say to that?" I asked him.

"She sounded annoyed with me."

"How do you mean?" My heart sank.

"She said—let me see if I can remember exactly what she said—she said that I was awful in bed. And, of course, she told me that my penis was one of the smallest she'd ever seen."

"Naturally," I agreed.

"And that the only time she'd seen a smaller one was on her two-month-old nephew and it was no wonder I'd had so many girlfriends because it was obvious I was trying to prove that I was a man.''

All the usual small member allegations that were par for the course from a woman scorned, but there was a danger that Daniel could be upset by Karen's version of the No Fury That Hell Hath. From the way he grinned, he didn't *look* upset.

''And what else did she scream at me?'' He stared thoughtfully. ''I wish I could remember because it was really good, but I can ask everyone else in the office because they heard it too.''

''I thought you said she called you.'' I was puzzled.

''She *did* call me. But everyone in the office *still* heard. Oh I remember—she swears she saw two gray ones in my pubic hair and that she only went out with me because I drove her to work most mornings and saved her having to pay for the train, and that my hair is thinning at the back of my head and I'll be bald by the time I'm thirty-five and no girl will go near me.''

''The bitch!'' I said. ''And what nasty stuff did she say about me?'' I tried to brace myself.

''Nothing.''

''Really?''

''Really.''

He was lying. When Karen was inflamed, she attacked indiscriminately.

''I don't believe you, Daniel. What did she say?''

''Nothing, Lucy.''

''I know you're lying. I bet she told you that sometimes I stuff my bra with cotton balls.''

''She did but I knew that anyway.''

''How?! No, don't tell me, I don't want to know. Okay, I bet she told you that she guesses I must be hopeless in bed because I'm too inhibited. She knows that would upset me."

Daniel looked mortified.

"Was that it?" I demanded.

"Something like that," he muttered.

"Exactly what did she say?!"

"She said we'd be well matched, because we're probably as bad as each other in bed," he admitted.

"The fucking bitch," I said in admiration. "She's so good at knowing what hurts most. But she didn't mean what she said about you," I continued, anxious to reassure him. "She always told me that you were great in bed, and that your penis is lovely and big."

The two construction workers at the next table stared at us with open interest.

"Thanks, Lucy," Daniel said warmly. "And I have it on good authority that you're good in bed, also."

"Gerry Baker?" I asked. Gerry Baker was a colleague of Daniel's that I'd had a short-lived fling with.

"Gerry Baker," confirmed Daniel. Foolishly.

"I *told* you not to talk to Gerry about what I was like in bed," I said angrily.

"I *didn't*," protested Daniel nervously. "All that happened was that he said that you were good in bed and . . ."

One of the workers winked at me, and said, "I can well believe it, darling."

The other worker looked appalled and hastily said to Daniel, "Sorry, mate, sorry about him. He's had a few. No disrespect meant to you or your lady."

"It's okay," I said quickly, before Daniel was forced to defend my honor. "I'm not his girlfriend."

Which meant it was fine to insult me.

The construction workers smiled with relief but it took

a little while to persuade Daniel that I hadn't been offended by them.

"*You're* the one I'm pissed off at," I explained.

"I didn't *ask* Gerry, you know," muttered Daniel. He looked suitably shamefaced. "It just slipped out accidentally and he said it without even . . ."

"Shut up," I said. "You're in luck. I'm too upset about what Karen said to worry about you and Gerry discussing my panties."

"He didn't even mention your panties," Daniel reassured me.

"Good."

"From what I heard they weren't on you long enough for him to even notice . . . I'm joking," he said hastily, as I turned a face burning with rage upon him.

Back to Karen.

"She doesn't really think anything's going on with us," I said. "She knows we're only friends."

"Exactly," Daniel said eagerly. "That's just what I said to her, that you and me are only friends."

And we both laughed heartily.

 60

If I hadn't been so pissed off with Karen I'd never have taken part in the Great Bitching Session which followed.

It wasn't an honorable, noble thing to do, to bitch about my friend, roommate and fellow female, and especially to do it with a *man*, but I was only human.

Bad in bed, indeed! The nerve of her!

Of course, no good ever came of gossiping. I'd hate myself later, what goes around comes around, my bad karma would be returned to me three-fold, and so on and so on. But I decided I could live with it.

Gossiping was a kind of McDonald's for my psyche. Irresistible at the time, but I always felt sort of disgusting afterward. And hungry again ten minutes later.

"Tell me about you and Karen. What have you done to make her hate you so much?" I asked him.

"I don't know," he said.

"I suppose it's because you're an egocentric, selfish bastard who broke her heart."

"Am I, Lucy, is that what you think?" He looked upset.

"Well . . . yes, I suppose."

"But, Lucy," he insisted. "I'm not, I didn't. It wasn't like that."

"So what *was* it like? I want to know why you didn't tell her that you loved her," I said, rolling up my bitching sleeves.

I'd teach her to suggest that I was useless in bed!

"I didn't tell her that I loved her because I didn't love her." He sighed.

"*Why* didn't you love her?" I asked. "What was wrong with her?"

Then I held my breath. In spite of what Karen had said about Daniel—and me—it was very important that he didn't say mean things about her, that he treated her with respect, that he behaved like a gentleman.

I hadn't forgotten that he was a man, and so was basically the enemy. It was fine for *me* to destroy Karen's reputation with the airing of a few well-chosen secrets, but Daniel wasn't allowed to treat her with anything other than the utmost respect. At least not until I said otherwise.

"Lucy," he said carefully, choosing his words slowly and watching my face for my reaction, "I don't want to say anything about Karen that could be misconstrued as nasty."

Right answer.

We both smiled with relief.

"I understand that, Daniel." I nodded gravely.

That was enough of that. He had observed the formalities, and now I wanted to hear *everything* about Karen. The more awful the better.

"That's fine, I won't misconstrue anything." I was brisk. "You can tell me all about it."

"Lucy," he said awkwardly. "I'm not sure . . . it hardly seems right . . ."

"It's okay, Daniel, you've convinced me that you're really a nice guy," I reassured him.

"Really?" he asked.

"Yes," I promised insincerely. "Now tell me!"

Daniel, like all men, had to be coaxed. They like to pretend that it isn't in their nature to be bitchy, but of course, they love a good character assassination, the bloodier the better.

Men make me laugh when they throw their eyes to heaven and sanctimoniously say, "Meeee-*yoww!*" whenever a woman makes an unkind comment. Men are *worse* gossips than women.

"Lucy, *if* I tell you anything—and I'm not saying that I will, mind—it's to go no further," he said sternly.

"Of course." I nodded earnestly. I wondered if Charlotte would still be up when I got home.

"Not even Charlotte," he added.

Bastard!

"Oh go on, let me at least tell Charlotte," I said sulkily.

"No."

"Please."

"*No,* Lucy. If you don't promise, I'm not going to tell you anything."

"I promise," I said in a singsong voice.

No problem. Talk was cheap and I wasn't under oath.

I took a quick look at him and he had trouble maintaining the straight, stern face. He tried not to smile, but he couldn't stop himself. I felt a surge of pleasure that I could still make him laugh.

"Okay, Lucy," he took a deep breath and finally started. "You know I don't want to say anything bad about Karen."

"Good," I said stoutly, "I wouldn't want you to."

Our eyes met and again his mouth twitched. He looked sideways over his shoulder, pretending to look around the pub, but I knew he was trying to hide his grin.

It had been a mistake on Karen's part to insult Daniel and me together because it had united us against her. Until the sting of her allegations stopped smarting, we would be close allies. Nothing unites two people as warmly and lovingly as a shared grievance against a third party.

Eventually Daniel cleared his throat and spoke.

"I know it sounds like I'm trying to put all the blame onto her," he said. "But Karen didn't really care about me. She didn't even like me very much."

"It sounds like you're trying to put all the blame onto her." I eyeballed him steadily.

"But it's true, Lucy, honestly! She didn't care about me."

"You lying bastard!" I scoffed. "She was besotted with you."

"No, she wasn't," he said, with a bitterness that surprised me. "She was besotted with my bank balance—at least what she thought my bank balance was. She must have mistaken my overdraft for savings."

"Oh Daniel, no woman goes out with a man for his money. It's an Old Husband's Tale," I said.

"Karen did. Size mattered to her—the size of my wallet."

I would have laughed except he looked so miserable.

"And she kept trying to change me," he said miserably. "She didn't like me the way I was. She was disappointed because she got a pig in a poke."

"A pig who gave her a poke, more like." I was unable to resist the cheap joke.

"I'm not a pig," he said huffily.

"In what way did she try to change you?" I asked kindly. I didn't want him to get so huffy that he would stop telling me things.

"She told me that I didn't take my job seriously enough. She said that I should be more ambitious. And she was always on at me to learn to play golf, she said that more deals are done on the golf course than in the boardroom."

"But you're a research person thingy." I was confused. "You don't *do* deals, do you?"

"Exactly!" he said.

"And do you remember when I took her to that work party at the end of July?"

"No," I said, managing to bite my tongue and not shout at him, "How the hell would I know *what* you took her to, it's not as if you called me or anything to keep me abreast of what was going on in your life."

"Well, you should have seen the way she carried on at that!"

I felt a cheap thrill and drew nearer, all the better to hear whatever awful thing he was about to tell me.

"The way she behaved with Joe . . ."

"Joe, your boss, *that* Joe?" I asked.

". . . Yes. It was horrible, Lucy. She practically offered to sleep with him if it would enhance my promotion prospects."

"God, that's awful," I said, blushing for her. "Joe, of all people! But didn't you try to stop her?"

"Of *course* I tried to stop her, but you know what she's like, she's so headstrong."

"How excruciating." I squirmed.

"Lucy, I was badly embarrassed for her," said Daniel. He looked pale and sweaty at the memory. "I felt awful for her."

"I bet."

Joe was gay.

We sat in silence. Our thoughts occupied by a mental image of poor Karen, as she flashed her tits, but flashed in vain.

"But apart from the career stuff and the money, did you have fun?" I asked. "Did you like her?"

"Oh, yes," he said firmly.

I was silent.

"Well, she was all right, I suppose." He sighed. "She didn't have much of a sense of humor. None, in fact."

"That's not true." I felt I *had* to say it.

"No, you're right, Lucy. She did have a sense of humor, the kind where you laugh at people who slip on banana skins."

Guilt wrestled with my desire to really trash her.

Guilt won.

"She's beautiful though. Isn't she?" I asked.

"Very," he agreed.

"She has a great body, hasn't she?" I asked, pressing him.

He looked at me oddly. "Yes," he said. "I suppose she has."

"Then why have you given all that up?"

"Because I just wasn't attracted to her anymore."

I laughed mirthlessly. "Ha! As if. A large-breasted blonde."

"But she was cold," he protested. "It's a terrible turn-off if you feel your lover doesn't even *like* you. Lucy, contrary to the terrible things you think about me—and all men, from what I can gather—big breasts and lots of sex aren't the highest things on my list of priorities. There are other things too."

"Like what?" I asked suspiciously.

"Well, a sense of humor. And it would have been nice if I hadn't had to pay for everything."

"Daniel, why are you suddenly so weird about money?" I was surprised. "It's not like you to be stingy."

"It's not the principle, it's the money." He grinned. "No, Lucy, I don't really care about the money, it was the way she never even offered to pay that pissed me off. It would have been nice if *she* had taken *me* out for a change."

"But maybe she doesn't have much money," I suggested doubtfully.

"It didn't have to be someplace that costs lots. Just the gesture would have been enough.

"But she had a dinner party for you."

"No, she didn't. You and Charlotte did most of the work."

Suddenly I had a very vivid memory of the Night of the Long Preparations. "*And* we each had to pay a third of the cost," I said, my integrity a shadow of its former self.

"So did I," he said.

"What?" I screeched. "I don't believe you!"

You had to admire her nerve, all the same.

"She probably got Simon and Gus to pay a third each also," I exclaimed. "She must have made a huge profit on the bloody thing."

"She'd have had a long wait trying to get any money out of Gus," said Daniel.

But I didn't tell him to fuck off and leave Gus alone. We had just spent the last hour destroying his ex-girlfriend's character. It was only fair that Daniel got a go at my ex-boyfriend.

"And she never read anything except that stupid magazine that has photos of lady this and countess that and Ivana Trump," he added.

"That's bad," I agreed.

"I prefer the one with the articles about men who have babies and 'I married a child molester,' what's that one called, Lucy?"

*"The National Enquirer?"*

"No, Lucy, a girl's one."

*"Marie Claire?"*

"That's it!" He was enthusiastic. "I love that. Did you see the report about the women who were imprisoned for having abortions? I think it was the February one. Jesus, Lucy, it was . . ."

I interrupted. "But Karen does read *Marie Claire*," I exclaimed in her defense.

"Oh." That brought him up short. He was silent and thoughtful for a while.

"No," he finally said.

"No, what?"

"I still don't think I love her."

I laughed. I couldn't help it. God would punish me.

"I suppose," Daniel said sadly, "what it comes down to is I was bored with Karen."

"Again?" I exclaimed.

"What do you mean, Lucy? Again?"

"That's just what you said about Ruth—that she bored you. Maybe you have a very low boredom threshold."

"No, I don't. You don't bore me."

"Neither does auto racing. But that's not your girlfriend either," I said smartly.

"But . . ."

"This mysterious new woman that you haven't managed to get into bed yet—she doesn't bore you?" I asked nicely.

"No."

"Give it time, Daniel. I bet in three months time you'll be complaining to me about how tedious you find her."

"You're probably right," he said. "You usually are."

"Good. Now take me somewhere and feed me."

We went to the Indian restaurant next to the pub.

I wanted to be serious and offload onto Daniel about Gus. But I couldn't nail him down for a serious conversation. Every time I asked him a question, he sang songs about the food. Which, no doubt, was very endearing, but I wanted to talk about matters of the heart. *My* heart. *And* he couldn't sing. Not like Gus. But there was a good chance that Daniel wouldn't fleece me for every penny I had. There was a bright side.

"Do you think Gus and I saw too much of each other?" I asked, as the waiter put the pilau rice on the table.

"Lay your head upon my pilau," sang Daniel tunelessly, "Ah, here's the bhajees. Lay your warm and tender bhajee close to mine." He lined up our onion bhajees side by side. "I don't know, Lucy, I really don't."

Such high spirits were a bit out of character. Although maybe they weren't. Daniel *used* to be fun, before my roommates went after him. In fact he was still fun, but I had no time to have fun with him, it was my job to discipline him. Let's face it, no one else would do it.

"But I really don't think we did, you know. If anything I wanted to see him less than he wanted to see me . . ."

"Your turn," he interrupted. "You have to sing something."

"Er, popadom, don't preach, I'm in trouble deep," I half-sang awkwardly. I pointed to my popadom so that he'd know what I was singing about. "So do you think I'll ever get over him?"

"Here's the chicken korma," he said, as he saw the waiter coming.

"Korma, korma, korma, korma, kor-ma, chameleon! You come and go, you come and go," Daniel sort-of-sang, moving the dish close to me and then moving it away again, moving it closer, moving it away. "Course you will. Your turn."

I pointed to the bowl of aloo gobi on the next people's table and sang absently, "Aloo, is it me you're looking for? But when?"

"Let me see," he said carefully. "I'll have to think about this one, Lucy. Oh yes, I know!"

My heart leaped. Daniel *knew* when I'd get over Gus?

"Tikka chance, tikka chance, tikka, tikka, tikka chance, tikka chance on me," he sang. "That was a good one, wasn't it?" He beamed. "Chicken *tikka*," he explained kindly to my puzzled face. "You know, tikka chance on me—Abba sang it."

"But what about me and Gus?" I asked faintly. "Oh fuck it! I can see it's pointless trying to have a serious conversation with you. What's this?"

"Vegetable curry."

"Okay. You can't curry love, you just have to wait. Your turn."

It took him a moment or two before he thought of one.

"It's my paratha, and I'll cry if I want to, cry if I want to, cry if I want to," he tone-deafed at me.

I stopped a passing waiter and asked him to bring me a bowl of dhal tarka, then I turned to Daniel.

"Got myself a crying, walking, sleeping, talking, living dhal!" I sang.

"Stand by your naan," he replied.

We spent the rest of the evening in convulsions. I know we had fun because the people at the next table complained about us. I couldn't remember the last time I'd had such a laugh. Well, it had probably been one night with Gus.

And when I got home Karen wasn't waiting up for me.

That was one of the great advantages of her having no respect for me. It meant that I could fly in the face of her orders, actively disobey her and it would never even *occur* to her that I might do so.

 61

The next morning when I arrived at work, Megan said, "That slime merchant Daniel just rang, he said he'll call back later."

"What's he ever done to you?" I asked in surprise.

"Nothing." It was her turn to sound surprised.

"So why are you calling him names?" There was a defensive edge to my voice.

"But that's what *you* always call him," she protested.

"Oh." I was shaken. "I suppose I do."

Technically she was right, yes, of *course,* I was nasty to Daniel all the time but it wasn't as if I really *meant* it.

"It's what we both call him, Lucy," she reminded me. She sounded concerned and well she might. When Megan had first met Daniel and she said that she didn't like him and couldn't see what all the fuss was about, I had been thrilled. I held her aloft as an example of intelligent womanhood to anyone who would listen. "She says that Daniel wouldn't stand a chance in Australia," I gleefully told everyone, including Daniel. "She says he's too slimy and she likes her men to be rougher and tougher than him."

And now Megan was concerned that I had changed the rules. It was no longer open season on Daniel.

I *hadn't* changed any rules, I thought uncomfortably, but it sounded funny to hear Megan call Daniel a slime merchant. Horrible, actually. I felt as if I was being disloyal to him, especially after he'd been so nice and paid for my dinner.

But then Meredia lumbered in, followed by Jed. And I forgot about Daniel because Jed was so funny. He hung up his coat, stared around at the office, rubbed his eyes and said, "Oh no, so I didn't dream it, it wasn't a nightmare! It's horrible, HORRIBLE!"

He did that most mornings. We were so proud of him.

The day proceeded.

I barely had my computer switched on (which meant that it was about ten to eleven) when my mother phoned and said that she was on her way up to town; it would be nice to meet me.

I couldn't have agreed less, but she was insistent.

"I've something to tell you," she said mysteriously.

"I can't wait," I said patiently. Her "somethings" were usually about the next-door neighbors stealing our trash can lid, or the birds continually pecking the tops of the bottles of milk even though she had repeatedly told the milkman to close the gate after him, or something equally earthshattering.

It was odd that she was coming up to town. She didn't ever, even though she was only twenty miles from central London.

Twenty miles and fifty years.

I didn't really feel up to meeting her but I felt that I should because I hadn't seen her since the start of the summer. Not that that had been my fault—I'd been out to the house lots of times—well, once or twice anyway—but only Dad had been there.

I agreed to meet her for lunch, although not in so many words. I didn't think she was au fait with the concept of "lunch." She was more of a "cup of tea and ham sandwich" kind of woman.

"Meet me in the pub across the road from my office at one o'clock," I said.

But she was appalled at the suggestion that she sit in the pub on her own and wait for me.

"What would people think?" she asked in alarm.

"Okay." I sighed. "I'll get there first and you won't have to wait on your own."

"But no," she said, sounding panicked. "Sure, that's just as bad, a single woman in a public house . . ."

"What's wrong with that?" I scoffed and began to tell her that I was always going into pubs on my own, but stopped myself in time, before she started wailing, "Oh, what kind of girl have I reared?"

"Someplace where we can have a cup of tea," she suggested, again.

"All right then, there's a café near . . ."

"Nothing too fancy," she interrupted anxiously, terrified that she might be caught in a "which one of these five forks should I use" scenario. But she needn't have worried, I wasn't too comfortable in those kinds of places either.

"It's not too fancy," I said. "It's nice, relax."

"And what kind of things do they have there?"

"Normal food," I reassured her. "Sandwiches, cheesecake, that kind of thing."

"Black Forest gâteau?" she asked hopefully. She knew about Black Forest gâteau.

"Probably," I said. "Or something very similar, anyway."

"And do I ask for my tea at the counter or do I . . . ?"

"You sit down, Mum, and the girl takes your order."

"And can I just march on in there and sit wherever I like, or should I . . . ?"

"Wait until they seat you," I advised.

When I arrived she was already sitting at the table, looking like a hick up from the sticks for a day, all awkward, as if she felt she had no right to be there. She was wearing a nervous "I'm just fine" smile and had her handbag clenched tightly against all the muggers. "They won't get the better of me," her grim little hands seemed to say.

She looked slightly different—slimmer and younger than usual. For once Peter had been right—she *had* done something funny to her hair. But it suited her, I grudgingly admitted.

And there was something strange about her clothes, they were . . . they were . . . what was it? They were *nice*.

And, to top it all, she was wearing red lipstick. She never wore lipstick, except to weddings. And sometimes to funerals, if she hadn't liked the person who died.

I sat down opposite her, smiled awkwardly and wondered what it was she wanted to tell me.

 62

*She was leaving my father.*

That was what she wanted to tell me. (Although it was probably overstating the case to say that she *wanted* to tell me, it was more accurate to say it was what she *had* to tell me.)

The shock was nauseating, literally. I was surprised that she waited until after I had ordered a sandwich to break the news to me, because she deplored waste.

"I don't believe you," I croaked, searching her face for a sign that it wasn't true. But all I· saw was that she was wearing eyeliner and she had it on crooked.

"I'm sorry," she said humbly.

My world felt as if it was falling apart, and that confused me. I had thought I was an independent twenty-six-year-old woman who had left home and established her own life, one who had no interest in whatever sexual shenanigans her parents might get up to. But right at that moment I felt afraid and angry, like an abandoned four-year-old.

"But why?" I asked. "Why are you leaving him? How could you?"

"Because, Lucy, it's been a marriage in name only for years and years. Lucy, surely you know that?" she asked, urging me to agree with her.

"No, I didn't know that," I said. "This is all news to me.'·

"Lucy, you must have known," she insisted.

She was overdoing the calling me "Lucy" bit. She kept trying to touch my arm in a pleading sort of way.

"I didn't know," I insisted back. She wasn't going to get me to agree with her, no matter what.

What's going on? I wondered in horror—other people's parents split up, but mine didn't. Especially because mine were *Catholics*.

A stable home life was the only reason I had put up with Catholic parents and their nonsense for so long. It had been an unspoken deal. My part involved, among other things, going to Mass every Sunday, not wearing patent shoes on a date and abstaining from candy for forty days every spring. In return for which, my parents were supposed to stay together even though they might have hated each other's guts.

"Poor Lucy." She sighed. "You could never face up to anything unpleasant, could you? You always ran off or stuck your nose in a book when the going got rough."

"Just fuck off," I said angrily. "Stop picking on me, you're the one in the wrong here."

"Sorry," she said gently. "I shouldn't have said that."

Now that really shocked me, it was one thing for her to tell me that she was leaving my father, but this was another thing entirely. Not only had she not shouted at me for using bad language, but *she'd* apologized to *me*.

I stared at her, sick with dread. Things must be very serious.

"Lucy," she said, even more gently. "Your father and I haven't loved each other for years. I'm sorry this has come as such a shock."

I couldn't speak. I was witnessing the destruction of my home, and me with it. My sense of self was amorphous enough as it was. I was afraid I would completely vanish into thin air if one of my main defining features disintegrated.

"But why now?" I appealed to her, after we had sat in silence for a few moments. "If you haven't loved each other for years, which I don't believe anyway, why have you picked now to leave him?"

And suddenly I knew why—the hairdo, the makeup, the new clothes—they all made sense.

"Oh Christ," I said. "I don't believe it—you've met someone else, haven't you? You've got a . . . a . . . boyfriend!" I had teased my brother with such a possibility, never dreaming it could be true.

She wouldn't meet my eyes, and I knew I was right.

"Lucy," she implored. "I've been so lonely."

"Lonely?" I asked in disbelief. "How could you be lonely when you've got Dad?"

"Lucy, please understand," she begged. "Living with your father was like living with a child."

"Don't!" I said. "Don't try and make out that it was his fault. You've done this, it's *your* fault."

She stared unhappily at her hands and didn't say anything to defend herself.

"So who is he?" I spat, the taste of bile in my mouth. "Who is this . . . this . . . *boyfriend* of yours?"

"Please, Lucy," she murmured. Her gentleness unsettled me, I was much more comfortable when she was scathing and sharp-tongued.

"Tell me," I demanded.

She just stared mutely, tears in her eyes. Why wouldn't she tell me?

"It's someone I know, isn't it?" I said in alarm.

"Yes, Lucy. I'm sorry, Lucy, I never meant for it to happen . . ."

"Just tell me who it is," I said, my breaths coming short and quick.

"It's . . ."

"Yes?"

"It's . . ."

"WHOOOO?" I almost screamed.

"It's Ken Kearns," she blurted out.

"*Who?*" I thought, dizzily. "Who's Ken Kearns?"

"Ken Kearns. You know, Mr. Kearns from the dry cleaners."

"Oh, *Mr.* Kearns," I said, vaguely remembering a bald old codger with a brown cardigan and plastic shoes and false teeth that seemed to have a life of their own.

The relief! Ludicrous as it seemed, I had been gripped with fear that her boyfriend was *Daniel*. What with the way he'd been boring on recently about his mysterious new woman, and the way Mum had flirted with him when he came to visit, and the way that Daniel had said that Mum was pretty . . .

Okay, so I was glad it wasn't Daniel, but, honestly, *Mr. Kearns from the dry cleaners*—she couldn't have picked anyone more awful if she had tried.

"Tell me if I've got this right," I said, in a daze. "Mr. Kearns, with the false teeth that are too big for him, is your new boyfriend."

"He's getting new ones," she said tearfully.

"You're disgusting," I said, shaking my head. "You are truly disgusting."

She didn't shout at me or berate me like she would normally have done when I said something disrespectful to her. Instead she acted all martyrish and humble.

"Lucy, look at me, please," she said, tears jostling at the corners of her eyes. "Ken makes me feel like a teenager, can't you see—I'm a woman, a woman with needs . . .''

"I don't want to hear about your disgusting needs, thanks very much," I said, shutting out the appalling mental image of my mother and Mr. Kearns rolling around amongst the coat hangers.

And still she made no move to defend herself, but I knew her. Sooner or later she'd run out of cheeks to turn.

"Lucy, I'm fifty-three years old, this could be my last chance of happiness. Surely you can't deny me that?"

"You and your happiness! Well, what about Dad? What about *his* happiness?"

"I've tried to make him happy," she said sadly. "But nothing works."

"Rubbish," I sputtered. "You've always tried to make his life a misery! Why the hell didn't you just leave years ago?"

"But . . ." she said feebly.

"Where are you going to live?" I interrupted, feeling sick.

"With Ken," she whispered.

"And where's that?"

"It's the yellow house across from the school." She tried, but failed, to keep the hint of pride out of her voice. Ken, the Dry-Cleaning King, obviously had accumulated a fair bit of money.

"And what about your wedding vows?" I asked. I knew that would really hit her where it hurt. "What about the promises you made, in a church, that you'd stay with him for better, for worse?"

"Please, Lucy," she said in a little voice. "I can't tell you how I've wrestled with my conscience, I've prayed and prayed for guidance . . ."

"You're such a hypocrite," I exclaimed—not that it

mattered to me on any moral ground, but I knew it would upset her, and that was my highest priority. "You've rammed the teachings of the Catholic Church down my throat all my life and stood in judgment over unmarried mothers and people who've had abortions, and now you're no better yourself! You're an adulterer, you've broken your precious seventh commandment."

"Sixth," she said, her usual self making a guest reappearance.

Hah! I knew I'd break her.

"What?" I asked in disgust.

"I've broken the *sixth* commandment, seventh is stealing, didn't they teach you anything in catechism classes?"

"You see, you see!" I crowed in bitter triumph. "There you go again, standing in judgment, setting yourself up as a moral watchdog. Well, let he·who is without sin cast the log out of his own eye!"

She hung her head and twisted her hands. Back to being a martyr.

"And what has Father Colm to say about all of this?" I demanded. "I bet he's not so friendly with you now, now that you've become a . . . a . . . a *home wrecker*. . . . Well?" I asked again, when she didn't answer.

"They've told me not to do the flowers for the altar anymore," she finally admitted. A single tear ran down her cheek, leaving a little white line as it washed through her inexpertly applied foundation.

"Quite right," I snorted.

"And the committee wouldn't take the apple tart that I'd made for the sale of work," she said, more tears streaking down her face. She looked like a deckchair.

"Quite right too," I said hotly.

"I suppose they thought it might be catching," she said

with a little smile. I stared coldly at her and, after a few seconds, her smile vanished.

"*And* you picked a great time to tell me," I said nastily. "How am I supposed to go back and do an afternoon's work after hearing this?"

That was unfair of me because Ivor was out and I wouldn't have done anything anyway, but it wasn't the point.

"Lucy, I'm sorry," she said quietly. "But I wanted to tell you right away. And I couldn't have you finding out from someone else."

"Okay," I said briskly, picking up my bag. "You've told me. Thanks a lot and goodbye."

I put no money on the table. She could pay for my sandwich as she was the reason that I hadn't been able to eat it.

"Wait, please," she urged. "Don't go yet, Lucy. Please just give me a chance to say my piece, that's all I ask of you."

"Go on then," I said. "This should be good for a laugh."

She took a deep breath and started.

"Lucy, I know you've always loved your dad more than you've loved me . . ."

She paused, in case I needed to contradict her. I stayed silent.

". . . but it was very hard for me," she continued. "I had to be the strong one, I had to be the disciplinarian, because he wouldn't. And I know you thought that he was a great laugh, and that I was mean and miserable, but one of us had to be a parent to you."

"How dare you," I demanded. "Dad was twice, *ten* times, the parent you ever were."

"But he was so irresponsible . . ." she started to protest.

"Don't talk to me about irresponsible," I interrupted. "What about your responsibilities? Who's going to take care of Dad?"

Although I already knew the answer to that one.

"Why should anyone need to take care of Dad?" she asked. "He's only fifty-four and there's nothing wrong with him."

"You know he needs to be taken care of," I said. "You know he can't look after himself."

"And why's that, Lucy?" she asked. "Lots of men live alone, men much older than Dad, and they're well able to take care of themselves."

"But Dad's not like other men, and you know it," I said. "Don't think you can get off the hook that way."

"And why isn't your dad like other men?" she asked.

"You know why," I said angrily.

"No, I don't," she said. "Tell me why."

"I'm not having this discussion with you any longer," I said. "You know Dad needs looking after and that's that."

"You can't face it, can you, Lucy?" she said, looking at me with this infuriating saintlike, doe-eyed expression, all faux compassion and social-workeresque concern.

"Can't face what?" I asked. "There's nothing I can't face, you're talking even more nonsense than you usually do."

"He's an alcoholic," she said gently. "*That's* what you can't face."

"Who's an alcoholic?" I asked, disgusted by her manipulations. "Dad is *not* an alcoholic. I see what you're up to, you think you can call Dad names and say terrible things about him just so people will feel sorry for you and say that it's okay for you to leave him. Well, you can't fool me."

"Lucy, he's been an alcoholic for years and years, probably before we even got married, but I didn't know the signs then," she said.

"Rubbish," I snorted. "He's not an alcoholic, you must take me for a complete fool. Alcoholics are those men in the street with dirty coats and big beards, who talk to themselves."

"Lucy, alcoholics come in all shapes and sizes, those men in the street are men just like your dad, except they were a bit more unlucky."

"They couldn't have got more unlucky than being married to you," I threw at her.

"Lucy, do you deny that your father drinks a lot?"

"He drinks a bit," I admitted. "And why wouldn't he? You've made him miserable all these years. You know, my earliest memory is of you shouting at him."

"I'm sorry, Lucy," she said, tears spilling down her face. "But it was so hard, we never had any money, and he wouldn't get a job, and he'd take the money that I had put aside to buy food for you and your brothers and he'd drink it. And I'd have to go down to the local shop and give them some made-up story about not getting to the bank on time and would they give me a bit of credit. And they knew damn well, and I had some pride, Lucy, you know. It didn't come easy to me to do that, I was brought up to expect more from life than that."

She was crying hard now, but it meant nothing to me.

"And I loved him, so I did," she sobbed. "I was twenty-two and I thought he was gorgeous. He kept telling me that he'd give it up and I kept hoping that things would get better. I believed him every single time, and every single time he let me down."

On and on she went, a catalogue of accusations. How he was drunk the morning of their wedding; how, when she went into labor with Chris, she had to make her own way to the hospital because he was missing, presumed drunk; how he stood at the back of the church at Peter's Confirmation and sang Irish drinking songs . . .

I didn't even listen. I decided that it was time for me to go back to work.

When I stood up to leave, I said, "Not that you're worried about it, but I'll take care of him, and I'll probably do a far better job than you ever did."

"Is that right, Lucy?" She sounded unimpressed.

"Yes."

"Good luck," she said. "You'll need it."

"What do you mean?"

"Are you any good at washing sheets?" she asked cryptically.

"What are you talking about?"

"You'll see," she said wearily. "You'll see."

 63

I went back to work in a state of shock.

The first thing I did was call Dad to make sure he was okay, but he sounded incoherent and dazed, which worried me sick.

"I'll be out to you right after work this evening," I promised. "Everything will be all right, please don't worry."

"Who will take care of me, Lucy?" he asked, sounding very, very old. I could have killed my mother.

"I will," I promised fervently. "I'll always take care of you, don't worry."

"You won't leave me?" he asked pathetically.

"Never," I said, meaning it as I'd never meant anything before in my life.

"You'll stay the night?" he asked.

"Of course I will, I'll stay with you always."

Then I rang Peter. He wasn't at work, so I presumed that Mum had already broken the news to him and, Oedipal idiot that he was, he had gone home to lie down in a darkened room, waiting to die of a broken heart. Sure enough, when I rang him at home, he answered the phone in a hoarse, grief-sodden voice. He, too, said that he hated our mother. But I knew it was for an entirely different reason and that he and I didn't share any common cause. Peter was devastated, not because my mother had left Dad, but that she hadn't left Dad for him.

Then I called Chris and discovered that Mum had informed him of her news that morning. I was annoyed with Chris because he hadn't called and tipped me off. So we had a brief argument, which was nice because it took my mind off Dad for a while. Chris was wildly relieved when I said that I was spending the evening with Dad. ("Jesus, thanks, Lucy, I owe you one.") Chris and Responsibility weren't on the best of terms, they had never really seen eye to eye.

Then I called Daniel and told him what had happened. He was a good person to tell because he was so sympathetic. And besides, he'd always been fond of my mother. I was glad to give him an opportunity to see what a bitch she really was.

He didn't comment on my runaway mother. He suggested that he'd drive me out to Dad.

"No," I said.

"Yes," he said.

"No way," I said. "I'm very upset, I'm no company, it's a long, boring drive and, when we get there, I just want to be with my dad."

"Fine," he said. "But I'd still like to be with you."

"Daniel." I sighed. "It's obvious that you need to seek psychiatric help, but I really don't have the time at the moment to deal with your mental problems."

"Lucy, be sensible," he said firmly.

We both had a little laugh at that.

"Daniel, you're asking the impossible," I said. "Stop building failure into your expectations of me."

"Now listen," he shouted. "I have a car, you have a long way to go, you'll have to stop at your apartment to get clothes and things. I'm not doing anything else this evening, I will drive you to Uxbridge and I want to hear no more about it!"

"Woooh!" I said, amused and slightly impressed, despite the awful circumstances. "It's my hero! Check your thighs, I bet they've gotten all muscular."

He didn't really know what I was talking about.

It was odd, I'd never thought about Daniel's thighs before. I had a vague suspicion that they were already muscular. I felt a bit funny, sort of nervous, so I stopped.

"Thank you, Daniel." I gave in. "If you really don't mind, then it would be a help if you could take me."

The awfulness of Mum leaving Dad hadn't overridden my fear of Karen, and what she would do to me if she found out that Daniel was escorting me to Uxbridge. But luckily she hadn't come home from work by the time Daniel and I left my apartment.

We stopped at a supermarket on the way to buy supplies for Dad. I spent a fortune, buying everything I could possibly think of that he had ever liked—hobnobs, tarts, alphabetti-spaghetti, mini-trifles, sugar puffs, colored polo mints and a bottle of whiskey. I didn't give a damn about what my mother had said about him being an alcoholic. I didn't believe it. And even if I did, I didn't care. I would have given him *anything,* to help him feel better, to feel that someone still loved him.

I would create a loving home for him, I thought with missionary zeal. I was looking forward to it. I'd show my mother how it should be done.

When Daniel and I arrived, we found Dad slumped in his armchair, drunk and crying. I was shaken to see how upset he was because, in a way, I'd thought he would be pleased that Mum had gone and left him in peace. I had almost expected him to be relieved that it was just me and him.

"Poor, poor Dad." I dumped the bags on the table and rushed to his side.

"Oh Lucy," he said, shaking his head slowly. "Oh Lucy, what will become of me?"

"I'll take care of you. Now, have a drink, Dad," I urged, gesturing at Daniel to bring the bottle of whiskey.

"I might as well, Lucy," agreed Dad, sadly. "I might as well."

"Are you sure, Lucy?" asked Daniel quietly.

"Don't you start," I hissed quietly. "His wife has just left him, let him have a bloody drink."

"Calm down, Lucy," he said, picking up an empty bottle of Jameson from the floor beside Dad's chair and thrusting it at me. "I just don't want you to kill the man."

"One more can't hurt him," I said stiffly.

Suddenly I felt very sorry for myself and Dad. Before I knew what was happening I was in the midst of throwing a mini-tantrum. "Oh for God's sake, Daniel," I screeched.

Then I marched out of the kitchen and slammed the door behind me.

I shoved open the door of the "good" front room and flung myself in a tantrumy rage on the "good" metal and brown corduroy couch. The room had always been kept for visitors. But as we had never had many visitors, it was in pristine, 1973 condition. It was like being in a time warp.

I sat and cried, at the same time feeling daring for sitting on the good furniture that only priests and visitors from Ireland were permitted to sit on. And, in a few moments Daniel came in as I had known he would.

"Did you give him a drink?" I asked accusingly.

"Yes," he said, and skirted the smoked glass coffee table. He sat beside me on the fossilized couch. He put his arm around me as I had known he would. Daniel was good at that kind of thing, Daniel was nice and predictable, I could always rely on Daniel to do the right thing.

Then he pulled me onto his lap, one hand around my shoulders, the other under my knees. I hadn't been expecting that, but I was quite happy to go along with it. Lots of affection was just what I needed.

I indulged myself and snuggled up to him and cried a little more. Daniel was a great person to cry on, there was something very reassuring and protective about him. I really got into it and snuffled around with my face on the shoulder of his suit, while he put a hand up and gently stroked my hair and said comforting things like, "Shush, Lucy, don't cry." It was very nice.

He smelled lovely—my nose was stuck in his neck, his scent was overwhelming. Manly and sweet. Quite sexy, actually, I thought in surprise—at least it would have been sexy if it wasn't Daniel's.

Idly, I wondered what he tasted like. Lovely, probably.

In fact, I was so close to him that all I had to do was stick out my tongue and touch the smooth skin of his neck with it.

Quickly I stopped myself. I couldn't just go around licking men, not even if they were Daniel.

He continued caressing my hair with one hand and slipped the other under the hair at the nape of my neck, where he did some kind of funny manipulation with his thumb and index finger. I sighed and relaxed closer to him. It felt really soothing.

Mmmmm, I thought, soothing in a shivery kind of way. Soothing and sort of . . .

Suddenly I became aware that I was no longer crying. I panicked, realizing I had to extricate myself from Daniel's arms immediately. I was only allowed to cuddle up to men if we were romantically involved, or if one of us was comforting the other. As neither was the case with Daniel, I was in his arms under false pretenses, my tenancy had run out with my tears.

Hoping that he didn't think I was ungrateful, I tried to jerk away from him.

He smiled at me, his face close to mine, as if he knew something that I didn't. Or perhaps something that I *should* know. Sometimes his clichéd good looks really get on my nerves, I thought, annoyed. And surely his teeth looked whiter than usual, he must have just been to the dentist. That annoyed me too. I felt hot and uncomfortable. I wasn't sure why.

It must have been because we had reached the awkward stage of an emotional outburst. The flash flood of happiness or misery had passed, and the hand-holding or hugging or tear shedding or whatever suddenly became excruciatingly embarrassing. *That* was probably why I felt as if I had to escape from him, I thought, scrambling around for a reason. I wasn't at my most comfortable with displays of affection.

At least not sober ones. But Daniel didn't seem to realize I wanted to break up our clinch. I tried to push myself out of the circle of his arms but nothing happened. Another wave of panicky fear swept over me.

"Thanks," I sniffed up at him, hoping that I sounded normal. As, once again, I made another attempt to wrench myself free from him. "Sorry about that."

I *had* to get away from him, I thought, frantically. I felt embarrassed and awkward in his arms, but it wasn't the usual sort of embarrassed and awkward.

He was *disturbing* me. I was aware of all sorts of things about him that I hadn't noticed when I'd been busy crying. Like, he was so *big*—I was used to small men. It felt funny to be held by someone as big as Daniel.

The scary kind of funny.

"Don't be sorry," he said.

I waited, expecting him to flash me his usual slightly mocking smile, but he didn't. He stared down at me, his eyes dark and serious, and didn't move. I stared back at him. A stillness settled on us. A waiting. Moments before, I had felt safe, now I felt anything but. And I couldn't seem to catch my breath, it wouldn't go the whole way down.

Daniel moved slightly, and I jumped. But he was only stroking my hair back off my forehead. The touch of his hand sent a little thrill through me.

"But I have to be sorry," I managed to blabber nervously, unable to look him in the eye. "You know me— I love to feel guilty."

He didn't laugh.

A bad sign.

And he didn't let me go either.

A worse sign.

To my horror, I felt a powerful rush of sexual attraction for him which nearly knocked me off his lap. I made another attempt to scramble away from him. I suppose it wasn't a very diligent effort.

"Lucy," he said, putting his hand on my chin, and gently moving my face, so that I had to look at him. "I'm not going to let you go, so stop trying."

Oh God, I thought. The gloves were off. I didn't like his tone. Well, actually I liked it very much. If I hadn't been so scared of what it meant, I would have loved it. Something very weird was going on—why was Sexual Attraction calling to see if Daniel and I were coming out to play? Why now?

"Why won't you let me go?" I stammered up at him, trying to buy time. I was vaguely distracted by his eyelashes—they were so long and thick it was indecent. And had his mouth always been that sexy? He was such a lovely color, slightly tanned against the whiteness of his shirt.

"Because," he said, staring down at me, "I want you."

Fuck it! My insides lurched with a scary thrill. We were approaching a border, about to cross into unknown territory. If I had any sense, I would stop us. But I didn't have any sense. I couldn't stop myself. And, even if I had wanted to, I certainly couldn't stop *him*.

For a long time before it happened, I knew he was going to kiss me. We hovered in space, our mouths almost touching, moving infinitesimally closer.

For years his face had been so familiar to me, but now he looked like a stranger, a very attractive one.

It was horrifying.

In a very nice way.

Finally, when my nerves were stretched to the screaming point and I was sure that I couldn't wait another second, he bent his head and put his lips to mine and kissed me. His kiss flooded through me like a sparkling drink.

I kissed him back. Because—shameful admission—I *wanted* to kiss him back.

I hated it because it was perfect.

It was the nicest kiss I'd ever had in my entire life and it was from Daniel. How awful—if he ever found out, his ego would go into orbit. I had to make sure that he never knew, I thought urgently.

I noticed all kinds of things that I'd never noticed before. How big and hard his back felt as I ran my hands along the grown-up-person's fabric of his suit.

No wonder he's such a good kisser, I thought, trying to make myself disgusted, he's had so much practice.

But then he kissed me again and I thought, well, the damage is done, might as well have another one.

He was delicious. He had such a perfect mouth and the smoothest *skin*. He tasted musky and sexy.

He was a *man,* a real man.

Oh Christ, I thought, I'll never, ever live this one down. He'll never let me forget this. The shame! After all the abuse I've hurled at him and his philandering ways. If I hadn't been so turned on, I might almost have laughed at myself.

Karen would kill me, I realized. I was as good as dead. How could I do this? I asked myself in shock.

But how could I not?

All these thoughts rushed through my head, and then out the other side as I became overwhelmed with desire for him.

Every now and then a little voice would say, Do you know who this *is?* This is *Daniel,* in case you hadn't noticed. And have you noticed *where* you are? Yes, exactly, you're in your mother's good room. On Father Colm's *couch*.

I was shaking because I was so attracted to him. I wanted to have sex with him there and then, on Father Colm's couch, with Dad in the next room. I didn't care.

And all he was doing was *kissing* me. Kissing and caressing me in totally chaste places. I didn't know whether to be impressed or annoyed that he wasn't trying to grope me, that he hadn't tipped me back on the couch and inched his hand up my skirt.

Finally he pulled away from me and said, "Lucy, you don't know how long I've waited to do this."

I had to hand it to him—he was good. He sounded intense and passionate. He *looked* great. His pupils were dilated. His eyes were nearly black and his hair was all messy and sexy, very different from its normal well-groomed look. The expression on his face was the best— he looked like a man in love, or in lust, at the very least.

No wonder so many women fell for him.

"Yes, Daniel," I said, in a shaky voice, trying to smile, "I bet you say that to all the girls."

"I'm serious, Lucy," he said in a serious voice with serious undertones, looking at me seriously.

"So am I," I said lightly.

Sanity, such as it was, had started its reluctant return to my wayward head. Although my whole body still shook with unsated desire.

I looked at him, wanting to believe him, knowing I couldn't.

We sat beside each other, close but separate, him looking sad, me looking sad, me still in his arms, having overstayed my welcome but loath to leave.

"Please, Lucy," he said, and put both hands on my face, holding it as gently and carefully as if my head was a brimming bucket of sulfuric acid.

Then the door opened. Dad shambled in. Even though Daniel and I sprang apart with the high-jump ability of spring lambs, he still saw what was in progress and looked shocked and annoyed.

"Good God," he roared. "You're all doing it! It's like Sodom and Begorrah around here."

 64

My life changed very quickly in the following days. Suddenly I had a new home, or an old one, depending on how you looked at it. I was keen to hand in the notice on my apartment immediately, eager to begin my new life, anxious to show how committed I was to it.

Someone had to move in to take care of Dad. I was the obvious candidate.

If Chris or Peter had offered to, I would still have insisted on doing it myself. Not that they *did* offer, the lazy bastards. They were both appalled at the prospect. It wasn't as if they'd have been any good at it either—my mother had done everything for both of them since the day they were born, so they hardly knew how to run a bath, never mind run a house. It was a miracle that they'd ever even learned how to tie their own shoes. Not that I was much better myself at housekeeping, but I knew I'd manage somehow. I would *learn* how to cook fish fingers, I thought passionately, it would be a labor of love.

Everyone tried to talk me out of going back to live in Uxbridge. Karen and Charlotte didn't want me to leave—and not just because of the hassle of having to find a suitable new roommate either.

"But there's nothing wrong with your dad," said Karen, puzzled. "Lots of men are on their own. Why do you have to go and actually *live* with him? Can't you just visit him every couple of days, you know, get a neighbor to look in on him, get your brothers to take turns, that kind of thing?"

I couldn't explain why to Karen. I felt that nothing less than the whole hog would do. I had to do it right. I would move back and take care of Dad, as he'd never been taken care of before, as he should always have been. I was *glad,* glad to have him to myself, that it would be just the two of us. I was bitter and angry with my mother for her fickleness, but it was nothing more than I expected from her. I was relieved that, finally, she was out of the picture.

"But how awful for you, moving back home to live with your parents," said Charlotte, sounding horrified. "Parent, I mean," she added quickly. "Think about it, Lucy—when will you be able to have sex with boys? Won't you be afraid of your dad bursting in and catching you at it, telling you that you can't do that kind of thing under his roof?

"And will he tell you what time you must get home by?" she chattered on, not noticing me squirm. "And say 'You're not going out in that' and 'You look like a prostitute with all that makeup' and things like that?" she exclaimed. "You're bonkers!"

Charlotte's problem was that she had made her escape from her familial home too recently. The memory of being under her father's thumb was very fresh in her mind. She still reveled in her new-found freedom. On the days that she wasn't suicidal with guilt about it, that was.

"Or what if your dad gets a new girlfriend?" she demanded. "Won't it be disgusting if you burst in and catch *him* having sex?"

"But . . ." I tried to interrupt. The idea of poor Dad

having a girlfriend was laughable. Almost as funny as the idea of me having a boyfriend.

A boyfriend was not in the cards. Daniel's kiss had been a one-off. A never-to-be-repeated, once-in-a-lifetime opportunity. Hurry now, while stocks last.

After Dad had caught us, he glared at us both for a little while. We cringed, as befitted us, under his disapproving look. Then he withdrew from the room and Daniel and I rearranged ourselves. I waited for my heartbeat to slow down and my breathing to return to normal. Daniel waited for his erection to subside and his gait to return to normal (I found that out some time later).

We sat side by side on the couch, a vision of mute sheepishness.

I wanted to die.

It was all so awful.

Kissing Daniel! *Kissing* Daniel. Kissing *Daniel*. And getting caught by Dad—the mortification! There was a part of me that would always be fourteen.

I was in a state of shock anyway, what with Mum having left Dad. And, in a way, I was *beyond* being shocked by Daniel's kissing me.

It was too weird to think about.

I didn't know why he'd had such an effect on me—I decided I was probably feeling vulnerable because of the disintegration of the familial unit.

And as for Daniel's motive, well, who knows? He was a man, I was a woman (well, sort of, more of a girl, really, I felt). Basically, I had been *there*.

Everything was topsy-turvy. I'd had enough upheaval for one day and I wanted Daniel and me to be back to normal. And the best way to do that was to *act* normal. So I insulted him.

"You took advantage of me," I grumbled.

"Did I?" he asked in surprise.

"You stupid bastard," I added, just for insurance.

"Yes," I said. "You knew I was upset about poor Dad. And then you insult me by feeding me your usual smoothie lines and kiss me."

"Sorry," he said, sounding horrified. "That wasn't my intention. . . ."

"Forget it." I sighed self-righteously. "Let's just forget it. But don't let it happen again."

Mean of me, I know. It takes two to tango, etc., etc., but I had enough on my mind, without wondering if I liked Daniel that way.

I wouldn't think about it, I decided. I was good at not thinking about unpleasant things. At the time, I didn't know just how good I was.

After about ten minutes, Daniel shamefully slunk off. Dad stood at the front door, almost shaking his fist after him and watched until he was sure Daniel was gone. We hadn't even given him a valedictory cup of tea. My mother would turn in her grave.

I wished.

 65

Daniel came to Uxbridge to see me a couple of nights after the great shame-fest. I was so embarrassed and confused that I would have been quite happy never to have seen him again, but he had pestered me.

First he called me at work the day afterward and asked me to meet him for lunch. I told him I didn't want to.

"Please, Lucy," he said.

"Why?" I asked. "Oh no."

"Oh no, what?"

"If you say we have to talk, I'll kill you," I said.

Megan, Meredia and Jed nearly gave themselves whip-lash looking up with interest.

"Actually, we do have to talk," said Daniel. "About your apartment."

*My apartment?* "What about it?" I was surprised.

"Just let me talk to you."

It was obviously an excuse, but I decided to go along with it.

"Come out to the house tomorrow night," I finally agreed.

To my alarm, I felt warm and glad at the thought of seeing him. A stop would have to be put to that.

"I'll come and meet you after work," he offered.

"Oh no!" I said quickly. There was no way I could bear an entire train journey with him. I would spontaneously combust from unspoken embarrassment.

When I hung up the phone, Megan, Meredia and Jed descended on me like vultures.

"Who was it?"

"Was it Gus?"

"What's going on?"

"Are you together again?" they had clamored.

I was frighteningly nervous as I waited at home for Daniel to arrive.

My head raced with the pros and cons—well, actually the cons and cons—of it all. Kissing Daniel had been a big mistake. Any further liaisons of this kind would be careless in the extreme.

Okay, so I felt as if I was incredibly attracted to him, but I knew that I wasn't really. The shock of my mother leaving my father had addled my emotions and I just *thought* I did. Daniel's kissing me had been the product of an unusual set of circumstances.

Let's look at it dispassionately, I thought, as I frantically brushed my hair. Dad watched me benignly. He wouldn't be quite so benign when he realized who I was brushing my hair for.

On the one hand, I thought dramatically, there was me. Confused, vulnerable, needy, a child from a freshly broken home, ready to love the first person who showed her affection.

On the other hand, there was Daniel—a man who was used to a lot of sex, and who hadn't had it in a couple of days. So naturally he wasn't choosy about who he interfered with. I had been there. He had interfered with me.

See. Not choosy.

And Daniel was a man who loved a challenge. What Karen had screeched at me on Sunday night had confirmed what I had always known. Daniel probably just went after me because I was the only girl in town who didn't have a crush on him.

But I would not succumb, I thought grimly.

For once I would resist the impulse to self-destruct. I would not love Daniel. I would be different.

As soon as I opened the front door to him, my resolution to not be attracted to him wavered, then dissolved.

"Hello," I said to the knot of his tie.

He bent to kiss me and a roar came from the kitchen.

"Hey you!" yelled Dad. "Leave my daughter alone!"

Daniel backed off hurriedly. I felt like a starving person who'd had a bag of chips waved under her nose and then whisked away.

"Come in," I invited the collar of his shirt.

I was horribly awkward. As I led him through the hall,

I banged my hipbone on the telephone table and then had to pretend it didn't hurt. I didn't want him to offer to kiss it better. Because I might have let him.

"Take off your coat." I stared his breast-pocket in the eye.

I was disgusted by the effect he was having on me. It was obvious that I was way out of my depth, only temporarily, of course. Only because my parents had split up. But all the same I had to protect myself.

I decided that I wouldn't be alone with him and, after he left that evening, I wouldn't see him again, *ever*. Well, maybe not ever, but for a while at least. Until I was back to normal, whatever that was.

As part of my cunning plan, I forced Daniel into the kitchen, where Dad sat glaring.

"Hello, Mr. Sullivan," Daniel said nervously.

"Haven't you a lot of nerve?" growled Dad. "Coming back here after you treating my home like a . . . like a . . . like a *hoor house*."

"Shush, Dad." I was mortified. "It won't happen again." Thankfully, he shut up.

"Would you like a cup of tea?" I asked Daniel's shoulder.

"When are we getting the crispy pancakes?" Dad interrupted rudely.

"What crispy pancakes?"

"We always have crispy pancakes on a Wednesday."

"But today's Thursday."

"Is it? Well, when are we getting the stew?"

"Do you always have stew on Thursdays?"

He looked at me mournfully.

"Sorry, Dad, I'll get into a routine next week. Can you make do with a pizza for this evening?"

"A pizza that you call for?" He suddenly perked up.

"Yes." What other types were there? I wondered.

"Not one from the freezer?" The look of hope on his face was heart-rending.

"God, no."

"Great," he said with glee. "And can we get beer?"

"Of course."

I suspected that he was fulfilling a lifelong ambition. My mother would have frowned on such extravagance.

When I called the pizza company, Dad insisted on speaking personally to the man who made the pizzas to discuss what toppings he should have.

"What are anchovies? Go on, sure I'll have a couple. What are capers? Sure, you might as well fling a few on." I had to admire Daniel's patience, although I still couldn't look him in the eye.

When the pizzas and beer arrived, the three of us sat around the kitchen table. As soon as the food was eaten, Dad recommenced glaring at Daniel. The tension was dreadful.

Dad wouldn't look directly at Daniel. He stared viciously at him whenever Daniel was looking at something else, but looked away quickly whenever Daniel flicked a glance at him. Daniel suspected that Dad was giving him dirty looks, so then *he* started to try and catch Dad at it. One microsecond he'd be idly drinking his beer, then, in a blur, he'd whip his head around to where Dad was staring at him. Then, in another blur, Dad whipped *his* head away and slurped *his* beer with a face as innocent as an angel's.

It went on for hours. At least, that was how it felt.

The atmosphere was so loaded that, when we finished the beer, we started, with gusto, on the whiskey.

The few times that Dad turned away to shout insults at a politician on the television, Daniel made all kinds of energetic gestures with his face and head, winking and jerking his head toward the door, indicating that we should exit by it and go to another room. Probably the living room, for a repeat performance.

I ignored him.

But finally Dad decided to go to bed.

We were all quite drunk by then.

"Are you going to be here all night?" he demanded to Daniel.

"No," said Daniel.

"Well, off with you, so," he said, standing up.

"Would you mind if I had a word with Lucy in private, Mr. Sullivan?" Daniel asked.

"Mind? Mind!" Dad sputtered. "After the way you two were carrying on the other night, you can be damn sure that I mind."

"I'm sorry about that," said Daniel humbly. "And I can assure you it won't happen again."

"Do you promise?" Dad asked sternly.

"I promise," said Daniel solemnly.

"All right, then," said Dad.

"Thanks," said Daniel.

"Now, I'm trusting the two of you, mind," said Dad, waggling his finger at us. "No high jinks, right?"

"None," promised Daniel. "Not a jink of any level, low, medium or high."

Dad shot him a suspicious glare. Daniel put on his ultra-earnest, you-can-trust-me-with-your-daughter-Mr.-Sullivan face. Not quite convinced, Dad shuffled off to bed.

Of course, I expected Daniel to try and jump me the minute the door closed after Dad. I was put out when he didn't. All evening, I had been looking forward to fighting him off and calling him a pervert. But he confused me by tenderly taking my hand and speaking gently.

"Lucy," he said. "I want to talk to you about something important."

"Oh yes," I said sarcastically. "About my"—little snigger—"apartment."

I knew a pretext as well as the next woman.

"Yes," he said. "I hope you don't think I'm interfering—actually I *know* you'll think I'm interfering—but please don't take your name off the lease just yet."

That floored me—I hadn't *really* expected him to want to talk about my living arrangements.

"But why not?" I asked him.

"All I'm saying is, don't rush into something that you can't get out of," he said.

"I'm not," I said.

"You are," he said. The nerve of him. "You're too upset at the moment to make a rational decision."

"No, I'm not," I said as my eyes filled with tears.

"Yes, you are," he said. "Just look at you."

Maybe he had a point, but I couldn't give in without a fight. I gulped a mouthful of whiskey. "But what sense does it make?" I asked him, "to live with my dad and pay rent on a flat?"

"But you may not *want* to stay with your father after a while," he suggested.

"Don't be silly," I said.

"Well, your mother may come back. She might make up with your dad," he said.

That thought filled me with alarm. "Unlikely," I blustered.

"Well, what about when you go into town and you've missed the last train home and you don't want to spend a thousand pounds on a taxi back to Uxbridge? Wouldn't it be sensible to have a little pied-à-terre in Ladbroke Grove?" he suggested.

"But Daniel," I said desperately, "there won't be any

nights out on the town anymore. That part of my life is over. More whiskey?''

"Yes please. Lucy, I'm very worried about you," he said, putting on his concerned face.

"Don't be," I said, annoyed and frustrated. "And don't give me that cute face, I'm not one of your . . . your . . . *women*. You obviously don't realize the seriousness of what's happened to my family. My mother has left my father and I have responsibilities.''

"People's mothers leave people's fathers every day of the week," said Daniel. "And the fathers cope. They don't need their daughters to give up everything and act as if they've entered a nunnery.''

"Daniel, I *want* to do this, it's not a sacrifice. I have to do it, I have no choice in it. I don't care if I can't go out and have fun anymore. Besides I wasn't having fun anyway." I was nearly in tears at the idea of such goodness, such daughterly devotion.

"Please, Lucy, just wait a month or so." He didn't look as moved as I felt.

"Oh, all right then," I agreed.

"Is that a promise?" he asked.

"I suppose it is.''

And then I caught Daniel's eye. Christ, he was good-looking! I nearly knocked over my glass.

I was impatient for the molesting to begin. I was so sure that he'd arranged to see me just so he could try to kiss me that I was damned if he was leaving without trying.

 66

What I did next was very out of character for me.

I blame it on the amount I'd had to drink. Combined with the trauma. Plus the fact that I hadn't had sex in a long, long time.

The sort of willpower, where you really like someone but keep away from them because you know that they're bad news, doesn't exist in real life. Not in my version of it anyway. My heart ruled my head.

My lust ruled my head.

"Maybe it's time I started," I said slowly.

"Started what?"

"Fun. Having it."

Purposefully—if a bit unsteadily—I stood up, holding his gaze, and made my way around the kitchen table to Daniel. While he sat staring uncertainly at me, I coaxed a piece of my hair seductively over one eye and then wantonly wriggled onto his lap and put my arms around his neck.

I moved my face closer to his.

God, he was gorgeous. Just look at that beautiful mouth, and any second now it would be kissing me. What I needed was some wild abandoned sex, lots of affection. And who better to do it than Daniel?

Of course I wasn't in love with him. I was in love with Gus. But I was a woman. And I had my needs.

"Lucy, what are you doing?" he asked.

"What does it look like?" I tried to make my voice husky and sexy.

He didn't put his arms around me. I wriggled a bit closer to him.

"But you promised your dad." He looked worried.

"No I didn't. You did."

"Did I? Okay, *I* promised your dad."

"You lied," I said. More low, sultry tones. This seduction was great fun, I decided. And remarkably easy.

I was looking forward to this. I was going to enjoy myself like I hadn't enjoyed myself in months.

"Lucy, no," he said.

No? *No?* Was I hearing things?

He stood up and I sort of slid off his lap.

I landed on the floor, swaying slightly. Scorching humiliation hadn't arrived yet, as intoxication was blocking the road. But it was definitely on its way.

How excruciating. Daniel would make out with *anyone*. What was wrong with me? Surely I wasn't that revolting?

"Lucy, I'm flattered . . ."

Now, that annoyed me.

*"Flattered!"* I roared. "Fuck off, you patronizing fucker. You can give it but you can't take it. You flirt with me; then, when I call your bluff, you can't deliver the goods."

"Lucy, it's not that at *all*. But you're too upset and confused and I would be taking advantage . . ."

*"I'll* be the judge of that," I said.

"Lucy, I'm very attracted to you . . ."

"But you don't want to have sex with me," I finished for him.

"You're right, I don't want to have sex with you."

"God, how embarrassing," I whispered.

Then I rallied.

"Well, what were you playing at the other night?" I demanded. "That wasn't a pistol in your pocket—you certainly acted like a man on the make, *then*."

"Lucy, look at me," coaxed Daniel. "I want to tell you something."

I turned a face burning with shame to him.

"I'd like to make it clear that I don't want to *have sex* with you," he said. "But, when things are different and you're not so upset and your life isn't in such upheaval, I *would* like to make love to you."

Now *that* was funny.

I laughed and laughed.

"What have I said?" He looked confused.

"Oh Daniel, *please*. What a slimy, smooth-bastard thing to say. 'I'd like to make *love* to you,' but not at the moment. Please give me a little credit—I know when I'm being rejected."

"You're *not* being rejected."

"Let me see if I've got this right. You'd like to make *love* to me," I cruelly mimicked him.

"That's right," he said quietly.

"But not right now. If that's not rejection, I don't know what is." I laughed again. He had hurt me and humiliated me and I wanted to do the same to him.

"Please, Lucy, listen to—"

"No!"

Then I either sobered up or calmed down.

"I'm very sorry about all of this, Daniel. I'm not in the fullness of my mental health. It's all been a terrible mistake."

"No, it hasn't . . ."

"And now I think it's time you left; you've a long journey home."

He looked sadly at me.

"Are you okay?" he asked.

"Don't flatter yourself," I said grumpily. "I've been rejected by much more attractive men than you. As soon as the killer mortification wears off, I'll be fine."

He opened his mouth to begin a fresh stream of platitudes.

"Goodbye, Daniel," I said firmly.

He kissed me on the cheek. I stood as if made of stone.

"I'll phone you tomorrow," he said at the front door.

I shrugged.

Things would never be the same again.

God, I felt depressed.

 67

The following day I took official leave of my Ladbroke Grove residence, though, as I'd promised Daniel, I'd continue to pay rent to keep my room there. Charlotte and Karen waved goodbye, after Karen had forced me to leave a handful of post-dated checks for the rent.

"Goodbye. I may never see you again," I said, hoping to make her feel guilty.

"Oh don't, Lucy." Charlotte was nearly in tears. She was so sentimental.

"We'll contact you when the phone bill comes in," said Karen.

"My life is over," I said coldly. "But," I added. "If Gus calls, make bloody sure you give him my number."

 68

Living with Dad wasn't the way I thought it would be.

I thought that we wanted the same things—I would devote my life to taking care of him and making him happy, and he would reciprocate by letting himself be taken care of and being happy.

But something had gone wrong, because I couldn't make him happy. He didn't even seem to *want* to be happy.

He was always crying and I couldn't understand why. I thought he should be glad to be rid of my mother, that he was much better off with me.

I didn't miss her and I couldn't see why *he* did.

I brimmed with love and concern for him and I was quite prepared to do anything for him, spend time with him, cosset him, cook for him, get him anything he wanted or needed. Except I didn't want to listen to him tell me how much he had loved her.

I wanted to take care of him only if he was going to be happy about it.

"Maybe she'll come back," he said over and over.

"Maybe," I muttered, thinking *What's wrong with him?*

Although, luckily, he never did anything practical to try and win her back. He made no great displays of passion, like standing outside Ken's yellow house and shouting neighbor-waking abuse at him in the middle of the night. Or daubing "Adulterer" in green fluorescent paint on

Ken's front door. Or emptying the trash cans of the neighborhood in Ken's driveway, so that when he left in the morning for a hard day's dry cleaning, he would sink ankle-deep in rusty tin cans and potato peelings. Or picketing the dry cleaners with signs saying "This man stole my wife. Don't get your shirts cleaned here."

Although I couldn't understand his pain, I tried to lessen it. But all I knew to do was to force food and drink on him and treat him like a convalescent invalid and point out the (few) amenities and diversions offered by our home. Like asking him in gentle tones if he would like to watch TV. Football? Or suggesting that he get some rest.

Bed and TV were about the extent of our recreational facilities.

He barely ate, no matter how hard I coaxed him. Neither did I. But while I knew that I'd be okay, I was afraid that he had started on his terminal decline.

Even before the end of the first week I was exhausted.

I had thought my love for him would give me limitless energy, that the more he asked of me the better I would feel, that the more I did for him, the more I would *want* to do for him.

I tried too hard to please and that burned up an awful lot of energy.

I eagerly watched him, anticipated his every need and did things for him even when he said that I didn't need to.

And then I was surprised to find that I was shattered.

The mere practicalities, alone, took their toll.

Like the fact that it took me at least an hour and a half to travel to work every morning. I had become spoiled by the thirty-minute journey from Ladbroke Grove, where I had numerous trains, buses and taxis to choose from.

I had forgotten what it was like to commute from the suburbs, where there was only one train at my disposal and if I missed that there was a twenty-minute wait until the next one.

I had once been a master of the ancient art of commuting, but I had lived in the city for too long and had lost many of my skills. I had forgotten how to sniff the air and stare at the sky (and the electronic noticeboard) and feel that the train was leaving in about one minute and that I had no time to buy a paper. I was no longer able to sense the vibes of a packed platform and realize that three trains in a row had been canceled and, if I wanted any chance of getting on the next one, I should start kicking and squeezing my way to the front immediately.

I used to *know* such things instinctively. I used to commune with the trains, almost merging into one being with the Underground system, man and machines working synchronously, in perfect harmony.

But not anymore.

And even though I had always been late for work in the past, I *could* have been on time if I had wanted. Now I really had no choice. I was at the mercy of London Underground and their various delaying mechanisms, leaves on the track, bodies on the track, signal failures, someone leaving their cheese sandwiches on the train, causing a bomb scare.

I had to get up very early. And before the first week was over, I discovered that Dad had a little problem and it became obvious I would have to get up even earlier.

At work I worried all day long about him, because it soon became clear that he couldn't be left on his own for any length of time. Taking care of Dad was like taking care of a child. Like a child, he had no fear, no sense of the consequences of his actions. He thought it was no big deal to go out leaving the front door open. Not just unlocked, but swinging open. Not that we had much to steal, but nevertheless, it was a bit worrisome.

As soon as work finished I rushed home. Anything could have happened. Almost every day there was a crisis of some kind. I lost count of the times he'd fallen asleep, either leaving the bath running, or the gas on. Or with a pot bubbling and burning, forgotten, or with a cigarette slowly burning its way through the cushion he was sitting on.

I often came home from work, exhausted, to find hot water leaking through the kitchen ceiling. Or to the smell of burning and a blackened, burned-out pot on the stove while Dad lay slumped asleep in his chair.

There were no more nights out on the town for me. I had thought I wouldn't mind and I was ashamed to find I did.

And the early nights didn't mean that I got plenty of sleep, because Dad usually woke me in the middle of the night and I had to get up to help him.

Dad wet his bed the first night I was home.

The heartbreak that I felt very nearly pushed me over the edge to insanity.

"I can't bear it, I can't bear it," I thought desperately. "Please, God, help me to live through this pain." To see my father so stripped of his dignity was almost more than I could handle.

He woke me up at about three in the morning to tell me. "I'm sorry, Lucy," he said, looking mortified. "I'm sorry, I'm sorry."

"It's okay," I hushed, "stop saying sorry."

I had a quick look at his bed and realized that there was no way he could sleep there.

"Why don't you go and sleep in the boys' room and I'll, you know, tidy, er, up your bed," I suggested.

"I will so," he said.

"Do," I urged.

"And you're not mad at me?" he asked meekly.

"Mad?" I exclaimed. "Why would I be mad at you?"

"You'll come and say good night to me?"

"Of course I will."

So he got into Chris's single bed and pulled the covers up to his chin, his slack old person's chin rough with white stubble. I smoothed down his wispy gray hair and kissed him on the forehead and I was filled with a fierce pride, a sense of how well I took care of him. No one would ever look after anyone as well as I would look after Dad.

When he went back to sleep I pulled the sheets off the bed and wrapped them up to take to the laundromat. Then I got a basin of hot, soapy water and scrubbed and rinsed the mattress.

The only thing that worried me about the whole episode was that the next morning, when Dad woke up in Chris's bed, he was confused and frightened. He didn't know how he'd got there because he couldn't remember anything of the night before.

When he wet his bed on the first night I was there, I thought it was because he was so upset, and that it was an isolated event.

But it wasn't.

It happened nearly every night. Sometimes more than once.

Sometimes in Chris's bed, too.

When that happened, I got him to move to Peter's bed.

Luckily—because there was nowhere else for him to move to except mine—he managed not to wet Peter's bed.

He always woke me up to tell me and at first I got up and comforted and relocated him.

After the first few nights I was so exhausted that I decided to leave my nocturnal cleaning-up until the morning, before I left for work.

I didn't, *couldn't* leave it until the evening, and it was out of the question to ask Dad to help.

Instead, I reset my clock to half an hour earlier than the horribly early time it was already set for, so I could clean up whatever needed to be cleaned up each morning.

When he woke me to tell me that he had wet his bed, I just told him to move to another one and tried to go back to sleep.

But it was so difficult, because he was racked with guilt every time it happened and wanted to talk about how sorry he was and to make sure that I wasn't angry with him. Sometimes he would ramble on for hours, crying and saying he was a failure and that he'd try to make sure it never happened again. And because I was so tired I found it hard not to get impatient with him. And that would upset him and I'd feel destroyed with guilt, which meant I got even less sleep, which made me more impatient the next time. . . .

And, always, like little whispers in the corner of my head, was the memory of what my mother had said about him being an alcoholic. I watched everything he drank. And it seemed to be an awful lot. More than I remembered from when we were young. But then I wasn't sure if I was overreacting to what she had said, so I tried to put it out of my mind.

Maybe he was drinking a lot, but so what? His wife had just left him, so why shouldn't he?

 69

My life quickly developed a routine.

In the evenings I had to run to the laundromat to dry the sheets I'd left in before I went to work. Then I made his dinner, then there was usually some small crisis to deal with because he was forever burning things or breaking them or losing them.

I don't know when the tiredness turned to resentment. I kept it hidden for a long time because I was ashamed of it. Through guilt and misplaced pride, I even managed to hide it from myself for a while.

I began to miss my other life.

I wanted to go out and get drunk and stay up late and swap clothes with Karen and Charlotte and talk about boys and the size of their penises.

I was tired of having to be constantly vigilant, of always having to be there. A big part of the problem was that I had wanted to be perfect for Dad. I had wanted to be the one who took care of him better than anyone else. But I couldn't and then I didn't even want to. It wasn't a challenge anymore, it was a burden.

I was aware that I was a young woman, that looking after Dad wasn't my responsibility. But I would have died rather than admit it.

Taking care of the two of us seemed an awful lot harder than looking after just me. A lot more than twice as hard.

And a lot more than twice as expensive.

Before long, money became a real worry. In the past, I had *thought* it was a problem, I never felt as though I had enough to buy essentials like new shoes and clothes. But now I was horrified to find I was afraid that I wouldn't have enough to cover essentials like *feeding* the two of us.

I couldn't figure out where it was all going. For the first time in my life I was afraid of losing my job. I mean, *really* afraid.

Everything had changed, now that I had a dependent. I suddenly understood why they say in marriage ceremonies, "Till debt do us part."

Except, of course, that I wasn't married to Dad.

It was easy to be generous with the money when I had plenty of it. I had never imagined that I would begrudge my father anything. That I wouldn't have given him the cut-off lycra shirt off my back.

But it wasn't true. As money got tighter, I resented having to give him any. I resented him saying to me every morning before I dragged myself off to work, "Lucy, love, could you leave some money on the table?"

I resented the worry. I resented having to ask for an advance on my paycheck. I resented having no money for myself.

And I hated what it did to me—the pettiness, the watching of every bite that went into his mouth, the watching of every bite that *didn't* go into his mouth. If I go to the trouble of buying food for him and cooking it for him, the least he could do is eat it, I thought angrily.

Dad got welfare money every two weeks, but I wasn't sure what he did with it. I ran the household on my salary alone.

"Couldn't he even buy a pint of milk?" I sometimes thought, in impotent rage.

I felt increasingly isolated. Apart from the people at work, the only person I ever saw was Dad. I never went out with any of the people I used to see. I didn't have time, because it was so important to get home immediately after work. Karen and Charlotte kept saying they'd come out to visit me, but they made it sound like a trip to a foreign country. Anyway it was a relief that they didn't come—I didn't think I'd be able to act happy for an entire two hours.

I missed Gus terribly. I fantasized about him coming to rescue me. But I had no chance of running into him while I lived in Uxbridge.

The only person I saw from my old life was Daniel. He was always "dropping by" and I hated it.

Every time I answered the door to him my first thought was how big and sexy and attractive he was. Then my second thought was of the night that I threw myself at him and he'd refused to bed me. I burned with shame at the memory.

And, as if that wasn't hard enough to cope with, he constantly asked awkward questions.

"Why are you always so tired?" and, "You're going to the laundromat, *again?*" and, "Why are all your sauce-pans burned?"

"Can I do anything to help?" he asked over and over again. But my pride wouldn't let me tell him how bad things were with Dad.

I just said, "Go away, Daniel, there's nothing for you to do here."

The money situation got worse.

The sensible thing would have been to give up the apartment in Ladbroke Grove. After all, what did I gain by paying rent on a place I never stayed in? But, suddenly, I realized that I didn't want to, that I was terrified of having to do that. My apartment was my last link with my old life. If that went, it would be a sign that I was never going back, that I was stuck out in Uxbridge forever.

 70

In the end, out of desperation, I went to see our local doctor, who happened to be Dr. Thornton, the same man who had prescribed antidepressants for me all those years before.

Ostensibly I went to get advice about Dad's bedwetting, but in reality it was a good plain old-fashioned cry for help. In the hope that he would tell me what I knew to be true wasn't really.

I hated going to Dr. Thornton. Not only was he a cranky old man who should have been put out to pasture years before, but, because I knew he thought our entire family was nuts. He'd already had to deal with me and my depression. And there had been that time when Peter was fifteen and he'd got his hands on a medical encyclopaedia and became convinced that he had every disease he read about. Mum was in to the doctor's office almost daily with him as he worked his way alphabetically and hypochondri- acally through the book, exhibiting symptoms of Acne, Agoraphobia, Alzheimer's, Angina, Angst and Anthrax until finally someone blew the whistle on him. Even the Acne wasn't real. Although the Angst certainly was, by the time Mum had finished with him.

Dr. Thornton's waiting room was like the day of judgment, packed to the rafters with fighting children, screaming mothers and consumptive geriatrics.

When I was finally granted an audience with His Healingness, he was slumped across his desk, looking exhausted and bad-tempered, his pen poised over the prescription pad.

"What can I do for you, Lucy?" he asked wearily.

I knew what he really meant was, "I remember you, you're one of those crazy Sullivans. So? Losing it again, are you?"

"Well, it's not about me," I began hesitantly.

He immediately looked interested.

"A friend of yours?" he asked hopefully.

"Well, sort of." I agreed.

"Thinks she might be pregnant?" he asked. "Hmmmm, is that it?"

"No, it's . . ."

"Has a mysterious discharge?" he interrupted eagerly.

"No, nothing like that . . ."

"Very heavy periods?"

"No . . ."

"Lump in her breast?"

"No," I said, almost laughing. "It really *isn't* me. It's my dad."

"Oh him," he said, annoyed. "Well, why isn't *he* here? I don't do virtual diagnosis."

"What do you mean?"

"I'm sick of it," he burst out. "It's all mobile phones and internets, and computer games and simulated flights. None of you want to do anything real!"

"Er . . ." I said, shocked, not knowing how to respond to his outpourings of Luddite vitriol. He'd become slightly more eccentric since our previous encounter.

"You all think you needn't do anything," he went on in a high voice. His face was flushed. "You can just sit at home with your modems and your PCs and think you're living, that you needn't get off your lazy behinds and interact with other human beings. You just E-mail me your symptoms, is that it?'' Physician, heal thyself! Dr. Thornton seemed to be cracking up.

Then, as suddenly as it had arrived, the fight went out of him.

''Well, what about your father?'' he sighed, slumping back over his desk.

''It's a bit embarrassing,'' I said awkwardly.

''Why?''

''Well, he doesn't think there's anything wrong with him . . .'' I started to delicately pick my way through the complicated story.

''Well, if he doesn't think there's anything wrong with him, and you do, then perhaps you're the one with the problem,'' said Dr. Thornton bluntly.

''No, listen, you don't understand . . .''

''I do understand,'' he interrupted. ''There's nothing wrong with Jamsie Sullivan. If he cut out the booze, he'd be fine.

''Although maybe he wouldn't be,'' he added, as if he were talking to himself. ''God alone knows what shape his liver is in by now. Probably hexagonal.''

''But . . .''

''Lucy, you're wasting my time. I've got a waiting room full of sick people out there, *really* sick people, who need looking after. And instead I get the female Sullivans plaguing me, looking for cures for a man who has decided to drink himself to death.''

''What do you mean, female Sullivans?'' I asked.

''You. Your mother. Your mother is almost a permanent fixture here.''

''Really?'' I hooted with surprise.

''Well, actually, now that you mention it, she hasn't been here in a while. Sent you instead, has she?''

"Er, no . . ."

"Why not?" he asked. "What's happened?"

"She's left Dad," I said, expecting sympathy.

Instead he laughed. Kind of. He really was behaving oddly.

"So she finally did it," he chuckled, while I stared at him, my head on one side, wondering what was wrong with him.

And what was he talking about, saying that Dad was drinking himself to death? Why did everything come back to Dad and drinking?

Somewhere in my head, something had started its slow descent into place and I was frightened.

"And now you've taken over where your mother left off?" asked Dr. Thornton.

"If you mean, am I taking care of him, then, yes," I said.

"Lucy, go home," he sighed. "There's nothing you can do for your father; we've tried everything. Until he decides to stop drinking, nobody can do anything for him."

More things slotted into place in my head.

"Look, you've got it all wrong," I said, fighting against what I knew to be true. "I'm not here about his drinking. I'm here because there *is* something wrong with him and it's got nothing to do with drinking."

"Well, what is it?" he asked impatiently.

"He wets his bed."

There was a silence. That's shut him up, I thought, nervously, hoping that it really had.

"Bed-wetting's an emotional thing," I went on, hopefully. "It's nothing to do with drinking."

"Lucy," he said grimly. "It's got everything to do with drinking."

"I don't know what you mean," I said, feeling sick

with apprehension. "I don't understand why you're saying all these things."

"Don't you?" he frowned. "But you *must* know, of course you know. How can you live with him and not know?"

"I *don't* live with him," I said. "At least I haven't for years, I've just moved back."

"But hasn't your mother told you all about . . . ?" he asked, looking at my sick, anxious face. "Oh. Oh. I see. She hasn't."

I could feel a trembling in my lower thighs, I knew what he was about to tell me. This was the disaster that I'd been avoiding all my life and now here I was face to face with it. This was the big one. There was almost a sense of relief, I could stop evading and avoiding now.

"Well," sighed Dr. Thornton. "Your father is a chronic alcoholic."

My stomach lurched. I had known and yet I hadn't known.

"Are you sure?" I asked.

"You really didn't know, did you?" he asked, a little more kindly.

"No," I said. "But now that you tell me, I can't understand how I didn't know until now."

"It happens a lot," he said, wearily. "I see it over and over again, where there's something very amiss in a home and everyone acts as if there's nothing wrong."

"Oh," I said.

"It's as if they have an elephant in their living room and they all tiptoe around pretending not to see it."

"Oh," I said again. "Well, what can I do?"

"To be quite frank, Lucy," he said, "this isn't really my area. I only know about physical ailments. If you father had, let's say, an ingrowing toenail or maybe an irritable bowel, I could suggest all kinds of treatment. But this family therapy, psychodrama, confrontation kind of stuff isn't something I'm familiar with. It came after my time."

"Oh."

"But are *you* feeling all right?" he asked hopefully. "Has all of this come as a shock? Because I can do shock, that's something I *do* know about."

"I'll be fine," I said, getting up to leave. I had to get away to deal with what he'd told me, I couldn't get out fast enough.

"No wait," he said urgently. "I could give you a prescription."

"What for?" I asked. "A new father? One that isn't an alcoholic?"

"Don't be like that," he said. "Sleeping tablets? Tranquilizers? Antidepressants?"

"No thanks."

"Well, I've another suggestion that might be of help," he said thoughtfully.

Hope ricocheted in my chest.

"Yes?" I asked breathlessly.

"Plastic sheets."

"Plastic sheets?" I asked faintly.

"Yes, you know, to protect the mattress from . . ."

I left.

I went away in a state of shock. When I got home, Dad had fallen asleep in his chair, leaving a cigarette burning into the armrest. He jerked awake when I came in.

"Will you run down to the liquor store for me, Lucy?" he asked.

"Okay," I said, too shell-shocked to argue. "What do you want?"

"Whatever you can afford," he said humbly.

"Oh," I said coldly. "You want me to pay for it?"

"Weeelll," he said vaguely.

"But you got your check only two days ago," I said. "What did you do with it?"

"Oh Lucy," he laughed, kind of nastily. "But you're your mother's daughter and no mistake.

I left the house, subdued, feeling sick. Was I just like my mother? I wondered. At the liquor store I bought him a bottle of real whiskey instead of the funny cheap stuff from Eastern Europe that he usually got. But I was still edgy, still desperate to spend money on him, so I bought cigarettes and four bars of chocolate and two bags of tortilla chips.

When my expenditure hovered around the twenty-pound mark, I was able to breathe easy again, secure in the knowledge that my extravagance had destroyed any similarity to my mother.

I couldn't stop thinking about what Dr. Thornton had told me. I didn't want to believe him, but I couldn't help it. I tried looking at Dad in the old way and then in the light of him being an alcoholic. The alcoholic light fitted better. Fitted perfectly.

Dr. Thornton's revelation had knocked down the first domino, the rest were hitting the deck at high speed. Like red wine spilled on a white tablecloth, the knowledge poured through my life, back to my earliest memory, tainting everything.

And it *should* be tainted. It *was* tainted.

I had been looking at my life, my father, my family from upside-down, and suddenly it had come upright. I couldn't cope with the way everything really was.

The worst thing was that Dad *looked* different to me. Like someone I'd never met before. I tried not to let it happen. I didn't want the man I loved to waver and disappear right before my eyes. I had to love him. He was all I had.

That evening, I kept sneaking looks at him, at all the things that had happened, all the signs. I tried to control it, just to look at a little bit of my life at a time, to dole out the unpleasantness in easy-to-manage, bite-size pieces. I tried to protect myself, not to overwhelm myself with the loss of it all.

But I couldn't stop seeing him differently.

He no longer seemed lovable and cute and cuddly and great fun. But drunk and lopsided and slurred and incapable and *selfish*.

I didn't want to think that way about my father, it was unbearable. He was the person I'd loved most, maybe the only person I'd ever really loved. And now I found that the person I had adored didn't even exist.

No wonder he was always such fun when I was young. It's easy to be playful if you're drunk. No wonder he sang so much. No wonder he cried so much.

The one thing that stopped me from really going crazy was the hope that maybe I could change him. I could reluctantly admit that he had a drinking problem, only if I could say that it was a solvable problem. I'd heard that people with drinking problems got better. All I had to do was find out how to go about it. I'd fix him. My father would be back and everyone would be happy.

 71

So I made another appointment to see Dr. Thornton. I was full of hope, convinced that there would be a way to save Dad.

"Can you prescribe something for him so that he won't

want to drink?'' I asked, confident that there would be something on the market for that.

"Lucy,'' he said. "I can't prescribe anything for *you* to give to *him*.''

"Okay,'' I said eagerly. "I'll get him down here in person and then you can give him a prescription.''

"No,'' he said annoyed. "You don't understand. There's no cure for alcoholism.''

"Don't call it that.''

"Why not, Lucy? That's what it is.''

"So what's going to happen?''

"He'll die if he doesn't stop drinking,'' he said.

Fear made me dizzy.

"But we've got to make him stop,'' I said desperately. "I'm sure I've heard of heavy drinkers who've managed to stop. How have they done it?''

"The only thing that sometimes seems to work is AA,'' he said.

"What's tha . . . ? Oh, you mean Alcoholics Anonymous,'' I said, understanding. "Well, I don't think he needs to go there. I mean, it's full of . . . of . . . *alcoholics*.''

"Exactly.''

"But seriously.'' I almost laughed. "Smelly old men, with strings around their coats and plastic bags around their feet? Come on now, my father is nothing like that.''

Although on second thought, he *was* fairly smelly, he never seemed to actually *have* the numerous baths that he ran, but I wasn't going to tell Dr. Thornton that.

"Lucy,'' he said. "Alcoholics come in all shapes and sizes, men and women, young and old, smelly and fragrant.''

"Really?'' I asked with skepticism.

"Yes.''

"Even women?"

"Yes. Women with homes and husbands and jobs and children and nice clothes and high heels and perfume and pretty hair. . . ." he trailed off sadly. He seemed to be thinking of someone in particular.

"So they go to this AA place and what happens?"

"They don't drink."

"Ever?"

"Never."

"Not even at Christmas and at weddings and on holidays and things like that?"

"No."

"I'm not sure he'd go for that," I said doubtfully.

"It's all or nothing," said the doctor. "And with your father, it'll be nothing."

"Okay," I sighed, "if it's our only option, let's tell him about this Alcoholics Anonymous thing."

"Lucy," said Dr. Thornton, sounding annoyed again. "He *knows*. He's known for years."

I broached the subject that evening. Eventually. I kept putting it off and in the end Dad was drunk before I brought it up.

"Dad," I quavered nervously. "Did you ever think that maybe you were drinking too much?"

He narrowed his eyes at me. I'd never seen him like that before. He looked different. Like a nasty, vicious, drunk old man, one you'd see on the street, flailing about, shouting slurred insults and trying to hit someone, but being too drunk to do any real damage.

He was watchful, eyeing me as if I was the enemy. "My wife has just left me," he said aggressively. "Are you going to deny me a drink?"

"No," I said. "Of course not."

I wasn't very good at this.

"You see, Dad," I went on cautiously, hating every second of it. I wasn't his parent, I was his *daughter*. He was supposed to tell me off, not the other way around.

"It's a question of money," I forged ahead, wimpily.

"I see, I see," he said in a raised voice. "Money, money, money. Always whining about money. You're just like your mother. Well, why don't you leave me too. Go on, get out. Go on, there's the door."

That put an end to that conversation.

"Of course I won't leave you," I whispered. "I'll never leave you."

I was damned if I was going to admit that my mother had been right.

But shortly after that Dad seemed to get far worse. Or maybe it was just that I was aware of it now. That he drank in the mornings became obvious. And that he caused fights in the local pub. And a couple of times the police brought him home in the middle of the night.

But still I held myself together. I couldn't go to pieces because I had no one to help me pick them up.

I went to Dr. Thornton again and he just shook his head abruptly when he saw me and said, "Sorry, no miracle cures have been invented. Unless it's happened since ten o'clock this morning."

"No, wait," I said eagerly. "I've been reading about hypnosis—couldn't Dad be hypnotized to stop drinking? You know, the way people are hypnotized to stop smoking or eating chocolate?"

"No, Lucy," he said, sounding annoyed. "There's no proof that hypnosis works and, even if there was, the person being hypnotized has to *want* to give up the cigarettes or whatever. Your father won't even admit that he drinks to excess so there's no chance that he'll decide that he wants to give up. . . . And if he says he wants to give up, then he's ready for AA,'' he added smugly.

I rolled my eyes. Him and his damn AA.

"Okay." I wasn't disheartened. "Never mind hypnosis. What about acupuncture?"

"What about it?" he asked wearily.

"Couldn't he have that done? Couldn't he have a little pin stuck in his ear? Or someplace?"

"Someplace indeed," he muttered. Quite nastily, actually. "No, Lucy."

So, as a last resort, I found the number for Alcoholics Anonymous in the phone book and called to ask them what I should do with Dad. And although they were very nice and sympathetic, they told me that I could do nothing for him, until he himself admitted that he had a problem. That rang a vague bell with me, I'd picked that up from popular culture at some stage. And something else. If the person admits they have a problem, that's half the battle. But I didn't believe it.

"Come on," I said annoyed. "You people are supposed to stop people drinking, so stop him drinking."

"I'm sorry," said the woman I was speaking to. "No one can do it except him."

"But he's an alcoholic," I burst out. "Alcoholics aren't supposed to be able to stop by themselves."

"No," she said. "But they must *want* to stop for themselves."

"Look, I don't think you understand," I said. "He's had a very hard life and his wife has just left him and, in a way, he *has* to drink."

"No, he doesn't," she said. Nicely.

"This is ridiculous," I said. "Can I speak to your boss? I need to speak to an expert here. He's a very special case."

She laughed. And that made me even more annoyed.

"We all thought that we were special cases," she said. "If I had a pound for every alcoholic who said that to me, I'd be a rich woman."

"What are you talking about?" I asked coldly.

"Well, I'm an alcoholic," she said.

"Are you?" I asked in surprise. "You don't sound like one."

"What did you think I'd sound like?" she asked.

"Well, . . . drunk, I suppose."

"I haven't had a drink for nearly two years," she said.

*"Nothing?"*

"Nothing."

"I mean, nothing at *all?*"

"No, nothing at all."

She can't have drunk very much, I thought, if she's been able to abstain for two years. She was probably a two-spritzers-on-a-Friday-night type of person.

"Oh, well, thank you," I said, getting ready to hang up. "But I don't think Dad is anything like you. He drinks whiskey and he drinks it in the mornings." I said it almost boastfully. "He'd find it very hard to stop. He'd never be able to go without a drink for two years."

"I drank in the mornings," said the woman.

I swallowed. I didn't believe her.

"And my favorite drink was neat brandy," she went on.

"A bottle a day," she added when I still didn't say anything. "I was no different from your dad."

"But he's old . . ." I said desperately. "You don't sound old."

"There's people of all ages in AA. Lots of old people."

"I can send someone by to talk to him," she suggested.

But I thought of how angry he'd be, how humiliating he would find it and thought better of it.

Then she gave me the phone number of another group of people called Al-Anon and said that it was for friends and families of alcoholics and that they might be able to help me. So, as a last resort, I called them. I even went to one of their meetings, expecting to be given all kinds of tips to help Dad stop drinking—how to hide the booze in the house, how to water the drinks, how to persuade him not to drink until after eight in the evening—that sort of thing.

And I was outraged to find that it was nothing like that.

Everyone there talked about how they were trying to leave their alcoholic husband or boyfriend or wife or daughter or friend or whatever to their own devices and simply get on with their own lives. One man talked about his mother being a drunk and how he always fell in love with helpless women who had drinking problems.

They were all talking about something called "co-dependency," which I knew about, because I'd read so many self-help books, but I couldn't see how it applied to me and my father.

"You can't change your dad," one woman said to me. "And by trying to, you're just avoiding your own problems."

"My dad is my problem," I said huffily.

"No, he isn't," she said.

"How can you be so heartless?" I asked. "I love my father."

"Don't you think that you're entitled to a nice life?" she asked.

"I couldn't just abandon him," I said stiffly.

"It might be the best thing that you ever did," she said.

"The guilt would kill me," I said self-righteously.

"Guilt is a self-indulgence," she said.

"How dare you," I said. "You haven't a clue what you're talking about."

"I was married to an alcoholic," she said. "I know exactly what you're going through."

"I'm just a normal person who happens to have a father with a drinking problem. I'm not like you . . . losers who have to come to these stupid meetings and talk about how you're managing to *detach* from the alcoholic in your lives."

"That's what I said in the beginning too," she said.

"God!" I said, angrily. "I just want to help him to stop drinking. What's so wrong with that?"

"Because you *can't* help," she said. "You are powerless over him and his alcohol. But you're not powerless over your own life."

"I have responsibilities."

"To yourself. And it's never as simple as getting the other person to stop drinking and then you'll suddenly be fine."

"What do you mean?"

"Well, what kind of relationships do you have with other men?"

I didn't answer.

"Lots of women like us have a really hard time having successful relationships," she said.

"I'm not a woman like you," I said scornfully.

"You'd be amazed how many of us have the wrong kind of relationships with the wrong kind of men," she said gently. "Because our expectations of the relationship is based on what we learned from dealing with the alcoholic in our lives."

"Here's my phone number," she said. "Ring me if you ever need to talk. Any time."

I walked away before she gave it to me.

Another avenue explored. Another dead end.
Now what was I going to do?

I tried to give him less money. But he begged and cried
and the guilt was so awful that I gave it to him, even
though I really didn't have the money to spare.

I swung from feeling furious to feeling so sad I thought
my heart would break. Sometimes I hated him and sometimes I loved him.

But I felt increasingly trapped and desperate.

 72

Christmas was horrible. I couldn't go to any of the hundreds of parties. While everyone else was putting on short,
black, glittery dresses (and that was just the men) I was
on a train home to Uxbridge. While everyone else was
puking or making out with their boss, I was begging Dad
to go back to sleep, telling him it really didn't matter that
he'd wet his bed again.

Even if there had been someone else to take care of
Dad, I still couldn't have gone because I was too broke
to buy a round of drinks.

Dad's drinking got even worse in The Festive Season.
I didn't know why—it wasn't as if he needed an *excuse*
to drink. To compound my self-pity, I only got two Christmas cards. One from Daniel and one from Adrian in the
video shop.

Christmas Day itself was truly awful. Chris and Peter didn't even come to see Dad and me.

"I don't want it to look as if I'm taking sides," was Chris's excuse.

"I don't want to upset Mammy," was Peter's.

It was a horrible day. The best thing about it was that Dad was comatose by eleven in the morning.

I was so desperate for someone else to talk to, anything to dilute Dad's presence, that I almost looked forward to going back to work.

 73

Because Christmas had been so awful, I foolishly approached the new year with hope.

But on the fourth of January, Dad went on a massive bender. He had obviously planned it because when I tried to buy a pack of gum at the station on my way to work, all my cash had disappeared. I could have run home and tried to stop him, but somehow I just couldn't be bothered.

When I got to town, I tried to get money from an ATM and it swallowed my card. "You are heinously overdrawn, contact your bank," the flashing message advised. I will not, I thought. If they want me, they'll have to come and get me. (They'll never take me alive, etc., etc.)

I had to borrow money from Megan.

When I got home from work, there was a scary-looking official letter just inside the front door. It was from my bank instructing me to return my checkbook.

Things were out of control. I tried to suppress the icy fear. Where would it all end?

As I made for the kitchen, something crunched under my foot. I looked down and saw that the hall carpet was covered in broken glass. And so was the kitchen floor. The kitchen table was scattered with broken plates and saucers and bowls. In the front room, the smoked-glass coffee table was in smithereens, books and tapes scattered all over the floor. The whole downstairs was in a shambles.

Dad's handiwork.

He'd done some drunken breaking and smashing in the past, but nothing as spectacular as this.

Naturally, he was nowhere to be found.

I went from the kitchen to the front room and back again, unable to believe the extent of the damage. If it was breakable, he had broken it. Even if it wasn't breakable, he had *tried* to break it. There was a yellow plastic bucket in the kitchen that he had obviously attempted to smash the living daylights out of, judging by the number of dents in it. In the front room there was a whole shelf of disgusting china boys and dogs and bells that my mother had doted on, that he had wiped out. I felt a spasm of sadness for my mother. He knew what they had meant to her.

I didn't even cry. I just began to clean it up.

While I was on my knees picking shards of broken china boy out of the carpet, the phone rang. It was the police calling to say that Dad had been arrested. I was cordially invited to come to the police station and bail him out.

I had no money and no more energy.

I finally decided to cry.

Then I decided to call Daniel.

Miraculously he was in—I don't know what I would have done if he hadn't been.

\*     \*     \*

I was crying so much he couldn't really understand what I was saying.

"It's Dad," I wailed.

"What's dead?"

"Nothing's dead, it's Dad."

"Lucy, either it's dead or it's not, it can't be both at once."

"Oh, for God's sake, just get over here, will you?"

"I'll be with you as soon as I can," he promised.

"Bring lots of money," I added.

He arrived two china dogs, a china bell and half a coffee table later.

"Sorry, Lucy," he said, as soon as I opened the front door. "I figured it out. It's your Dad?"

He went to put his arms around me but I skipped nimbly away. The last thing my melting pot of emotions needed was sexual attraction.

"Yes," I said, as tears poured down my face. "But he's not . . ."

"Dead," he finished for me. "Yes, I'd gathered that much. Sorry, I couldn't hear you very well. Christ, has there been an earthquake out here?"

"No, it's . . ."

"You've been burgled! Don't touch a thing, Lucy."

"We haven't been fucking well burgled," I wept. "My stupid, drunk bastard of a father has done all this."

"Oh no, Lucy." He looked genuinely horrified, which made me feel even worse. "But why?" he asked, running his hands through his hair.

"I don't know. But it gets worse. He's been arrested."

"Since when can they arrest you for breaking things in your own house? God, this country becomes more and more like a police state every day. Next it'll be illegal to burn the toast and to eat ice cream straight from the carton and . . .''

"Shut up, you bleeding-heart liberal.'' I laughed despite myself. "He hasn't been arrested for breaking his own dishes. I don't know *why* he's been arrested.''

"So he needs to be bailed out?''

"He does.''

"Okay, Lucy, to the chick-mobile. Let's go and rescue him!''

Dad had been charged with about a million things—being drunk and disorderly, causing a public nuisance, causing damage to property, intention to cause actual bodily harm, obscene behavior and on and on. It was horrific. I had never imagined that the day would come when I'd have to bail my father out of jail.

When Dad was led from the cells, he was as meek as a lamb—the fight had gone out of him. Daniel and I took him home and put him to bed.

Then I made Daniel a cup of tea.

"Okay, Lucy, what are we going to do about this?'' he asked.

"Who's 'we'?'' I asked defensively.

"You and me.''

"What's it got to do with you?''

"For once, Lucy, just for once, Lucy, could you try not to fight with me? I'm only trying to help.''

"I don't want your help.''

"You do,'' he said. "You wouldn't have called me if you didn't. There's no *shame* in it,'' he added. "Lucy, there's no need to be so touchy.''

"You'd be touchy if your Dad was an alcoholic,'' I said, as tears splashed down my face—*again*. "Well, maybe he's not an alcoholic . . .''

"He's an alcoholic." Daniel was grim.

"Call him what you bloody well like," I sobbed. "I don't give a shit whether he's an alcoholic or not. All I care about is he's a drunk and it's ruining my life."

I sobbed a good bit more, the burden of months of worry spilled down my cheeks.

"Did you know?" I asked. "You know, about Dad?"

"Er, yes."

"But how?"

"Chris told me."

"Why didn't anyone tell me?"

"They did," he said.

"Well, why didn't anyone help me?"

"They tried. You wouldn't let them."

"What am I going to do now?"

"How about moving out and letting someone else take care of him?"

"Oh no," I said in fear.

"Fine, if you don't want to move out, you don't have to, but there's lots of people who can help you. Apart from your brothers, there's live-in helpers and social workers and all kinds of people. You'll still be able to take care of him, but you won't have to do it on your own."

"Let me think about it."

At midnight, while Daniel and I were still sitting gloomily at the kitchen table, the phone rang.

"What now?" I asked in fear.

"Hello?"

"Might I have a word with Lucy Sullivan?" roared a familiar voice.

"Gus?" I asked, as joy flooded through me.

"The very fella," he shouted.

"Hello," I wanted to dance. "Where did you get my number?"

"I met the scary, blond woman in McMullens and she said you were living out in the middle of nowhere. I'd been thinking about you and missing you anyway."

"Had you?" I was almost in tears with joy.

"Indeed I had, Lucy. So I says to her, 'give me the phone number, I'll call her and take her out.' So here I am, Lucy, calling you and asking to take you out."

"Great!" I said in delight. "I'd love to see you."

"Okay, give me the address and I'll be right out to get you."

"You mean, *now?*"

"When else?"

"Oh, now isn't a good time, Gus." I felt very ungrateful.

"Well, when is?"

"The day after tomorrow?"

"Right you are. Thursday, after your work, I'll come and get you."

"Great."

I turned back to Daniel with shining eyes.

"That was Gus," I said breathlessly.

"I gathered."

"He was thinking about me."

"Was he?"

"He wants to see me."

"He's very lucky that you're so obliging."

"What are you pissed off about?"

"Couldn't you have made him work a bit harder, Lucy? I wish you hadn't given in so easily."

"Daniel, Gus calling me is the nicest thing that's happened in months and months. And I don't have the energy to play games with him."

He gave a tight little smile.

"You'd better have plenty of energy for gameplaying on Thursday night," he said curtly.

"And so what if I do?" I asked angrily. "I'm allowed to have sex, you know. Why have you gone all Victorian-dad on me?"

"Because you deserve better than him."

He got up to leave. "Are you sure you don't need me to stay the night?"

"I'm sure, thanks," I answered.

"And you'll think about what I said about getting help for your Dad?"

"I'll think about it."

"I'll call you tomorrow. Bye."

As he bent to kiss me—on the cheek—I said, "Oh, er, Daniel, can you loan me any money?"

"How much?"

"Er, twenty, if you don't mind."

He gave me sixty.

"Have a nice time with Gus," he said.

"This money isn't for Gus," I said defensively.

"I didn't say it was."

 74

I was beside myself about seeing Gus. Obviously, be-cause I hadn't been out for about three months, some of the excitement was good plain old-fashioned cabin fever. But it wasn't just that—I was still crazy about him. I'd never given up hope that it might work out for us. I was so excited that I was able to put my worry about Dad on hold.

When I told the others in the office that I was meeting Gus, there was mayhem. Meredia and Jed gasped with delight, then linked arms and skipped around the office, knocking over a chair in the process. Then they changed direction and Meredia's generous hip sent a desk organizer flying onto the floor, scattering paper clips and pens and highlighters everywhere.

They were almost as excited as I was—probably because their social and romantic lives were as uneventful as mine, and they were glad of any diversion, personal or vicarious.

Only Megan looked disgusted.

"Gus?" she asked. "You're going out with *Gus?* But what happened? Where did you meet him?"

"I didn't, he called me."

"The little bastard!" she exclaimed.

There was a chorus of disagreement from the rest of us.

"No, he's not," yelled Meredia.

"Leave him alone, he's a great guy," shouted Jed.

"So what happened?" demanded Megan, ignoring them. "He called you and then what?"

"He asked me to meet him," I said.

"And did he say why?" she quizzed. "Did he say what he wants from you?"

"No."

"And *are* you going to meet him?"

"Yes."

"When?"

"Tomorrow."

"Can we come too?" begged Meredia, as she crouched on the floor, scooping up handfuls of staples.

"No, Meredia, not this time," I said.

"Nothing nice ever happens to us," she said moodily.

"Oh, come on now," said Jed jovially, trying to cheer her up. "What about the fire drill?"

We had had a fire drill about a week before, and in fairness, it *had* been great fun. Especially as we got advance warning of it—Gary in Security leaked details of it to Megan in a fruitless attempt to advance himself sexually with her. So, for two hours before the bell went off, we had our coats on and our bags on our desks, ready to go.

According to the memo that had been circulated, I was a Fire Monitor, but I didn't know what that was, and no one had explained it to me. So, instead, I took advantage of the bedlam and confusion and went to Oxford Street and took in a couple of shoe stores.

"Don't meet him, Lucy," said Megan. She sounded upset.

"It's okay," I reassured Megan, touched by her protectiveness. "I can look after myself."

She shook her head, "He's bad news, Lucy."

And then she was unusually silent.

The following day when Jed came into work, he said he hadn't been able to sleep the night before with excitement. Then he complained all day long that he had butterflies in his stomach.

He insisted on personally vetting my appearance before I met Gus. "Good luck, Agent Sullivan," he said. "We're all depending on you."

It had been a long time since I had felt this young and happy. As if life had possibilities.

Gus was waiting outside the building for me, swapping insults with Winston and Harry (which I later discovered were real). When I saw him my stomach did a flip—

he looked so good, his black, shiny hair falling into his green eyes.

The passage of four months had done nothing to diminish his attractiveness.

"Lucy," he shouted when he saw me and lounged sexily over to me, opening his arms wide.

"Gus." I smiled breathlessly, hoping he wouldn't see that my legs were wobbling from exhilaration and nerves.

He threw his arms around me and wrapped me tight, but my soaring happiness came to a screeching halt as I got a whiff of alcohol from him.

It was nothing unusual for Gus to reek of alcohol—in fact it was more unusual for him *not* to reek of alcohol. That was one of the things I found attractive about him.

Or rather, *had* found attractive about him.

Not anymore, it seemed.

For a moment I felt a flash of anger—if I'd wanted to spend the evening with a smelly drunk I could have stayed at home with Dad. My evening with Gus was supposed to be The Great Escape, not more of the same.

He moved back slightly so he could look at me, but kept his arms around me and smiled and smiled and smiled. And I cheered up. I felt dizzy to be within kissing distance of that sexy, handsome face. *I'm with Gus,* I thought in disbelief, *I'm holding my dream in my arms.*

"Let's go for a drink, Lucy," he suggested.

There was that feeling again—a surge of annoyance.

Well, surprise, surprise, I thought, pissed off. I had hoped he might have planned something a bit more imaginative for our reconciliation. Silly me.

"Come on," he beckoned and started walking briskly. In fact, he almost broke into a run. He must be dying for a drink, I thought, as I traipsed behind him. He led us to a nearby pub, which we had been to lots of times in the past. It was one of Gus's favorite pubs, he knew the barman and most of the clientele.

As I passed over the threshold behind the speeding Gus, I suddenly thought—*I hate this pub*. I had never noticed before, but I always felt uncomfortable there.

It was dirty and no one ever wiped off the tables. It was full of men who all stared at me when I came in, and the staff were downright rude to women. Or maybe it was just me.

But I tried to think positive.

I was with Gus and he looked beautiful. He was cute and funny and sexy. Even if he was still wearing that awful sheepskin coat that I was sure had fleas.

There was a momentous break with tradition when the time came to buy the first drink—it was paid for by Gus.

And what a production he made of it. Naturally, as soon as we were sitting down, I had reached for my purse, as I always had to with Gus. With everyone, I thought gloomily. But instead of placing his order with me, like he usually did, he jumped up and practically roared, "NO, NO! I won't hear of it!"

"What?" I asked, slightly irritated.

"Put your money away, put your money away!" he urged, waving his arm in a "put your money away" fashion at me, like drunk uncles do at a wedding. "I'm getting this round."

It was like the sun coming out from behind the clouds— Gus had money. It was a sign telling me that everything would be fine, Gus would take care of me.

"Okay." I smiled.

"No, I insist," he said loudly, making flapping movements in the direction of my purse.

"Fine," I said.

"I'll be insulted if you won't let me. I'll take it as a

personal *insult* if you won't permit me to get this round,"
he insisted, with great magnanimity.

"Gus," I said, "I'm not arguing."

"Oh. Oh. Right then." He sounded a bit put out. "What
do you want?"

"A gin and tonic," I muttered humbly.

He arrived back with my gin and a pint of lager and a
measure of whiskey for himself.

His face was dark with annoyance.

"Jesus," he complained. "It's daylight robbery! Do you
know how much that gin and tonic was?"

Not as much as I'll have to spend on you for the next
round, I thought. Why do you always have to order two
drinks at once, when everyone else has just one at a time?

But all I said was a meek "sorry" because I didn't
want to cast a blight on the evening that I had looked
forward to so much.

His bad mood didn't last long, though; they never did.

"Cheers, Lucy." He smiled, clinking his pint against
my extortionate gin.

"Cheers," I said, trying to sound as if I meant it.

"I drink, therefore I am," he announced, with a grin,
and drank half the pint in one gulp.

I smiled, but it was an effort. Usually I was delighted
by his witty remarks, but not this evening.

It wasn't going the way I had wanted it to.

I didn't really know what to talk to Gus about, and he
didn't seem to be bothered talking at all. In the past, we
had always had so much to talk about, I thought wistfully.
But suddenly it was awkwardness and tense silences—at
least on my part.

I desperately wanted to make it all right, to push us
through the tension barrier, but I hadn't the heart to kick-
start the conversation.

Gus made no effort either. In fact he seemed oblivious of the silence. Oblivious of me too, I realized after a while.

He was a man at peace with himself and the world, settled in his armchair with his drinks and his cigarette, comfortable, pleased with himself, surveying the pub, nodding and winking at the people he knew, watching the world go by.

As relaxed as a newt.

He grinned and finished his two drinks in record speed, went back to the bar and got himself another couple.

He didn't offer to get me another drink. Not even one. I hadn't minded this behavior before. I certainly minded now.

We sat there in silence, me mute with expectation, while he drank his two drinks and smoked a cigarette. Then he threw the remaining half pint or so down in one gulp and, before he had even finished swallowing, gasped, "Your round, Lucy."

Like a robot, I got out of my seat and asked him what he wanted.

"A pint and a small one," he said innocently.

"Anything else?" I asked sarcastically.

"Thanks very much, Lucy," he said, sounding delighted. "Fine girl you are, I could do with some smokes."

"Smokes?"

"Cigarettes."

"Cigarettes? What flavor?"

"Benson and Hedges."

"How many? A thousand?"

He seemed to find that hilarious. "Just twenty will do, unless you really *want* to buy me more."

"No, Gus, I don't," I said coldly.

While I waited at the bar, I wondered why I was so pissed off.

It was my own fault, I decided. I had set myself up for disappointment. I had come with so much expectation. And too much need.

I yearned for Gus to be nice to me, to pay me attention, to tell me he'd missed me, that I was beautiful, that he was madly in love with me.

And he hadn't. He hadn't asked how I was, he didn't explain where he had been, why he hadn't contacted me for nearly four months.

But maybe I was asking too much of him. I was so unhappy with the rest of my life that I had hoped Gus would be my savior. Someone to take care of me, someone to whom I could hand over my life and say "Here, fix this."

I wanted it all.

Relax, I advised myself, as I tried to catch the bartender's eye, enjoy yourself. At least you're *with* him. Didn't he show up? And he's still the same witty, entertaining person he always was. So what more do you want?

I came back to the table, loaded down with drinks and renewed hope.

"Good on you, Lucy," said Gus, and fell on the drinks, like a starving man to food.

Shortly after that he announced, "I'll have another drink."

Almost as an afterthought he added, "And you're buying."

Something slipped from a shelf inside me and went crashing to the floor.

I was not a charity. At least, not anymore.

"Oh really," I said, unable to hide my anger. "Since when have they started accepting fresh air as legal tender?"

"What are you talking about?" he asked, looking at me warily. There was something unfamiliar about me.

"Gus," I said, with grim delight. "I don't have any money left." That wasn't quite true. I had enough left to get me home and even to buy a bag of chips on the way, but I wasn't telling him that. He'd wheedle it out of me if he knew.

"You're a terrible woman," he laughed, "trying to scare me like that."

"I'm serious."

"Go on out of that," he joshed. "You've got one of those magic little cards that gives you money from the hole-in-the-wall."

"Yes, but . . ."

"Well, what are you waiting for—off with you, Lucy, there's no time to waste. Run down and get the loot and I'll wait here and watch our seats."

"What about you, Gus?"

"Well, I suppose I could manage another pint while you're gone, thanks very much."

"No, I mean, don't you have a cash card, Gus?"

"Me?" he yelled and laughed and laughed. "Are you serious?" He laughed and laughed again, and then made a face to convey that he thought I'd gone crazy.

I sat in silence, waiting for him to finish.

"No, Lucy." He cleared his throat and finally calmed down, but his mouth kept twitching. "No, Lucy, I don't."

"Well, neither do I, Gus."

"I *know* you do," he scoffed. "I've seen you use it."

"I don't have it anymore."

"Give me a break. . . ."

"Really, Gus."

"Well, why don't you?"

"It was swallowed. Because I didn't have any money in my account."

"Didn't you?" He sounded stunned.

I'll show him, I thought with satisfaction. Then I felt ashamed. It wasn't right to take it out on Gus just because I was annoyed with Dad.

I suddenly felt that I wanted to tell Gus all about it, to explain why I was in such a bad mood. I wanted understanding and forgiveness, sympathy and affection. So, without further ado, I launched into the whole saga about living with Dad and having to give him money and having none left for me and . . .

"Lucy," interrupted Gus urgently.

"Yes?" I said hopefully, looking forward to a bit of sympathy.

"I know what we'll do," he said with a brilliant smile.

"You do?" Great! I thought.

"You've a checkbook, right?" he said.

Checkbook, I thought? *Checkbook?* What's that got to do with how unfortunate I am?

"Well, I know the bartender," continued Gus, eyes shining. "And he'll cash your check if I vouch for you."

I swallowed. That wasn't what I'd wanted to hear.

"So write the check, Lucy, and we're in business." He beamed.

"But, Gus." Even though I shouldn't have, I felt like a spoilsport. "I don't have any money in my account; in fact I'm overdrawn over my overdraft limit."

"Oh, never mind that," said Gus. "It's only a bank, what can they do to you? Property is theft! Come on, Lucy, let's beat the system!"

"No," I said apologetically. "I really can't."

"Well, good riddance to you, Lucy, and the horse you

rode in on; we might as well just go home," he said sulkily. "Bye, nice seeing you."

"Oh, all right," I sighed, reaching for my handbag and my checkbook, trying not to think of the terrifying phone call from my bank that was certain to follow.

Gus was right, I thought, it was only money. But I couldn't help feeling that I was always having to give and give and that, for a change, I wanted someone to give to me.

I wrote a check and Gus went to the bar with it. From the length of time he was gone and the expression on the bartender's face, he wasn't finding it too easy to cash.

He eventually came back, loaded down with drinks.

"Successful mission." He grinned, stashing a handful of notes into his pocket. I noticed that the fly of his jeans was held together with a safety pin.

"My change, Gus," I said, trying to keep the anger out of my voice.

"What's wrong with you, Lucy?" he grumbled. "You've gotten very stingy and cheap."

"Really?" I was nauseous with inarticulated fury. "What's cheap and stingy about me? Haven't I bought you almost every drink this evening?"

"Well," he said, all indignant, "if you're going to be like that about it, just tell me what I owe you and I'll give it back to you when I get it."

"Fine," I said. "I will."

"Here's your change," he said, slamming a bundle of bills and coins down on the table.

That was the point where it was obvious that the evening was ruined, beyond redemption. Not that it had been a wild success before that. But at least before that, I still had hope that it would get better.

I knew it was a deeply insulting thing to do, but I picked up the bundle and began to count it.

I had written a check for fifty pounds and he had returned about thirty. A round of drinks for two—even a round including Gus—didn't cost twenty pounds.

"Where's the rest of my change?" I asked.

"Oh that?" He was annoyed, but tried not to show it. "I didn't think you'd mind, but I bought Vinnie—that's the bartender—a drink for facilitating us, I thought that was only fair and decent."

"And what about the rest?"

"While I was up there, Keith Kennedy came along and I felt that I should see him right too."

"See him right?"

"Buy him a drink, he's been awful good to me, Lucy."

"That still doesn't account for it all," I said, admiring my tenacity.

Gus laughed, but it sounded a bit high-pitched and forced.

". . . And I, er, owed him some money," he finally admitted.

"You owed him money and you gave it to him out of my change?" I asked calmly.

"Er, yes. I didn't think you'd mind. You're like me, Lucy, a free spirit. You don't care about money."

On and on he went, and then he started to sing John Lennon's *Imagine*, except the only line he seemed to know was the one about imagining no possessions. He put on quite a show—stretching out his arms beseechingly and making meaningful faces at me. "Oh, Lucy, imagine no possessions, imagine no possessions, sing along! Imagine no poss-eh-SHUNS! Do, do, do, do, doo-oooooh-oooooooh!"

He paused and waited for me to laugh. I didn't, so he kept singing.

In the past, I would have been touched and charmed by his singing. I would have laughed and told him that he was a terrible man and forgiven him.

But not this time.

I didn't say a thing. I couldn't. I really couldn't. I was beyond anger. I felt too much like a fool. I was too ashamed of myself to be angry. I didn't *deserve* to be angry.

The whole evening had been an exercise in damage control, with me trying to hide from myself just how upset I was. Now the awfulness of it all was right out in the open.

Why did I feel as if this was constantly happening to me? I wondered. So I did a quick review of my life and realized it was because it *was* constantly happening to me.

It happened every day with my father. I had gotten myself into financial trouble so that I could give money to him. No wonder it felt so familiar.

Hadn't Gus always depended on me for money? He had never had a penny. I had been glad to give it to him in the beginning. I had thought I was helping him, that he needed me.

The knowledge made me feel sick. I was a fool, a bloody idiot. Everyone knew it, except me. I was a soft touch. Good old Lucy, she's so desperate for love and affection that she's prepared to buy it. She'll give you the shirt off her back because she thinks that you deserve it more than she does. You'll never go hungry with Lucy, even though *she* might. But so what? What does she matter?

Gus hadn't been the only boyfriend that I had taken care of financially. Most of them hadn't had jobs. And the ones who had jobs still managed to borrow money from me.

The rest of the evening, I felt as if I was outside my body, looking at me and Gus.

He got really drunk.

I should have gotten up and left but I couldn't. I was fascinated, repelled, appalled at what I was seeing, but I couldn't look away.

He burned my tights with his cigarette and didn't even notice. He slopped his beer on me and didn't notice that either. He slurred, he started stories and meandered and forgot about them. He talked to the man and woman at the next table and kept on talking to them even when it became obvious that he was annoying them.

The drunker he got, the more sober I became. I barely spoke and he either didn't notice or didn't care.

Had he always been like this? I wondered.

And the answer was, of course, yes.

He hadn't changed. But I had. I saw things differently. It barely mattered to him that I was there. I was merely a source of money.

Daniel had been right. As if I wasn't feeling bad enough, I had to admit that that smug pig had been right. He'd never let me forget it. Although maybe he would— he wasn't as smug as he used to be. He wasn't really smug at all. He was nice. At least he bought me an occasional drink. And an occasional dinner . . .

I sat with an empty glass in front of me for over an hour. Gus didn't notice.

He went to the men's room and was gone for twenty minutes and didn't explain or apologize when he eventually returned. There was nothing unusual in such behavior. Nights out with Gus were always like that.

Somehow I was always surrounded by men who drank a lot and took advantage of me and I couldn't understand how it had happened.

But I knew I'd had enough.

At closing time, Gus had an argument with one of the bartenders—a fairly regular occurrence. The bartender shouted "Have you no homes to go to?" in an effort to get everyone to leave and Gus decided that was a terrible thing for him to say because there had been an earthquake in China a few days previously. "What if a Chinese person heard you?" shouted Gus. To describe the rest of the incoherent drivel that came out of his mouth would be too tedious for words. Suffice it to say that the bartender physically hustled him toward the door, as Gus struggled and shouted. To think I once *admired* that kind of behavior; that I'd thought Gus was a rebel.

We stood in the street as the door slammed behind us.

"Okay, Lucy, home we go," said Gus, swaying slightly and looking bleary.

"Home?" I asked politely.

"Yes," he said.

"Fine, Gus," I said smoothly.

He smiled the smile of a victorious man.

"And where are you living now?" I asked.

"Still in Camden," he said vaguely. "But why . . . ?"

"Well, off to Camden we go," I said.

"No," said Gus in alarm.

"Why not?" I asked.

"Because we can't," he said.

"Why can't we?"

"Because we just . . . can't."

"Well, you're not coming out to my father's house."

"But why not? I'd say your old man and I would get along just fine."

"I'm sure you would," I agreed. "That's what I'm afraid of."

Something was up, I'd known it all along. He probably had a girlfriend in Camden, one that he lived with, something like that.

But I didn't care. I wouldn't have touched him with a ten-foot pole. I couldn't see how I had ever fancied him. He looked like a little gnome, a little, drunk leprechaun. With his stupid sheepskin jacket and his filthy brown sweater.

The spell was broken. Everything about him revolted me. He even smelled funny. Disgusting, like a carpet the morning after a really rowdy party.

"Save your excuses," I said. "Don't tell me why you won't take me to your apartment. Why you never did, in fact. Save your ridiculous stories."

"What ridiculous stories?" he asked. He had difficulty saying "ridiculous."

"Let's see," I said. "You'll probably tell me that you're taking care of a cow for your brother and that it has nowhere to stay except in your bedroom and that it's shy and afraid of strangers."

"Would I?" he asked, thoughtfully. "Well, you might be right, that sounds like me, so it does. You're an exceptional woman, Lucy Sullivan."

"Oh, I'm not," I smiled. "Not anymore."

That confused his already alcohol-addled head.

"So you see," he said, "we have to go back to your place."

"*I'm* going," I said. "You're not."

"But . . ." he said.

"Goodbye," I sang.

"No, wait, Lucy," he said in alarm.

I turned and smiled benignly on him. "Yes?"

"How am I going to get home?" he asked.

"Do I look like I can foretell the future?" I asked innocently.

"But Lucy, I don't have any money."

I put my face up to his and smiled.

He smiled back.

"Frankly, my dear," I beamed, "I don't give a damn."

I had always wanted to say that.

"What do you mean?"

"I mean—in language that you'll understand"—I paused for impact and put my face right into his—"FUCK OFF, GUS!"

There was a little pause while I took another deep breath. "Extort money from someone else, you drunken little bastard. I'm no longer open for business."

And I swung off down the road, leaving Gus staring after me.

A few seconds later I realized I was walking the wrong direction for the tube station and had to slink back the way I had come. Luckily the little swine wasn't still there to see me.

 75

I was exhilarated with anger.

I went to Uxbridge, but only to pick up my things. The other passengers on the train looked at me oddly and kept their distance. I kept remembering how mean I'd been to Gus and a triumphant voice in my head reminded me that *you've got to be cruel to be cruel.*

With bitter amusement, I wondered what my father had managed to destroy in my absence. The drunken fool had probably burned the house down. And, if he had, I just hoped that he'd managed to burn himself with it.

I thought of what a conflagration there'd be, and in spite of everything, I laughed. More funny looks from the other passengers. It would take about a week to put him out. He'd burn so brightly he'd probably be visible from outer space, just like the Great Wall of China. Maybe they could harness him up to an electricity generator and he could power the whole of London for a couple of days.

I hated him.

I had seen how badly I had let Gus treat me and it was an exact copy of the way my father treated me. I only knew how to love drunk, irresponsible, penniless men. Because that's what my father had taught me.

But I didn't feel as if I loved him anymore. I'd had enough. He could take care of himself from now on. And I wouldn't give him any more money—either of them. Gus and Dad had merged into one in the melting pot of my anger. Dad had never stroked Megan's hair, but, nevertheless, I was furious with him for doing it. Gus hadn't cried all over me when I was a little girl and told me that the world was a terrible place, but that was still no reason to forgive him for it.

I was actually grateful to both Dad and Gus for being so horrible to me. For pushing me into a place where I didn't care about them anymore. What if I'd never found out? If they'd been just a bit nicer, it could have gone on forever. With me forgiving them again and again and again.

Memories of other relationships rushed back, ones that I thought I'd forgotten. Other men, other humiliations, other situations where I'd made it my life's work to take care of a difficult, selfish person.

With the unfamiliar anger, another strange emotion had surfaced. This new one was called Self-Preservation.

 76

"You're so lucky," sighed Charlotte enviously.

"Why?" I asked in surprise. I couldn't think of anyone less lucky than me.

"Because you're all straightened out now," she said.

"Am I?"

"Yes, I wish *my* dad was an alcoholic, I wish I hated *my* mother."

This bizarre conversation with Charlotte took place the day after I had left my dad's and returned to my apartment in Ladbroke Grove. It was nearly enough to make me consider moving back in with Dad.

"If only I could be like you," Charlotte went on. "But my father can hold his drink and I love my mother. . . . It's not fair," she added bitterly.

"Charlotte, please tell me what you're talking about."

"Men, of course." She was surprised. "Boys, lads, fellas, the ones with the love truncheons."

"But what about them?"

"You're going to meet Mr. Right and live happily ever after."

"Am I?" That was nice to hear, but I wondered where she was getting her information from.

"Yes." She waved a book at me. "I read it here. It's one of your crazy books. About people like you, how you always pick men just like your dad—you know, ones that drink a lot and don't want any responsibility and all that.''

I felt a twist of pain, but I let her go on.

"It's not your fault," she said, consulting her book. "You see, the child—that's you, Lucy—senses that the parent—that's your dad, Lucy—is unhappy. And because—well, I don't really know why—because children aren't too wise yet, I suppose, the child thinks it's her fault. That it's up to her to make him feel better. See?''

"I suppose so.'' She *had* a point. I had so many memories of Dad crying, and I never knew why. But I remembered the overwhelming need to know that it wasn't my fault. And the fear that he'd never be happy again. I would have done anything to help him feel better.

Charlotte continued blithely to slot my round life into the round hole of her theory.

"And as the child—that's you again, Lucy—grows older, she is attracted to situations where the feelings of childhood are . . . what the fuck's this? Re . . . re . . . rep . . . ?''

"Replicated,'' I supplied helpfully.

"Wow, Lucy, how did you know?'' She was impressed.

But of course I knew. I had read that book many times. Well, at least once. And I was fully conversant with all the theories in it. It was just that I had never thought they applied to me before now.

"It means 'copied,' doesn't it, Lucy?''

"It does, Charlotte.''

"Okay, so you sensed that your dad was an alkie, and you tried to make him better. But you couldn't. Not that it was your fault, Lucy,'' she added hurriedly. "I mean, you were only a little girl and what could you do? Hide the bottles?''

*Hide the bottles.*

I heard a bell ring, it was a long way away, more than

twenty years. And suddenly I remembered a day when I was very young, maybe four or five, and that's what Chris said to me. "Come on, Lucy, we'll hide the bottles. If we hide the bottles then they'll have nothing to fight about."

A wave of heartbreak washed over me, for the little girl who hid a bottle of whiskey that was almost as big as herself in the dog's basket. But Charlotte kept chattering, so I had to file it away for later.

"So the child—that's still you, Lucy—grows into adulthood and meets all kinds of men. But the ones she's attracted to are the ones with the same problems as the child's parent—that's still your dad. See?"

"I see."

"The grown-up child feels comfortable and familiar with a man who drinks to excess or is irresponsible with money or who routinely uses violence . . ." she read aloud.

"My father was never violent." I was nearly in tears.

"Now, now, Lucy." Charlotte calmly wagged her finger at me. "These are only examples. It means that if the father always ate his dinner wearing a gorilla suit, then the child feels comfortable and familiar with boyfriends who wear fur coats or have hairy backs. See?"

"No."

She sighed with exaggerated patience.

"It means that you met men who were always drunk and didn't have jobs and sometimes were Irish and they reminded you of your dad. But you weren't able to make your dad happy, so you felt like you'd been given a second chance and you thought 'Oh good, I can fix *this* one, even if I wasn't able to fix my dad.' See?"

"Maybe." It was so painful I nearly asked her to stop.

"Definitely," said Charlotte firmly. "Not that you did it on purpose, Lucy. I'm not saying that it was your fault. It was your conscience that did it."

"Do you mean my *subconscious?*"

She consulted the book. "Oh yes, your *sub*conscience. I wonder what the difference is?"

I didn't have the energy to explain.

"And that's why you always fell in love with crazy drunks like Gus and Malachy and . . . who was the one that fell out of the window?"

"Nick."

"That's right, Nick. How is he, by the way?"

"Still in the wheelchair, as far as I know."

"Oh, that's terrible." She spoke in suddenly hushed tones. "Is he *crippled?*"

"No, Charlotte." I was brisk. "He's completely better, but he says the wheelchair is much handier for getting around, seeing as he's drunk the whole time."

"That's okay." Charlotte sighed with relief. "I was worried his willy was kaput along with the rest of him."

It wouldn't have made any difference if Nick *had* lost the use of his genitals. Most of the time I'd been with him he'd been too drunk to even get it up. If his wallet hadn't been stolen early one Saturday evening, I don't think we'd ever have consummated the relationship.

Charlotte continued.

"And now that you know why you always pick the wrong men you won't do it anymore." She beamed at me. "You'll tell all the drunk spongers like Gus to get lost and you'll meet the right man and live happily ever after!"

I couldn't return her dazzling smile.

"Just because I know why I pick the wrong men doesn't mean that I'll stop doing it, you know." I laughed in exasperation.

"Nonsense!" she declared.

"I might become mean and bitter and hate men who drink."

"No, Lucy, you will allow yourself to be loved by a man worthy of you," she quoted. "Chapter Ten."

"But first I'll have to relearn the habits of a life-time."—Let's not forget that I had read the book too. "Chapter Twelve."

My ingratitude upset her.

"Why are you being so difficult?" she said. "You don't know how lucky you are. I'd give *anything* to have a dysfunctional family."

"Believe me, Charlotte, you wouldn't."

"Yes, I would." She was firm.

"For God's sake, why?" I was becoming more and more upset.

"Because if there's nothing wrong with me and my family, how can I explain why all my relationships are disasters? I've nothing or no one to blame, except me."

She stared at me again, with resentful envy.

"You don't think my father's a bully, do you?" she asked hopefully.

"No," I said. "I don't know him well, but he seems to be a very nice man."

"You don't think he's weak and ineffectual and a poor leader, inviting disrespect?" she asked, reading aloud from the book.

"On the contrary," I said. "He seems to command a lot of respect."

"Would you say he's a control freak?" She begged. "A melagomaniac?"

"It's megalomaniac, and no, he isn't."

"Sorry," I added.

She was annoyed.

"Well, Lucy, I know it's not really your fault, but you invented all these things . . ."

"Invented what?" I demanded, poised to be annoyed.

"Okay, well, not invented them exactly," she back-tracked. "But I wouldn't know about them if it weren't for you. You've put ideas in my head," she added sulkily.

"In that case I should get a medal," I muttered.

"That's mean," she said, her eyes bright with tears.

"Sorry," I said. Poor Charlotte. How awful to be just bright enough to know how stupid you are.

But she never stayed down for long.

"Tell me again how you told Gus to fuck off," she demanded excitedly.

So, not for the first—or last—time, I told her.

"And how did you feel?" she exclaimed. "Powerful? Victorious? I'd love to be able to do that with that pig Simon."

"Have you spoken to him lately?"

"I had sex with him on Tuesday night."

"Yes, but have you spoken to him recently?"

"No, not really."

That made her laugh.

"Oh, I'm so glad you're back, Lucy," she sighed. "I've missed you."

"I've missed you too."

"And now that you're back we can have lovely talks about Frood . . ."

"Who? Oh, *Freud.*"

"Wha . . . ? Say it again, how does it go?"

"Like 'fried,' but in an Australian accent. Froyd."

"Froyd," she murmured. "Yes, I was reading about Froyd . . . Now, Froyd says that . . ."

"Charlotte, what are you doing?"

"Practicing for the party on Saturday." She was suddenly bitter. "I'm sick to death of men thinking that just because I've got big tits, I'm stupid. I'll show them. I'll go on and on about Frood, I mean, Froyd. Although they probably won't even notice, men never listen to me, they just have conversations with my chest.''

She was gloomy for only a moment.

''What are you wearing to the party? It must be so long since you've been out.''

''I'm not going to the party.''

*''What?''*

''Not yet. It's too soon.''

Charlotte laughed and laughed.

''You silly woman,'' she roared. ''You make it sound as if you're in mourning.''

''I am,'' I replied primly.

 77

The anger that I'd felt that night I saw **Gus** propelled me out of my father's house, with the minimum of anguish and soul-searching. I moved back in with **Karen** and Charlotte and waited for normal life to resume.

I don't know how I thought I'd get off so lightly.

It took less than a day for the hired gun of Guilt and his henchmen to track me down. They worked me over good and proper and continued to do so every day. I was almost unrecognizable, beaten to a pulp by Grief, Anger and Shame.

I felt as though my father had died. In a way he had— the man that I thought had been my father no longer existed. Had never existed, in fact, except in my head. But I couldn't mourn him because he was still alive. Worse than that, he was alive, and I had chosen to abandon him. I had surrendered my right to grieve.

Daniel was wonderful. He had told me not to worry about a thing, that he would figure something out. But I couldn't let him do it. It was my family, my problem and I had to be the one to fix it. First of all, I yanked Chris's and Pete's heads out from where they were buried in the sand, and in fairness to the pair of lazy bastards, they said that they'd help to look after Dad.

Daniel had suggested contacting social services and there was a time when I would have thought that that was the most shameful thing I could do to Dad. But I was beyond feeling shame, I was all shamed out.

So I called lots of numbers. The first number I called told me to call a second number and when I called the second number they told me it was the people at the first number that should help me. Then when I called the first number again they told me that the rules had been changed and it really was the people at the second number that should be helping me.

I spent about a million hours of my employer's time on the phone and heard the words, "That's not our area" over and over again.

Eventually, because Dad was such a danger to himself and others, they made him a priority case and allocated him a social worker and a home help.

I felt wretched.

"He's okay, Lucy," Daniel promised me. "He's being taken care of."

"But not by me." I was lacerated by a sense of failure.

"It's not your job to take care of him," Daniel gently pointed out.

"I know, but . . ." I said miserably.

*     *     *

It was January. Everyone was broke and depressed.

No one went out much, but I didn't go out at all. Apart from with Daniel.

I thought about my father constantly, trying to justify leaving him alone.

It had come down to a choice between me and him, I decided. One of us could have had me, but there wasn't enough of me to be shared between two.

I chose me.

Survival was an unpleasant thing to witness. Survival at someone else's expense was an unpleasant choice to make. There had been no room for love or nobility or honor or feeling for my fellow man—in this case, Dad. It was about me and only me.

I had always thought I was a nice person, a kind, generous, selfless person. It was a shock to find that when the chips were down, the kindness and generosity were only a veneer. That I was a snarling beast just like everyone else.

I didn't like myself very much—although that was nothing new.

Meredia, Jed, and Megan were intrigued by my state of mind. Or rather, my states of mind. Every day I had a different emotion and they were eager to know all about it and offer advice and opinions.

As I said, it was January and no one got out much.

"What is it today?" they chorused when I walked into the office.

"Anger. Anger at not having had a real father when I was a little girl."

Or . . .

"Grief. I feel like the man I loved, the man I always thought was my father has died."

Or . . .

"Inadequacy. I should have been able to take care of him."

Or . . .

"Guilt. I feel so guilty for abandoning him."

Or . . .

"Jealousy. I'm jealous of people who had a normal childhood."

Or . . .

"Grief . . ."

"What, again?" demanded Meredia. "We had grief only a couple of days ago."

"Yes, I know," I said. "But it's a different kind of grief; this time it's grief for me."

We had all kinds of wonderful, metaphysical discussions.

I instigated a lot of conversations about survival in extreme circumstances.

"Remember those boys that were in the plane crash in the Andes?" I asked.

"The ones who ate the other passengers?" asked Meredia.

"And the survivors were shunned by the rest of the town when they got home for eating their neighbors?" asked Jed.

As an office, we had never stinted on reading the tabloids.

"That's right," I said. "So do you think it's better to die with honor or to get your hands good and dirty in the base, ignoble struggle for survival?" We argued it back and forth for hours, and pondered vital moral issues.

"What do you think human flesh tastes like?" asked Jed. "I think I heard someone say it was a bit like chicken."

"Chicken breast or chicken thigh?" asked Meredia

thoughtfully. "Because if it was chicken breast I wouldn't mind, but if it was chicken thigh I don't think I could."

"Me neither," I agreed. "Not unless it was in barbecue sauce."

"Do you think they cooked it or ate it raw?" asked Megan.

"Probably raw," I said.

"Shut up or I might puke," said Megan.

"Really?" We all looked at her in surprise. Megan wasn't the squeamish type.

"But you weren't out drinking last night." I was confused.

She *did* look pale. But that could have just been because her tan had finally faded.

She placed her hand on her chest and made heaving kind of actions.

"Are you really going to puke?" I asked in alarm. Jed thoughtfully placed a wastepaper basket on her lap.

The three of us stared at her, delighted with the drama, hoping that she might throw up and add some excitement to our day. But she didn't. After a few minutes she flung the basket on the floor and said, "Okay I'm fine. Let's have a show of hands. All those in favor of eating the corpses for survival?"

Three hands shot up.

"Come on, Lucy," said Jed. "Put your hand up."

"I'm not sure . . ."

"Lucy, who did you allow to survive? You or your father? Eh?"

I shamefacedly put my hand up. Then while Meredia still had her hand up, Jed tickled under her arm. She squealed and giggled and said, "Ooooh, you little . . ." Oblivious of their audience, they called each other names and pretended to wrestle. I raised my eyebrows meaningfully at Megan, and she raised hers back at me.

Gray January limped along. And my social life remained barren.

I recommenced my close relationship with Adrian in the video shop.

I tried to take out *When a Man Loves a Woman* and came home instead with Krzysztof Kieslowski's *The Double Life of Veronique*. I wanted to rent *Postcards from the Edge* and somehow ended up with *Il Postino* (the undubbed, unsubtitled version). I begged Adrian to give me *Leaving Las Vegas* but instead he gave me something called *Eine Sonderbare Liebe*, which I didn't even bother to watch.

I didn't really need to go out because there was a real life soap opera taking place in my office. Meredia and Jed had become very close. Very close *indeed*. They always left at the same time—although that was no great surprise because every employee in the building bolted from their desks the second it was five o'clock. But, more tellingly, they always *arrived* at the same time. And their behavior in the office was very loving and couply. Giggly and coy and constantly simpering and blushing—Jed seemed to have fallen hard. And they had a private little game that no one else was allowed to play, where Meredia threw Rolos or grapes in an arc across the office at Jed and he tried to catch them in his mouth, then flapped his arms together and made seal noises.

I envied them their happiness.

I was delighted that *they* were falling in love before my very eyes. Because I could no longer depend on Megan to provide me with romantic drama. She had changed. She didn't look like Megan anymore, as the sharp fall-off in the number of young men hanging around the office was testament to—now we could get out the door without having to push and shove grimly and say, "Excuse me, do you *mind?*" I couldn't figure out what was different about her and then I realized. Of course! The tan—it was no more. Winter had finally run her into the ground and stripped her of her golden, lit-from-within translucence. It had faded her from a magnificent goddess to an ordinary, sturdy girl whose hair sometimes looked greasy.

But I realized that it wasn't just her good looks that had been muted. She wasn't the breezy, happy, energetic person she used to be. She no longer tried to find out Meredia's real name. She was often sullen and snappy, and it worried me.

That was quite an achievement, considering how busy I was feeling sorry for myself, but I cared about her.

I tried to find out what was wrong—and not just out of morbid curiosity either. I drew blanks until the day I tentatively asked her if she missed Australia. She turned to me and yelled, "Okay, Lucy, I'm bloody homesick! Now, *stop* asking me what's wrong."

I knew how she felt—I had spent my whole life feeling homesick. The only difference between the two of us was that I didn't know what or where home was.

As soon as I realized that Megan's happiness was solar powered, I was anxious to give her some sun. Although I couldn't buy her a trip to Australia, I *could* buy her a gift certificate from the tanning salon near work. But when I gave it to her, she looked appalled. She stared at it like it was a warrant for her death, then finally choked out, "No Lucy, I couldn't."

And then I was *really* worried about her—it's not that Megan was a stingy woman, but she had a great deal of respect for money and especially for things that were *free*.

But, no matter how hard I tried, she continued to insist that it was far too decent of me and that she couldn't possibly accept.

So, in the end I went myself and all it did was give me eight million more freckles than I already had.

 78

The only person I saw in any kind of a social sense was Daniel. He was always available because he was still without a girlfriend, which must have been the longest gap since the day he was born. I didn't feel guilty about the time he spent with me—I reckoned I was keeping him out of harm's way and saving some poor woman from falling in love with him.

I always felt really glad to see him, but I knew it was just because he filled the fatherless vacuum in my life. And I thought it was very important to tell him that—I didn't want him to get the idea that I might, God forbid, be *attracted* to him. So every time I met him, the first thing I said was, "I'm very glad to see you, Daniel, but only because you're filling an empty space in my life." And he showed unusual restraint by not making some vulgar comment about which one of my empty spaces he'd like to be filling. Which made me sad for the days when he made suggestive remarks to me all the time.

I said the empty space thing so often, that in the end he used to beat me to it. Whenever I said, "Hi Daniel, it's lovely to see you . . ." he'd interrupt, "Yes, yes,

Lucy, I know, but it's only because I'm filling the father figure gap in your life.''

We went out two or three times a week, and somehow I never got around to telling Karen about it. I *meant* to, of course, but I was so concerned with trying to ration the number of times I saw Daniel that I didn't have the energy to tackle Karen.

At least that was what I liked to believe. And it *was* hard work trying to not see Daniel every night.

"Stop asking me out!" I scolded him, one evening while he cooked dinner for me at his apartment.

"Sorry, Lucy," he said humbly, as he chopped carrots.

"I can't let myself become too dependent on you," I complained. "There's a danger it could happen, you know, because without Dad there's a big gap in my life . . .''

". . . And your immediate instinct is to fill it," he finished for me. "You're very vulnerable right now and you can't afford to become too close to anyone."

I looked at him with admiration.

"Very good, Daniel. Now finish the sentence. Especially not who? Who should I especially not become too close to?"

"Especially not a man," he said proudly.

"Correct," I beamed. "Top marks."

I was delighted with him for knowing so much psychobabble. Especially when you considered that he was a good-looking man who enjoyed great success with women and didn't need to read up on pop psychology.

"Oh, while I think of it," I said. "Will you come to the movies with me tomorrow night?"

"Of course I will, Lucy, but didn't you just say you can't get too close to a man . . .''

"I don't mean *you*," I said airily. "*You* don't count as a man."

He threw me a hurt look.

"Oh, you know what I mean." I was exasperated. "Of course you're a man for *other* women, but you're *my* friend."

"I'm still a man," he muttered. "Even if I'm your friend."

"Daniel, don't sulk. Think about it—isn't it far better for me to be with you than with some other man that I might fall for? Well, isn't it?"

"Yes, but . . ." he trailed away. He sounded confused.

He wasn't the only one. I didn't know whether it was safe to be with Daniel because it was keeping me out of harm's way or whether I was putting myself in mortal danger of becoming too close to him. On balance I thought I was safer with him than not with him. And I kept the barriers up simply by constantly reminding him that they were there. It was okay to be with him as long as I reminded us both that it wasn't okay. Or *something* like that. All in all, it was easier not to think about it.

Occasionally I remembered the time he had kissed me, then banished the memory immediately. Because whenever I remembered it—and it really was very rarely—quick as a flash, I immediately remembered the night when he *wouldn't* kiss me, and the rush of shame that followed put an end to my reminiscences good and fast.

Anyway, Daniel and I were back on our old footing, so relaxed with each other that we could laugh together at our brief romantic-sexual encounter.

Well, almost.

Sometimes when he said to me, "Would you like another drink?" I forced a laugh and lightly replied, "Oh no, I've had enough. After all we don't want a repeat of that night out at Dad's when I tried to seduce you."

I always laughed heartily, hoping to laugh away any residual shame and embarrassment. He never really laughed at all, but then again, *he* didn't need to.

 79

January became February. Crocuses and snowdrops started to appear. People emerged from their cocoons, especially around the time they got paid and had money for the first time since the financial holocaust of Christmas. Meredia, Jed and Megan lost interest in my personal life now that they had money to go out drinking and create lives of their own. Which was a terrible shame because I still had so much to offer—not a day passed that I wasn't tortured by self-loathing and shame.

I went to see Dad once a week. Every Sunday—because I always felt suicidal on Sunday *anyway,* and it seemed a shame to waste it. And, acute and all as my self-loathing was, it was nothing compared to the hatred that Dad had for me. Of course, I warmly welcomed his disgust and venom because I felt that it was all that I deserved.

February edged into March and I was the only living thing still in hibernation. Even though Dad was being well taken care of in a physical sense, I felt *filthy* with guilt. And Daniel was the only person left that I felt comfortable whining to. No matter what people say, there *is* a time limit to the amount of time you're allowed to be in mourning, be it for a father, a boyfriend or a pair of shoes that they didn't have in your size. And Daniel's time limit was a lot longer than everyone else's.

No one at work even *listened* to me anymore. On Mondays when someone asked, "Hi, nice weekend?" and I replied, "Awful, I wish I were dead," no one lifted an eyebrow.

I think I would have gone crazy without Daniel. He was just like a therapist, except he didn't charge me forty pounds an hour, or wear beige corduroys or socks with sandals.

It wasn't always doom and gloom when I met him but, when it was, he was great. Time after time he listened to me covering the same ground, going over the same anguish again and again.

I could meet him for a drink after work and flop onto the seat beside him and say, "Don't stop me if you've heard this, but . . ." and launch into yet another saga of—let's just say—a sleepless night, or a tearful Sunday, or a miserable evening I'd had worrying or feeling guilty or ashamed about Dad. Daniel never once complained about my lack of new material. He never held up his hand like a policeman stopping traffic and said, "No, hold on! Wait a minute, Lucy, I think I know this one!"

And he would have been perfectly entitled to. Because if Daniel had heard my story of woe once, he had heard it a million times. Sometimes the wording was slightly different, but the punch line was always the same. Poor him.

"Sorry, Daniel," I said. "I wish my misery was a bit more varied. It must be very boring for you."

"It's okay, Lucy." He grinned. "I'm like a goldfish, I have a very short memory. Every time I hear it, it's as if it's for the first time."

"Well, if you're sure," I said awkwardly.

"I'm sure," he said cheerfully. "Come on and tell me again about the imaginary bargain that you've made with your father."

I flicked him a quick glance to see if he was making

fun of me, but he wasn't. "Okay," I said awkwardly, trying (once again) to find the right words to say how I felt. "It's like I've made a bargain with Dad."

"What kind of bargain?" Daniel asked, in the same kind of voice that music hall comedians said, "But how does he smell?" Straight man to my funny man. We made a great double act.

"It's all in my head," I said. "But it's like I've said, 'It's okay, Dad, I know I abandoned you, but my life isn't worth living because I hate myself so much for saving me instead of you. So, we're equal. Quits.' Am I making any sense, Dan?"

"Absolutely," he agreed, for the umpteenth time.

It surprised me to realize how highly I thought of Daniel. He had been so good to me through the whole Dad crisis.

"You're a good man," I told him, one evening, when I had paused for breath.

"No, I'm not. I wouldn't do it for anyone except you." He smiled.

"But, even so, I mustn't become too dependent on you," I added hurriedly. I hadn't said it in at least five minutes and his smile had unnerved me. I had to neutralize it. "I'm on the emotional rebound, you know."

"Yes, Lucy."

"I'm getting over the loss of my dad, you know."

"Yes, Lucy."

I wanted that twilight life to continue forever, where I didn't have any real contact with anyone except my therapist—by which I mean Daniel. Until Daniel decided that he'd had enough, which threatened to destroy the nice safe world I'd created.

He gave me no warning.

One evening we met and I said the usual, "Hi Daniel,

it's lovely to see you but only because you're filling a gap in my life,'' he held my hand and very gently said, ''Lucy, isn't it about time that this stopped?''

''Wh-what?'' I asked, feeling as if the ground had swayed beneath my feet. ''What are you talking about?''

''Lucy, the last thing I want to do is upset you, but I've been thinking and I wondered if the time has come for you to try and get over this,'' he said, in an even *more* gentle tone. The expression on my face was on the rigor mortis end of the stricken scale.

''Maybe I shouldn't have indulged you so much,'' he said. He looked sick. ''Maybe I've even been bad for you.''

''No, no,'' I hastened to say. ''You've been *good* for me.''

''Lucy, I think you should start going out again,'' he suggested in gentle tones, which did nothing but scare me.

''But I'm out now.'' I was apprehensive. Not to mention defensive. I sensed that my days in the safe haven were coming to an end.

''I mean, *out,* out,'' said Daniel. ''When are you going to start living again? Seeing other people? Going to parties?''

''When the guilt about Dad goes away, of course.'' I looked at him suspiciously. ''Daniel, you're supposed to *understand.*''

''So you can't have a life because you feel guilty about your dad?''

''Exactly!'' I hoped that meant that the subject was closed. But it wasn't.

Daniel said, ''Guilt doesn't go away on its own. You've got to make it happen.''

Oh no! I didn't want to hear that.

I decided to sway him with my womanly charms so I gave him a coy little glance from under my eyelashes.

"Please don't look at me like that, Lucy," he said. "It won't work."

"Fuck you," I muttered, then I sat in embarrassed, sullen silence.

I tried a nasty glare, but no luck with that either. I could see he meant business.

"Lucy," he said, "I don't want to upset you, so please let me help you." In fairness to him, he *did* sound as if he was in terrible anguish.

I sighed and gave in. "Okay, you mean bastard, help me then."

"Lucy, your guilt will probably get less, but it won't ever disappear completely. You'll have to learn to live with it."

"But I don't want to."

"I know, but you're going to have to. You can't just opt out of life until some time in the distant future when you don't feel guilty—it might never happen."

I had been quite happy to do just that.

"You're like the Little Mermaid," he said, suddenly changing the subject.

"Am I?" I glowed with pleasure. This conversation was much more to my liking. And my hair *did* look long and curly and sleek, now that he mentioned it.

"She had to suffer the agony of walking on blades in exchange for being able to live on dry land. You've made the same kind of bargain—you've paid for your freedom with guilt."

"Oh." No mention of my hair.

"You're a good person, Lucy, you haven't done anything wrong and you're allowed to have a nice life," he explained. "Think about it, that's all I ask."

So I thought about it. And thought about it. And thought about it. I smoked a cigarette and thought about it. I drank my gin and tonic and thought about it. While Daniel was at the bar buying me another one, I thought about it. I finally spoke.

"I've thought about it. Maybe you're right, maybe it's time to move on."

The whole truth was that perhaps I was finally becoming bored of so much unadulterated misery. *Bored* with being so self-indulgent. And I could have gone on for a lot longer than I already had—years probably—if Daniel hadn't pulled me up short.

"Great, Lucy." He was delighted. "And while I'm being mean to you, maybe you could give some thought to visiting your mother."

"What are you?" I asked sharply. "My bloody conscience?"

"And seeing as you're already pissed off at me," he grinned, "I think I might as well tell you that it's about time you stopped taking any more abuse from your dad. Stop punishing yourself. You've repaid your debt to society and your sentence is at an end."

"I'll be the judge of that," I said angrily. Stop punishing myself, indeed! It was obvious that *he* hadn't been brought up as a Catholic. I couldn't even *begin* to contemplate a life that didn't involve lots of self-flagellation.

Although now that I thought about it, maybe going easy on myself was a good idea, a very pleasant option, in fact. And, as I wavered on the brink, Daniel said something that changed everything for me.

He said, "You know, Lucy, if you feel that guilty, you can always go back to your father. Anytime you like."

The suggestion appalled me. I wouldn't do that. Not ever. And it was only *then* that I realized what Daniel had been talking about. I'd chosen freedom because that was what I had wanted. I might as well enjoy it.

I stared at him as realization dawned.

"You're right, you know," I said faintly. "Life is for living."

"God, Lucy." He sounded shocked. "There's no call for clichés."

"Bastard." I smiled.

"You can't be afraid forever," he said, making the most of my good humor. "You can't hide from your feelings, from other people." He paused for emphasis, "Lucy, you can't hide from men."

Now, that was going too far. He was trying to make me run before I could walk.

"A *boyfriend!*" I said in alarm. "You want me to get a boyfriend after all the disasters I've been through."

"Christ, Lucy, hold on," said Daniel. He grabbed my arm as if I was just about to run out into the street and proposition the first man I met. "Not immediately. I mean *sometime*, not now . . ."

"But Daniel," I wailed. "I'm such a bad judge of men. You, of all people, know how hopeless I am."

"No, Lucy, I only want you to *think* about it . . ." he said anxiously.

"I can't believe you think I'm ready for a boyfriend," I said in surprise.

"Lucy, I don't mean . . . all I'm saying is . . ."

"But I trust your judgment," I said doubtfully. "If you say it's the right thing for me, then it must be."

"It's only a suggestion, Lucy." Daniel sounded nervous.

But something had tickled the back of my brain, the memory of the fun of being in love. I vaguely remembered how nice it had been. Maybe, along with being bored by my misery, I had also become bored with being without a man.

"No, Daniel," I said thoughtfully. "Now that you mention it, maybe it's not such a bad idea."

"Wait, Lucy, I only said . . . Now that I think about it, it's a bad idea, a very bad idea, I'm sorry I ever mentioned it."

I held my hand up authoritatively.

"Nonsense, Daniel, you were right to say all this to me. Thank you."

"But . . ."

"No buts, Daniel, you're quite right. The next time there's a party going on, I'll go!" I finished decisively.

After a few triumphant minutes I said in a little voice, "But we'll still see each other, won't we? Not all the time, or anything, but you know . . . ?"

And he replied, "Of course we will, Lucy, of course we will."

It never occurred to me, not even for a moment, that Daniel might have had another reason for wanting to ease me away from him, for setting me free to fly on my own. That his concern for my independence mightn't have been entirely altruistic. That, perhaps he might have had a new girlfriend impatiently fidgeting in the wings. Anxiously waiting for me to take my final bow and exit stage left so that she could take her rightful place in the spotlight. I never doubted that his concern for me was genuine and sincere and selfless. I trusted him utterly. And because of that, I decided to go along with what he suggested.

 80

The new me. Oozing strength. Independent. Reborn. Back out there. Fighting Fit. Firm handshake. Meeting new people. Social interaction. Flirting. Strong woman. Knows her own mind.

God, it was *exhausting*.

And so *boring*. As far as I could see, what Learning to Live Again *really* meant was just staying away from Daniel. Or at least cutting down drastically on the amount of time I spent with him. And I missed him terribly. No one was as much fun as he was. But it was for my own good, even *I* could see that, and rules were rules. Anyway, it wasn't the awful cold turkey that I'd expected because he still called me every day. And I knew that I'd see him the following Sunday because I was taking him out for lunch for his birthday.

This Learning to Live Again business was easier said than done—I'd been out of circulation for too long and I had no one to play with. I gatecrashed a post-work drink with Jed and Meredia and what a mistake that was. They both behaved as if I were invisible.

The following night I went out with Dennis and, even though he had promised me a wild night, that was also a disaster. First of all he refused to go to any pubs except gay ones and I spent the night desperately trying to make eye contact with him as he twitched in his seat, watching young boys in tight white T-shirts over my shoulder. I could barely get a word of conversation out of him. And when he *did* bother to talk to me, all he spoke about was Daniel. Which was very irresponsible of him—he was feeding my habit, instead of weaning me off it.

Megan was still laid low with her Seasonal Affective Disorder because, when I suggested going out and getting drunk and picking up men, she just sighed and said she was too tired.

So that left Charlotte and Karen. And with all due respect, roommates were a bit of a last resort. I could have got drunk with them *anytime*.

"Can't you think of anything better for us to do than go to the Dog's Bollix and have drinks spilled on us by Scottish construction workers?" I complained. "Not that there's anything wrong with Scottish men," I said quickly, as Karen's face darkened.

"Leave it to me." Charlotte mysteriously tapped the side of her nose. And, with the flair of a magician pulling a rabbit out of a hat, she produced a party for us to go to on Saturday night. Her workmate's roommate's boyfriend's brother's colleague's cousin was having a party because he hadn't gotten laid in forever. For this very reason Charlotte, Karen and I were extremely welcome.

On Saturday night the preparations for the party were just like old times. Charlotte and I opened a bottle of wine and got ready together in my bedroom.

"I wonder if there'll be any nice guys there tonight?" asked Charlotte, as she tried to put mascara on her bottom lashes with a slightly drunken hand.

"I wonder if there'll be any guys there at *all*," I said doubtfully. "Especially if the guy is only having the party so that he can get a girl."

"Don't worry," said Charlotte, her hand wobbling.

"There'll *have* to be some men, and one or two of them will probably be nice."

"I don't care, as long as they're not like Gus," I said. Karen marched into the room and opened my wardrobe.

"You mean the days of you bringing home drunk, penniless lunatics, who steal our bottles of tequila, are over?" she demanded as she efficiently flicked through my hangers.

"Yes."

"Oh damn!" exclaimed Charlotte. "Give me a tissue someone, it's gotten all over my face."

"And it's all because of this business with your dad?" asked Karen, ignoring Charlotte.

"Who knows? Maybe I would have grown out of penniless musicians anyway," I said.

"Hardly," said Charlotte, as she licked a tissue and dabbed it at the mascara streaks on her cheekbones. She was loath to give up on her theory. "Let's face it, Lucy, you weren't getting any younger. Froyd says . . ."

"Oh shut up, Charlotte," snapped Karen. "Lucy where's your suede jacket, I want to wear it tonight."

I resentfully handed it over.

Eventually we were ready.

"Lucy, you look *beautiful,*" said Charlotte.

"No, I don't."

"You *do*. Do I look like I'm wearing gray blusher?"

"Not really. Anyway, you're beautiful."

Actually, you *could* still see faint traces of where she'd rubbed the mascara into her face, but the taxi was on its way and we didn't have time for Charlotte to redo her makeup. I'd send her to the bathroom when we arrived at the party.

"Karen, we must watch Lucy in action tonight," said Charlotte. "She'll find the best-looking, richest man in the room and get together with him."

"No, I won't." I didn't want to disappoint Charlotte.

My transformation couldn't be the immediate, miraculous one that she expected. "Decent men are in short enough supply as it is—why should I suddenly meet a gorgeous one who worships the ground that I walk on just because I've found out my father's an alcoholic?"

"You will." She was adamant.

"Listen to me," said Karen. "If there's a rich, good-looking man there, he's got my name on him."

The word *Daniel* hovered unspoken between Karen and me.

Then fearless Karen spoke it.

"Do you remember when I thought there was something going on with you and Daniel?" she asked with a menacing laugh. "Although I'm still not convinced that you haven't secretly got the hots for him.

"Not that it'll do you any good," she continued. "Let's face it, Lucy." She flicked her sophisticated blond glance over my short, flat-chested body. I automatically obliged her by feeling ashamed and worthless. "You're not exactly his type, are you?"

Indeed I wasn't. It was official—he had told me so. The memory of the night he had turned me down was at the forefront of my mind.

 81

At the party I spotted him immediately—the one I would have picked in my former existence. He was young, with sun-bleached surfer's hair, which was long enough to indicate that he wasn't a stockbroker. He was handsome and unreliable looking, with bright sparkly eyes. The sparkliness of his eyes had probably been achieved by chemical means. You could tell, just by looking at him, that he had never been on time for anything in his life.

His sweater was what I would have once described as individual and unique, when the word horrible would have sufficed. He was loud and lively and in the middle of telling a story that involved great sweeps of his arms. The group of people around him were all laughing uncontrollably but then again they all looked like drug addicts. He was probably telling them about one of the times he was arrested, I thought uncharitably.

I pulled myself up short. When did I get to be so bitter? It wasn't right to lump every badly dressed, long-haired young man in the same category as Gus. This blond guy might be kind and generous with a good heart and lots of money.

I stared at him, and thought, "You know, he *is* cute."

He caught me looking at him, and winked and grinned at me. I turned away.

A few minutes later, someone tapped me on the shoulder. I turned around and it was him—the cute, loud, sun-bleached jailbird.

"Hello," he said loudly. His eyes were an amazing glittery silver color. The pattern on his sweater could have brought on an epileptic fit.

"Hello." I smiled. I couldn't help it, it was completely automatic.

"I spotted you from across the room." He grinned. "And I spotted that you were spotting me too. I wondered if you'd like to come out to the conservatory with me to smoke a joint or twenty . . ."

His voice trailed away as I just stared at him. I didn't

mean to be rude but I had to check my vital signs to see if I was attracted to him. But nothing happened, I was stone cold.

"Er . . . maybe not . . . just a suggestion." He backed away from me, his smile replaced by a look of nervous apprehension. "Stupid thing to say, because I don't have any drugs, never touch them—'Just say no,' that's my motto. . . ."

He bolted back to his friends and I heard him telling them that I was an undercover policewoman. They looked collectively ashen and, as a single body, shuffled from the room.

Whatever he thought he had seen in me—the signal that I used to give out to attract men like him—had gone. It was only the ghost of it that had flickered briefly and lured him in error.

Pity, though, because he really was very cute.

Later on, I heard someone complain that there was no one at the party to buy any drugs from. I had the grace to feel guilty.

It was an awful party, the neighbors didn't even call the police. The music was terrible, there was almost nothing to drink, and not a single attractive man.

None that I liked the look of anyway.

Karen got her knickers all in a twist because of some big, beefy guy whose dad was rumored to be loaded. And, in her usual determined manner, she found someone who knew someone who knew someone who knew the big, beefy guy and ended up speaking to him.

Charlotte and I sat on the sofa while all the people milling around completely ignored us. I was bored out of my skull. Charlotte kept up a running commentary on everyone there. "See him, Lucy, the way he's got his arms by his side—a classic anal tentative," and, "See her,

Lucy, desperate for affection—probably wasn't breast-fed.''

And I muttered, "It's retentive," and, "That's her husband she's holding hands with.''

How I rued the day Charlotte had ever gotten her hands on my Psychology for Miserable Women books.

The tedium continued. But at least there was the walk to find a cab to look forward to.

Karen flitted by with the human steak.

"Girls," she said to Charlotte and me, in her put-on I'm-so-charming voice, "this is Tom. He wanted to be introduced to the two of you—God knows why!''

Charlotte and I laughed. Because we knew there would be trouble later if we didn't.

"Tom, this is Charlotte and this is Lucy.''

Up close he wasn't so bad, really. Brown eyes, brown hair, quite a kind face. It was just that I couldn't stop imagining him covered with pepper sauce.

The person beside me on the couch got up because their friend had collapsed in the bathroom. And Tom asked Karen if she wanted to sit down.

"No," she said. Because she wanted to stand beside him, of course.

"Are you sure?" he asked puzzled.

"Quite.'' She laughed gaily up at him. "I love to stand.''

"Okay," he said, *really* puzzled by then. And, to Karen's slack-jawed horror, he sat down beside me.

Quick as a flash, in a damage control exercise, Karen perched on the arm of the sofa, beside Charlotte. Actually, she really sat *on* Charlotte. Then she leaned across us so that she could talk to T-bone, almost obscuring Charlotte and me.

But she was wasting her time.

"I'm so glad I met Karen," said Tom to me.

I smiled politely.

"Because," he continued. "I've been watching you all evening and I've been trying to pluck up the courage to come and talk to you."

I smiled politely again.

*Christ!* Karen would *kill* me.

"So I couldn't believe my luck when I ended up speaking to your friend."

"What's this?" Karen smiled.

"I'm just telling Lucy how glad I am that I got talking to you," said Tom.

Karen tossed her hair back in a gesture of triumph.

"I've spent the whole night wondering how I could get to meet Lucy," he continued.

Karen froze mid-toss. Even the strands of her hair were rigid. She turned a Lucy-you-will-die-for-this-you-bitch face on me.

I shrunk back into the couch. A few days later I heard that all the plants in the house died that night.

And it wasn't as if I found Tom even remotely attractive—after all, I was almost vegetarian.

"I'm glad I was of use to you, Tom," said Karen corrosively. She stood up and stalked across the room.

Tom and I looked at each other, him in shock, me in fear. Then we both burst out laughing.

It was typical that Tom liked me. Because I didn't like him. I hadn't even noticed him. I had always found that the best way to get men interested in me was not to like them. But I had to mean it—faking it never worked. Men always knew that when I ignored them and lifted my chin haughtily, I was actually dying for it. (I quote.)

Charlotte—obviously on a death wish—ran after Karen, so I talked to meaty Tom. I was touched by his little confession about being too nervous to talk to me, etc., etc. And he seemed nice. But of course he did—he wanted to get me into bed. I almost shuddered at the thought—he was so *big,* it would be like having sex with a bull.

Not like Daniel—*he* was big, but nice big. Idly, I wondered where he was that evening. I suddenly had a horrible thought—maybe he was at another party, doing a Tom, trying to persuade a girl to come home with him. My stomach clenched in fear and I had a panicky urge to call him in the hope that I might find him at home in bed—alone.

"Oh no," I said to myself in horror, "I *warned* you this might happen." After all I'd said, had I become too dependent on Daniel?

I forced myself to sit still—I couldn't just call him and ask if he was in bed with someone. And, while I was on the subject, why did I want to?

That scared me into calming down. I had *never* been possessive about Daniel. I had never minded who he talked to, who he seduced, who he took home to his bed and whose clothes he took off and . . .

The panicky fear began to rise again. He had been without a girlfriend for a long time—and it couldn't go on forever. He was bound to meet some nice woman at some stage. But if he started going out with someone, what would happen to me? Where would I fit into his life?

What was going on, I wondered in fear. I was acting as if I was jealous, as if . . . as if . . . as if *I liked him.* No, no, I wouldn't think it! I WOULD NOT THINK IT. I nearly screamed it out loud.

My mind lurched back to the present. I tried to focus on poor Tom, because he had asked me a question and seemed to be eagerly waiting for an answer.

"What?" I asked. I felt slightly sick.

"Lucy, can I take you out some night?"

"But I don't like you, Tom," I blurted out. In fact, what I actually said was, "I don't like *you*."

He looked a little bit taken aback.

"Sorry," I said. "I wasn't thinking . . ."

But I *had* been thinking. I had become too possessive of Daniel and Daniel obviously knew it. He probably thought I had a crush on him. The nerve of him.

"I only want to take you out for dinner, Lucy," Tom said humbly. "Do you have to like me for that?"

"Sorry, Tom."

I could barely speak to him. Daniel wanted to get rid of me, I realized. That was what all that about me having to start living again was about. Little mermaid, indeed! He was just trying to prize my clinging hands from him, finger by finger. I felt a fierce burst of humiliation, which quickly became anger. Fine then, I thought in fury, I'd have nothing further to do with Daniel. I'd get a new boyfriend and that'd show him. I'd go out with Tom and we'd fall in love and be really happy.

"Tom, I'd be delighted to go out with you," I said. I wished that I was dead.

"That's great." Tom beamed. If I hadn't felt so sorry for him, it would have been nice to hit him.

"When?" I tried to force some enthusiasm into my voice.

"Now?" he asked hopefully.

With a scathing raise of an eyebrow I managed to convey that Tom was in danger of dying shortly.

"Sorry," he said in fear. "Sorry, sorry, sorry. Tomorrow night?"

"Okay."

It was a done deal. And just in time, for the party keeled over and died.

 *82*

I had every intention of never seeing Daniel again. The only problem was that the following day I was supposed to take him out for his birthday lunch. I felt that I couldn't cancel it—not only had it been arranged for weeks, but it was his *birthday*.

Perhaps I felt relieved, but I tried not to think about it. That was easy because the atmosphere between Karen and me was terrible. She wouldn't speak to me and she did regular tours of the apartment where she went to the time and trouble to open all the doors· just so she could slam them shut again.

It was very unpleasant. And I bitterly regretted having said that I'd go out with Tom. I must have been out of my mind—he was *awful* and Karen was welcome to him. I knew for a fact that I wouldn't fall in love with him and prove anything to Daniel.

The terrible fear that Daniel had met a new woman had come sneaking back while I slept. I was sure that the terror that I'd felt the previous night had been a premonition. It was no longer just a thought—it had mutated into a *premonition*.

I tried to talk sense into myself as I got ready to go out. I was fairly sure that I didn't like Daniel, *as such*. It wasn't a romantic or sexual thing that I felt for him. Immediately, memories of The Kiss flooded back uninvited but I blanked them out. (I was still so good at blanking things out—it really was a wonderful ability.) But perhaps I had come to depend on him too much as a friend? In the aftermath of the disintegration of my family had I become too fond of him?

Well, if I had, it must stop.

I was pleased with myself for being so sensible. Although it only lasted a moment. The panic started again immediately.

But what if he's in bed with her *right now?* I thought.

In the end I called him. I simply couldn't stop myself. I pretended that I had called to check where I was meeting him—even though I knew it was Green Park tube at two o'clock. And, to my relief, it didn't *sound* as if there was a woman in bed beside him. Although it was hard to be certain—Daniel's life wasn't a porno film where women shriek and giggle while they're in bed.

It was a godsend being in the doghouse with Karen, because I didn't have to make up some elaborate excuse when I left to meet Daniel. If she had been speaking to me she would have definitely been suspicious because, in an attempt to show Daniel that I wasn't a clingy loser, I was dressed to the nines. My very short dress and matching swingy coat were hardly appropriate protection from the bitterly cold March day, but I didn't care. Pride would keep me warm.

He was waiting outside Green Park tube at the appointed time. As I wobbled, shivering, toward him on my high snakeskin sandals he gave me a smile of such dazzling intensity that it nearly knocked me over. I was annoyed—and very suspicious. What was he grinning about? Was it the delight of having a new girlfriend that made his smile so broad? Was it a post-coital glow that made him look so gorgeous?

"Lucy, you look beautiful," he said. Then he kissed me on the cheek and my skin tightened and tingled. "But aren't you cold?"

"Not at all," I said vaguely, as I discreetly examined him for lovebites, chapped lips, scratches, etc.

"Where are we going, Lucy?" he asked.

I couldn't see any obvious signs of recent sexual activity on him, but as most of him was bundled up in a winter coat, that was no reason for me to breathe a sigh of relief.

"It's a surprise," I said, as I wondered if he had his coat collar up to hide a neckful of hickeys. "Come on, let's hurry, I'm freezing!"

Damn! Our eyes met and his mouth twitched as he tried not to laugh.

"Don't even think about it," I threatened.

"I wouldn't," he said humbly..

I led him to Arbroath Street and when we reached the glass front of Shore, I said "Dah, daah!"

He was impressed and I was happy. Shore was one of London's newest, grooviest restaurants, frequented by models and actresses. Or so the magazines said—this would be my first and probably my last visit.

As soon as we walked in, I realized that I had gravely underestimated *just* how groovy and happening a place Shore was. The rudeness of the staff gave it away.

The host, a young saturnine man, stared at me as if I had just squatted down in the entrance and urinated.

"Yes?" he hissed.

"A table for two in the name of . . ."

"Do you have a reservation?" he snapped.

Immediately I wanted to say, "Look, you little asshole, you're only a *receptionist,* you know. I'm *sorry* that I'm going to spend more on a meal than you get paid in a week, but ruining our lunch isn't going to bring about a redistribution of wealth. Have you thought about night classes? You could go back to school and try passing a couple of exams. Then you might get a real job.''

But because it was Daniel's birthday and I wanted everything to go beautifully, I humbly said, ''Yes, I made a reservation. The name is Sullivan.''

But I spoke to thin air. He had emerged from behind his little podium and was air-kissing a woman in Gucci flares who had come in after us.

''Kiki, darling,'' he fawned. ''How was Barbados?''

''You know—Barbados.'' She pushed past me. ''We're just off the plane. David's parking the beemer.''

She surveyed the restaurant. Daniel and I obligingly pressed ourselves back against the wall.

''Just the two of us,'' she said. ''A window table would be nice.''

''Did you . . . er . . . make a reservation?'' He discreetly coughed.

''Oh, naughty me.'' She smiled icily. ''I should have called you on the car phone. But I have every faith in you, Raymond.''

''Er, it's Maurice,'' said Raymond. He pronounced it ''Mor-eece.''

''Whatever.'' She waved a hand dismissively. ''Just get us a table and fast. David's starving.''

''Don't worry, we'll squeeze you in somewhere.'' He giggled. ''Leave it to Mor-eece.''

He consulted his book. Daniel and I merged with the wallpaper. Even though there wasn't any.

''Let's see,'' muttered Maurice anxiously. ''Table ten should be just about leaving . . .''

He continued to ignore Daniel and me.

I hate you, I thought.

If I had been alone I would have waited forever. But

because we were there for Daniel's birthday, and I wanted him to have a good time, I decided to take matters into my own hands.

"Excuse me, Maurice"—I pronounced it "Morris"—"Daniel's starving, in fact he's nearly as hungry as David. We'd like to go to our table, please. The one we *reserved.*"

Daniel burst out laughing. Maurice glared at me, snapped up two menus and gave Kiki a "Christ, can you believe it?" look. He set off across the restaurant at high speed. For some reason he seemed to have a penny between his tiny buttocks, and he took great pains not to drop it. Clenched. Very clenched.

He slung the menus on a little table and disappeared. He couldn't get away from us quickly enough. Ordinary people, ugh!

Daniel and I sat down. Daniel laughed and laughed.

"That was great, Lucy," he said.

"Sorry about that, Daniel." I felt quite tearful. "I want you to really enjoy this because it's your birthday and you've been very good to me and I've so much to thank you for and what did you do last night?"

"Sorry?" He looked confused. "What did I do last night?"

"Um, yes," I said. I hadn't meant to blurt it out like that.

"I went for a couple of pints with Chris."

"And who else?"

"No one else."

Phew.

The relief was great for about thirty seconds. Until I realized that there were thousands more Saturday nights in the future, stretching out into infinity. And on every single one of them there was a chance that Daniel would meet a woman.

That subdued me so much that I could barely listen to him. He was saying something about us going to see some comedian that evening.

"No, Daniel, wait," I said quickly. "I can't go out with you tonight."

"Can't you?"

Was he disappointed? I wondered hopefully.

"I've got a hot date," I said.

"Really? That's great, Lucy." Did he have to sound so bloody happy for me?"

"Yes, it *is* great." I felt defensive and angry. "He's not drunk and penniless. He has a job and a car and Karen even liked him."

"Great," he said—again!

I nodded curtly.

"Well done," he said enthusiastically.

*Well done?* I thought angrily. Have I been that pathetic?

The day had suddenly clouded over. I sat in silence. Birthday or no birthday, I felt much too angry to be nice to him.

"So I won't be seeing quite so much of you from now on," I said.

"I understand, Lucy," he said nicely.

I wanted to cry.

I sat and sullenly stared at the table. Daniel must have picked up on my mood because, unusually for him, he also became very subdued.

Despite the rudeness of the staff, the lunch was not a success. The food was nice, but I didn't want to eat it. I was too pissed off with Daniel. How dare he be glad for me? As if I was handicapped or something.

Luckily, the horribleness of the staff gave Daniel and me something to talk about. Every single one of them was so patronizing, condescending and good, plain, old-fashioned rude that toward the end of the meal we began to tentatively communicate again.

"Asshole." Daniel gave me a little smile as our waiter ignored us when we wanted to order coffee.

"Stupid bastard," I smilingly agreed.

When the bill came we scuffled over it.

"No, Daniel," I insisted. "This is on me, for your birthday."

"If you're sure?"

"I'm sure." I smiled. But not for long when I saw how much I had to pay.

"Let me pay half," suggested Daniel when he saw my appalled expression.

"No way."

More scuffles. Daniel tried to grab the bill from my hand, I pulled it away from him, etc., etc. In the end he graciously let me pay.

"Thanks for a lovely lunch, Lucy," he said.

"It wasn't lovely, though, was it?" I asked sadly.

"Yes, it was," he said stoutly. "I wanted to come here and now I know what it's like."

"Promise me something, Daniel," I asked fervently.

"Anything."

"That you will never knowingly, willingly come here again."

"I promise, Lucy."

I walked him to the tube station, then I walked to the bus stop. I felt very depressed.

Tom was the perfect gentleman.

He rang my doorbell at seven exactly, as arranged. And, as arranged, he didn't come up to the apartment. What he lacked in graceful, elegant, emaciated good looks he more than made up for in the instinct of self-preservation. He was no fool, and he suspected that Karen was a sore and vengeful loser.

I ran downstairs to where he waited in his car. I got a slight shock when I saw him sitting behind the wheel. There was nothing wrong—it was just that he looked as if he'd be more at home hanging from a butcher's hook. He made it worse by wearing a red shirt. I hoped he would never get his nose pierced.

He took me to a restaurant—the *same* Emperor's New Clothes restaurant that I'd taken Daniel to for lunch. Maurice was still on duty. He stared with loathing and disbelief when Tom stampeded through the door and pawed the ground with me at his side.

Tom wined and dined me, then tried to get me to go back to his apartment, with a view to sixty-nining me, I suppose.

He didn't have a chance.

Nice guy, but I wouldn't have bedded him if he was the last man on the planet. And he *loved* me for it. His eyes shone with admiration as I turned him down.

"Would you like to go out during the week?" he asked eagerly. "We could go to the theater."

"Maybe," I agreed doubtfully.

"Well, it doesn't have to be the theater," he said anxiously. "We could go bowling. Or go-karting. Whatever you like, really."

"I'll see," I said. I felt bad. "I'll call you."

"Okay," he said. "Here's my number. And here's my work number. And here's my mobile. And here's my fax number. And here's my e-mail address. And here's my real address.

"Thank you."

"Call anytime," he said, fervently. "Anytime at all. Day or night."

 *83*

Charlotte dropped the bombshell on Thursday evening. She rushed in from work, all agog.

"Guess who I met?" she screeched.

"Who?" Karen and I asked in unison.

"Daniel," she beamed. "And he was with his new girlfriend."

I couldn't see my face, but I *felt* myself go pale.

"His new what?" hissed Karen. She didn't look too hot herself.

"Yes," said Charlotte. "And he looked gorgeous. And he seemed really glad to see me . . ."

"What's she like, the bitch?" hissed Karen.

Thank God for Karen. She asked all the awful questions that I couldn't.

"Beautiful!" enthused Charlotte. "Really tiny and dainty, I felt like an elephant next to her. And she has lots of dark, curly hair. She's like a little doll, a bit like Lucy. And Daniel is *crazy* about her, you should have seen his body language . . ."

"Lucy isn't like a little doll," Karen interrupted.

"Yes, she is."

"No, she isn't. There's a difference between being short and being a little doll, you fool."

"Well, her face looked like Lucy. And her hair," shouted Charlotte.

"I thought you said she was beautiful," sniffed Karen.

At first I thought she was sniffing dismissively. But when sniff followed sniff, followed by heaving shoulders, followed by outright sobbing, I realized that she was crying.

Lucky her. In her position of ex-girlfriend she was allowed. I had no rights.

"The rotten, stinking, lousy bastard," she fumed. "How dare he be happy without me? He wasn't supposed to meet someone else, he was supposed to find out that he couldn't live without me. I hope he loses his job and that his house burns to the ground and that he gets syphilis, no wait . . . AIDS, no wait . . . *acne,* he'd hate that, and that he's in a car crash and his fuck-truck is totaled and that he's arrested for a crime he didn't commit and . . ."

The usual kind of things you say when your ex-boyfriend has the audacity to meet someone new.

Charlotte patted and shushed her, but I just walked away. I felt nothing for her, I was too busy feeling for me.

I was in shock.

I had just realized that I was in love with Daniel.

I could hardly believe my stupidity, not to mention my poor judgment. I had suspected for some time that I was actually attracted to him. That had been very careless of me. But to be in love with him, to *love* him—that was nothing short of criminal negligence.

And to think of how I had laughed at all the other women who had fallen for him over the years. Little did I think it would happen to me. Doubtless there was a great lesson to be learned from it—don't mock lest ye be mocked yourself, or something like that.

I couldn't think straight because the sharp tearing pain of jealousy was driving me demented.

Worse than the jealousy was the fear that I had lost

Daniel forever. It had been such a long time since he'd been out with anyone, that I had started to think of him as *mine*.

Big mistake.

I did the most foolish thing I could think of—I called him.

He was the only one who could comfort my pain, even though he was the one who had caused it. It was an unusual situation to cry on a friend's shoulder about my broken heart, when the person whose shoulder I was crying on was actually the one who had broken my heart. But I never seemed to do things normally.

"Daniel, are you alone?" I expected him to say no.

"Yes."

"Can I come over?"

He didn't say, "It's late" or "What do you want?" or "Can't it wait until tomorrow?"

He just said, "I'll come and get you."

"No," I said. "I'll get a taxi, I'll see you soon."

"Where are you going?" Karen caught me trying to sneak out the front door.

"Out," I said, with a soupçon of defiance. Misery had made me less afraid of her.

"Out where?"

"Just out."

"You're going to see Daniel, aren't you?"

She was either very perceptive or else highly paranoid and obsessed.

"Yes." I met her eyes.

"You stupid bitch, you haven't got a chance with him."

"I know." I made for the stairs.

"Are you still going?" she asked in angry surprise.

"Yes."

*"DO NOT GO,"* she barked in staccato fashion.

"Says who?" By then I was halfway down the stairs, where it was a lot easier to be brazen.

"I forbid you to," she said.

"I'm going."

She was incandescent with rage. She could barely speak.

"I don't want to make you see a fool of yourself," she finally managed to sputter out.

"Maybe not, but you'd love to see me make a fool of myself."

"Come back here!"

"Get lost," I said bravely and bolted.

"I'll wait up for you!" she screamed. "You'd better come home. . . ."

 84

In the taxi, on the way over, I decided that the only thing I could do was tell Daniel why I was so upset—despite the Greek chorus in my head begging me not to.

"You know that the last thing you should ever do is tell the man you're in love with, that you're in love with him!" they sang. "*Especially,* when he's not in love with you."

"I know," I said in exasperation. "But it's different with me and Daniel. He's my friend, he'll talk me out of it. He'll tell me how horrible he is to his girlfriends."

"Get someone else to talk you out of it," they sang. "There's a world full of people—why pick on him?"

"He'll take away the pain, he'll make me feel better."

"But . . ."

"He's the only one who can," I said with firm finality.

"You're not fooling us," the chorus sang. "We know you're up to something."

"Shut up, I'm not," I protested.

I understood that Victorian stuff about, "He must never know how much I love him, I could not bear his pity." Especially if the man wasn't very nice and would laugh and tell his friends about it when they went shooting grouse. But it didn't apply to me, I decided. I didn't need my dignity with Daniel.

When he opened the door to me, I was so happy to see him that my heart leaped.

Dammit, I thought, so it's true, I really *am* in love with him.

I ran straight into his arms—being his friend had lots of advantages that I had no intention of giving up just because he had gotten himself a new girlfriend.

I clung to him tightly and—to give him credit—he clung on to me pretty tightly also.

He must have thought that I was behaving most oddly but, being the decent kind of guy he was, he went along with it. I would explain in a little while, I decided. But for the moment I was staying where I was. He was still my friend, I was still allowed to be hugged by him. And for a few moments I could pretend that he was my lover.

"Sorry about this, Daniel, but I need you to be my friend."

A lie of course—but I couldn't really say, "Sorry about this, Daniel, but I want to marry you and have your children."

"I'll always be your friend, Lucy," he murmured as he stroked my hair.

Thanks for nothing, I thought uncharitably. But only briefly. He was a great friend—it was hardly his fault that I'd been foolish enough to fall in love with him.

After a while I felt strong enough to disentangle myself from him.

"So what's wrong?" he asked. "Is it your dad?"

"Oh no, nothing like that."

"Tom?"

"Who? Oh no, poor Tom, not him. Why do the ones we don't love always fall in love with us, Daniel?"

"I don't know, Lucy, but they do."

You don't know the half of it, I thought nervously. I took a deep breath. "Daniel, I need to talk to you."

But when I actually tried to tell him what was wrong with me, it wasn't as easy as I had thought it would be. In fact, it was really awkward and embarrassing.

The romantic idea I had harbored of flying to him and expecting him to magically kiss away my pain had evaporated. He had a girlfriend, for God's sake. I was only his friend. I had no rights over him. What could I say?—"Daniel, I want you to break up with your new girlfriend." Hardly.

"Lucy, what do you want to talk to me about?" he asked, after the seconds had ticked by and I still hadn't said anything.

I looked at my hands for ages before I found the right words.

"Charlotte said she met you with a girl and I was, um, jealous," I finally managed to blurt out. I couldn't meet his eyes, and I *cringed*.

Maybe telling him hadn't been a good idea.

Maybe it had been a very bad idea.

I shouldn't have come, I realized, I must have been

crazy. I should have just gone to bed and waited it out. The pain would have gone eventually.

"Only because she was short with dark hair," I added quickly, in an attempt to recover lost ground and lost dignity. I had been wrong about the dignity—I *did* need it with him. "I've no problems with you screwing around with big blond girls, but I keep remembering that night out at Dad's when you turned me down and I thought it was because I wasn't your type. And it didn't feel very nice when Charlotte said that the girl she met you with looked a bit like me, because what was wrong with me . . . ?"

"Oh, Lucy." He kind of half-laughed. At me or with me? Was it good or bad?

"I suppose Sascha does look a bit like you," he said. "I hadn't noticed, but now that you mention it . . ."

*Sascha.* Why couldn't she have been called Madge?

"Anyway, that's all that was wrong with me," I said briskly, in a very belated attempt to recover lost ground. "Nothing at all the matter, I've overreacted as usual. You know me. Well, it's been good to get it off my chest. But I must be off now . . ."

I stood up to leave and if I had left then, that second, I would have missed the arrival of my anger. But no, I met it at the door as it staggered in, gasping and panting, worn out from the crosstown journey. "Sorry, I'm late," it wheezed, clutching its chest. "Awful traffic. But I'm here now . . ." And with that I turned around on Daniel with sudden fury.

"You could have just told me, you know, that you had a new girlfriend. Instead of giving me all that . . . that . . . *crap,*" I spat, "about me needing to get out more. You only had to tell me that I was cluttering up your life and that *Sascha* needed you more than I did. I would've understood, you know.''

He opened his mouth to say something but I beat him to it.

''If you wanted me out of the way, then you only had to say. Did you think I'd mind, did you think I'd be jealous? The nerve of you! You think you're gorgeous, don't you? That every woman is crazy about you.''

Once again he tried to say something, it seemed to be some sort of denial, but he didn't stand a chance.

''We're supposed to be friends, you know, Daniel. So how could you pretend that you were *concerned* about me? That you cared about me?''

''But . . .''

''When it's obvious that the only person you care about is yourself!''

That was the part in most arguments when the angry shouting changes into tearful wobbling. This one was no exception—you could have set your watch by it. My voice veered off the trembly end of the scale and I realized that I was dangerously close to crying. But still I didn't leave. Like a fool I was waiting in the hope that he might be nice to me, that he might say something to make me feel better.

''I wasn't pretending,'' he protested. ''I really *was* concerned for you.''

I hated the look of pity on his face.

''Well, there's no need,'' I said nastily. ''I can look after myself.''

''Can you really?'' He sounded pathetically hopeful.

How dare he! ''Of course, I can,'' I threw at him.

''That's great,'' he said.

How could he be so cruel, I wondered, as pain tore through me.

Easily, I realized. Very easily. He'd done it lots of times

to lots of other women, why should I get special treatment?

"Goodbye, Daniel. I hope things work out for you and the beautiful Sascha," I said sarcastically.

"Thanks, Lucy, and the best of luck with rich Tom." He matched my sarcasm.

"What are *you* being so nasty about?" I asked in angry surprise.

"What do you think?" His voice had suddenly gone up several decibels.

"How the fuck should I know?" I shouted back.

"You're not the only one who's jealous." he yelled. He looked furious.

"I know I'm not!" I said. "But, to be quite honest, Daniel, Karen isn't really my concern right now."

"What the hell are you talking about?" he asked. "I'm talking about *me!* I'm fucking jealous too! I've spent months waiting for the right time, waiting for you to get over your dad. I did everything I could think of to stop myself making a pass at you. I was so patient, it nearly killed me."

He paused for breath. I stared at him, unable to speak. Before I could take it all in he began shouting again.

"And then!" he roared into my face. "And then, when I finally manage to convince you to start thinking about having a relationship with a man, you go and get off with someone else. I meant *me,* I wanted you to think about having a relationship with *me,* and instead some rich, lucky bastard gets you!"

My head raced as I tried to take it all in.

"Wait a minute, wait a minute, why is Tom a lucky bastard?" I asked. "Because he's rich?"

"No!" Daniel shouted. "Because he's going out with you, of course!"

"But he's not going out with me," I said. "I only went out with him once and that was just to annoy you. Not that it worked."

"Not that it worked!" sputtered Daniel. "Of course it worked. I got so drunk on Sunday night that I was too sick to go to work on Monday."

"Really?" I asked, momentarily sidetracked. "Were you throwing up? That kind of sick?"

"Couldn't eat a thing until Tuesday evening," he said.

There was a little silence and for a moment we were just Daniel and Lucy again.

"What was that part that you said about wanting to make a pass at me?" I asked.

"Nothing, forget it," he said sulkily.

"Tell me!" I shouted.

"Nothing to say," he muttered. "It was just that I could hardly keep my hands off you, but I knew I had to because you were so vulnerable. If anything had happened with us I'd always be afraid that you had only done it because you were all mixed up.

"That was why I gave you that talk about coming back to the land of the living," he said. "I wanted you to know your own mind and be able to make decisions so that when I asked you out and if you said yes, I wouldn't feel like I was taking advantage of you."

"Ask me out?" I said, carefully.

"Out, *out*," said Daniel, sheepishly. "As in boyfriend and girlfriend out."

"Really?" I asked. "Are you serious? So all that stuff about me meeting people wasn't just to get me out of the way to make room for Sascha."

"No."

"Who's this Sascha anyway?" I asked jealously.

"A girl from work."

"And does she look like me?"

"I suppose there's a superficial resemblance. Although she's not half as beautiful as you," he said idly. "Or as funny or as sexy or as cute or as smart."

I sat very still. That sounded promising. But not promising enough.

"How long have you been going out with her?" I asked.

"But I'm not going out with her." He sounded annoyed.

"But Charlotte said . . ."

"Please!" Daniel put his hand to his forehead, as if he had a headache. "I'm sure Charlotte said plenty and you know how fond of her I am, but she doesn't always get things right."

"So, you're *not* going out with .Sascha?" I asked.

"No."

"Why not?"

"I didn't think it was fair to go out with her when I'm in love with you."

My brain went into shock. The words hit home long before the feelings arrived.

"Oh," I said in surprise.

I couldn't think of anything to say. I would have settled for him having a little crush on me.

God, this was great.

"I shouldn't have said that." Daniel looked miserable.

"Why not? Isn't it true?"

"Of course, it's true. I don't go around telling women I love them at the drop of a hat. But I don't want to scare you. Please, Lucy, forget I said it."

"I will not," I said irritably. "That's the nicest thing anyone has ever said to me."

"Really?" he said hopefully. "You mean you . . ."

"Yes, yes." I waved my arm distractedly. I wanted to think about what he had said to me. I had no time to bother with him.

"I love you too," I added. "I think I must have for a really long time."

Happiness and relief began to trickle through me, increasing to a steady flow, then gushed as though from a broken pipe. But I had to be sure.

"Are you really in love with me?" I asked him suspiciously.

"Oh God, yes."

"Since when?"

"For a long time."

"Since Gus?"

"Since long before Gus."

"Why didn't you ever tell me?"

"Because you would have screeched with laughter and humiliated me . . ."

"I would *not* have!" I was outraged.

"Yes, you would."

"Would I?"

"Oh yes, Lucy."

"Well, maybe I would," I reluctantly agreed. "Oh, sorry, Daniel." I was passionately apologetic. "But I *had* to be mean to you, because you were just too attractive. And that's actually a compliment," I added.

"Really?" he asked. "But all the guys you went out with were completely different from me—how could I compete with someone like Gus?"

He was right—until recently I couldn't have coped with a boyfriend who didn't have a terrible credit rating and a drinking problem.

I thought about it some more.

"Are you really, *really* in love with me?"

"Yes, Lucy."

"No, I mean *really?*"

"Yes, really."

"In that case, can we go to bed?"

 85

Astonished by my brazenness, I took him by the hand and led him into his bedroom.

I was torn between acute lust and acute embarrassment. Because I was afraid that it could still go horribly wrong.

It was all very well for him to go around telling me he loved me, but the real test, the real issue was the bed one.

What if I was terrible in bed?

What about the fact that we'd been friends for more than ten years? The potential cringe factor was high. How could we possibly be all gooey and romantic about each other and not laugh?

What if he thought I was hideous? He was used to women with huge breasts. What would he say when he saw my fried eggs?

I was so nervous that I almost changed my mind.

But not quite.

I had a chance to sleep with him and I fully intended to avail of it. I loved him. But I also lusted after him.

However, after the flying start where I brazenly took his hand, I ran out of trollopy steam. Once I got him into the bedroom, I didn't really know what to do. Should I drape myself seductively on his duvet? Should I shove him onto the bed and jump on top of him? But I couldn't, it was too mortifying.

I perched on the edge of his bed. He sat down beside me.

God, this was so much easier when I was drunk.

"What's wrong?" he whispered.

"What if you think I'm hideous?"

"What if you think *I'm* hideous?" he asked.

"But you're gorgeous." I giggled.

"So are you."

"I'm so nervous," I whispered.

"I am too."

"I don't believe you."

"But I am, honestly," he said. "Here, feel my heart."

That made me edgy. In the past I had submitted my hand for the alleged feeling of a heart and instead my hand had been placed on the young man's erect member and then rubbed up and down said member at high speed.

But Daniel really did place my hand on his heart. And, yes, there did seem to be a fair amount of commotion going on in his chest.

"I love you, Lucy," he said.

"I love you, too," I said shyly.

"Give me a kiss," he said.

"Okay." I turned my face up to his, but I closed my eyes. He kissed my eyes, and my eyebrows, and along my hairline and all the way down to my neck. Light, tantalizing kisses that were almost unbearably pleasurable. Then he kissed the corner of my mouth and gently pulled at my lower lip with his teeth.

"Knock off the arch-seducer stuff," I complained, "and kiss me properly."

"Well, if my form of kissing is not to Madam's satisfaction . . ." He laughed.

Then he did the smile thing that he did so well. And I kissed him—I couldn't help myself.

"I thought you said you were nervous," he said.

"Shush." I put a finger to my lips. "I nearly forgot about it for a second."

"How about if I lie down on the bed and you lie here next to me in my arms?" he asked as he pulled me down next to him on the bed. "Is that too arch-seducery for you?"

"No, that was nice and clumsily done," I said to his chest.

"Any chance that you might kiss me again, Lucy?" he whispered.

"Okay," I whispered back. "But I don't want any slick moves from you—like you taking my bra off on the first try."

"Don't worry, Lucy, I'll fumble."

"And you're not to say 'What's that, Lucy?' and take my panties out from behind my ear. Do you hear?" I said grumpily.

"But that's my party trick," he said. "It's the most spectacular thing I do in bed."

I kissed him again and I relaxed a bit. It was wonderful lying so close to him, inhaling the Daniel smell, touching his beautiful face. God, he was sexy.

"Do you really love me?" I asked again.

"Lucy, I love you so much."

"No, I mean, do you really, *really* love me?"

"I really, *really* love you," he said, looking into my eyes. "More than I've ever loved anyone, more than you can imagine."

I relaxed for a second. But only for a second.

"Really?" I asked.

"Really."

"No, Daniel, I mean, really, *really?*"

"Really, *really.*"

"Okay."

There was a little pause.

"You don't mind my asking, do you?" I asked.

"Not at all."

"It's just that I've got to be sure."

"I completely understand. Do you believe me?"

"I believe you."

We lay smiling at each other.

"Lucy?" asked Daniel.

"What?"

"Do you really love me?"

"Daniel, I really love you."

"No, but, Lucy," he said awkwardly. "I mean do you *really* love me? As in really, *really?*"

"I really, *really* love you, Daniel."

"Really?"

"Really."

Very, very slowly, he took off my clothes, skillfully managing to snag zippers and yank things that shouldn't have been yanked. Every time he opened a button he kissed me for about an hour before he opened the next one. He kissed me everywhere. Well, almost everywhere, thankfully he left my feet alone. Fergie had a lot to answer for—men seemed to think that they had to suck toes before they had fulfilled their bedtime duties. A few years ago, it had been cunnilingus—the watching paint dry of sex, I always felt. I didn't like men going near my feet, not unless I'd had plenty of warning—enough of a warning to have had a pedicure. He kissed me and opened buttons, kissed me and peeled my shirt off one shoulder, kissed me again, peeled my shirt off my other shoulder, kissed me again, didn't comment on the grayness of my white panties, kissed me again, said my breasts weren't like fried eggs, kissed me again, said they were more like hamburger buns, kissed me again. "You're so beautiful, Lucy," he said, over and over again. "I love you."

Until I had nothing on.

There was something very erotic about being naked while he was still dressed.

I clamped my arms around my chest and wrapped my-self up in a ball.

"Get your clothes off," I giggled.

"You're so romantic, Lucy," he said, peeling one arm off my chest, then the other.

"Don't hide yourself," he said. "You're too beautiful."

He gently forced my knees away from my chest.

"Get lost," I said, trying to hide my excitement. "How come I'm not wearing a stitch and you're still fully dressed?"

"I can take my clothes off, if you want," he teased.

"Do it then," I said, trying to be brisk.

"Ask me."

"No."

"*You'll* have to do it, in that case."

I took off his clothes. My fingers were trembling so much that I could hardly open the buttons of his shirt. But it was worth it.

He had such a beautiful chest, such smooth skin, such a flat stomach.

I traced the line of hair from his bellybutton with my fingernail, as far as the waistband of his trousers and a shiver ran through me when I heard him gasp.

Out of the corner of my eye, I had a quick look at the groin area of his pants, and was appalled and thrilled when I saw the way the fabric strained.

Eventually I plucked up enough courage to slowly start

opening his pants. But I wasn't used to men in suits. Daniel's trousers had a system of buttons and zips that could rival Fort Knox.

Eventually we liberated his straining erection.

He passed the underpants test. Which was more than could be said for me. My panties had seen better days, most of them inside a washing machine, mistakenly put in with a black wash.

He was gorgeous—and something that made him even more attractive to me—he wasn't perfect. Although his body was beautiful, it wasn't one of those muscular elaborately patterned ones that Chippendales seem to have.

The feel of his skin on my skin was indescribable. Everything felt so sensitive, the skin on the inside of my arms tingled as I wrapped them around his back. The feel of the roughness of his thighs against the softness of mine made me weak, his hardness against my wetness was explosive.

All embarrassment had gone. Only desire remained. When I caught his eye I no longer felt a hysterical urge to laugh. We'd passed over the line—we were no longer Daniel and Lucy, we were a man and a woman.

We hadn't mentioned birth control, but when the time came we were both responsible adults living in the HIV positive nineties.

He produced a condom and I helped him put it on. And then, we . . . um, you know . . .

He came in about three seconds. It was mind-blowingly erotic to see Daniel's face scrunched up in ecstasy, ecstasy that I'd caused.

"Sorry, Lucy," he gasped. "I couldn't stop myself, you're so beautiful and I've wanted you for so long."

"I thought you were supposed to be great in bed,"

I complained teasingly. "I never heard that you were a premature-ejaculation merchant."

"I'm not," he protested anxiously. "I haven't done that since I was a teenager. Just give me five minutes and I'll prove it to you."

I lay in the circle of his arms and he kept up the constant volley of kisses and stroked my back and my thighs and my stomach.

And in an admirably short time, he made love to me again.

The second time lasted for much longer and he did it achingly slowly and tantalizingly and with all the attention focused on me and what I wanted. No one had ever been as selfless and giving in bed to me before. And I climaxed as I never had before, shuddering and trembling, my eyes wide with shock and pleasure.

This time when he came, he kept his eyes open and looked at me. I nearly dissolved, it was so erotic.

We hugged each other fiercely, we couldn't get close enough.

"I wish I could unzip my skin and put you inside me," he said. And I knew what he meant.

We lay in silence for a while.

"There now, that wasn't too bad, was it?" asked Daniel. "What were you afraid of?"

"Lots of things," I laughed. "That you might think I had a horrible body. That you might make me do weird stuff."

"You have a *beautiful* body. And what kind of weird stuff?"

"Well," I explained, "there are some men who say things like, 'Can you just stand on your head, here, don't worry about the pain, I'm told it gets easier to bear after a while. Now, keeping your legs at a one-thirty-degree angle to each other, I'm going to enter you from behind, now you can move your entire body in a kind of pincer like movement, approximately eight inches, no, I said *eight* inches, that's more like ten—stupid bitch, are you trying to kill me?'—that kind of thing.''

He laughed and laughed, and that felt wonderful too.

And then, more sleepily, more relaxed, we made love again.

"What time is it?" I asked later.

"About two."

"Do you have to work in the morning?"

"Yes, do you?"

"Yes, I suppose we should get some sleep," I said.

But we didn't.

I was starving, so Daniel went to the kitchen and came back with a packet of chocolate cookies, and we lay in bed and ate them and hugged each other and kissed each other and talked about nothing in particular.

"I should join a gym," he said ruefully, poking a finger into his stomach. "If I had known that this was going to happen, I would have joined months ago."

That, more than anything, endeared him to me.

When we finished the cookies, he commanded me, "Sit up."

I sat.

He brushed the sheets with vigor.

"I can't have my woman sleeping on chocolate cookie crumbs," he said.

As I smiled at him, the phone rang and I jumped about a foot. Daniel answered it.

"Hello, oh hello, Karen, yes, I *am* in bed actually."

A pause.

"Lucy?" he asked slowly, as if he'd never heard such a name. "Lucy *Sullivan?*"

Another pause.

"Lucy Sullivan, your *roommate? That* Lucy Sullivan? Yes, she's right here beside me. . . . Yes, right here beside me in bed," he said. "Would you like to speak to her?"

I made all kinds of frantic denial actions and made a cross of my two index fingers and held them toward the phone.

"Oh yes," said Daniel cheerfully. "Three times. Wasn't it three times, Lucy?"

"Wasn't what three times?" I asked.

"The number of times I've made love to you in the last couple of hours."

"Um, yes, three," I said faintly.

"Yes, it was definitely three, Karen. Although we might do it again before the night is over. Is there anything else you need to know?"

I heard screaming and ranting from Karen. Even *I* heard the crunch when she banged down the phone.

"What did she say?" I asked.

"She said she hopes we give each other AIDS."

"Is that all?"

"Er, yes."

"Come on, Dan, what else did she say?"

"Lucy, I don't want to upset you . . ."

"You've *got* to tell me now."

"She said that she slept with Gus when you were going out with him."

He looked at me anxiously. "Have I upset you?"

"No, I'm kind of relieved. I always felt that there was someone else. But are *you* upset?"

"Why would I be upset? I wasn't going out with Gus."

"No, but you were going out with Karen when I was going out with Gus. If she slept with Gus, then . . ."

"Oh, I *see*," he said cheerfully. "It means that she two-timed me."

"Do you mind?" I asked anxiously.

"Of course I don't mind. I couldn't care less about Karen sleeping with him. It was *you* sleeping with him that bothered me."

We lay in silence, the circle of bliss ruptured.

"I'll have to move out," I said finally.

"You can move in here," he offered.

"Don't be ridiculous," I said. "We've only been going out with each other three and a half hours. Isn't it a bit soon to be talking about living together?"

"Living together?" Daniel sounded shocked. "Who mentioned living together?"

"You did."

"No, I didn't. I'm far too frightened of your mother to suggest living in sin with her only daughter."

"Well, in that case, what *are* you talking about?"

"Lucy," he said sheepishly, "I was, er, you know wondering if . . ."

"What?"

"Would there be any chance . . . ? You know . . . ?"

"Any chance of what?"

"You'll probably think I have an awful nerve asking, but I love you so much and . . ."

"Daniel," I begged. "*Please* tell me what you're on about."

"You don't have to give me your answer straight away, or anything."

"My answer to what?" I pleaded.

"Take forever to think about it, as long as you like."

"To think about WHAT?" I yelled.

"Sorry, I didn't mean to annoy you, but, it's just that, um, well, er . . ."

"Daniel, what are you trying to say?"

He paused, took a deep breath and blurted out, "Lucy Carmel Sullivan, will you marry me?"

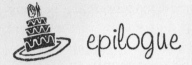 epilogue

Hetty never came back to work. She divorced Dick, left
Roger, got rid of the tweed skirts, bought lots of leggings,
enrolled in Women's Studies and is now happily romantically involved with an earnest Swedish woman called Ag-
netha. According to Meredia neither of them shave under
their arms.

Frank Erskine never came back to work either, he took
early retirement and left without fanfare. Apparently he
plays a lot of golf.

Adrian now only works weekends at the video shop
because he's taking a film-making course, where I hope
he meets a nice girl who knows her Walt Disney from her
Quentin Tarantino.

Daniel's Ruth, the woman he was going out with before
Karen, was in the *News of the World* for having sex with
a politician.

Jed moved in with Meredia and they both seem to be
blissfully happy. Despite his small stature he is very protective of large Meredia, and gets many opportunities to
prove it.

Meredia's real name is Valerie and she's thirty-eight. I
found out by accident when I was called to Personnel for
being late once too often. Her record file was just lying open
in Blandina's filing cabinet and I couldn't help but see.

I haven't told Megan. In fact, I haven't told anyone.

Charlotte still hasn't found a man to take her seriously and is talking about having a breast reduction. She is going to apply to study psychology. Just as soon as she's learned how to spell it.

Karen started going out with Simon shortly after Daniel and I got together, and the pair of them have matching His'n'Hers lifestyles. They buy a lot of expensive clothes and go to bars that have only been open a week and that are photographed for architectural magazines.

Dennis still hasn't found Mr. Right, although he's having a lot of fun looking. He had a bad knock when Michael Flatley left the cast of Riverdance, but he's over it now.

Megan is pregnant.

And Gus is the father. Apparently they've been together since the summer that I was allegedly going out with him. Megan even wrote Gus's farewell speech to me. Although I haven't seen Gus, I gather that imminent fatherhood hasn't made him any less irresponsible. Poor Megan looks constantly exhausted and miserable. I feel really sorry for her and I'm not saying that in the way that you do when you don't feel sorry for the person at all and instead you really hate them. My heart genuinely goes out to her.

My mother is still living with Ken Kearns and they're like love-struck teenagers. Ken has new false teeth, they look like expensive, deluxe, top of the line ones. My mother looks younger and younger every time I see her. Soon they won't serve her in pubs. Mum and I have had a tentative reunion. And although we're not the best of pals yet, we're working on it.

My father is still drinking, but he's being taken care of. He has a social worker and home help. Chris, Peter and I take turns visiting him. Whenever it's my turn, Daniel comes with me, which is great because it means that Dad has to divide his insults between the two of us. I still feel guilty, I suppose I always will, but it's only guilt and it's not going to kill me.

Daniel keeps asking me to marry him. And I keep telling him to get lost. "Be practical," I say. "Who would give me away? Even if Dad didn't hate me he still wouldn't be sober enough to lurch up the aisle with me." But the real reason that I won't agree to marry Daniel is because I'm afraid of being jilted at the altar. I obviously haven't got used to a guy being nice to me yet. But Daniel says that he'll always love me and never leave me and that, short of lopping off his penis and presenting it to me in a jar of preservative, getting married is the most extreme thing he can think of to convince me of his unending devotion.

I've told him I'll think about it. The getting married part, I mean. Not the lopping off of his . . . oh, you know what I mean.

And if we do get married I want Mrs. Nolan as my matron of honor.

Daniel swears he loves me. He certainly *acts* as if he does.

And, you know, I'm halfway to believing him.

One thing I'm sure of, I love Daniel.

So, watch this space. . .

*Wm* WILLIAM MORROW        ▦ Perennial

## New in hardcover from Marian Keyes:

### ANGELS

ISBN 0-06-000802-4 (hardcover)

Margaret Walsh's sisters Rachel (of *Rachel's Holiday*) and Claire (of *Watermelon*) may be hilariously dysfunctional, but Margaret has always been the family good girl. Then she loses her husband and job in quick succession, and finds herself with the overwhelming urge to run away—something good girls never do. From the moment her plane hits the runway, Los Angeles—and Margaret herself—will never be the same.

## Also by Marian Keyes:

### LAST CHANCE SALOON

ISBN 0-380-82029-3 (mass-market)

Tara, Katherine and Fintan have been best friends since legwarmers were cool. Now, in their early thirties, Fintan extracts a promise from Tara and Katherine that will change all their lives—and loves—in wholly unexpected ways....
**"Deeply hilarious… and unexpectedly deep."**—*Newsday*

### LUCY SULLIVAN IS GETTING MARRIED

ISBN 0-06-009037-5 (paperback)

A psychic predicts that Lucy will be walking down the aisle within a year. But Lucy has secrets that she hides even from herself, and until they are revealed, the identity of the man who'll walk beside her will be impossible to foretell.
**"Enchanting."**—*The Chicago Tribune*

### RACHEL'S HOLIDAY

ISBN 0-06-009038-3 (paperback)

The fast lane is much too slow for Rachel Walsh, who loves to party. Then she finds herself in the emergency room one morning, and is forced to begin a journey of self-discovery both heartbreaking and hilarious… and ultimately full of hope.
**"Unforgettable."**—*Boston Globe*

### WATERMELON

ISBN 0-06-009036-7 (paperback)

On the day Claire delivers her first child, her husband delivers some news that will turn her life upside down....
**"Irresistible."**—*The Houston Chronicle*

**Available wherever books are sold, or call 1-800-331-3761 to order.**